Queen Eleanor's Legacy

Queen Eleanor's Legacy

Atarah Ben-Tovim

PIATKUS

First published in Great Britain in 1994 by
Judy Piatkus (Publishers) Ltd of
5 Windmill Street, London W1

**The moral right of the author
has been asserted**

*A catalogue record for this book is available
from the British Library*

ISBN 0-7499-0226-4

Set in 11/12pt Times by
Phoenix Photosetting, Chatham, Kent
Printed and bound in Great Britain by
Mackays of Chatham PLC, Chatham, Kent

Author's Note

The Castle of Châlus, where Richard the Lionheart died, still stands. The treasure which caused his death there is historical fact.

With the exception of SS General Lammerding who commanded the Division Das Reich at the time of the massacre of Oradour, all modern characters in this book are fictitious. Any resemblance to any person, living or dead, is entirely coincidental.

Part 1

Chapter 1

The ornate silk-wound ormolu clock on a marble Adam overmantle struck noon. It was a discreet and delicate sound in keeping with the oak panelling, the valuable Persian carpet on the floor and the polished Sheraton chairs of the luxuriously appointed office above busy Baker Street in London's West End.

Sir Ewan Sinclair took a large key from a drawer in his desk and gently wound the mechanism of the clock – exactly twelve turns of the key and not a fraction more. It was a weekly ritual that he found soothing. He found everything in his office soothing, otherwise it would not have been there. The panelled walls were lined with photographs in which he beamed at the camera, wearing immaculate evening dress and a cherubic expression. Beside him in each picture stood a star of the concert platform. Singers, conductors, soloists – all stood frozen at the moment of shaking the hand of the short, chubby man who was the doyen of London's impresarios and personal managers.

The photographs of honour were behind his desk – in the best position to impress visitors. They showed the same face beaming at the camera beside the Queen, the Queen Mother, Prince Charles, Princess Anne... If the entire Royal Family had disappeared overnight, the police could have made up the Missing Persons poster right there in Sir Ewan's sanctum.

The owner of this gallery of fame was staring not at the royals but at a picture of himself standing on the stage of the Royal Festival Hall with a tall blonde girl in a long gown, holding a flute and a bouquet of flowers. On the other side of her stood André Previn and in the background the London Symphony Orchestra. She had been just twenty-seven when the picture was taken, two years before, but stood poised and confident, enjoying the glamour of the moment. A big future ahead of her, though Sir Ewan. No doubt of that.

With a glance at the clock, he pressed the Play button on the expensive Revox tape-deck set into the wall behind his desk. The reel was marked

3

in felt pen JAY FRENCH: ROUGH MIX (PREVIEW COPY).

For the second time Sir Ewan listened to his favourite client playing the Badinerie from Bach's Suite in B Minor – a bagatelle which she had turned into a short masterpiece. He pressed the Fast Forward button to spin on fast in order to sample a few bars from each of the other pieces of music on the tape.

On the tooled morocco leather of his otherwise empty desk were a copy of that day's *Times* and three glossy 10 x 8 photographic enlargements. The lead story of 9 March 1991 was all about the ecological implications of the burning oil wells in Kuwait, set on fire by retreating Iraqi forces at the end of the Gulf War. In the photographs beside the paper, Jay French's face stood out from the musicians surrounding her in the studio, with its high cheek bones and intelligent eyes.

Sir Ewan recalled her getting angry with the photographer who had dogged her throughout the recording session to get what he called 'working shots'.

'Do we have to?' she had asked the PR man for whom the photographer was working. 'I've got no make-up on.'

'Black-and-white, grainy,' the photographer had said, camera clamped to his eye, motor-wind whirring. 'You look fantastic, Jay – really zing! Action shots with the mixer in the background, that's all. Who needs make-up?'

'In jeans and an old sweater?' she had asked, unconvinced. 'What's it for?'

'Album cover for the States,' someone mumbled from the back of the room.

And the fact was, thought Sir Ewan, that the photographer was not kidding: this client of his actually did look stunning at the end of a long day's recording, with no make-up and in old casual clothes, chosen for comfort at a studio session where she had not expected to be on view.

Sir Ewan pressed the Stop button and turned to his junior secretary who had sat silently waiting, her thoughts elsewhere. He rattled through a dozen letters at machine-gun speed, signed a folder of outgoing correspondence and collected from his senior secretary a slim attaché case which contained his passport, traveller's cheques and currency for three different countries. Running five minutes late, he took his private lift to the underground garage where his chauffeur was sitting at the wheel of a monogrammed Bentley with maroon coachwork.

A waiter at Wheeler's oyster bar in Old Compton Street was already holding open the door of the restaurant as the Bentley drew up outside.

'Good morning, Sir Ewan,' was the greeting. 'Your guest is waiting at your usual table.'

4

'I've a plane to catch.' The impressario spoke on the run to the maître d'hôtel who hurried to take the order of this important regular client as they climbed the winding stairs to the upper restaurant. 'I think just a dozen oysters each and something very light to follow.'

'Perhaps the sole meunière?' the maître d'hôtel panted.

'And a bottle of that Chablis I had the other day, nicely chilled.'

Jay French was seated, sipping a glass of Tio Pepe and ignoring the looks she was attracting from men at the other tables. Sir Ewan kissed her on the cheek. A connoisseur of charisma, he always felt a surge of near youthful excitement when his jaded eyes met Jay's piercing green ones. He took in her flawless complexion, the long blonde hair, the simple silk blouse and long skirt she was wearing. It was rare in his experience to find physical beauty and genuine talent so perfectly balanced in one person. In another couple of years, he thought, she'll be pursued by half the eligible millionaires in Europe...

'I'm late,' he apologised. 'I got carried away, listening to the preview tape of your new album.'

'I'd like to know how you got hold of a copy already.' Jay was coolly amused. 'I haven't even got one myself yet. We only finished mixing the master in the early hours of this morning.'

'It was a personal favour.'

'There's a playback organised for this afternoon at the studio,' she said.

'I was hoping to be there, but I have a first performance in Tokyo to attend, so I'm afraid, if you'll forgive me...' His hand brushed her arm to show the apology was sincere. 'By the way, I've ordered us oysters, and sole to follow.'

He licked his lips, an over-grown cherub looking forward to a birthday feast. 'I hope that's all right? My flight leaves in less than two hours but I wanted to have a little chat before I left.'

He tasted the wine, nodded to the waiter and carried on talking.

Jay interrupted him calmly. 'A little chat? I know what you're building up to, Ewan. You don't have to be devious.'

'Oh dear!' The innocent smile was accompanied by one of Sir Ewan's habitual gestures: two plump, well-manicured hands raised in surrender. 'After all my years in the business, Jay, I'm not sure I know how to be otherwise. Ah... here are the oysters.'

'You're going to bully me again,' she said.

He slurped an oyster out of its shell. 'My, these are good.'

The waiter hovered discreetly, slipping a fresh plate of brown bread onto the table at just the right moment and topping up the glasses unobtrusively. It was the kind of personal service that a tipper of Sir Ewan's lavish scale expected. He tasted the fish and pronounced it excellent.

5

His hand brushed Jay's arm again. 'Now I know you won't like this, but I'm going to ask you one more time to stop performing with your Early Music group.'

'You're managing my recital career, Ewan...'

'Exactly.'

'... and Early Music with my own ensemble is a different scene altogether.'

'Give it up,' he said. 'Please.'

'I've got commitments, Ewan.' Jay refused to get excited. 'I've agreed dates and signed contracts. I'm not going to break them.'

'Leave that to me,' he begged. 'I'll sort everything out. You see, doing too many things confuses people. Your public wants you to be a star soloist backed by an orchestra. They don't want to see you as one of a group of musicians playing rather monotonous old music on reproduction instruments.'

'Now you're being nasty.'

'It was a fashion, that's all.' Sir Ewan dismissed the genre with a wave of his hand. 'Way past its peak now, and you know it.'

'Money's not the only reason to make music.' Jay put down her knife and fork, placed a hand on his sleeve, delaying the fork that was halfway to his mouth. 'Now listen, Ewan. I don't give way on this, no matter how much I respect and value the way you manage my solo career. I started the Chinon Ensemble when I was at music college. It's still made up of the same musicians. We've played together for eight or nine years now and we've got that ensemble rapport that comes of working together for a long time and not counting the hours – like a good string quartet. Apart from anything else, I can't let the others down by dropping the whole thing now. They've worked bloody hard, believe me.'

'Oh, I know they're your friends.' He smiled in a last attempt to disarm her. 'But...'

'No buts,' she said firmly. 'My understanding with you is that I can keep chunks of the calendar free for things I want to do. Well, playing Early Music is one of them. I get a kick out of it.'

The waiter was standing at the head of the stairs with Sir Ewan's driver beside him, pointing at his wrist-watch.

'I respect you the more, Jay.' He sighed. 'So there's an end on 't. Now about tomorrow at Canterbury... Refresh my mind, what's the programme?'

'I'm playing the Blessed Spirits in the first half and the Mozart G Major in the second – with some young Hungarian conductor I've never heard of.'

Sir Ewan twinkled cherubically, sharing a secret with her. 'Zoltan looks marvellous from the back – all anguish and arm-waving.'

6

'Is that your way of telling me he's awful?'

'I think the public will love him.' He smiled, a gambler on to a good tip. 'Anyway, if you drive your conductor and orchestra tomorrow like you did the session musicians on the tape I've just been listening to, nobody'll know whether our young Hungarian friend is good or bad, will they?'

Chapter 2

On the platform of the ancient Chapter House of Canterbury Cathedral the chamber orchestra was tuning to the harpsichordist's A.

Backstage, there was hardly room to move. Camera cables snaked across the floor and through doorways. Empty instrument cases lay across chairs with articles of clothing draped over them. The entrance to the platform itself was half-blocked by a camera and a colour monitor on a pedestal, beside which the cameraman was talking to one of the television stage managers, both wearing headphones. The SM, wearing headphones and a dinner jacket, was watching the monitor screen as last-minute adjustments were made to the lighting.

Jay blocked out all the noise and people, to concentrate on the sound of the harpsichord. She blew a note, pulling out the head-joint of the flute minutely to flatten the sound. Satisfied, she peered through a gap in the screens at the edge of the staging and looked at the packed rows of seats. Somewhere in the audience were her father and mother, but she could not see them.

'It's a good house.' The comment came from Carl Moritz, Sir Ewan's orchestral manager. Resplendent in impeccably cut dinner jacket and scarlet cummerbund, he had counted at a glance what was called in the business 'the bums-in-seats'.

To Jay, he added, 'Your name on the bill is a good draw.'

'I went to school here,' she said, recognising a few faces. 'And Dad still practises in Herne Bay, ten miles away. He's a pillar of the community.'

'Local girl makes good?' Carl teased. 'Don't be modest, Jay. You're filling the house all over England.'

He looked away swiftly, but not before Jay caught a hint of pain in his eyes. Poor Carl, she thought, it still hurts him to be close to me...

The SM was asking, 'The director wants to know when the conductor will be ready for his entrance.'

'Where is the man?' muttered Carl.

'In the loo,' said Jay, 'for the sixth time.'

'The bloody Magyar's been shitting himself with nerves ever since the rehearsal,' Carl muttered so that only Jay could hear. 'I don't know why Sir E was conned into booking him.'

'In return for some favour,' Jay snapped. She was normally icy calm before a performance but resented that the tyro conductor Sir Ewan had foisted on her was going to get part of the credit for her performance with the orchestra that evening.

Carl turned at the sound of footsteps, beaming. 'Ah, there you are, Zoltan. You look wonderful, Maestro!'

The young Hungarian was sweating with tension, Jay saw. He mopped his face on a towel and tried to smile at her. She looked away; his nerves were his problem – if he could not cope with them, he'd never make it as a conductor.

'He's here,' the SM said into the mike on his headphones.

Over the headphones, Jay heard the director's voice, sounding calm. 'Standby VT. Standby cameras. Here we go, folks. Start the tape. House lights and cue applause.'

The house lights dimmed. Another SM on the side of the stage cued the applause. The conductor sucked in a deep breath and walked on to the platform in a spotlight. As the lights came up, he bowed to the public, raised his arms majestically and turned to welcome Jay.

Carl held her back until the applause had built. 'At least the Magyar looks good,' he murmured.

For the first time that evening, he let himself look at Jay. He took in the green satin evening dress that brought out the colour of her eyes. Long sleeves gathered at the wrists emphasised the décolleté.

'You look stunning tonight, Miss French,' he said quietly.

'If there's ever an award for the best orchestral manager, Carl,' she murmured, 'you'll get it.'

'In your case, I meant it.' He kissed the back of her hand and let her go.

Jay stepped on to the platform and allowed the conductor to lead her to the front. She felt good in her new dress. It had cost a fortune but was worth every penny at that moment. In the pool of light between the orchestra and the front of the platform, she acknowledged the applause and raised her flute. The clapping hushed and died. Jay retuned to an A note on the Leader's violin. It was not necessary, but audiences liked a little fussiness in a soloist. She gave the conductor a nod to indicate that she was ready. As she closed her eyes, breathing in on the up-beat, she caught a glimpse of her father's wavy grey hair six rows back from the front.

Then time stood still.

Jay's ears rang with the reverberation of a sound she could not identify. It was like the echo of a door closing at the end of a long corridor, but without the initial crash. She had the feeling that the closing door had cut off the sound of a voice with something very important to say. Her brain strained to catch the words, while at the same time knowing that it should be concerned only with her flute and Gluck's music.

In one corner of her field of vision, Jay saw a look of alarm in the orchestral flautist's eye as they played the opening duet together, with the strings and harpsichord discreetly supporting the melody. She was aware that her own sound was wrong; the notes were correct, but voiced as though a child had learned the part without grasping its sense.

Twenty-eight... twenty-nine... she counted in her head, praying that the echo of the slamming door would die away in time. But as it receded towards silence, so her mind strained after it.

The solo in the Dance of the Blessed Spirits began on bar thirty-three. It was perhaps the most beautiful piece of music ever written for flute and one which was a joy to play, each time Jay performed it.

Thirty-one... thirty-two, she counted to the end of her bar's rest. Her fingers shook and refused to open or close the keys of the flute. Instead they jerked spasmodically in front of her eyes. The flute, instead of lying comfortably below the lower lip, slipped away sideways and down however much she tried to pull it back to the proper position. For a moment she thought she was going to drop it altogether. It slid through hands moist with perspiration and she caught it awkwardly, halfway to the floor.

Dizzy, Jay thought she was going to fall off the platform. The cameraman immediately in front of her had the same thought. She saw him look up, alarmed, and track the camera back out of the way. People in the front row were staring, knowing that something was wrong.

Jay tried to step away from the edge of the platform but her legs refused to obey. The musicians hesitated and stopped playing one by one. In the audience every pair of eyes was locked on to her. In the mobile control room, the director stared at the monitor screens, gazing from the output of one camera to another, all confirming that Jay was staring blankly into space with an expression of anguish on her face.

The conductor lowered his baton and turned to her, a tense smile glued in place for the benefit of the public. With a huge effort, Jay regained control of her legs, turned and walked off the platform in a daze. She stumbled off-balance and had to catch at chair-backs and the shoulders of the musicians for support on her slow and painful way through the orchestra to the back of the platform; it took all her concentration to place one foot in front of the other twelve times.

Carl was standing just off-stage, a hand out-stretched to guide her last paces. As she collapsed against his broad and comforting chest, Jay felt tears welling in her eyes.

'Oh Christ!' she said. 'I can't play a note, Carl!'

He led her to a chair, then hissed to the back-desk fiddles: 'Go on to the Handel.'

The message was passed forward to the conductor. There as a rustle of paper and the scraping of chair legs on bare boards as the orchestra turned to the next item in the programme: a concerto grosso in which Jay was not involved.

Carl knelt by her chair. Behind him the television SM was looking anxious, being bullied for news by the director but not knowing what to say.

'Now take it easy,' Carl said soothingly. 'Tell me what happened.'

He tried to take the flute from Jay but fingers that had refused to play refused now to let go, staying locked tightly around the instrument in spasm.

Jay shook her head in bewilderment. 'I don't know what happened, Carl. I just couldn't play a note.'

He stood up, thinking fast. 'Are you going to be all right by the end of the Handel? If so, I'll give Zoltan the nod.'

Jay's hands unlocked suddenly. The flute fell into her lap. She looked at her hands. They were trembling now so strongly that ripples in the dress fabric were travelling right up her arms to the shoulder.

'Look at my hands,' she gasped, horrified. 'I'm like some damned old woman with palsy. Oh, Carl! Whatever's happening to me?'

He had an arm around her shoulders, trying to comfort her. 'Has this ever happened before?' he asked.

'No,' she said. 'No, of course not.'

But it had. Sitting there as the orchestra played the opening bars of the concerto grosso, she remembered something that had happened ten years before, on Easter Sunday of 1982.

11

Chapter 3

She remembered waking up that morning with no inkling of the terror that lay ahead.

If most nineteen-year-old girls on holiday slept late, Jay was the exception. Early rising was for her an unbreakable discipline. In term-time during her years at a specialist music school, work had begun at six o'clock, seven days a week. Although she was now a student at the Royal Academy of Music in London and free to decide her own schedule of work and practice, she still got up each day at six o'clock, did breathing exercises at the open window, had a short Yoga session and then practised for two hours solid.

On that morning Jay opened the windows of her bedroom and looked out at the view which she had known for every holiday she could remember. The garden of her parents' cottage in the Dordogne was over-grown but beautiful. A lawn, broken by mature shrubs and trees, merged into a vineyard. Through the leafless trees she could see the terracotta roofs of the little village of St Denis. The air was cold, with a trace of frost on the grass. Smoke was already rising from some of the chimneys. Jay shivered, forced herself to do some deep breathing and closed the window with relief.

In the other bedroom of the small cottage, her parents awoke and lay dozing to the sound of Jay's flute. She was playing not pieces of music, but scales and long notes and studies. By the time she had finished practising, her father and mother had breakfasted, packed the car and were ready to start the journey back to England.

At the last moment, Jay ran half a mile to the nearest neighbour, a woman artist with whom she had made friends during the holiday. As she ran back along the tow-path beside the placid Dordogne after saying goodbye, she was feeling fit, relaxed and happy.

'I've got a surprise,' her father announced. 'We're not going to take the motorway home, for once. We're going to head across country and spend the night at Chinon.'

'Where's that?' Jay asked.

Her mother passed a road map to her and pointed. 'In the Loire Valley, darling. There's a castle there. You'll like it. And the countryside is very different from the Dordogne.'

'I thought it would make a change,' her father said. 'A change from rushing back to Calais as fast as we can, like lemmings on wheels.'

The journey lasted two hours, during which Jay hardly spoke; she was practising in her head, eyes closed and fingers moving on the keys in her imagination. Her parents, used to her silences, did not intrude but chatted between themselves quietly. At Chinon they booked into a small hotel nestling beneath the frowning castle walls and walked up the hill to where the great fortress of the Plantagenets still brooded on its limestone spur. The atmosphere was hot and clammy, with thunder grumbling beyond the horizon.

They joined a small group of tourists at the main gate of the castle, waiting for the next guided tour. A lover of old buildings, Jay would have preferred to wander around the castle on her own, but her father, being a doctor, preferred facts and figures to guess-work and imagination.

The guide was a student who had only taken the job because a friend had said it was a good way of getting to chat up foreign girls. In this party Jay was the only girl but his efforts to make conversation were frustrated by her parents who saw him off like sheep-dogs each time he tried to get close.

In a light cotton dress and sandals, with her long blond hair falling loose on her shoulders, the boy thought Jay a typical English girl on holiday – an attractive, carefree nineteen year old. Only on second glance was there something about her piercing eyes and the set of her classical features that indicated a combination of intelligence and authority unusual in someone so young.

For her part, Jay thought it a pity that he was so unenthusiastic. The bored monotone in which he was delivering his commentary made it a soporific recital of dates and names, difficult to follow. In the sultry pre-storm heat, the group flocked after him from one point of interest to the next. Outside the Boissy tower Jay leaned against the sun-warmed stone, with her eyes half-closed, day-dreaming and letting her imagination people the castle for her as she half-listened to the guide's voice.

Most medieval history she could remember was about kings and battles but here at Chinon the name of one woman constantly intruded: Eleanor of Aquitaine. She had been queen of France and twice queen of England, yet was usually known by the title to which she had been born – Duchess of Aquitaine. It was in the Boissy tower that Eleanor had had her apartments.

The guide looked at his wrist-watch and hurried through his script, hustling his group along. This was his last tour before the two-hour lunch break.

'*S'il vous plaît...*' The interruption came from behind him.

He recognised the English girl's voice and turned as she stepped forward and put her hand on his bare forearm. She had her back to the rest of the group, so that only the guide saw her strained expression, or rather a hundred different expressions chasing each other across her face as she stepped closer to him.

Her eyes were not looking at him but right through him. It sent a shiver down his spine. Her lips opened as she took another step closer until their bodies were touching. He was too surprised to step back. Incredulously, he thought: She's going to kiss me...

Instead she fell gracefully into his arms. He felt the bare skin of her back above the cotton sun-dress and the softness of her breasts against his chest as the unexpected weight of her body nearly pulled him with her to the ground. Then she was lying at his feet, her skirt blown clear of a pair of shapely brown legs by the breeze.

Her parents pushed through the gawping spectators.

'*Je suis médecin,*' her father said to the guide. And to the crowd watching: '*Ecartez-vous, s'il vous plaît.*' Give us some room, please.

He felt Jay's pulse and beckoned to the guide: 'Give me a hand to carry her into the shade, will you?'

Jay felt herself being lifted by two pairs of hands, and then was aware of rising to head height and beyond until she was looking down on the scene as the body that was hers was carried into the shade of a wall. She stopped rising and found her view framed by a narrow window whose small leaded panes gave on to the courtyard, which was not peopled now by a small group of tourists but full of the hustle and bustle of medieval life, as the thousand inhabitants of the castle went about their daily tasks.

* * *

'Gold?' queried Richard Coeur-de-Lion.

He licked grease off his lips, threw away the chicken leg he had been eating and brushed aside the page-boy holding the rest of the dismembered bird before him on a pewter plate. As the page moved away, the king caught him by one ear lobe and tweaked it hard between the grimy nails of his index and thumb.

'Did I tell you to move, boy?' he hissed, bringing his mouth close to the ear with its now bleeding lobe.

The boy stifled an exclamation of pain. 'No Sire,' he whimpered.

'Then why did you?' The king's voice was full of menace.

'I thought, Sire...'

'You thought? What thought you?' Still gripping the lobe, Richard turned the boy to face him. He raised his hand until the unfortunate page was able to touch the ground only on tip-toe. The chicken slid off the plate and fell into the ankle-deep muck in which they were standing. A dog poked its head between the king's legs and grabbed the unexpected treat, but was attacked by another cur before it could swallow a morsel.

The monarch kicked the snarling dogs out of his way and brought his face close to the rosy cheeks and long lashes. 'You thought you were so pretty,' he whispered, 'that you could do as you wished, is that it?'

The boy was crying now. 'Sire, I meant no harm.'

Richard released him, bored with teasing his current favourite. 'No, you didn't. But I love to see you weep, boy. Were we alone, I should lick the tears from your sweet cheeks as tenderly as you lick my moist flesh. Forgive me.'

'I do, Sire,' the boy whispered.

With one of the lightning changes of mood for which the Plantagenets were famous, Richard stopped playing pederast and became the bluff and hearty man of war. Not as bandy-legged as his father Henry Plantagenet, but stocky and with the coarseness of manner acquired in a lifetime of warfare, he strode close to the armed rider who had just clattered through the gateway into the courtyard. 'You said gold?'

'Aye.' The man, exhausted from a long hard ride, dismounted from his lathered horse that stood, head down and lame in one foot.

Richard recognised him as one of the *routiers*, the mercenaries who served him when there was no war to justify an army for the king to command – and for just so long as they were paid.

'How much gold?' he asked roughly.

The man eased the helmet from his head. Like the king's, his hair was cut short, for long hair got tangled inside an iron helmet. Unlike the king, who wore a well-trimmed beard, the *routier*'s dirty face was covered with a three-day growth of stubble. He scooped a handful of water from a stone horse trough and swallowed thirstily, then poured another handful over his head. 'A king's ransom, Sire. No less. I swear I saw it with my own eyes.'

In a fit of rough good humour Richard embraced the man with both arms and kissed his travel-grimed cheek. He raised his face to the weak spring sunshine that was conjuring steam from the puddles between the flagstones and cried: 'Here stands a king unransomed yet! There's not a monarch in Christendom needs more gold than I. So speak, man. Tell me where it is, this king's ransom of yours.'

He turned to the thickset, battle-scarred captain of the *routiers* who had ridden into the castle with the messenger. Mercadier threw the reins of his horse to a stable-boy and dismounted, his greedy eyes narrowed at the thought of gold.

15

'You love the yellow metal more than me, Mercadier.' Richard cuffed the old warrior. 'If you could swear allegiance to an element, you would, my friend.'

Mercadier laughed briefly at the king's joke. 'My only loyalty is to you, Sire.'

You lie as smoothly as a bishop,' grinned the king, excited at the thought of gold. He led the two men out of earshot of the crowd that assembled so quickly at any unusual event. There was little privacy and no secrecy at the Plantagenet court.

Tethered to a well-head was an ox about to be slaughtered for the royal table. A wave of the king's hand scattered cook and scullions alike until only the ox was left to hear.

'Now...' The King seated himself on the rim of the well surround and spoke in a quieter voice. 'Tell me all you know.'

The *routier* looked to Mercadier. A nod from the captain bade him begin.

'In a village by name of Châlus, which lies in the fief of the Count of Limoges, a poor husbandman busy at the spring ploughing uncovered two days ago a massy treasure of gold that covered the floor of a hay-cart with precious objects and sacks of coin beside.'

When the man had finished his story, Richard asked: 'What proof do you bring me?'

From inside his jacket of mail, the *routier* pulled a gold coin. 'There are a thousand such. Nay, more. I brought this one as token of the rest.'

'And where is it now, this treasure of yours?'

'In the Castle of Châlus.'

'By what force is Châlus held, Mercadier?' queried Richard, weighing the heavy coin in his hand.

'The garrison is no more than three knights and a handful of men-at-arms, Sire. I know the place well.'

'Three knights only?' Richard mused. 'Then Aymar of Limoges is a fool if he doesn't send reinforcements swiftly. We must move fast. Have you a hundred men, Mercadier, that can ride with me within the hour?'

'Two hundred if need be, Sire.'

'A hundred will do.' The king was as mean as Mercadier was grasping; every man hired would have to be paid for.

'Bid them follow when I ride out,' he snapped. 'And, Mercadier, bring sappers and siege engines to reduce the tower at Châlus.'

He dismissed the two men with a gesture, clapped his hands for a steward and shouted for his horse to be readied, the baggage train to be harnessed immediately, his arms and armour to be brought. As the stream of orders was acted upon, the court came to life in a riot of noise and the confusion of servants running to their duties. Only the page with the bleeding ear stood still where the king had left him.

The cook and his helpers crept back to the ox which regarded them balefully, pulling futilely on its tether until it had backed itself into a corner between the well and the wall of the Boissy tower.

'Who speaks of gold at Chinon?'

The peremptory voice rang out clearly in the morning air, cutting through the hubbub of preparation. It belonged to the woman who had once styled herself in a letter to the Pope 'Eleanor, by the wrath of God, Queen of England!' She had been listening from one of the windows of her quarters in the tower.

As Mercadier clattered out of the courtyard to alert his men billeted in the town below, Richard turned to Queen Eleanor, his mother. After seventy-seven summers, she stood straight and proud in a time when most women were bent by toil and child-bearing before they were half her age. Her clear green eyes flashed with the intelligence that had outwitted popes and kings since she was crowned Queen of France as a girl of fifteen.

She did not deign to descend the stone steps, having no wish to soil the train of her velvet dress in the dung and urine that littered the courtyard. Instead she called the king to her and listened keenly to the tale of treasure trove.

Below them in the courtyard, the cook thrust once, then again. He found the jugular vein and twisted his knife. Blood gushed out of the wound. Dogs lapped at it. The ox bellowed feebly, sank to its knees and subsided without resistance in a pool of blood.

'My sword! My horse!' the king bellowed.

Misunderstanding the reason for the excitement, a hunt servant loosed Richard's hounds from the Dogs' tower. A pack of wolfhounds and four huge elkhounds from Ireland raced baying through the courtyard in a flurry of neighing horses, squawking chickens and cursing men.

'Richard, stay!' As the king turned to leave her, Eleanor shivered with a premonition.

She clutched his sleeve with one hand and the hilt of his jewelled dagger with the other. 'There are affairs of State here at Chinon which merit your attention more than this trivial seige.'

He turned on the carefree grin that had been Henry's and which he knew she could never resist.

'Come now, Mother!' he chided. 'There's gold to be had and fighting to be done – proper work for a king. Yet you bid me stay here like some shrivelled clerk, furrowing my brow over documents that bore me?'

He took his sword belt from a squire and buckled it on, ignoring the coat of mail he was offered. 'As I see it, Mother, most affairs of state boil down to affairs of gold. And there's an end to it.'

She held him, surprisingly strong for a woman, let alone one of her age. 'I beg you, despatch Mercadier's men to blockade Châlus and its treasure, if you will.'

'He'd steal every penny for himself.'

'Then send to Château Gaillard to summon William the Marshal. Trust him to conduct this siege, Richard. There is no hurry if County Aymar is in Paris, talking treason with the French king as they say.'

Richard pulled himself free.

'You bid me wait?'

He spun the gleaming coin in the sunlight. As he caught it, he punned, 'This is the only wait I acknowledge – the weight of gold in my hand. Where there's gold, there's always a hurry, woman. That's one thing I've learnt from life. In any case, Richard Plantagenet is known not for his pauses but for the speed with which he rides.'

And there's the truth, reflected Eleanor as the king leaped on to a mounting block and from there into the saddle. Her eldest surviving son spent his life trying to live up to his own reputation. If only, she thought, Richard had his father's shrewd brain as well as Henry Plantagenet's valorous heart. If only he had just a dash of his mother's sixth sense…

She stood unhappily at the head of the steps, attended by two ladies-in-waiting, an island of silent females surrounded by a noisy sea of men and horses and weapons. The king clattered through the gateway, heading down to the town and the bridge across the Loire which his father had built. He pressed on, heedless that most of his servants were still getting ready to follow. With a clanging of metal, weapons were hauled from the armoury and distributed. Saddle girths were tightened, draught animals were harnessed, men shouted at servants, swore and kicked and got in each other's way.

At the sound of the king's departure, the page-boy thought it must be safe to move at last. The only person near him was the slow-witted cook standing beside the huge carcass of the slaughtered ox and wondering what to do with all that meat.

The queen, a few paces away, was oblivious of him. She studied the coin Richard had pressed into her hand. On it was the head of the Roman emperor Augustus, crowned with laurel. She groaned aloud. No good would come of this venture, she was sure.

'He's so damned hungry for gold,' she declaimed to the world at large. 'If the devil opened the doors of hell and held out a coin, my Richard would reach inside to snatch it from the fiend himself.'

She clenched the coin in her fist and hit herself on the mouth repeatedly with the back of her hand until the lips bled, trying to take her mind off the premonitory pain in her heart.

* * *

As the sounds and images from the past faded, Jay opened her eyes to find her father kneeling on the ground beside her.

'Are you feeling better?' he asked.

Jay looked from him to the worried faces of her mother and the guide. They were all strangers. 'What happened?' she asked. 'Where have the other people gone?'

Thinking that she meant the other visitors in the tour group, her father said, 'We're the last ones left.'

Jay pulled herself up to a sitting position. She knew now who he was. 'What happened to me?' she asked.

'You fainted, that's all.' He smiled a professional smile to reassure the patient. 'You fainted from the heat, Jay. Nothing to worry about.'

'Oh no!' Jay touched her lips which were swollen. There was a trace of blood on her finger. 'I must have bruised my lips as I fell.'

'Not possible,' said her father. 'You didn't hit the ground. The guide caught you when you fell against him. There's no way you could have bruised your lips.'

'I have, I tell you!' Jay's voice rose in anguish. It was a flautist's nightmare: she could feel her lips swelling as she touched them. 'I won't be able to play for days!'

Chapter 4

The old man plodded steadily onwards, upwards and away from the city of Beirut. He had deliberately kept away from the bomb-pitted highways along which sped jeeps full of armed men, choosing instead to use a network of old tracks remembered from his youth. Now he was following paths along which the Crusaders once had ridden and which had been trodden by Greek, Persian and Egyptian merchants a thousand years before the Roman legions marched that way.

He recalled riding along the same track on a mule when he was a boy. It was after an illness when he had been sent to the mountains to convalesce. The servants had been laughing as they walked alongside their young master, happy to escape the heat of summer in the city as they headed for the cool of the Chakrouty family's mountain home.

The sea breeze had carried to the boy's ears the distant noises of the most prosperous city in the Middle East. Now as the old man climbed slowly upwards into the foothills, the sounds borne on the wind were of artillery belching from East Beirut answered by a salvo from West Beirut. A concrete apartment building split apart like a rotten fruit and subsided in clouds of dust. For no reason except boredom a sniper shot dead a woman who had left her shelter for one incautious moment in a search for water to give to the child clinging to her skirt. Then he shot the child.

From the south, a flight of Kfir fighter-bombers with Star of David markings screamed in low to drop their bombs precisely on a building vacated only ten minutes previously by Yasser Arafat.

In the refugee camps Palestinian teenagers manned outdated, hand-cranked anti-aircraft guns which loosed off a few shells, more for morale than anything else. An obsolete Russian-built SAM-7 missile got lucky, swerving between the decoy flares that littered the sky with puffs of smoke. It detonated with a flash near one of the Israeli aircraft, which turned seaward, trailing smoke. A dot ejected but no parachute blossomed and both plane and dot were swallowed by the blue waters of the Mediterranean.

High in the hills above the city, the village of Tel-el-Sultan had been a resort where the cosmopolitan rich of Beirut came to escape the hot weather of the coastal plain. It was now a pile of rubble, still smoking from the shells of the Syrian guns which had been turned on it when the PLO took possession the previous day. As the old man came in sight of the ruins, he was singing a song he had learned forty years before during another war: 'It's a long, long way to Tipperary, it's a long way to go.'

His English accent was surprisingly good for an old man in Arab robes who looked like a beggar.

'Halt! Where are you going, old father?' The challenge stopped him in his tracks.

A group of young men and boys, some of them barely adolescent, surged through a break in a cactus hedge. Armed with Kalashnikov sub-machine guns, old rifles and knives, they surrounded him threateningly, bombarding him with questions, jostling and slapping him more from habit than intent to harm.

He gave them his name and could see from their faces that it meant nothing, which told him that they were not from Beirut. Some had blood-stained bandages and dressings recently applied. By their accents he knew them for Palestinians.

'Where is your respect for my age?' he asked, but they only laughed.

He tried another question: 'Where are you going, my sons?'

'To kill the Jews and the Christians!' A dark-eyed, curly-haired boy of twelve swung his loaded AK 47 in a wild arc, pretending to pull the trigger. 'Bang! Bang! Bang!'

The others laughed. 'None of your business, old father,' said the leader, who looked no more than twenty years old.

As they headed noisily in the direction of the city, excited at the prospect of combat, he stood and watched them go. The sun was getting hot and he had not much food and no water left, but he was nearly at the end of his journey. He gathered his strength and ignored the pains in his chest and the difficulty in breathing which had prompted him to come to Tel-el-Sultan before it was too late.

Merlin Freeman lay on the filthy earthen floor of a cellar in one of the refugee camps that clustered around the periphery of the city of Beirut like flies around the eye of a dead dog.

For three months – it could have been longer, for he had soon lost count of the days and nights in the timeless dark – every day had been the same alternation of hunger, thirst, fear and boredom. Now fear replaced boredom as the crump-crump-crump of explosions walked steadily nearer to his underground prison like the footsteps of a terrifying giant. He felt the nervous sweat start on his skin and shivered with the cold.

The butt of a Kalashnikov beat on the cellar door and a voice shouted, 'Prisoner, face the wall!'

Merlin was not a person. People had names. He was just The Prisoner. It was always: 'Prisoner, do this!' or 'Prisoner, do that!'

Obediently he rolled over and faced the wall. His bed was one moth-eaten old blanket laid on the damp earth floor. Behind him, he heard the cellar door thrown open. Anonymous hands thrust over his head a thick, foul-smelling black hood which made it difficult to breathe. A handcuff was snapped round the prisoner's right wrist and ratchetted tight. The metal cut into the suppurating sores that made a bracelet of pain around his wrist. Merlin's groan earned him a savage jerk on the chain as the other cuff was clicked onto a ring of iron sticking out of the wall.

The explosions were still coming nearer. Merlin could feel them pulsing through the ground and shaking his whole body. Through the open cellar door came the sound of shouting. Then a direct hit collapsed the building next door and literally blew away the ramshackle house above the cellar. The floor beneath Merlin's thin blanket heaved like an animal turning over in its sleep and a tongue of fire curled through the cellar as the pressure wave of the explosion squeezed the breath out of his lungs.

He thought he was dead until he remembered the hood and pulled it off with his free hand. To his surprise the other hand was free too, the handcuffs dangling from his wrist. The iron ring in the wall had been cut cleanly through by a piece of white-hot metal that had missed amputating his hand by less than a centimetre. It lay now smoking on the ground behind him.

He blinked at the daylight shining through a great hole in the floor of the house above. Lying beneath the hole was the crumpled body of the guard who had been handcuffing him when the shell landed. Half the man's shirt was burnt off and the skin of his right shoulder looked like a well-done steak.

Silence changed to a ringing in Merlin's ears as his hearing returned. There were men moaning and a woman screaming not far away. Using muscles that were weak from disuse, he stood up and walked unsteadily to the hole. By standing on top of the inert body he could reach up far enough to see out. There were bodies lying everywhere.

The light hurt his eyes. He squinted and reached up to grasp a metal reinforcement bar sticking out of a piece of smashed concrete. It was just out of reach.

He panicked, then forced himself to think calmly. It was now or never; in a few moments somebody would come looking for him. He bent down to take the blood-stained head-dress from the body on which he had been standing and wound it around his wrist to conceal the handcuff. Then he reached up, using the guard's assault rifle, reversed, as a hook to pull himself up the ramp of rubble and out of the hole.

An armed Palestinian, blood streaming down his face from a scalp wound, mistook the dust-covered figure standing in the rubble and clutching a weapon for one of his comrades. He shouted urgently in Arabic for Merlin to run for help. To avoid having to reply, Merlin shook his head as though deaf or dazed. Around him, people with torn clothes, people clutching wounds and people in shock, were running and staggering in all directions through the smoke and dust. Merlin took advantage of the confusion to walk unsteadily away between the hovels of the camp, uncertain where safety lay.

The light, not his recent captors, was now the chief enemy. It beat into this brain through over-sensitive eyes that throbbed as though someone were showering them with fire-hot needles. It was this pain that brought him finally to his knees, sobbing, on a pile of dust and bricks that had been someone's home.

The woman was standing over him when he looked up. It was hard for Merlin to see her face against the background of the too-bright sky. Veiled from head to foot, her features were hidden. He was aware only of her eyes – compelling eyes that ordered him to obey.

'Come,' she said. 'You must get up. And hurry.'

She had none of the humility with which most Arab women talked to a man. Merlin thought she was talking French but with such a heavy accent that her speech was almost unintelligible.

'*Je suis blessé*,' he said. I am wounded.

'You will not die.' She spoke coldly, like a busy surgeon who had more important cases to attend to.

Eyes half-closed, Merlin staggered to his feet and followed her through the dust and shouting and confusion to a deserted building, roof-less and with walls holed by shellfire.

'Stay here,' she ordered. 'Hide yourself and wait until I come for you.'

The old man picked his way past what had been a luxury French restaurant and through the vandalised gardens of bombed-out villas once lived in by wealthy American, Swiss and French expatriates. At the far end of the village was an ancient house hidden among trees, thanks to whose concealment it had escaped the worst of the bombardment when the Syrian guns had bombarded the Palestinian positions.

The iron-bound door with its creaking, rusted hinges gave directly on to a courtyard around which the house was built. There, waiting by the dried-up fountain, was the old man's son.

Salem Chakrouty was dressed in civilian jacket and trousers with a Kalashnikov assault rifle slung over his back. Apart from the weapon, there was nothing military about him. His manner was gentle and his eyes were dead, as though the fire had gone out behind them. He embraced his father. Neither talked of the last time they had met, at the funeral of Salem's wife and two children.

After the earth had covered the three shrouded bodies in their shallow grave, they had walked between rows of graves whose makeshift head-stones were decorated with huge plastic-covered colour photographs, mostly of moustached young men looking serious for the camera. The pictures had put Salem in mind of the Biblical plague which had taken the firstborn son from every household in the land of Egypt.

The two men talked now of trivialities.

'The fountain is dry,' said Salem. 'Its basin is filled with leaves and rubbish.'

'One day the water will flow again,' said his father, Yussef.

'Perhaps.'

'But there is something here more precious than water.' Yussef knelt beside the basin and cleaned the mess away from the tiled surround.

It was a crazy paving of broken ceramics, tastelessly set in cement. One tile, more or less intact, drew his eye. It had a glaze of intense blue, broken up with white classical Arabic writing scrolling itself into intricate, indecipherable patterns. Before the war, tourist traps in the city had been full of tiles like this, bearing roughly written prayers or quotations from the Koran which tourists bought as souvenirs. This tile, however, was genuinely ancient, and the writing was not a prayer but a poem. In one corner, the glaze had been shattered by a bullet at some time in the fighting, but most of the verse was intact.

'This tile,' Yussef told his son, 'is your legacy which I bequeath to you as my father did to me and his father to him. Guard the secret well, for it is a precious thing.'

Salem watched his father, concealing the worry he felt. The old man had been ill for a long time and there were no medicines to be had. The obsession with an old tile which had brought them both to the house that day at risk of their lives sounded to him like a senile fixation.

'Can you read what the writing says?' Yussef asked.

To humour his father, Salem studied the scrolls and curlicues of the classical script which meant nothing to him.

For privacy, in case anyone was prowling about the ruins, the two men were speaking English. All the family spoke French and English as fluently as Arabic. In the days when Lebanon's prosperity and stability merited the title of Switzerland of the Middle East, they had been as much at ease walking down the Champs Elysées or Fifth Avenue as strolling

24

through the smart shopping streets of Hamra. Now the boutiques of Hamra were boarded and shuttered, the streets over-grown with weeds – and Paris or New York as remote as the moon.

'This,' said Yussef, caressing the tile, 'is the writing of an ancestor of ours. He was a great man known as Yussef El-Kebir – Joseph the Great. It has been in our family for forty generations. I shall read to you what it says.'

His eyesight was not good, but he knew the words from memory, since his father had taught them to him as a boy, as his father had taught him:

> 'Destroyed by fire is house and home.
> My sons with weapon in hand shall roam.
> The olive bears no fruit; the fig-tree dies.
> When all is lost, then shall arise
> My sons...'

The old man's voice faltered. 'Have you news of Kassim?' he asked.

'I heard that my brother is with a Shi'ite militia unit in the Beka'a Valley,' Salem answered. 'They are fighting men who were their comrades until last week when everyone changed partners in this crazy game we are all playing.'

Yussef finished reciting the text of the inscription, then stood and shuffled to the grated opening in the courtyard wall where long ago he had set up a telescope to look down on the city. The mounting was still bolted into the masonry, the telescope long stolen. He recalled using it years before to show his two excited young sons the illuminated sign with letters three metres high atop the Chakrouty International hotel near the British Embassy on the waterfront of West Beirut.

Proudly he had told them, 'One day all that will be yours, my sons.'

Now his eyesight was not good enough to see the city unaided and the hotel would not have been visible even with a telescope, for it was a pile of rubble surrounded by other piles of rubble.

He had the Syrians and the Israelis to thank: the Syrian Army for converting the lower floors and basement garage of the hotel into a command bunker and the Israeli Air Force for inserting a bomb with surgical precision through a first-floor window to implode the entire structure in a cascade of concrete and quick-broiled corpses.

South of the city, the Chakrouty family's citrus orchards, vineyards and olive groves were now all barren wasteland. The last remnant of the family wealth was the primitive lime-washed house in Tel-el-Sultan.

Yussef collected his thoughts. The first part of the prophecy on the tile was surely fulfilled a thousandfold: *Destroyed by fire is house and home. My sons with weapon in hand shall roam...*

All that had come to pass.

The olive bears no fruit; the fig tree dies… It was all true. The only thing of value left for him to bequeath to his sons was a tile. He knelt beside it again and stared at the bright blue glaze. What did the words mean? His own father had said: 'At the right time, the meaning will be clear to your son or his son or his son's son. That is the way with prophecies.'

Dimly and confusedly, he remembered saying farewell to Salem. The pains in his chest were worse now, but they no longer worried him. If his elder son survived, the message had been passed on and he had done his duty. If not, it no longer mattered.

Forgive me, he said to the other Yussef: forgive me if I have failed you.

He scattered debris and leaves over the tile and thought about the long journey back to the city. There was a trickle of rust-coloured water oozing from a broken pipe beside the basin of the fountain. He crouched beside it and filled the leather water bottle tied to his waist, using some more of the brackish liquid to moisten the last crust of bread from his waist-pouch which he swallowed morsel by morsel as once he had eaten caviare.

It was dark when Merlin awoke. He sighed with relief at the gloom of a moonless night, lit by fires burning out of control and the intermittent flashes of explosions. Crawling out of the hide he had burrowed in the rubble, he found the woman waiting, veiled in the doorway.

'Hurry,' she ordered. 'I have brought your friends, but you must be quick.'

Warily Merlin followed her outside. It was curfew. On either side of the street, whole apartment blocks towered, black and gutted by fire and explosion like sculptured cliffs. He looked for the woman but she had gone. Still clutching the Kalashnikov, he had gone no more than twenty paces when he was surrounded by a group of armed men in nondescript uniforms. In the poor light their blackened faces were hidden in the folds of the *keffiyeh*, the traditional Arab head-dresses they wore.

'Drop it!'

The command rang out in Arabic, given extra authority by the muzzle of a machine-pistol rammed against the back of Merlin's neck.

He obeyed, his spirit crushed by the sheer bad luck of being so swiftly recaptured. The Kalashnikov skipped from his hand and clattered to the rubble-strewn ground. A hand was clamped over his mouth, forcing his head back. He felt a knife dig into his back just above the kidneys, ready for a swift thrust before he could cry out. He stood still, hands above his head, wondering whether the men frisking him so expertly were Palestinians or a patrol of Shi'ite militia. Either way, the result would be the same.

Then a shaded torch shone briefly on his face. There was an intake of breath and an oath that was Russian, not Arabic: '*Yob tvoyú mat!*'

The light went out and a voice said quietly in English with an Israeli accent, 'Well, well well. Just when we don't want to see a newsman, who should crawl out of the woodwork but the famous Merlin Freeman?'

It took a couple of minutes of being dragged along the darkened streets over piles of rubble before the realisation sank into Merlin's mind that he was in the hands of a squad of Israeli paras on a clandestine mission. They led him through the black-out to where they had hidden their dark-camouflaged jeep. There was a muttered exchange in Hebrew.

A torch was flashed on Merlin's face again and a voice he recognised as belonging to an Israeli para captain said, 'Fuck you, Freeman. You're a goddam embarrassment. I ought to slit your interfering throat, that's what I ought to do.'

Merlin's brain could not lock on to reality. Despite the half-serious threat, his relief at being safe in Israeli hands was too much to handle. He felt a mad laughter bubbling up inside him. Someone passed him a water bottle from which he drank greedily. The action of swallowing helped to damp down the insane mirth.

'What happened to the woman?' he asked.

'What woman?'

'The one who came to fetch you.'

'No one came to fetch us.'

Merlin let that go.

'Question is, what are we going to do with you?' the captain asked.

The laughter was coming again. This time there was no way Merlin could stop it.

The captain grabbed a handful of Merlin's torn and stinking shirt and slapped his face hard with the other hand. 'Sober up, old buddy!' he hissed. 'We have to make a deal – and fast.'

'Okay,' he said weakly. 'Whatever you want.'

'Silence in return for your safety,' said the Israeli. 'That's the deal. We weren't here tonight, so you didn't see us. Got it? We'll dump you nice and near the Intercontinental Hotel where you *shikker* slobs in the Press corps hang out – but for the record, you walked home.'

Merlin fought the hysteria again. 'Right,' he agreed. 'There was no woman. I didn't see you. I walked home.'

Hustled into the jeep for the two-mile dash to the between-the-lines haven of the Intercontinental Hotel, Merlin could not stop alternately weeping and laughing uncontrollably. As the engine revved and the jeep progressed bumpily through the darkness, reversing back from junctions that suddenly lit up with streams of tracer and darting down narrow alleyways, the tears ran freely down his cheeks and it was hard to know what was real and what he had imagined.

Chapter 5

At the western end of the Mediterranean on the morning of Easter Monday 1982, early risers were staking their claims to favourite places on the beaches of the Costa del Sol. A few miles inland, hidden in the folds of the Sierra Nevada lay a remote, fenced-off private estate known as El Valle de los Cantos.

There was no road leading to the valley, only a dusty track which had once had a sun-bleached signpost at the end, now replaced by a notice painted with a skull and crossbones above the warning: QUARRIES! DANGER OF EXPLOSIONS. The occasional tourist who ignored the sign, was stopped at a check-point manned by a pair of athletic-looking young men in their twenties, each holding a Dobermann straining on its leash. They spoke in German with Austrian accents.

From the check-point, little could be seen of the valley itself. It was an arid bowl where only sage brush grew and half a dozen modern buildings were dotted in small plots of irrigated greenery. The buildings were odd in that all the windows on external walls were narrow shuttered slits. Video cameras enabled anyone inside to look out but there was no way of seeing in. Anyone curious enough to climb the nearby heights with a pair of binoculars would have been lucky to escape the Dobermanns that ran free after dark or the helicopter that made regular over-flights during the day. The only sound in the valley that morning was the howling of the Dobermanns, disturbed by the scent of a vixen lurking in the hills up-wind.

In the largest house, Hermann Kreuz was still at work. Usually the sexagenarian scholar followed a strict daily timetable, but excitement had stopped him sleeping that night. He had spent the small hours working on the translation of a letter discovered in the archives of a monastery high in the Austrian Alps. How it had got there was a mystery. It was a poem written eight centuries before by Richard the Lionheart to his mother, Eleanor of Aquitaine.

Satisfied with his translation of the poem, Kreuz broke off for a snack of nuts and fruit, eaten standing up because of his belief that eating while seated was bad for the digestion. He was something of an enigma in the art world, although widely respected for his erudition. Collectors and scholars who consulted him, or asked for an attribution, addressed him as Professor or Doctor Kreuz, but the highest rank he had ever held was *Sturmbannführer* in the SS.

The art collection that filled his house and overflowed into the other buildings was even more mysterious. Few of the rare visitors saw more than one or two of Kreuz's treasures. They were given to understand that their host was not so much the owner of all these precious objects, more of a learned curator acting for a consortium of owners. The truth was that hardly an item in the collection had been acquired legitimately. Most of it was loot from museums, monasteries, castles and private homes, taken at the point of a gun wherever the writ of the SS had extended during the Second World War. What Adolf Eichmann had been for the Jews of Europe, his comrade Hermann Kreuz had been for its medieval art – a transportation expert par excellence.

Kreuz was disappointed but resigned that morning. In scholarship, so many leads came to nothing. The Lionheart's letter, although in verse, was no more than a whining complaint to his mother, written in March of 1199, that the treasure tower in Chinon Castle was completely empty. '*Savies qu'a Chinon non a argent ni denier...*' the king had written.

...which, reflected Kreuz, must have been a large part of the reason for Richard's well-documented haste to grab the treasure of Châlus before Count Aymar could claim it as his own. In the spring of 1199, the English Crown was irretrievably in debt: the first instalment of the enormous ransom demanded by the Duke of Austria had procured the king's release from captivity but it had also drained the vast resources of his realm on both sides of the Channel. Not even Richard's extraordinary rapacity could squeeze more taxes from his ill-used subjects. The treasure tower at Chinon was indeed empty.

Kreuz was, like most scholars, an orderly man. He went methodically to file the poem and its translation in the appropriate drawer of his extensive filing system – and found himself looking at a parchment whose significance had eluded him until then. It recorded the disappearance – variously ascribed in the contemporary chronicles to a miracle or witchcraft – of the vizier to the emir of Granada, Yussef el-Kebir. The parchment was dated October 1199 – eight months after Richard's ill-fated expedition to Châlus.

As Kreuz knew, the ancestor of Yussef Chakrouty and his sons had been famous during the twelfth century for his work as an alchemist, a philosopher and a doctor, an economist and architect. Europe north of the

Pyrenees was still wallowing in the Dark Ages while in Moorish Spain all the arts and sciences of Greece and Rome, of India and Egypt, were flourishing thanks to minds like that of Yussef el-Kebir.

What interested Kreuz particularly was that the disappearance of the alchemist vizier coincided exactly with an undocumented gap in the otherwise well-chronicled life of Eleanor of Aquitaine which had long intrigued him. Feverishly he pulled out tome after tome from among the priceless ancient volumes which lined the shelves of his library. For the thousandth time he re-traced the contemporary accounts of the siege of Châlus with its great mystery: what had happened to Richard the Lionheart's gold? That it had been discovered was certain. Yet it had disappeared again shortly afterwards in the most mysterious circumstances and never seen the light of day again.

As the sun rose above the Sierra Nevada, Kreuz suddenly had a blinding revelation of what had happened to the treasure of Châlus. His excitement was such that he could hardly breathe. His pulse was racing and his vision kept clouding over. He ran to one of the narrow windows and stood by it, gulping in lungfuls of the cold morning air until he felt calmer.

Without flattering himself, he knew that only he could have unravelled such a mystery eight centuries after the event. He had solved an enigma that had baffled scholars and treasure-hunters alike for eight hundred years: who had re-hidden the hoard of gold that had cost the life of Richard the Lionheart? The prime suspect had always been his mother, Eleanor of Aquitaine.

After eight centuries, Kreuz had discovered her motive! He felt weak with excitement, seeing the whole picture so clearly. He knew everything except where she had re-hidden the treasure. And when he knew the answer to that, knowledge would be in his grasp that men had sought since the dawn of time.

Kreuz sat down with the two parchments in his hands, frustrated that he was so close and yet still so far from the end of the trail. He had no idea that it was going to be ten long years before he uncovered the next clue – which would be brought to him by Jay Francis as a result of her nightmare experience at the recital in Canterbury Cathedral.

Part 2

Chapter 1

Half-asleep, Jay tried to piece together what had happened in the Chapter House the previous evening. All she could recall was walking on to the platform – and then her memory was blank until she was sitting back-stage with Carl comforting her. Fragments of memories seemed to fit in between: the face of the cameraman below her, looking up… the conductor's arm frozen in mid-beat… the orchestral flautist's look of alarm. And there were other memories as well: of violence and anger, noises, shouting. These did not make sense because they could not have happened during a concert, so where had they come from?

Jay wondered what was in the injection her father had given her, and drifted off to sleep again.

In the dream, she was angry – no, furious with a man who had been a friend and then betrayed her, turning against his protectors not on any point of principle but from arrogance and greed. 'If Henry were here…' someone had cried.

Was it her own voice?

'If Henry were here, he would kill you with his bare hands.'

The dream faded into her mother's voice and a hand shaking Jay gently into consciousness. She opened her eyes and saw the familiar wall-paper of her childhood bedroom. She felt the clean sheets and the crisply laundered pillow case against her cheek. From the light coming through the Laura Ashley curtains, she guessed that it was about mid-morning. Outside there was the familiar cry of sea-gulls and a north-easter was hurling intermittent curtains of hail against the window-panes.

Her mother smiled. 'You were so deeply asleep, but Daddy said to wake you.'

Jay pulled herself up in the bed, took the large cup of sweetened tea and grimaced at the taste.

'You're to drink it all.' Her mother drew the curtains. 'You were muttering about a bucket. Whatever was that all about, I wonder?'

Not bucket, Jay thought. It was Becket! 'Damn Becket!' Those had been the words cut off by the slamming of the door...

She sat up in the bed and grasped at the cosy, boring familiarity of the scene in the bedroom: her in bed, her mother spoiling her with a cup of tea, always too sweet.

'I'm feeling fine now,' she said.

Her mother did not sit down to chat. She sniffed the air and departed with: 'I can smell something burning in the kitchen. Daddy's back from his morning calls. He said, if you want to chat with him, how about a pre-lunch sherry in the drawing room?'

'I'll be down,' said Jay.

Typical mother's understatement, she thought. Do I want to chat with him? After what happened last night, there are a million questions I want to ask him.

She shuddered at the memories but saw with relief that her hands held the cup and saucer without trembling. She put them down and held both hands horizontal, fingers outstretched. They were perfectly steady. Her ears heard only distant traffic and some birdsong from the garden. There were no compelling echoes of phantom voices.

Tentatively, Jay put her feet out of bed on to the thick pile carpeting and stood up with none of the giddiness and nausea of the previous evening. She crossed the room to the dressing table, opened the flute case and assembled the instrument. With a deep breath, she lifted the flute and played the first four bars of the solo from the Dance of the Blessed Spirits.

She put the flute down and looked at herself in the dressing table mirror. She was always pale. It went with being a musician, forever late in bed. Dark smudges under the eyes was all there was to show for the trauma in the Chapter House.

She remembered her mother looking over her shoulder in that same mirror years before. She had been brushing Jay's long hair when she wondered aloud: 'Where do your looks come from, Jay? There's no one on my side of the family or Daddy's with blond hair and green eyes.'

Then she had added: 'And where does talent like yours come from too? That's nothing to do with Daddy or me, either. He's tone deaf and I just about know where middle C is on the piano.'

Jay's thoughts returned to the present when the telephone rang downstairs. Through the open door she heard the same calm voice repeating a message as her mother wrote on the telephone pad, ending with the inevitable: 'I'll tell the doctor.'

There were three bunches of flowers in the hall, delivered by Interflora: one from Sir Ewan, one from Carl and the other from Zoltan, the conductor. Jay read the cards and felt like an invalid.

Her father put down his newspaper as she came into the comfortably furnished drawing room with its overstuffed armchairs, Persian carpets and chintz curtains. 'How are you feeling this morning?' he asked, as though Jay had been in bed with 'flu for a couple of days.

'Better,' she said, holding her hands out to show him. 'Look. No wobbles, Dad. I even blew a few notes on the flute.'

He eyed her non-committally above his half-moon spectacles.

Jay took the glass of sherry which her mother poured before leaving the room. Still her father said nothing. He never did lead the conversation.

'Can you tell me what happened?' she probed. 'Because I can't remember a thing.'

He sipped his sherry, taking his time about it. 'Well, I'll tell you what I saw. You walked out and smiled at the audience. Everything seemed fine.'

'And then?'

'You tuned up and nodded to the conductor.'

'And?'

'He's not very good, is he? All show and no brain.'

'So? That's what the public likes.' Jay was impatient; her father always took so long to answer a question.

'What happened next?' she asked. 'Tell me what happened.'

'The music started and your face went blank.' He gestured with both hands open, palms upwards.

'Was there a noise?'

'I don't think so. No, the audience was quiet, waiting for the music to begin.'

Jay sought a logical explanation for the noise: 'Perhaps a late-comer slammed a door or scraped a chair on the floor?'

He shook his head. 'You played the duet with a sort of wobble on the notes. At least that's what it sounded like to my ears. When it came to the solo, I thought you were going to faint and fall right off the platform. Your mouth hung open and you nearly dropped the flute. Then you turned around and walked off-stage in a daze. On the way, you banged into several of the fiddle-players' chairs, as though you couldn't see properly.'

'I was feeling my way through a thick fog,' she said, remembering that much.

'Has this happened before?' he asked neutrally, taking another sip of his sherry.

Jay wanted to ask about disseminated sclerosis, epilepsy, brain tumours. But it was impossible ever to ask him direct questions.

'No,' she said distantly. 'But I suppose I ought to have a check-up.

Can you recommend a specialist in town I could go to?'

'For what?' He ticked off on his fingers some of her worst fears: 'Cancer? A brain tumour? Muscular dystrophy?'

There was a twinkle in his eye as he spoke that reduced her fears to the level of figments of an over-active imagination.

Jay sniffed and let the tears come.

He finished his sherry calmly and stood up. 'Before you go to a consultant, I recommend a visit to Dr French in Herne Bay. Of course, he's only an old buffer of a GP, but he has been known to put patients' minds at rest from time to time. If you want me to give you a quick once-over, you know where the surgery is.'

Jay followed him along the corridor and through the baize door that divided the private part of the house from the doctor's surgery.

The examination was brief but thorough.

'There's nothing physically wrong with you,' he said. He glanced at his notes as though she were a new patient whose particulars he had not yet memorised. 'You're a very healthy woman of twenty-nine who...'

'Could it be some virus?' she tried.

'Could be,' he smiled. 'In the Middle Ages, they'd have said a demon had entered into you. Today, if we doctors can't explain something, we say it's due to a virus. It sometimes means about the same.'

'So what happened?' She felt like screaming at him, to make him take it more seriously. Something had happened...

'When did you last have a day off?' he asked.

'Musicians don't have days off, Dad. You know that.'

'And when did you last have a day without working or thinking about work?'

'Oh God,' she sighed. 'I suppose when I went skiing last Easter.'

'That was nearly a whole year ago. It's a long time without a break.'

'This is a crucial time,' Jay said. 'I've got a new album coming out. There's the tour with the chamber orchestra. And the American tour starts in two months.'

'It's always a crucial time in the music business. You can't ever let up, can you?' Her father was staring at a photograph on his desk. 'If you want my opinion as to what happened, I'd say you had a sort of black-out caused by over-work – nothing that a spot of holiday wouldn't put right.'

'A holiday?' Jay laughed. She felt enormously relieved that he had found nothing obviously wrong. 'I've got bookings right through till the end of August, Dad. I can't take a holiday.'

'Balls,' he said.

She had never heard him use bad language before. It was as surprising as if a bishop had farted at her.

He grinned like a naughty boy at his own vulgarity.

'Everyone needs a rest sometimes.' He turned around the photograph so that she could see it. It had been taken on her first day at the Mozart School when she was thirteen. In it, Jay was standing between her parents in the quadrangle, looking awkward and clutching her new flute case protectively in front of herself.

She recalled the loneliness of her years at the high-powered school for prodigies, the agony of learning that she was not the best, the determination to beat the competition and the relentless hours of practice starting at six o'clock each morning and ending late at night, every night. There had been no holidays or weekends, no days off then or since.

'Well?' Her father was watching Jay. 'I don't believe in telling my patients what to do, but – in my humble opinion – if you don't want to risk losing your nerve completely, you need to take a rest.'

'Is that what you think?' Jay's voice rose in indignation. 'You think I lost my nerve on the platform last night?'

'Stage fright,' he said.

Jay stood up. 'I don't get nerves,' she shouted, wanting to throw the photograph at him. 'I know myself well enough, Dad. I'm not the sort that cracks up from pressure.'

He raised his hands to calm her, eyes shrewd above the reading glasses. 'It's a tough life you have, Jay. The closer to the top you get, the tougher it is. I know how hard you work. And, though you won't like my saying this, you have no one to share the highs or lows with, have you? That's hard for a performer, exposed to criticism day after day. Psychologically it's a lot of pressure for one person to absorb.'

'I wondered when we'd get round to my status as a single woman,' she snapped.

'I'm not your mother,' he remarked calmly. 'The last thing I'd want is for you to marry the wrong man just to provide me with a grandchild. But I am saying that being single doesn't make it any easier on you to cope with the stresses of a very tough life-style.'

He grinned, ran his fingers through his hair and looked for a moment as she remembered him from childhood. 'You can't find a bloke who measures up to your old dad, is that the problem?'

Disarmed, Jay smiled back at him. 'Lots of blokes,' she said. 'But no one I want to live with on a permanent basis.'

'Oh, I nearly forgot.' He crossed through a note on his telephone pad. 'That nice man Carl Moritz rang earlier this morning to see how you were feeling. He sounded very concerned. And last night, he was so solicitous and competent that I felt almost superfluous.'

Jay laughed.

'Your probing may be more subtle than Mummy's,' she said, 'but it's just as obvious, Dad. So for your information, Carl is an old friend but nothing more. Not on my side, that is. We had what you'd call an affair a couple of years ago, but it didn't work out.'

She left it at that, not wanting to recall the jealousy that her success had brought out in Carl. At least, she thought, I helped him realise that he would never make it as a player, while as a manager he's one of the best...

Jay's father nodded sympathetically. 'I could help you unwind with a session of hypnotherapy after lunch,' he suggested. 'It used to do you a lot of good.'

'No need,' Jay shook her head. 'I feel fine now. Whatever it was that was troubling me, has gone.'

He stood up. 'Then it's time for lunch. D'you know what I'm looking forward to in my retirement?'

'Tell me.' Jay opened the door for her father and gave him a hug for being so solid, so boringly dependable, so sane.

'Eating curry at lunch-time,' he grinned, 'after a lifetime of being afraid to breathe garlic fumes into my patients' faces at afternoon surgery.'

The deserted promenade of an English seaside resort on a squally February afternoon was a good place to think.

In jeans and a head scarf and anorak borrowed from her mother, Jay walked along the prom past boarded-up amusement arcades and restaurants where last year's menus hung curled up in grimy glass cases displaying collections of dead flies. She stood in the shelter of a wind-break and watched the surf pounding the shingle beach. Great swathes of spray blocked out the view, isolating her in a world of whiteness.

Because she had spent so much of her childhood away at boarding school, Jay loved the cold, clean loneliness of the north Kent coast in winter. The truncated pier, the pavilion with the booths for fortune tellers and instant photo machines, the padlocked ice cream stalls and sordid amusement arcades exuded nostalgia for her. All the vulgarity of the summer season was missing, the pervasive stench of chip oil and fried onions blown away by the gales whose salt-laden air scoured the resort clean each winter.

She stepped from the shelter into the full force of the wind and let the spray numb her face and hands. A few hardy sea anglers in plastic oilskins and sou'westers were fishing from the promenade. They were old men who recognised her as the doctor's daughter and mouthed greetings as she passed, head down against the biting north-east wind.

Several phone calls had interrupted Jay's lunch. Her mind went back to the first one, during which the soup went cold. Sir Ewan had been on the line from Tokyo, to let her know that he was *au courant* and worried for her. At the end of the conversation, Jay had agreed that Carl should find a replacement solo flautist for the chamber orchestra engagements until Easter, which was four weeks away, while Jay took a break. And Carl had rung ten minutes later to say that it was all fixed and she must not worry about anything, leaving Jay feeling impotent, like a patient in hospital whose decisions are being made for her.

Two calls had been from journalists. To them Jay had used Carl's suggestion: sudden food-poisoning and, yes, she understood that the television recording would be rescheduled.

And a couple of musician friends had called. Jay had only realised to what extent the telephone had become her master when her mother commented: 'No wonder you're tired. If a musician can't ever eat a meal without being called to the phone half a dozen times, it's worse than being a doctor.'

Her father had suggested: 'Could you live without the sound of telephone bells for a week or so? It might make all the difference...'

It was worth a try, Jay thought. She didn't want a repeat of last night, ever. And she couldn't risk not being on form when the new album came out.

Mentally she went through her engagements diary, striking out the cancelled recitals and the television rehearsal and recording days.

A solitary seagull appeared as a dot in the leaden sky. It hovered overhead and swooped suddenly to grab something out of the water just below where Jay was standing, then wheeled in the air currents above the promenade, wings outstretched and calling almost plaintively. Jay fitted words to the notes. Come away, it seemed to be calling. Come away!

She made up her mind fast, as she usually did. A holiday was what she needed but at zero notice she would not find a friend to go with. So she'd go where she had a friend: to France. If she left straight away and drove fast, she could catch the evening car-ferry and be on the other side of the Channel by dinner-time.

Chapter 2

The old house on the edge of Tel-el-Sultan was dark, as were all the other ruined houses of the village, but below it, on the plain between the hills and the sea, lights flickered in windows of apartment blocks and headlights moved along roads into and out of Beirut. Navigation lights of ships decorated the sea and a civilian airliner roared low overhead with its landing lights on, passing across the face of the full moon like a huge bat.

As the once-familiar slight figure of his brother came through the courtyard door, Salem Chakrouty gave the traditional greeting: 'Kassim, my brother, welcome to our house.'

The two men embraced: Salem tall, well-built and outgoing despite a gaunt sadness that hung around him like a cloak – and Kassim, the shorter thin-faced younger brother, who before the war had been a studious introvert.

He was dressed now in nondescript battle fatigues, a wind-proof parachutist's smock thrown over the top against the cold. Above his left shoulder showed the butt of a Soviet assault rifle slung upside down on his back. A Czech-made Makarov 9 mm automatic pistol was in a holster on his belt, with the flap cut away for a quick draw. The smile of greeting did not stay long on his face.

As they ended their embrace with the ritual kiss on both cheeks, Salem asked himself: Is this hard, angry man my beloved younger brother or is it a stranger who bears his name?

Kassim turned to the two companions who had followed him into the courtyard, each holding a Kalashnikov AK 47 at the ready.

'It is well,' he said to them. 'Go now. Be back in one hour.'

They departed with a roar of exhaust from their jeep.

There was an awkwardness between the two brothers, alone for the first time in years. Salem asked about mutual friends, receiving answers in monosyllables. He led his brother to the grille and pointed at the lights of Beirut twinkling below. There were gaps – dark areas where no build-

40

ings stood any longer – but the city was nearly back to normal after a decade and a half of civil war, with services like running water and electricity available for several hours each day.

'Look at the city,' he said, pointing. 'It lives again, despite everything. You see? The war is over at last.'

'For you, perhaps,' said Kassim coldly. 'For me, the fighting continues until we have driven all the godless foreigners from our land.'

'There is no point in continuing the struggle,' Salem disagreed.

'How can you say that?' Kassim's voice was harsh, accusing: 'You of all people, who have lost your mother, your father, your wife, your children, your home, your business...'

'They are gone.' Salem wanted to convince, not argue. 'Killing more people will not bring back those already dead.'

'But you can avenge the dead, like a man should,' Kassim sneered. 'That would surely be more fitting than crawling on your belly to everyone you know, begging for loans.'

'Ah,' Salem sighed. 'So you have heard I am trying to re-start some kind of business?'

'Business?' Kassim sneered. 'How can you worry about making money when the south of our country is a tributary of Israel, the north is controlled by Syria, and the city down there is a whorehouse where two-legged pigs snuffle in the filth and grovel for scraps.'

'Stop!' Salem shouted. 'This is our father's house. I forbid such talk here – from you of all people, whose friends have become the biggest drug dealers in the entire world, a man who chooses to live in the Beka'a where nothing grows but hashish plants and fields of opium poppies.'

'So?' Kassim taunted him. 'Do you think that you city people without pride or religion or moral values are superior to us? You know that it is not for ourselves we grow the drugs. It is to finance the Islamic revolution and at the same time to destroy the decadent nations who crave cheap illusion.'

The years of savage internecine fighting had affected men differently, Salem thought. There were those like him who had survived each torment, praying for the war to end. They now rejoiced in each day without gunfire and murder. They were the people whose lights burned in the city below where they were trying to re-build their shattered lives.

But there were also many like Kassim, who had killed his first man, a Christian Falangist sniper, before his fifteenth birthday. Those men had survived the war physically but were now able to live only by a savage creed of primitive violence. Perhaps, Salem reflected, they were the real casualties, those who had changed so much during the fighting that they could not end the war within themselves.

For a moment the two brothers stood face to face in the darkness, neither giving way. Then Salem stooped and lit a portable gas lamp he had brought with him. It hissed and spread a warm yellow glow around the courtyard. Kassim looked at the once familiar scene. His brother had made an attempt to clean the courtyard – the filth of years had been swept into one corner and a new padlock gleamed on the hasp of the bullet-damaged door.

Salem took food from a vacuum container: *tabouleh* and some cold meats. There was a bottle of wine for himself – it had been made sixteen years earlier from the last grapes to be harvested in the Chakrouty vineyards before the war began in 1975. For his brother, there was a bottle of water.

'Let us eat,' he said.

They sat on the broken coping of the basin around the fountain and shared a meal together for the first time in years. The silence was broken by odd remarks that strangers might have exchanged.

When they had finished, Salem's foot scraped away the leaves he had left covering the blue-and-white tile.

'I need your help,' he said.

'I am your brother,' said Kassim coldly. 'What you need, I must give you. That is written. So tell me what you want. But hurry, for I have not long.'

Salem looked up. By the light of the gas lamp, his brother's eyes glittered in the thin, bearded face.

'I shall be brief,' he said. 'Our father – may peace be on his soul – left us a legacy to share. This tile…'

He placed the lamp on the ground beside it and prayed that the message fired into its glazed surface might have enough meaning to save his brother's life.

'What is so special about this tile?' Kassim asked.

'It is an heirloom,' said Salem, 'handed for forty generations from father to eldest son – as our father handed it to me. As our family travelled from country to country over the centuries, the tile came with us. It was our grandfather who placed it here when he bought this house to keep his favourite mistress in.

'He was a fornicator,' said Kassim shortly.

Salem thought of the anonymous mound beneath which his father lay. Forgive this lie, he prayed, clearing his throat. 'Our father charged me to share with you the knowledge of this tile which is our legacy.'

What the old man had said, was: 'On no account tell Kassim, or all is lost.'

But my duty to the living is greater than to the dead, Salem excused himself mentally. Aloud, he continued, 'This tile was made by our ancestor, Yussef el-Kebir, who was a great thinker, able to foresee the future.'

'That is an abomination!' snapped Kassim.

'I did not say he was a magician.' Salem kept his voice calm. 'Only that he could see the future. And if indeed he could do so, it must have been God's will, my brother. In any event, our ancestor made provision for his descendants in a time of need, which is an honourable thing, is it not?'

'Do you believe all this?'

'There is a great treasure, so our father said, to which Yussef el-Kebir left the clues in the writing on this tile.'

Kassim laughed. 'What does it say?'

'I cannot read it,' Salem confessed. 'To me, it looks like a prayer. Certainly the script is very ancient. I thought that you who were religious in your youth would be able to decipher it better than I.'

Kassim knelt and gazed at the tile. His finger traced the curving lines of calligraphy in blue on the white background. 'It is no prayer,' he said. 'The name of God is not mentioned once. It is the work of a blasphemer.'

'But can you read it?'

'Yes,' Kassim admitted grudgingly.

Salem could hear the noise of the jeep's exhaust returning.

'Read it to me,' he pleaded urgently.

When Kassim had finished, he sat back on his heels. 'A fairy story,' he said dismissively. 'A pack of nonsense.'

'No.' Salem caught his brother's sleeve to prevent him leaving. 'Father said it was all true.'

He tapped the tile between them. 'He said that this writing, if we can understand its message, will lead us to a great fortune which is ours by right and which we may now claim to re-build our shattered fortunes.'

Kassim stood as the jeep returned, stopping outside the ruined house with a squeal of brakes.

'Our father was an old man, senile and babbling,' he said. 'Now I must go.'

'Shall we meet again?' asked Salem. It seemed his plan had failed.

'*Insh'allah*,' grunted Kassim. If God wills it. He seemed not to care either way.

Next day Salem parked his battered and bullet-scarred black Mercedes outside the old house in Tel-el-Sultan. From the back seat he took a bundle of clothing and climbed over the rubble towards the house. He was half-expecting that his brother would not come to the rendezvous. The mysterious message which had reached him at dawn seemed a complete about-face, which was not in character for Kassim, whose stubbornness had been a family joke since he was a toddler.

Salem felt a great surge of hope when he saw his brother standing outside the old house, waiting for him. He was still dressed in the clothing of a Shi'ite militiaman but for the first time in years he carried no weapons. Kassim shifted uneasily as Salem approached. He felt naked without a Kalashnikov slung over his shoulder and another weapon in his belt.

As they embraced, the older man caught a flash of what looked like anger in his brother's eyes. He dismissed it from his mind. The only thing that mattered to him was that Kassim had come. He pulled back and studied his brother's face.

Kassim lowered his eyes. 'These are the clothes you found for me?'

'I hope they fit.' Salem felt apologetic for the shabby clothes he had brought for a man who had once worn Savile Row suits. 'But you are so thin that none of mine would do.'

Kassim stripped and threw his militia clothing in a pile behind the fountain. Salem noted the scars on chest and belly where bullets had torn his brother's flesh and the shiny burn patch as big as two outstretched hands that covered one shoulder. What about the wounds inside? he wondered. How deep do they go?

When Kassim was dressed, he said, 'Read to me what it says on the tile, as I used to read to you when you were a child.'

Kassim's shoulders relaxed.

It was going to work out, thought Salem. The tile was his legacy. If he used it to bring his brother back to life, that was his business.

'Destroyed by fire is house and home...' Kassim read slowly.

'Go on,' prompted Salem.

Kassim speeded up: 'My sons with weapon in hand shall roam, The olive bears no fruit; the fig-tree dies, When all is lost...'

'You see?' Salem let his excitement show in his voice. 'This tile, made centuries ago, foretells exactly what has happened to us.'

'Perhaps,' muttered Kassim. After a pause he continued reading the old script: 'When all is lost, then shall arise, My sons – to wrest from the brood of Ali Anor, What was my due so long before.'

He sat back on his heels.

'Read on,' urged Salem.

'There's a part here which is damaged,' said Kassim. 'I can't make it out. Something about a vale of muses, I think.'

Salem smiled sadly. 'Today there is no such place in Lebanon.'

Kassim stared at the tile, trying to fill in the missing curves. The calligraphy was so stylised that it was not hard to follow the lines of his ancestor's brush-strokes. He moved his right hand, holding an imaginary brush and mouthing the words.

'Here,' he said, 'something is missing completely, my brother. But here I can make out something about a secret fortress of the Cross.'

'...which in the twelfth century would mean a Crusader castle, like Krak des Chevaliers or Beaufort Castle,' Salem guessed.

'...where the Jews bombed us in 1982,' finished Kassim.

'So perhaps the treasure is hidden in a castle?'

'There is one more line.' Kassim squinted at the cracked surface of the tile. 'It looks as though this fortress of the Cross is in the land of the setting sun.'

'Which was the old Moorish name for the kingdom of Andalucia in southern Spain. Is there nothing else?'

'No more that is legible.'

'Then who is or was Ali Anor?' Salem wondered aloud.

'Ali, yes. But Anor? What kind of name is that? It's not Arabic.'

Kassim stood up and brushed the dust off his knees. He looked through the grille at the city below. From this distance, the war damage was not apparent. For a moment he recalled the atmosphere of childhood summer holidays spent in this cool old house looking down at the stifling city and the blue Mediterranean beyond.

'Will you come with me to Spain?' asked Salem softly behind him. 'Will you come with me to find this legacy of ours so we may rebuild our family fortunes?'

Chapter 3

Jay listened to her own voice on the answering machine and used the remote bleeper in her hand to activate the replay of recorded messages. Voices of friends were asking how she was. It was hard for a freelance musician like her, to whom the telephone was a professional umbilical cord, not to note down their numbers and call back immediately. She felt a delicious thrill that she had had the courage to cut herself off from the world for a whole week. Nobody apart from her parents knew where she was.

Outside the medieval farmhouse where her father planned to retire, the Dordogne sky was far from being the cloudless blue that tourists sought in summer. It was raining, with heavy black clouds racing in from the Atlantic coast only fifty miles away.

She found an old anorak of her father's, put it on and busied herself getting some warmth into the old stone walls and tiled floors with only a few mobile bottled-gas heaters to help. There was un unopened bottle of still mineral water among the mouse droppings in the pantry. She heated some of its contents to make herself a cup of instant coffee, wondering if her impulse to come to St Denis in the middle of winter had been a mistake.

Time I got a grip on myself, she thought. Shopping is always fun in France. There's just time to buy some food in the village before the shops close...

She backed her brand-new Renault Alpine carefully out of the barn and into the muddy driveway, avoiding the worst of the ruts. There was a break in the clouds as she was crossing the bridge over the Dordogne. The sun burst through and illuminated the little village of St Denis huddled beneath a ruined tower which had been a Templar outpost when medieval pilgrims forded the river there on their way to Santiago de Compostela, long before the bridge was built. The twisted streets of timbered houses leaning towards each other, the tiled roofs and ridges meeting at crazy angles, were all suddenly ablaze with sunlight reflected off wet tiles and stone. The river sparkled below the wide quay where the barrels of wine had been stacked for loading onto barges for shipment down-river to the sea.

The light bouncing off the wet cobbles of the quay itself made an oblique slash of dazzling brightness. Jay stopped her car to enjoy the view; in a minute the clouds would close up and it would be lost. There was a couple walking along the tow-path a quarter of a mile away. Even at that distance Jay recognised the woman. She got out of the car and called: 'Leila!'

The woman looked up in Jay's direction, blinded by the sunlight. Leaving the engine running, Jay scrambled down the wet grass of the embankment and ran to meet her only close friend outside the world of music. The other woman ran too so that they collided halfway and swung each other round, laughing with pleasure.

With her mass of dark curly hair, olive complexion, deep brown eyes and curvaceous figure, Leila Dor was often taken for an Egyptian but was a *pied noir* – a French citizen who had been born in Algiers, fled her troubled homeland in 1962 and then tried living in many countries before settling in the Dordogne.

She was dressed as usual in vibrantly colourful clothes: a hand-painted anorak and paint-spattered jeans above red and yellow shoes. She hugged Jay excitedly and called to her companion who was walking towards them along the river bank, 'What a wonderful surprise! Merl, come and meet my best girlfriend in the whole world.'

She hugged Jay again, scolding her. 'You should have told me you were coming, I'd have opened your house up and got some fires going.'

Leila's stream of words poured out in all directions. 'On second thoughts,' she contradicted herself, 'I'm glad you didn't ring. A surprise is better.'

Her throaty accent which mixed Bab-el-Oued, Brooklyn and Birmingham was only partly due to two packets of Gauloises a day. She coughed and blamed it on the weather. 'Everyone in St Denis has *la grippe*, you'll see. When did you get here?'

'An hour ago,' answered Jay. 'I was just going into the village to buy some provisions and then give you a call to see if you were free for dinner tonight.'

'Well, I would be,' Leila drawled. 'But you're the second surprise visitor I've had today.'

She switched to English and introduced her companion. 'Jay, this is Merlin Freeman, an American buddy of mine from way back – Greenwich Village, all that swinging scene, you know? And Merlin, meet an English friend: Jay French. Jay is a musician, a very good one too. She plays the flute.'

The man, who had been staring at Jay, turned on an easy smile and stretched out a hand to shake hers.

'I know you,' she blurted, taking in the tanned face, sexy brown eyes and dark, curly hair. From his looks, he could have been a relative of Leila's.

Merlin's shirt was open at the neck despite the cool wind, and his anorak was not zipped up. He stood just under six feet tall and had the easy stance of a man in good physical condition. There was something vaguely military about his bearing.

He grinned, showing perfect teeth, and shook his head: 'I don't think we've met. Music's not my scene at all. I'm the type of ignoramus that thinks serial music is what you hear on a corn flakes commercial.'

Jay stepped backwards. The sunlight bouncing off the river lit the scene like a floodlight. Her eyes searched Merlin's face.

'But I do know you,' she insisted. 'I know we've met.'

'On the box,' he apologised. 'You've seen me on the box.'

'Merlin's a television correspondent,' explained Leila. Her eyes tore themselves away from the freak lighting effect on the opposite bank and shifted from Merlin's face to Jay's. 'You've probably seen him reporting some happy event like the Gulf War.'

'Of course. I remember now.'

'Seriously…' Merlin's eyes held Jay's. 'It's a problem in my business. People recognise me but can't place me. They don't expect to meet a media personality in a shop or walking along the street, so I'm always meeting total strangers who launch into a personal conversation and get angry because I don't know what the hell they're talking about.'

'Big-time reporters like Merlin live in the best hotels and restaurants all the time on expenses,' said Leila. 'He'll buy us both a slap-up dinner tonight, won't you, Merl?'

'Correction.' Merlin had still not taken his eyes off Jay's face. 'For the first time in years I'm not on expenses. I'm here on a sabbatical trip.'

'Doing what?' asked Jay.

A shadow crossed his face, quickly erased by the professional smile. 'It's a long story. But it will give me great pleasure to take you two beautiful ladies to dinner and give you the abridged version. I have the name of a good place in St Emilion.'

Leila was amused at the effect Merlin was having on Jay, whose usually pale cheeks were flushed, but not from the exertion of running.

She waved to the opposite bank where a cluster of rain-sodden multi-coloured parasols advertised Cinzano. 'We don't need to go that far, Merlin. We're standing a hundred feet away from one of France's great restaurants.'

He looked surprised.

48

'You won't find it an any book,' she continued. 'It's called Chez Dominique and it's run by a seventeen-stone ex-Foreign Legion paratrooper who will cook the best meal you've ever eaten. Just don't get into a fight with him, that's all. Any trouble and Dom will roll the three of us as flat as one of his delicious crêpes. How about seven-thirty at my place for a pre-dinner drink, Jay?'

She licked her lips. 'Fine by me.'

Merlin spoke slowly as Jay turned away. 'I also have a funny feeling we've met before, but we can't have done, so there it is.'

'*A tout à l'heure*,' Leila called after her.

'*A tout à l'heure*,' Jay echoed.

She followed the tow-path, walking the long way round to get back to her car, aware of Merlin's eyes on her all the way.

Chapter 4

Leila's house was a mess.

Like its owner, it was a chaos of colours. Red-printed final demands were stuffed into jam jars bristling with paint brushes. One wall was part green and part yellow, as though Leila had run out of paint halfway. Sketches were tacked on to doors and window frames with drawing-pins. Clothes and half-finished canvases and empty frames covered the furniture and littered the terracotta tiles, making it necessary for Jay to pick her way across the room as though walking across a river on stepping stones.

The creator of all this chaos was '…running late as usual, darling.' Her voice came from the shower cubicle in one corner of the converted cottage which was one vast studio where Leila worked, ate and slept.

'Help yourself to a drink,' she called. 'There's some Cinzano in the satchel hanging on the big easel, I can't remember why. Oh, and there may be ice in the fridge, if it's working. Have a look, anyway. If the fridge isn't making a funny humming noise, hit it on the right side and it may go again.'

Jay lifted the pick-up which was scratching round and round the centre scrolling of a record on the turntable and switched off the hi-fi. She pushed the mound of dirty dishes in the sink aside and turned on the hot tap. The water ran tepid. There was a scream from the shower: 'For Chrissake, don't run the hot tap! It's turned to ice in here.'

The washing-up liquid container was empty. Jay rinsed a couple of glasses in cold water after emptying them of cigarette ends. Then she set out to hunt for Leila's satchel, which was not hanging on the easel. In a long mirror pinned to the half-painted wall by four nails, she caught sight of herself. She had changed twice before setting out and wondered if her black woollen dress was overdoing it for a dinner in St Denis. Perhaps a blouse or sweater and trousers would have been more appropriate, and trainers rather than heels?

In the shower Leila was singing one of Edith Piaf's songs, *Mon Légionnaire*. She sang off-key and rather loudly, making Jay wince. From time to time the performance was interrupted with bits of local gossip hurled at random over the screen. Jay cleared a chair and sat down. The mess in which Leila lived was the opposite of her own well-ordered flat. In every way the two women were as different as their looks, which was a large part of the reason why they had been friends for so long.

As the voice from the shower kept up a stream of non sequiturs, Jay thought how wonderful it must be for Leila to be free to choose when to go to bed or get up in the morning, when to work or even not to work if she felt so inclined. It was the antithesis of her own ordered life as a musician in which every hour of the day was pre-planned, sometimes years ahead.

After reading the latest threatening letter from France Telecom, Jay picked up the paint-stained telephone. The line was dead. Half-listening to Leila's exuberant chatter, she wondered what it was like not to care if the phone was cut off. The thought brought another twinge of unease that she had temporarily excommunicated herself.

And then Leila emerged from the shower swathed in a large orange beach towel and grabbed her glass of Cinzano. 'Isn't this the most amazing drink in the world, Jay? I sold a picture to a wine merchant and he paid me in vermouth. A dozen bottles. So have another one and another.'

Her infectious enthusiasm for the pleasures of the moment – a shower, a drink, a man – always began by making Jay regret being such a serious person herself. Then, after a while, she caught a mild form of Leilitis herself and stopped thinking about work and dates and schedules and the thousand pressures of her working life.

'He's a dish, isn't he?' Leila, half-dressed, was choosing a dress from her wardrobe, a metal pipe hung on wire from a beam. Each one she pulled out to examine was more screamingly colourful than the last.

'Orange and green? You like this one, Jay? No, I can see you don't, so I'll wear it. Merlin, I mean. I saw the effect he had on you. Not that you're the first. If that man knew what he did to women...'

She changed tack abruptly, finishing the drink in one gulp. 'We're late. Come on. Let's go.'

'Merlin isn't staying here with you?' Jay asked.

'He's got a room above the restaurant.' Leila laughed her low throaty laugh. 'I've no doubt Merl would like to spend the night here, darling, but Dom – you remember him? – well, he is a very jealous man and very violent. So, since Merlin always turns me on, I thought it would be better if he spent the night where Dom can keep an eye on him. Then no one gets tempted in the wee small hours.'

'I thought that sort of thing didn't bother you?' Jay queried.

'It doesn't bother me,' Leila agreed. 'It's the men who get uptight, haven't you noticed? By the way, have you got wheels?'

'D'you want to go in my car?'

'My faithful *deux-chevaux* –' Leila posed theatrically in the doorway, her orange and green kaftan screaming above a pair of vivid blue shoes, six-inch metal earrings jangling in her hair as she moved – 'is having a hysterectomy, darling. It suffered a fallen engine because I forgot to put oil in. That's just like machines, isn't it? You let 'em guzzle all the gasolene they want and they let you down because of some other damned thing.'

Jay laughed and finished her drink. 'Nobody else could wear that dress,' she decided. 'But on you it would make Barbra Streisand green with envy.'

She embraced her friend. 'Coming into your house is like breathing neat oxygen. You've got no phone, no car and no money by the look of it. But nothing bothers you.'

Leila's eyes swept round the mess in which she lived. 'I used to pretend to care,' she said, serious for a moment. 'I pretended to be what other people call normal, Jay. Oh I really did, so don't laugh at me. My God, if you knew how many times I wept, trying to be a dutiful daughter, a conscientious art teacher and even a good wife and mother. Then one day I woke up and realised that I was only fooling myself. Everyone else knew I was a fake, even my own child. So I renounced the world and stopped pretending. This...' She paused and swept an arm to encompass all the mess. 'This is me.'

Merlin kept them waiting five minutes and arrived at the reserved table in a dinner jacket with the excuse that he had had to wait for a call to New York to come through. Jay thought she had caught a glimpse of him in a roll-neck sweater looking out of the restaurant window as she was parking the car. She wondered if he had gone back to his room to change in her honour.

The meal was a masterpiece, as Leila had promised. Her lover – the *patron et chef de cuisine* – was showing Merlin, a potential rival, just how good a cook he was. He insisted on serving their table himself.

The conversation flowed easily, a mixture of Leila's scandalous revelations and anecdotes from Merlin's limitless fund of stories about famous people whom he had interviewed. Jay laughed at Leila's scandal and Merlin's jokes as they enjoyed the superb food and a sublime locally bottled wine. She gazed out of the window at the moonlit river flowing past only a few feet away and thought, as she always did, how beautiful France was. With each breath she could feel the tension of months drain away.

As the meal progressed, she found it harder and harder to keep her eyes off Merlin's face. Whatever chemistry was gong on seemed to be affecting him equally. Their hands brushed repeatedly as they reached for a glass or the condiments.

Leila watched with amusement the reaction they were having to each other. After the dessert, she excused herself to go to the washroom and returned with: 'I've just got myself a lift home. Dom says, as we're the last diners, he'll be delighted to drive me back. He says to help yourselves to drinks.'

She stood looking down at Jay and Merlin. 'Well, one of you could say: Don't go, Leila. We'll miss you.'

They both said it together and laughed.

Leila kissed them goodnight. 'The way you two are looking at each other, I'll be in the way very shortly. No, don't protest – not that you are. I actually feel like death, because I can't shake off this 'flu bug. So *bonne nuit, mes enfants*. Have fun. *Ciao*.'

She was gone in a final whirl of colour. Merlin went to the bar and poured himself a generous measure of 1937 Armagnac and another coffee for Jay.

She nodded thanks and started with surprise when he said softly, 'We haven't spoken for three whole minutes.'

Since Leila had gone, Jay had been acutely aware of being alone with him. She stopped toying with the coffee cup and observed, 'After two hours with Leila, silence can be fun.'

'Depends who you're with,' he said.

There was another pause, both of them listening to the music coming from the bar where a local folk singer was entertaining a small crowd of regulars.

Merlin shifted in his chair. 'Silences can be hard to handle if you're with the wrong person – and very comfortable with the right one.'

'It's the same in music,' Jay suggested. 'Without dynamics, it doesn't exist.'

'Dynamics?'

'The loud and soft. The silences between the notes. The pauses. All that.'

He nodded. 'I've just realised that I know nothing about music. I never thought about it before meeting you today. And now it seems a terrible thing to have missed out on.'

Jay looked at him, trying again to remember where they had met. It was not possible that she would remember so strongly a face she had seen only a few times on television. And the soft-brown voice that matched his eyes… that tugged at her memory too. It reminded her of a line in a poem by Lamartine she had learned for 'A' level French.

Something about *'les voix chères qui se sont tues'*: the beloved voices that we hear no more...

Jay started. 'What did you say?'

'I said, tell me what it's like to be a musician at the top. Tough, I guess.'

She laughed, 'I'll tell you when I get there.'

'Don't be modest,' he warned. 'I've done some research on you.'

Jay reminded herself that, beneath the lazy manner, the man across the table was a reporter.

'I put in a couple of calls before dinner to friends in London,' he said. 'They tell me you're pretty famous on the recital circuit, that you pull good audiences wherever you play and that your meteoric showbiz career has been more like that of an opera singer than a flute-player.'

Jay was amused and flattered that he had taken the trouble. 'Do you do that with every girl you meet, Mr Freeman? Make enquiries before you take her to dinner?'

'No, Miss French,' he apologised with a grin. 'But then you don't exactly come across as Miss Average Dinner-Date, if you'll pardon my saying so. My friends tell me you were a prodigy. What's that like? I've always wondered.'

He was an easy man to talk to. Once started, the story of her life flowed.

Merlin hardly spoke. Chewing a tooth-pick, he watched her face and listened fascinated as Jay told him about the rigid, monastic discipline of the Mozart School, the dedication of being a prodigy and the relentless competition that had never let up since her first professional performance when she was fourteen.

'Not so very unlike my scene,' he commented at last. 'A correspondent is only ever as good as his last despatch.'

He paused. 'But now something's gone wrong,' he prompted.

Jay was on her guard. 'Did your reporter friends in London tell you that?'

Merlin replied with a question. 'Do you want to tell me about it?'

The hair on his scalp tingled as Jay recounted what had happened in Canterbury Cathedral. From his own experience, he knew that some things happen for which there is no rational explanation.

Somebody switched out most of the lights in the restaurant. They were the only clients left. Merlin leaned forward. He was playing with a book of matches to avoid disturbing Jay by looking directly at her. As she finished talking, he looked up and asked, 'You say this wasn't what musicians call "losing your nerve"? So what's the difference?'

'I've had friends who lost their nerve...' Jay hesitated; it was a difficult thing to explain to someone who lacked the vocabulary of a musician.

'At the time, they looked normal. They weren't giddy or anything like that. It's just that they couldn't play the notes without a sort of wobble. They couldn't control the sound they were making. The whole orchestra breaks out in a sweat when it happens.'

'I've got the picture,' said Merlin. 'Now tell me again what happened to you in Canterbury Cathedral, so I can compare.'

Jay took a long drink of water. She shut her eyes to concentrate. 'I walked on to the platform...'

'No butterflies in the tummy?'

'I've never had nerves in my life,' she said shortly. 'Everything was normal until I blew the first note and heard this noise and the voice...'

By osmosis his professional ability to manipulate words put the right image into her head: 'Then I felt someone's hands pulling my fingers away from the keys.'

Merlin studied her hands on the table close to his, taking in the long sensitive fingers, the nails trimmed short for playing.

Jay was wishing she had been able to tell her father what it had felt like. 'This illusion,' she continued, 'only lasted for a second or two. But... you have to understand that playing professionally is like being an Olympic athlete. Every part of your body -- every muscle and nerve – is tuned to top performance.'

He nodded.

'So when my fingers refused to do what my brain was telling them, my brain flipped – like blowing a fuse.'

The memory hurt. Jay gripped Merlin's clasped hands tightly, willing him to understand. 'I've performed the Blessed Spirits in public maybe a hundred times, Merlin, and suddenly I couldn't play a note. I nearly dropped the flute. I was giddy. I thought I was going to fall and staggered off the platform, unable to see properly or hear anything except that echo. I was trembling from top to toe. I thought I was going mad.'

The memory made her feel sick. At that moment she could have collapsed against his chest as she had instinctively sought physical reassurance from Carl when it happened. With the next breath came the fighting response to her own panic – the strength that had made her a performer.

Merlin returned the pressure of her hand. 'You say there was a noise?' he prompted gently.

'...like someone slamming a door.' Jay thought of telling him about the voice that had shouted, 'Damn Becket!', but it seemed over-dramatic.

Merlin was trying to find a rational explanation. 'Perhaps there really was a noise that put you off your stride? A sudden noise at the wrong moment, just when the audience had hushed for the music to start? That must happen sometimes.'

Jay had asked her father the same question.

'There was no noise, Merlin – except inside my head. And this voice... Oh, damn!' She pulled her hand away from his. 'I don't want to talk about it any more.'

'You didn't lose your nerve,' he said.

'How would you know?' Jay was angry with him for spoiling the evening by making her recall the trauma. The magic that had been building was all gone now. 'You just said you didn't know a thing about music.'

The restaurant was silent, except for a distant noise of washing up in the kitchens. In the bar the singing had stopped. There were sounds of someone locking up.

He stood up. 'I think they're trying to get rid of us.'

He pulled back Jay's chair for her and said softly, 'I apologise for being so intrusive. I have a social disease: I can't stop myself asking questions.'

'My fault,' said Jay briskly. 'I didn't have to answer, did I?'

They looked at each other for a long moment, each regretting the change of mood, but unable to take the one step forward that might have bridged the gap. If Jay's moment of weakness had won over her performer's toughness, she would have let Merlin take her in his arms, but she had fought it and been strong without him, so he had no role except to offer politely: 'Can I drive you home?'

'I've got my own car.'

'Ah, yes, the red monster I saw you drive up in.' He followed her outside and dutifully admired the sleek lines of the Alpine. They talked about styling, gears and engine capacity for a few minutes before parting like strangers.

Chapter 5

'Have you got any batteries?' was Leila's greeting next morning. She was shaking an ancient transistor radio whose cracked casing, like most of her other possessions, was accidentally daubed with oil paint in several colours.

There was a burst of France Inter as she hit the radio and jolted a loose solder joint. She put the tranny down carefully beside her easel, talking to it like a dog. 'There now. Stay still and don't move.'

To Jay, she confided: 'Machines are like men. To make them work, you hafta know the vital spot on which to land the blow.'

She seated herself at the easel in front of a painting of the village of St Martin in blues and greys under lowering storm clouds.

'Winter landscape,' she sniffed into a handkerchief.

'It's powerful,' said Jay.

'That's the sort of remark friends make when they mean: I don't like it. Oh hell, why should you? I don't know if I do yet. Do you want coffee? Help yourself.'

Leila picked up her palette. 'It's in that red pot on the stove. Chuck another log in the fire while you're there. And how was your night of love?'

Jay rinsed a cup from the crowded sink and poured herself a coffee. It was never obvious when Leila expected a reply to the questions she broadcast in all directions.

'That picture on the easel wasn't there yesterday,' she said.

'I lied.' Leila squeezed paint from a nearly empty tube. 'I didn't come back here to eat aspirins and feel sorry for myself. I left because I couldn't take any more of that intense gazing into each other's eyes that you and Merlin were indulging in. I spent the night painting.'

'You've been working all night?'

'You're saying all the things that get up an artist's nose.' Leila sat back on her stool and stared at the canvas. 'I wanted to capture the light during

57

that break in the storm yesterday afternoon when I was walking along the tow-path with Merlin.'

The words cued a *déjà vu*. It was a while since Jay had had one. And they were always such trivial moments: the cup of coffee in her hand – the picture on the easel – Leila turning on the stool, palette and brush in hand and saying: '… along the tow-path with Merlin yesterday afternoon'.

'You look as though you've seen a ghost.' Leila stared at Jay.

'I'm fine.'

'I never know with you. Your musician's pallor worries me. You ought to get outside more and collect some free vitamin D. I'd like to paint your portrait one day, you know. An action portrait – while you're playing. I see you… I don't know quite how, but not in modern clothes at all.'

'I've got a lot of medieval costumes I wear with my Early Music ensemble.'

'That's it!' Leila's excitement bubbled over. She lit a Gauloise and stared at Jay through the smoke, devouring the lines of her face, then stabbed a paint brush as her friend. 'You should be wearing one of those pointed hats with muslin they used to wear then.'

'A hennin. Strictly speaking, they're rather late: fourteenth, fifteenth-century, but I do have a couple.'

'Is that what I call a wimple?' asked Leila.

'No, a wimple is simpler – like a nun's veil.'

Leila studied Jay's face. 'It's a deal. Let's do it.' She spun back to her easel. 'You didn't tell me how it was with Merlin.'

'Nothing to tell,' said Jay.

Leila bent towards the easel, intent on adding some detail with a small brush, the large one clenched between her teeth. 'What a waste! You're crazy. How often do you meet a dish like Merl?'

'That camping-car of his,' said Jay. She watched her friend concentrate on applying the paint. 'It wasn't parked outside the restaurant when I drove past.'

'It has wheels. That's the idea.'

'I wanted to thank him for dinner last night.'

'Mm.' The grunt was hardly audible through the two brushes now clamped between Leila's teeth as she used a third one on the painting.

'He's gone to Oradour.' She removed the brushes and dragged a mouthful of Gauloise smoke into her lungs.

'Doesn't mean a thing to you, does it?' she exhaled and picked tobacco off her lip, leaving smudged of red oil paint decorating her chin like badly applied lipstick. 'I forget you ignorant musicians only read what Bach and Mozart wrote. If you ever read newspapers, you'd know that one of the worst atrocities of the Second World War happened at Oradour-sur-Glane.'

'I remember the name now,' said Jay. 'What's Merlin doing there?'

'He didn't tell you?'

He didn't tell me anything about himself, Jay thought. He seems so open and yet he's really quite a private person, hiding behind the questions he asks people and the stream of amusing anecdotes…

Leila flicked the cigarette into the sink. 'He's using up some leave that's due to him after three months of sitting out there in Saudi Arabia, covering the Gulf War. There's a book he's been writing for years. So he's working on that for a few weeks. That's what the camper's all about. My mobile office, he calls it.'

'What's the book about?'

'Massacres,' said Leila.

Jay recoiled. 'Are you serious?'

Leila dumped the cigarette end into her coffee cup. 'Have you got a road map?'

'Why d'you ask?'

'The English,' Leila shook her head sadly, 'were invented on the sabbath. It was God's day off, so He let one of the apprentices do the job – hence the missing part between the ears. Now get out of here and let me paint in peace, will you? And give my regards to Merlin.'

'How did you know I'd go after him?'

Leila put down her palette. She crossed the room and took both Jay's hands in hers. 'You're a musician, Jay, you listen to people's voices. I'm a painter, so watch their faces. Something changed in your face, the moment you met Merlin. You look different than you did before. And I think he's the same about you, so go for it, huh?'

Jay picked her way down the street where life had stopped in mid-afternoon on 24 June 1944.

She looked around the village of Oradour. In a workshop lay the tools abandoned where the saddler had been working when the SS arrived and cordoned off the village from the rest of the world. Next door a carpenter's tools lay where he had put them down in mid-task. The scales in the butcher's shop had been weighing meat rations that afternoon until the butcher and his customers were rounded up for slaughter themselves; the useless machine now stood rusting on the counter of the shop. Outside the grocer's, prams were parked where mothers had snatched their babies from under the muzzles of the rifles. And in the main square the doctor's car was still parked where he had left it that day after arriving for a routine medical examination of the children in the little school, to find them all standing in the open air with their hands up.

59

When the main body of troops left four hours later, all the inhabitants of Oradour, with the exception of a handful of terrified and wounded survivors, were dead: shot, battered to death, asphyxiated by smoke or simply burned alive.

Jay shuddered. She did not need to read the details in the leaflet she was holding. Just looking at the village where the clocks had stopped forty-seven years before, she could feel the echoes of horror and violence numbing her mind. It started to drizzle and she wondered whether the sun ever shone on this desolate village of the dead.

Further along the main street was a now roofless church. There, she read, 543 women and children had been murdered by men who spoke their own language. Most of the SS troopers were men from Alsace; many of the children they killed were refugees from the neighbouring province of Lorraine. Setting fire to a churchful of screaming victims, the soldiers had played music on their radios and cracked jokes as they went about their hideous task that balmy June afternoon.

Jay found Merlin in the church. He was standing before a huge mass of melted bronze. The furnace fuelled by the body fat of the hundreds of victims had generated temperatures so high that the church bell had melted and fallen like a blob of wax on to the floor below, with the iron clapper protruding intact from the shapeless mass.

There was a pair of Pentax cameras slung around Merlin's neck but he was not using them. He stood motionless, head bowed, beside the melted bell as though in prayer and seemed unaware of Jay's arrival. She stepped back outside the church, leaving him to his vigil. There were no other visitors in the village. When five minutes had passed and he still had not moved, she went back into the church and walked quietly up to him. His face was haggard and seemed ten years older. He looked at her without reaction or recognition, consumed by some inner conflict.

'Merlin?' Jay kept her voice low. It was both a church and shrine where they stood. 'Are you all right?'

He did not reply but scanned the desolate scene of the massacre with head lowered, as though the cameras were a burden made of lead.

Jay was puzzled. Surely he must have seen worse things in his career as a war correspondent – or at least fresher scenes of bloodshed than this memorial to a crime half a century old?

She took Merlin's arm and tugged gently. Without bothering to protect his cameras from the rain, he let her lead him out of the church and along the tram-lines of the cobbled street that led to the car park. They were halfway back when he spoke for the first time. His voice was hollow and hoarse.

'I was here,' he said. And again: 'I was here.'

'You were here?' Her face screwed up against the rain, Jay tried to follow his meaning.

'... when it happened.'

In 1944? It wasn't possible. 'No, Merlin,' she said uncertainly.

He turned his face to her and she saw that some of the tears running down his cheeks were not from the rain.

'I was... I was at My Lai,' he said.

Chapter 6

The chapel in the Valle de los Cantos had been stripped empty and decorated with long red banners that reached from roof to floor. On them the black swastikas stood out boldly in their white roundels. Carved into the top of the wall was the legend: *Ein Führer! Ein Volk!* The huge oaken table in the centre of the chapel was surrounded – like Arthur's round table – by twelve high-backed chairs. In front of each, instead of a place setting, was a silver dagger bearing the runes of the SS.

Hermann Kreuz was pleased with the decoration. Now that Germany was re-united, half the motto on the wall was again true. He pivoted on one heel, reading aloud the other words carved into the stone: *Ich schwöre dir, Adolf Hitler...*

The words of the sacred oath of the SS faded into shadow, but everyone present that evening would know them by heart. Adolf Hitler might be dead but the *Führerprinzip* lived on.

Kreuz barked commands to the two guards responsible for the décor, making them level a banner here and straighten a chair there. There was the sound of a car horn outside, which brought a smile to Kreuz's thin lips. Isolated by his cold intellect, he had no true friends, but once a year he enjoyed the ritual reunion with old comrades, recalling the time when they had briefly ruled more of the globe than the Romans had ever conquered. That night they would sing the old songs, renew their oaths and re-dedicate themselves to an ideal greater by far, in their view, than the lily-livered democracy which had temporarily replaced it.

The Dobermanns were tied up and howling mournfully as the small convoy of dusty chauffeur-driven BMWs and Mercedes with German and Austrian number plates drove slowly down the track into the valley. As each vehicle drew level with the checkpoint, a guard directed the driver to the correct guest house, in which were laid out a selection of the drinks and food most enjoyed by the guest in question. The television set was linked to the satellite antenna on the roof of the main house and tuned exclusively to stations 'back home'.

The passengers got out and stretched, enjoying the warm winter sunshine after the long motorway drive. The youngest were past seventy now and some considerably older.

Kreuz looked twenty years younger than his guests. An almost skintight crew cut disguised the thinning of his hair. His well-massaged face and neck were nearly wrinkle-free. As each car arrived, he trotted forward in his track suit to shake another old comrade's hand, to slap the aged shoulders and drink a toast in the open air. The guests' glasses were filled with Veuve Cliquot champagne. Kreuz's held sparkling mineral water; he never drank anything else.

One after another he evaluated the physical fitness and mental capacities of his old comrades. None of them kept anything like as fit as he did; two now walked with sticks, almost all wore glasses and several had pot bellies. Kreuz concealed his revulsion for the way they were letting themselves age. They have forgotten, he thought, that the brain controls all; fighting the physical process of ageing is but another triumph of the will...

The yearly reunion of Das Reich had two functions. In the daytime it was the annual general meeting of a company whose assets included a dozen tourist hotels and nightclubs on the nearby Costa del Sol, plus shares in several of the new thousand-yacht marinas. Kreuz was the legal president and managing director of the company. He knew that the following day they all had a busy agenda to work through, with a huge cash-flow problem caused by the recession in tourism, aggravated by the arrival on the Costa del Sol of new money from the Arab countries, Hong Kong and Korea.

But the first priority was the ritual swearing-in of the new generation of Das Reich so that the spirit and ideals of the SS would walk the earth long after its founder-members had been promoted to Valhalla. And that was something about which Hermann Kreuz cared very deeply.

Merlin's camper was a rented US model. It had cruise control, a shower, a flush toilet and thermostatically controlled heating but, as Jay discovered, it did not have food.

She drove to a small local supermarket for supplies and then headed south to a camp-site which the check-out girl had thought was open in winter. On the journey along the bank of the winding River Glane she made repeated checks of her rear-view mirror to make sure that Merlin's huge vehicle was still lumbering along behind.

He did not speak while she prepared the meal, but sat immobile and grey-faced at the table. Mentally Jay compared this behaviour with the engaging, outgoing man with whom she had dined the previous evening. In the hard light of the overhead fluorescent tubes, she noticed odd lines in Merlin's face that were not from smiling or laughing. Inside the self-assured, handsome television reporter with the tooth-paste smile, was another Merlin Freeman very different from the man the viewers knew.

They ate in silence: ham and eggs, washed down with a bottle of the local red wine, followed by bread and cheese. Merlin chewed the food automatically and without apparent appetite. When Jay had finished, she reversed the roles they had played in St Denis and placed her hand very lightly on his. 'You made me talk a lot about myself yesterday, Merlin. It's my turn to ask the questions tonight.'

He was eating the American way, using a fork in his right hand. He stabbed the fork at her and said harshly, 'Reporter's caveat: answers can damage your mental health.'

Jay searched his eyes. She could read nothing there. 'I'll take that risk,' she said.

Merlin waited. What is it about Jay? he wondered. To her, I won't lie. Is it because she's tough enough to take it? Or is there something else?

'Wasn't that the real you, last night?' she asked.

'Oh, sure,' he mocked her. 'The amusing cynical correspondent, that's me.'

'Well, was that the real you in the church?'

He was silent.

'I'm not much good at asking questions,' she said. 'You could help.'

'Unfortunately I'm not much good at giving answers.'

There was a pause while she sought some clue in his face.

'Leila told me you're writing a book about massacres.'

'*The* book of massacres,' he said.

Jay thought how much more easily Leila would have pried her way towards the truth. It had never been her nature to intrude on other people's privacy, but in Merlin's case she felt that there was both a right and an obligation to do so. It was something to do with that first moment of recognition on the river bank... like a debt to be repaid, she could not quite put a finger on it.

'You said you were at My Lai?' she began.

'So what's the next question?' Merlin interrupted her harshly, wanting to get it over with.

'Did you kill people there?'

'Yeah.' Merlin glanced up at Jay's face then lowered his eyes again.

She had to know now: 'Women and children?'

'Yeah.'

He waited for her to reject his hand that was stained with blood. Instead, he saw and felt Jay's fingers curl and grip his wrist with a firm pressure.

Saving a drowning man... was the image in her mind. Hold on, Jay. Don't let go of him...

'Then the book is a kind of atonement,' she suggested.

'Jesus!' Merlin exploded, jerking his hand away from hers and standing up. 'Do you think atoning is as easy as that? You sound like some cheap shrink telling me to talk about it and it'll go away...'

He was shouting now. 'That My Lai shit wasn't some bad dream! It was a real walk in hell we took that day.'

Jay watched him pacing around the camper. 'But what's the good of reminding yourself again and again? It was a long time ago, Merlin. You must have been a kid.'

'I was nineteen.'

He took a deep breath and tried to speak calmly. 'Look. I want to explore in print what it is that makes these things happen, Jay. What we looked at this afternoon was a rare excess – a fortissimo extravaganza, in musical terms. A festival of violence. But massacres on a smaller scale happen all the time.'

He pulled a pile of research papers from the shelf above Jay's head and unfolded a map on the table between them. 'See these places marked in red? There are over a thousand sites in France alone where civilians were deliberately killed during the Occupation – a few Jews, or a dozen members of the local Resistance rounded up and just blown away... There's nothing rare about a massacre, believe me. You have to understand that the men who did that – ' He jerked his head in the direction of the village of death. ' – were not *inhuman*. What they did was uniquely human because no beasts do it.'

What have I got myself into? Jay wondered. How can I be sitting here listening to a man who has done *that* – and feel neither shocked nor revolted but just concerned?

Merlin folded the map and poured himself another glass of wine. Jay covered her glass with her hand.

'Except for his uniform,' he continued, 'there was no way you could have looked at one of those SS guys at Oradour in June '44 and said: "That man's a killer. This one's a pathological sadist." You know why? Because whatever women and pacifists like to believe, Jay, the seeds of violence that blossom as massacre are implanted in the psyche of most men. They germinate fast, given the right conditions, and they are in all of us – a part of our human inheritance, like walking upright.'

'I don't believe you,' she said.

He laughed wryly, 'Nobody does.'

Jay could see that the crisis was past.

'That,' he said tiredly, 'is exactly why I have to write *The Book of Blood* – to try and make people like you understand. Maybe, just maybe, it'll help prevent some terrible event one day. So I think it's worth a try.'

'I think you're very brave to go back to these places, Merlin.'

Merlin, Jay thought, was a name like a seagull's cry borne on the north-east wind: Merlin... Merlin... Merlin.

'Aren't you frightened the way it carves you up, each time you go mentally back to that day at My Lai?'

He grinned crookedly. 'I'm actually pretty sane, considering. I've talked to shrinks, so I know. A lot of vets who went through what I did in 'Nam are still living on welfare twenty years later, in short-let rooming houses, married to a bottle or a needle.'

'Perhaps your book will help them too?'

'So they can live happily ever after? Yeah, wouldn't that be nice for everybody?'

She ignored the sarcasm, wondering instead: 'How can a man who's done what you have, bear to spend his life as a war reporter? Of all the jobs in the world... If it was me, I'd never want to be reminded of what had happened.'

'There isn't any choice,' he said again. 'I've tried to break away, believe me. I've moved into other areas of journalism, done sport and politics, but each time...'

He paused. 'Each time, something happens to drag me back to war and the pity of war. Do you believe in destiny?'

'Yes.'

'Then my destiny is to live with my memories and guilt.'

Jay stood up to tidy away the plates and cutlery. The dashboard clock read 2205.

'I was going to find a hotel room,' she said, 'but it's a bit late. Do you mind if I spend the night in your camper?'

For a moment she thought Merlin was going to say no. Instead he grunted: 'There's no privacy, but there's a spare bunk and plenty of blankets, if you want to stay.'

'That's fine.'

He looked up at her, the lines etched deeper on his face. 'You're not worried at the idea of spending the night with a murderer? Or does it turn you on?'

She put the dishes in the sink and flinched as the hot water scalded her wrist. 'You're not a murderer,' she said with her back to him.

'That's exactly what I am,' said Merlin harshly. 'And you better believe it.'

Kreuz looked magnificent. His black *Sturmbannführer* uniform fit him like a glove, the jack boots gleaming in the light of the huge candles which were the chapel's only lighting, now that dusk had faded in the narrow slit windows.

If some of the others present fitted their re-tailored uniforms badly when standing, seated at the table in the poor lighting they passed muster. And their voices had been lusty enough, belting out the territorial boast of *Deutschland Uber Alles*, which had more meaning now than for forty years past. They had sung all the old marching and drinking songs and now it was time to blood the daggers they wore at their belts.

There were four young men to be sworn in that night. All were sons of old comrades who had died or could no longer be present. All wore black SS ceremonial uniform. Three were from the ranks of Kreuz's guards, as blond and blue-eyed as their master. The other was a fair-haired man in his late-twenties whose hair hung over the collar of the uniform jacket. He held himself awkwardly, a civilian dressed as a soldier, and would have liked to be somewhere else.

In each case, the ritual was the same. The initiate pulled up his left sleeve and bared his arm. Kreuz's dagger was drawn deliberately across the skin. The blood spurted and Kreuz gripped the wounded arm to rub it against the slash on his own forearm, mixing their blood.

Someone started singing the *Horst Wessel Lied*. Kreuz clasped each of the initiates round the shoulders in a rare moment of emotion.

'Well done,' he said to each man. 'You are the young blood which renews our ageing corpus. Through you and your descendants the ideals of the SS will live a thousand years until destiny calls and we rise again to a new greatness.'

Chapter 7

There was sunshine and blue sky next morning. Jay drove into New Oradour for fresh rolls and returned to be greeted by the aroma of coffee wafting out of the open door of Merlin's camping van.

'I've got croissants,' she called, 'and *pains au raisins* and *chocolatines...*'

Merlin stuck his head out of the doorway. He had shaved and put on a clean bush shirt and khaki trousers. The haggard lines that had transformed his face the previous evening were gone. 'A feast,' he said.

'... and the newspapers you ordered, sir,' she said, passing them up.

'It's an occupational disease,' he apologised. 'I have to read several newspapers each morning or I get withdrawal symptoms – even in a country where the headlines don't mean a damn thing to me.'

He immersed himself in a copy of *Le Figaro*, from time to time asking Jay the meaning of a word. She ate a couple of croissants dunked in her coffee French-style and watched him surreptitiously. She had lived with a couple of lovers for short periods but could not recall feeling so peaceful and relaxed in the morning with either of them, despite the revelations of the previous day.

Above Merlin's head was the shelf packed with research maps and books for his travels. Jay pulled down the green Michelin guide to the area and leafed through it idly.

'Châlus,' she said, surprised. 'We're very near. And I never even knew where it was.'

Merlin was concentrating on something in the paper. 'What's special about that?'

'There was a massacre...' She half-hesitated but he gave no reaction so she carried on reading aloud from the Michelin. 'In 1199 Richard the Lionheart met his death there, below the castle ramparts.'

'Châlus?' Merlin looked up, searched his memory and drew blank. 'What was an English king doing in a place like that?'

Jay put down the booklet. 'Although King of England, Richard was a Norman. He didn't even speak English and only went to Britain twice, each time to raise taxes. But – to answer your question – at Châlus he was indulging two of his favourite pastimes: besieging a castle and trying to get his greedy hands on a treasure. He slaughtered the defenders apparently to the last man.'

Merlin shrugged. 'And did good King Richard get the treasure?'

Now there's a mystery.' Jay scanned the brief paragraph in front of her. 'It apparently disappeared, but some scholars believe that his mother, the Duchess Eleanor of Aquitaine buried the treasure at the village next to Châlus, which is called Oradour-sur-Vayre.'

'I've heard of that place.' Merlin put down the newspaper.

'There are several villages called Oradour,' Jay continued reading. 'The name is a corruption of the Latin *oratorium*, meaning a place where the pre-Roman Gauls came to pray for their dead.'

Merlin was staring right through her. 'You sound very knowledgeable,' he said absently.

'Blame Mr Michelin,' she said. 'But actually, I am more clued-up than most. I've done a lot of research of the twelfth century for my Early Music group. We sing several songs of the period.'

'Why?' he asked distantly.

She laughed. 'I like the music of the Plantagenet period – and I'm the boss of the Chinon Ensemble when it comes to selecting the repertoire.'

'Go on.'

'Plus, I did medieval history for "A" level and got hooked on the subject.' She paused, made uneasy by his unfocused stare.

'And?' he urged.

'That's all there is.' Jay looked puzzled.

'No, it's not all.' Merlin felt the buzz that comes when a story opens up right under a newsman's nose. 'It's coming back to me. Listen...'

He grabbed a ball-pen and started scribbling on a piece of typing paper. 'One – there has never been an adequate explanation of why the SS wiped out Oradour. Two – there has to be some very compelling reason why the Das Reich Division was here from the tenth through the twelfth of June 1944.'

He underlined the dates on the paper. 'For Christ's sake, tenth June was the fourth day of the Allied invasion! Rommel needed every goddam German tank and every soldier he could lay hands on up north. So what the hell was an SS armoured division doing, farting around here, killing civilians when it should have been belting its way flat-out towards the Normandy beach-head?'

'You tell me.'

'I'm groping my way.'

69

Merlin looked up from the paper covered in cryptic notes. 'Another oddity about Oradour is that most SS massacres of civilians were well-publicised. That was the whole point of them.'

Merlin circled the words 'No publicity' on the paper. Two days before in nearby Limoges, he remembered, the Germans had hanged ninety-nine hostages from lamp-posts all over town as a warning to the civilian population. Yet at Oradour...

'Here, the SS tried to conceal what had happened by burying a lot of the corpses in rough graves and imposing a news black-out.'

Jay was going to speak, but Merlin circled the word 'Motive?' and continued: 'There was no reason for reprisals here, because there had been no *maquis* activity at Oradour-sur-Glane. In fact there was a rumour the SS picked the wrong Oradour on a map, that they had meant to take out Oradour-sur-Vayre, where there had been Resistance activity.'

'Surely the SS could read a map?' Jay interrupted. 'They were professional soldiers...'

'Ever heard of friendly fire?'

'No. What's that?'

Merlin laughed shortly and lifted the hair behind his left ear. Jay could see a scar several inches long where no hair grew.

'Friendly fire is what the military call an own goal. The guys who did that to me were professional soldiers on my own side who couldn't read a map.'

Merlin changed tack. 'I did a story on Lammerding a few years ago.'

'Where's that?' Jay was lost.

'Not a place, a man. SS General Lammerding was in command of Das Reich division at the time of Oradour.'

Merlin circled the name 'Lammerding' on his sheet of paper. 'He had been using his troops to harvest gold for several months previous to the invasion. Hitler and Goebbels may still have been ranting about ultimate victory, but the Waffen SS generals were soldiers; they knew which way the tide was flowing. Certainly Lammerding and his pals knew the writing was on the wall. So they were shipping gold from all over German-occupied Europe to Switzerland for use after the inevitable defeat. It was this gold which financed *Odessa*, *die Spinne* and *die Kameradschaft* – the organisations which funnelled the top Nazis out of Germany via Italy to South America.'

Merlin paused. 'You with me so far?'

Jay smiled at his excitement. This is a third Merlin I'm seeing, she thought. I've known the smiling media man and the veteran weighed down by a burden of guilt. This is Merlin the reporter. I like him best...

'You'll see what I'm getting at, Jay.' His voice was tense. 'A few years back I picked up an item on a tape...'

70

'A tape?' She queried the word which obviously meant something else to him.

'The agency tape in a newsroom,' he explained. 'I always notice anything to do with a massacre. This was a rumour that the true reason which drew Das Reich to this harmless village in June '44 was that they were after a treasure buried here.'

It all came back to him. A book had been published suggesting that the real reason why the inhabitants of Oradour were killed and every house set on fire was because the SS were looking for a hoard of gold and wanted to conceal the evidence of the search in which they tore every home in the village to pieces.

Merlin leaned towards Jay. 'Does history repeat itself so closely?' he asked. 'Two massacres due to two treasures at two places with the same name, within a few miles of each other?'

'Or was it the same treasure?' Jay wondered, intrigued by the way his mind worked.

Merlin grabbed the paper in both hands and crumpled it into a ball. 'You're the navigator. Work us out a route,' he ordered. 'We'd better take both cars in case we don't come back from Châlus.'

Exploring ancient sites was one of Jay's favourite relaxations. She lost count of time as her imagination ran free, trying to picture who had trodden a Roman flagstone on which she stood or who had passed through a now ruined medieval doorway – and wondering what the faint figures from the past had worn and felt and thought and said. Aged fifteen, she had spent an entire afternoon lost in imagination, sitting in the colonnade of the temple of Hephaistos at Athens while her worried parents scoured the Roman forum and the Akropolis, looking for her.

Well, she thought, looking up at the remains of Châlus Castle, this place has none of the magic of Athens, but it'll do. Any ruin is a place to dream and escape from the present for a while...

The tower that claimed King Richard's life was a squat, sullen pile of stone, like so many minor castles and donjons of the period dotted all over France – although in this case ruin and decay had given it a melancholy charm that the builders never intended.

Jay scrambled up the uneven hillside where the Lionheart's sap had fallen in eight hundred years before and collapsed the castle wall above. Much of the dressed stone from the damaged walls had afterwards been looted to rebuild the houses of the nearby village but, at the top of the mound, the blank face of the castle keep still towered intact, its only feature the arrow slit from which the fatal arrow had been fired.

It drew Jay like a magnet. She stumbled into some leafless brambles and found an old cobbled path beneath her feet. The thorns tore at her thick jeans. She was glad she had brought a pair of walking boots, her normal gear for exploring ruins.

There were no other visitors, which made conditions ideal. To savour the atmosphere of ruins, Jay needed to be alone, with no ice cream wrappers on the grass or coach parties posing noisily for photographs.

There was a shout from Merlin, a hundred feet below. No ruin-lover, he had opted to sleep off the heavy, five-course lunch they had eaten in a nearby workmen's restaurant and now lay stretched out on a sun-lounger beside the camping van. Jay turned and waved back. Although the crumbling walls were obviously dangerous, she scrambled precariously higher and higher up the keep, making for the arrow slit.

At the top she clambered on to the narrow, wind-eroded ledge behind the slit and knelt where the bowman had taken aim that fateful day in 1199. Breathing hard from the climb, Jay tried to put herself into the mind of the unknown archer sighting on the English king far below, pulling the string back, loosing it and...

There was again the sound in her head of a door closing and the voice that had cursed Becket cut off in mid-speech before she could hear what it had to say.

With the same ringing in her ears that had stopped her playing in the cathedral, Jay lost her balance. Vertigo grabbed her and she felt herself leaning farther and farther out into space, unable to do anything about it. A hundred feet below her lay a pile of fallen stones and below that, at the foot of the mound, she could see the camper where Merlin was asleep, with her own car parked beside it.

She knew that he would never hear her cry until it was too late.

Chapter 8

At the last moment, Jay felt her left arm twist behind her as though someone had grabbed it, enabling her to find an awkward hand-hold in the masonry.

The scene below faded to blackness and remembered noises bore in on her. There were men shouting, a strange rhythmic thudding, the sound of arrows tearing the air, an injured horse screaming like a man. And there were smells – of burning and, much closer a stink a putrefying flesh that was nauseating.

* * *

King Richard hurled the rotten carcase of the sheep on to the bucket of the trebuchet and straightened up, wiping filth off himself. 'Loose!' he bellowed.

With a groan of twisted sinews, the trebuchet arm described an arc, hit the padded stop with a thud and catapulted the stinking putrid mass over the castle walls.

The king roared with laughter at his practical joke. 'They want food, I'll give it to them,' he said to the sweating mercenaries who manned the battery of trebuchets and mangonels, catapults whose design had not changed much since Roman times.

Stepping deliberately clear of the protecting wickerwork screens, he shouted at the blank walls towering above: 'Eat that, you bastards!'

Still laughing, he ducked back into shelter as a volley of arrows shredded the air, *shew-shew-shew*, and bounced off the screen.

'Their aim is getting keener,' he remarked to Mercadier.

'They know there's not long to go,' the mercenary captain said dryly. It was common knowledge that the king intended to give no quarter on the morrow: every living soul in Châlus Castle was to be put to the sword.

From the mouth of the tunnel dug into the hillside came the noise of pick and shovel. The local peasantry, pressed into service at the point of a sword, had dug the sap far beneath the castle walls. Already men were piling huge faggots of twigs and branches smeared liberally with pig-fat against the pitch-soaked timbers which supported the roof of the cavern. When this mass was fired, the roof of the sap would collapse and the wall with it. Into the breach would leap five score of Mercadier's ruthless mercenaries, against whom the three knights defending the fortress with their men-at-arms would stand no chance.

Mercadier's eyes flicked from the sappers in the tunnel to his small battery of mobile catapults, thudding in the still, damp air with a repetitive rhythm as they hurled over the ramparts rocks, fire and filth of all descriptions.

A cry went up as a group of defenders were sighted trying to put out a fire in the castle stables. Mercadier barked a hoarse command and his bowmen loosed a volley. The same savage screaming, *shew-shew-shew*, and more arrows arched over the ramparts to impale living flesh within the walls. One of the distant figures in the smoke fell to the ground, which raised a rough cheer among the band of archers.

There was a thud and a scream of agony not ten paces from where Richard stood talking to Mercadier. A huge boulder had been thrust over the ramparts by the defenders and rolled down the hill to smash its way through the screens and crush one of the peasants carrying faggots. Two mercenaries tried to roll the rock off the man's body, then desisted as he screamed in agony from the broken ribs puncturing his lungs. Another boulder bumped and crashed its way down the hillside, carrying away more of the screens and crushing to death a faggot-laden mule.

The king who had taken pleasure in the slaughter of three thousand Muslim prisoners at the siege of Acre eight years before paid no heed to a single dying peasant. 'Good work.' Richard clapped Mercadier on the shoulder. 'Tomorrow the gold of Châlus is mine.'

Side by side, monarch and mercenary strode towards a stone horse trough where the king's mount was waiting safely out of bow-shot. At a cry of warning from the men by the catapults, they turned to face the castle and raised their kite-shaped shields to fend off a volley of arrows from the desperate defenders. Most fell short, one impaling another mule which had just been unloaded. It whinnied and bucked and reared, trying vainly to bite the thick shaft sticking out of its withers. One bounced feebly off the king's shield, its energy spent, and fell to the ground.

Twenty paces on, thinking himself safe in the poor light of dusk and well out of bow-shot, Richard handed his shield to the squire who was walking behind him. He lifted the iron helmet off his head and handed that to the squire, then slipped the coif – the hood of his mail hauberk – back from his head in order to scratch the itching at the base of his neck. The mail armour protected the wearer from casual blows and projectiles but it also protected the royal lice from their hosts's scratching.

'Ah!' he sighed with the pleasure and yawned. Besieging a castle – even a small one – was always a race against the arrival of reinforcements. In this case, there was no news of Count Aymar coming to the rescue so it seemed to Richard that the treasure would be his next day.

The king of England and half of France grabbed the reins from the peasant boy who was holding them, placed one foot on the edge of the horse trough and vaulted into the saddle. He turned his horse and reached down for the shield. As the squire passed it up to him, Mercadier turned back to the sap where he would drive his men hard all night long, if need be. He heard a gasp and a thud and turned to see the king stretched full-length on the ground, the horse rearing in fright. A short metal bolt from a crossbow had penetrated deeply into the mass of muscle at the base of the king's neck.

'Mercadier, I'm hit.' The king sounded more surprised than in pain. A professional in the business of warfare, he had failed to allow for the extra range of the newly-invented crossbow. He allowed the squire and the mercenary captain to pull him upright into a sitting position, from where he could see the castle. There was a white blur at the arrow-slit where the marksman's face peered down to see who his lucky shot had felled.

'Pull it out,' said Richard hoarsely, clutching at the bolt in his flesh.

As Mercadier's strong hands gripped the short missile and pulled uselessly, the king's face went white. Then, with a huge effort, he showed why he had been dubbed Lionheart. He thrust Mercadier aside and hauled himself painfully to his feet, to be half-lifted into the saddle, where he sat swaying, his sword arm held uselessly against his chest.

'No one is to know I'm hit, Mercadier,' he groaned. He did not want the mercenaries fading away in the night.

He grimaced with pain as the horse moved under him. Through gritted teeth he ordered the squire, 'Ride fast to my lodging in the village and tell Chaplain Milo to prepare infusions and unguents for my wound.'

The youth stood, mouth agape.

'Ride, I said,' snarled Richard, his face drawn with pain.

The squire leaped into his own saddle and whipped his mount into a gallop, scattering a path through the peasants carrying fuel for the fire in the sap.

A hundred miles away in the Boissy tower of Chinon Castle the sound of voice, recorder and rebec stopped abruptly in the queen's apartments.

'Stop!' Eleanor commanded. 'I am suddenly in no mood for melody.'

The troubadour and two ladies-in-waiting put down their instruments. The queen shivered and pulled a fur-lined cape round her shoulders for warmth. Troubled, she went to the window and peered out in the direction of Châlus. She felt again the premonition she had had on the day when Mercadier's man had clattered into the courtyard at Chinon with news of the treasure. She recalled how she had tried vainly to stop or at least delay her impetuous son.

The door closed quietly as her companions left the room. Outside, dusk was drawing in. The reflection in the glass of Eleanor's face, lit by the last rays of the setting sun, was lighter than the scene outside.

'Who are you, old woman?' she wondered aloud. 'How have I come to be trapped in your weak and withered body, while my spirit is yet so youthful and vigorous?'

In the reflection, she saw her left hand clench suddenly and clutch at the folds of the wimple above her right shoulder, as though pulling something through the fabric. She took the hand away and looked with distaste at her arthritic knuckles. Coloured by the last rays of sunlight, the skin of her hand was blood-red.

* * *

Jay was staring at the blood-red sun through clouds of smoke. Then the colour changed, the smoke thinned and vanished in front of her eyes. She found herself staring at the sun in order not to see the void below. Blinded, she shut her eyes and clutched with her right hand at a thick stem of ivy growing on the wall.

Although it peeled away from the stone almost instantly, the moment's resistance gave her the time to regain her balance. She pulled herself back to safety, heart pounding from the narrow escape, and fell back on to the ledge where she lay regaining her breath. Her left hand was bleeding where she had cut it. She wound a handkerchief roughly round it, closed her eyes and fell into a restless sleep peopled by figures who had been dead eight hundred years. On waking, she remembered only fragments of the dream but the narrow escape from falling to her death was a vivid memory.

Looking at the stone where the ivy had been, she found a line of stylised Gothic letters carved into the wall. It was part of an inscription still largely obscured by greenery. Warily, Jay wedged one foot and one hand into the arrow slit, found a narrow foot-hold between the stones for her other foot and reached out to tug the remaining ivy away from the wall. The carving was hard to read, even thrown into sharp relief by the angle of the sun. It looked like six lines of a song.

But why, Jay asked herself, would anyone carve a song high up on a castle wall?

In a pocket of her anorak she found a pencil and a scrap of paper and began carefully copying down the inscription: *'Savies que la pucelle...'*

Chapter 9

Merlin insisted on dressing the gash in Jay's hand. Only after he had re-packed the first aid case, would he let her show him what he called: 'This crazy poem you found.'

He squinted at the sheet of paper and passed it back. 'Doesn't mean a thing to me. The words look like French, but I can't recognise more than a couple of them.'

'It isn't modern French,' she explained. 'It's the old southern tongue called Langue d'Oc.'

'How come you can understand all this stuff?' he asked.

'The Chinon Ensemble, you remember? I told you we play Early Music. Many of the songs we perform are in Langue d'Oc.'

'So you can read it just like I read the *New York Times*?'

'More or less,' she agreed. 'It helps that I was bilingual in French to start with. My family comes from France, way back – refugees from the Terror. Hence our surname.'

'Wow! Scarlet Pimpernel stuff. This I gotta hear.' Merlin fixed his deep brown eyes on Jay.

Once again he made it easy to talk. Jay found herself telling him about family holidays in St Denis, her father's obsession with genealogy, and the research she had done with him on the family tree which stretched back to the Plantagenet period and – give or take a few guesses – to the royal line itself.

When she had finished, Merlin took the paper in his hand again. 'Where did you say this was carved?'

She pointed. 'Up there, to the right of the *meutrière* where the fatal bolt was fired from.'

'And how d'you know that's the right arrow-slit?'

She waved the green booklet. 'According to Michelin…'

Merlin shielded his eyes against the light but could make out nothing apart from a patch of lighter-coloured stone where the ivy had kept the weather at bay.

77

'There's nothing visible from the ground,' he commented. 'So tell me what would be the point of carving an inscription up there. Who's going to see it?'

'I don't know.'

She stared at the words on the paper. They had the familiar look of a well-known quotation or a verse of a song learnt in childhood. Merlin, she saw, had dozed off again in the warm sunshine. It took her an hour's work to make a proper translation, sitting in the shade on the step of the camper.

'Listen to this,' she called.

'Know that the maid with green eyes bold
And the great seer from Arthur's court
From beneath waters all unsought
Shall find why King Peter did not grow old.
As light and dark unearth the lion's bait
Which through the centuries doth wait.'

'Clever,' he commented.

'What is?'

'To translate it as verse. Isn't that difficult?'

'Sometimes,' Jay admitted, 'I spend a month working on the words of a song. This came out very easily in comparison.'

'The rhyme's odd,' he said, chewing a blade of grass.

'It's a *sirventès*.'

'What's that?' He had both eyes open now.

'A form of medieval verse.' Jay knelt in front of him on the grass and turned the paper over to show him the side copied from the original. 'See? It rhymes ABBACC. That's a *sirventès*. I kept the rhyming pattern in English to try and give it the same feel.'

'Sounds a bit like one of Nostradamus' quatrains,' he commented. 'You know, those sixteenth-century prophecies that some people believe have predicted the rise of Napoleon, the death of Hitler, the Gulf War and so on.'

Jay looked at the paper in her hand. 'If it's a prophecy...' she said playfully '...then that line about the great seer at Arthur's court has to mean Merlin.'

'Reading Nostradamus' verses is like doing crossword puzzles.' He took the paper from her. 'You get a knack for it and it's easy. Now here... The maid with green eyes bold is you, but who the hell's King Peter?'

Jay racked her memory. 'I never heard of a King Peter – French or English.'

Merlin lay back on the lounger studying her notebook. 'That's what happens with Nostradamus: just when you're getting somewhere, you meet a brick wall.'

He paused. 'You know the most uncanny line of all?'

'The one about "the seer at King Arthur's court"?'

He grunted. 'Actually it's the next one. "From beneath waters all unsought" could mean in plain speech: from Atlantis.'

'It probably does. In the Middle Ages they were preoccupied with the legend of the land beneath the sea.'

'Remember the song *Marching Through Georgia*?' Merlin asked. 'Well, I was born in Fair Oaks. It's a piece of nowhere just across the Chattahoochee River from the city of Atlanta.'

'And line 5,' said Jay banteringly. 'That fits too. I'm blonde and your hair is dark.'

Merlin yawned and handed back the notebook. 'You see how these things work on people who want to believe? It's like fortune-telling. You talk the facts into fitting the wording.'

'In line six,' Jay continued, "Unearth the lion's bait" must mean digging up the treasure that lured Richard the Lionheart right here to his death.'

Merlin laughed. 'It's a good game, isn't it? We solved all the clues. Now we've got the whole crossword filled in, except for nine down...'

He put on a spooky voice: 'Whereabouts of treasure map marked "Dig Here".'

Jay closed the notebook and lay down on the second lounger. She still felt drowsy despite falling asleep in the castle. Merlin was right: the meal had been wonderful but heavy... and they had drunk quite a bit of wine with it.

'All the same,' she said, closing her eyes, 'it's weird how many possible references there are to you and me in a *sirventès* which was carved up there very soon after the siege that cost Richard his life.'

'How can you be so sure of the date?' Merlin leaned across the gap between the loungers and shook her. 'The date. How can you be so sure?'

She pushed sleep aside with difficulty. 'The *sirventès* died out soon after. But Richard and his mother, Queen Eleanor, used to exchange whole letters rhyming ABBACC.'

'Why?'

'A sort of code. In those days you could never tell who would intercept a messenger, so they wrote to each other in cryptic poems full of allusions that would mean little or nothing to strangers.'

'That figures,' he commented.

'King Richard was both a poet and a composer.'

Merlin nodded, not looking at her. 'There's that story of his minstrel

79

singing outside the castle in Austria – a song which only the king would know because he had written it.'

'It was a *tenso*.'

'What's that?'

'A two-part song. The whole point was that only Richard knew the descant to sing to Blondel's melody.'

'Positive identification. Clever.'

Through half-closed lids, Jay saw Merlin pick her notebook off the ground and study it.

'Dürnstein,' he said. 'Where Blondel sang outside the castle. I just remembered.'

Another memory tugged at his consciousness, just out of reach. He stood up and stretched. 'I need some exercise. Why don't we both climb up there, so I can take a look at this carving for myself?'

'Because I'm asleep.'

'Come on.'

They climbed in silence. As the going became difficult on the crumbling top of the wall, Merlin drew further and further ahead.

'Wait for me,' Jay called. 'I'm stuck.'

He turned, balanced on the narrow stone ridge at the top. 'You're doing fine. Just keep coming straight towards me.'

'I'm sorry, I get vertigo.'

Merlin clambered back and saw that her eyes were closed.

'You're okay now.' He sounded sympathetic. 'Here, grab my hand.' He pulled Jay up to the ledge behind the arrow slit where she sat as close to the wall as possible, refusing to look down.

'If you're as bad as that,' he asked, 'how did you manage to get up here before, all on your own?'

'I don't know.'

'Dutch courage from all that vino at lunch?' he grinned.

'Maybe.'

'I don't see any carving,' he said. 'Where is it?'

Jay forced herself not to think about the height. 'You have to wedge yourself into the arrow-slit and swing out in front of the wall to read it.'

He shot her a doubtful look. 'So it can only be read by the angels? That really makes sense.'

Merlin squeezed through the eroded slit and thrust himself into space, causing Jay to scream at him, 'What the hell are you doing?'

'It's okay.' His face reappeared outside the slit, looking puzzled.

'How are you holding on out there?'

'A hand-jam. Relax! You shove your hand into a slit in the rock and clench your fist. Bingo! Safe as if there was a handle to hold on to. But I can't make out this mysterious carving of yours.'

'You're clinging too close to the wall to see it. Lean out further,' she instructed. 'You've got to be at the correct angle to see the lettering.'

Merlin hung for a couple of minutes over the sheer drop before he swung himself back through the slit.

'Well?' asked Jay, when he was safe.

He looked sceptical. 'I couldn't make out more than a word or two. It looks like there was some carving there once, but it could just be the way the stone has weathered.'

Puzzled, Jay pushed herself through the narrow slit and leaned out as far as she dared. It was true. The sun had moved more than she had realised since the first time she had climbed the tower. Instead of throwing the carved words into sharp relief, the indifferent lighting revealed only the faint trace of a few Gothic letters – and even those would not be clear to an untrained eye that did not know what it was looking for.

As Merlin helped her back to safety, she shuddered. 'You think I made the whole thing up.'

They climbed down in silence, Merlin helping Jay until they were nearly at the bottom. With a sigh of relief, she sat down on a pile of tumbled stones. Her legs were still trembling.

Then he said: 'No, I don't think you made it up. Tell me about this medieval poetry and the songs you sing.'

Jay wondered if he was listening; his mind seemed far away. She was in the middle of telling him something when he snapped his fingers and said: 'Got it! Whilst we were climbing up there I was trying to recall the name of an SS officer I interviewed years ago. It was no big deal – in fact the piece got spiked – but I remember the guy made no secret of the fact that he had served in the Das Reich division. For all I know he was at Oradour. And he lives – guess where?'

'Tell me.'

'Dürnstein, in Austria.' Merlin looked pleased with himself. 'Now how's that for a coincidence?'

'Creepy.'

'...is the word. Kempfer was his name. I think I'm going to drop in on ex-Major Kempfer and ask him what he and his pals were doing, hanging around here on tenth June 1944 instead of racing northwards to push the Allies back into the sea.'

'D'you think he'll answer?' she asked.

Merlin grinned, 'You'd be amazed what questions people will answer if you roll up out of the blue and catch them off their guard.'

'Why?'

He laughed. 'Well, rationally I should say: Because we newsmen always promise to protect our sources.'

'But in fact?'

He paused. 'You'd make a pretty good reporter yourself, you know that? I suspect it's because – as every taxman, detective and priest knows – a lot of people just want to spill the beans. The right question at the right moment and they'll tell you how they killed their wife or swindled the shareholders or rigged an election. You'd be amazed what secrets people have freely divulged to me in off-the-record conversations.'

Merlin squatted down to bring his head level with Jay's. 'How d'you feel about coming along for the trip? It'll be fun.'

'Just like that?' she asked, to gain time. 'You take off for the other end of Europe on the spur of the moment and expect me to come with you?'

He seemed impatient to be off. 'I like to move fast when I get an idea.'

Jay could feel him willing her to say yes. To break the eye contact she turned and picked up the notebook which had fallen out of her hip pocket when she sat down. He was still waiting for an answer.

I'm on holiday, she thought. I can do what I want. There's no reason not to go... But it seemed better to play safe with: 'Thanks, I'm supposed to be taking a break. Catching planes and staying in hotels is something I can do without for a while.'

Chapter 10

Like most musicians, Jay drove long distances several times a week and normally had a good sense of direction. She had gone several miles along the Paris-Bordeaux motorway before she realised from the road-signs that she was heading in the wrong direction. She pulled her car into a service area and opened the window to breathe some cold air, wondering what she had been thinking about to get lost in a part of France she knew well.

Merlin, was the answer. He was not like any other man she knew. But then, she reasoned, they were all musicians or connected with the world of music, whereas he was… What was he? Just when she thought she had him pigeonholed, he revealed another aspect of his complex personality.

She had known him only forty-eight hours and yet she missed him already. At Châlus she had jumped into her car and driven off without saying goodbye properly because she had felt an irrational anger at the way he had suddenly decided to head for Vienna on the spur of the moment. And yet, she thought rationally, why shouldn't he go to Vienna if he wanted? He didn't owe her anything, any more than she owed him, so why had she been angry? It didn't make sense, but then nothing made sense about Merlin.

Ah well, she sighed, if he wanted to play reporters, she could do that too – and research the *sirventès* carved on the castle at Châlus. There was a specialist bookshop in Bordeaux which Jay remembered visiting with her father years before when they were working on the family tree. If she pushed the three-litre turbo-charged engine of the Alpine to the limit, it should be possible to get to Bordeaux before the shops closed…

She broke all the motorway regulations, enjoying the thrill of speed and the concentration of overtaking everything else on the road. Arriving in Bordeaux, all the lights were green. She sailed through the outskirts and headed by memory into the maze of narrow streets that made up the old quarter of the town, to find the shop with ten minutes to spare before closing time. There was a space on a yellow line right in front of the door, where she left the car unlocked and ran inside.

It was the right place. A pale and monkish assistant unearthed three books from a top shelf and blew the dust off them. Jay left the shop clutching Amy Kelly's scholarly biography of Eleanor of Aquitaine and two books of early medieval poetry which included a number of *sirventès* attributed to Eleanor and to Richard the Lionheart.

She began the drive back to St Denis, only to find every light red and every street blocked solid with rush-hour traffic. It was easier to park and let the commuters get away than fight them for road-space so she pulled up in a part of the town she had never visited to order a cup of coffee on the glassed-in terrace of a pavement café. There she fidgeted with the books, unable to concentrate on them, putting her mood of suppressed excitement down to the adrenalin of the long drive against the clock.

Across the street was an ugly ancient building which she had never visited. It was the Cathedral of St André. To kill time, Jay crossed the street and plunged into the cold gloom within. She shivered and pulled the collar of her anorak round her neck. The dressing which Merlin had strapped to the back of her hand rubbed against her chin, reminding her of Châlus.

The interior of the cathedral was uninspiring. Jay had played in many great churches but this building had none of the soaring elegance of Canterbury or the architectural poetry of Bourges. It was a hotch-potch of many periods of architecture, each fighting the others.

A chord rang out from the massive organ which was being tuned for a recital. The noise drew Jay's eye to the magnificently carved organ screen from which a life-size wooden flute-player gazed down at her.

Another chord, louder. And another louder still. The entire volume of air in the building resonated, amplifying the sound to a level that hurt Jay's sensitive musician's ears. She made for the nearest door and was just passing a hugely ugly wooden pulpit when the organ tuner pulled out all the stops. She stopped in her tracks, hands clamped over her ears, almost screaming with pain at the noise.

A late shaft of sunlight from a hole in one of the high stained glass windows led her eye along its golden path full of dancing dust-motes to the head of a woman carved at the top of a column which was set into the wall behind the pulpit.

In the silence after the organ chord died away Jay heard the echo of her books falling to the stone floor. The sound echoed back and forth across the nave of the empty cathedral. To her trained ear, that echo was frighteningly familiar; it was a harmonic of the door slam that had drawn a gauze veil over her eyes and left her spinning with vertigo in Canterbury Cathedral.

*   *   *

'Dear God, Chaplain Milo, to what have we come? The king stinks worse than a week-old corpse!'

Queen Eleanor felt ill with fatigue. She clung to the arm of Richard's chaplain outside the hovel in which the stricken king lay on his bed of pain.

She had started from Chinon Castle within the hour of receiving news of the king's condition, and covered the hundred miles to Châlus in two days and two nights of non-stop travel on horseback, by boat and in a litter suspended between two horses, taking whatever means was quickest for each stage. The only stretch of paved carriageway had been the few miles where her route ran along an old Roman road. She swayed now with fatigue and clutched the chaplain's arm more tightly.

A harsh grating sound of metal on stone made her look up to where two bodies were suspended in chains from the battlements of the castle, where they swung grotesquely in the wind. Several dwellings in the village were burning. A cloud of sparks rose into the damp air as a cottage roof fell in.

'I have cut the missile from the king's flesh.' The chaplain was eager to show that he had fulfilled his duty as physician to Richard's body as well as his soul.

'It took four men to hold King Richard down, though it was by his own command that I cut and gouged until I could pull out the bolt. By the time I was done, the king's neck was nearly severed from his shoulder. I washed the wound with infusions of herbs, applied poultices soaked in unguents and bound it...'

'He'll die,' she said.

Milo bent his head. 'God's will be done, Madam.'

Eleanor's face spasmed with repressed tears. A part of her mind wanted to throw herself on the bed where her adored favourite son lay wounded and simply howl with grief.

'You,' she had told Richard so many times when he was a child, 'will be the greatest king that Christendom has ever known.'

'You,' she had caressed him by word and touch so many times as he grew into manhood, 'are the bravest knight, the most handsome poet, the most gifted of musicians, most beautiful of men.'

'You, chaplain,' she said now, 'went with Richard on Crusade.'

'I did.'

'You've dressed his wounds before.' She caught the priest by both arms and shook him. 'You are skilled in these things. Think once again, lest there be something else we can do for the king!'

The chaplain spoke wretchedly, betraying his own love for his royal master. 'Once the black evil has entered mortal flesh, there is nothing anyone can do, Madam.'

Eleanor shook him with a man's energy. 'Think, Priest. Think hard. I'll build you a chapel in Chinon Castle if you can save the king's life. I'll build you an abbey if you want, so think!'

Milo gestured helplessly. 'In the Holy Land, they say some Saracen magicians have the art to cast out the infection that stinks.'

'Would that such a magician were here this day,' she groaned. 'Oh, Richard, I would pay the devil himself all the gold in Christendom to save you.'

Milo sank to his knees sighing, 'Let us pray.'

Instead of joining him, Eleanor raised her face to the sullen clouds scudding on from the Atlantic and addressed Him as an equal: 'You bastard! You've taken away the only man this old woman loves.'

'Get up!' She pushed the priest roughly. Later she could be a mother and give way to grief for the suffering of flesh that was born of hers; first she had to be a queen.

'Damn praying,' she said angrily. 'You've worn the knees out of your hose and it hasn't saved my son's life. As for Richard's soul, you'll have all eternity to pray for that, Chaplain. No, the time for praying's past. You'll write instead.'

'To whom?'

'To history,' Eleanor threw at him. 'You're a clerk, so go fetch pen, ink and paper. I'll dictate you the king's testament while he can still sign and press a seal on wax with his own strength.'

She put a hand on the door of the hovel in which the King of England and half of France lay dying, then turned as another question struck her: 'Where's the gold, Milo? Where is the gold that lured my son here? Tell me that.'

The chaplain indicated a house more substantial than the rest, one of the few that had not been plundered and burnt to the ground in the routine orgy of destruction that had accompanied the siege of the castle itself. It was here that Mercadier had quartered himself. There were candles showing behind the parchment in the window frames. A confusion of shouts, blows and screams came from within. On the doorstep lay a huddle of naked, broken, blood-streaked bodies.

'Mercadier has the surviving prisoners in there,' said Milo. 'He hanged half the garrison and put the rest to torture but none have talked of gold. Or so I'm told.'

* * *

Jay felt a hand take her elbow.

'*Vos livres, madame. Vous les avez laissés tomber.*' It was Milo's voice, or another similar: soft and priestly. The sacristan beside her was holding the books he had picked up off the floor.

She took them from his with a murmured: '*Merci.*'

'Are you feeling all right?' he asked. 'You look pale. Perhaps you would like a drink of water?'

Jay let him lead her through the gloom to a chair by the door where she sat down. On a small shelf by the offertory box stood a carafe of water and some glasses.

As he poured the water there was a final chord on the organ. In quick succession she saw again the dying king, the kneeling priest, the bloodied corpses. As the last echoes of the chord reverberated and died, so the images grew fainter and vanished.

'Whose head?' she asked the sacristan.

He smiled and passed her the glass. 'Now that is one of the cathedral's treasures. Perhaps the greatest. It's a pity the pulpit hides it. I'm often asked to show tourists where it is. You English call her Queen Eleanor, and know her as the wife of your King Henry II, but to the French she is the Duchess of Aquitaine.'

Jay took a sip of the water. It tasted flat and stale. His voice had the monotone of men who spend their time whispering in churches.

'The carving – ' he was obviously pleased to talk to someone interested. ' – is supposedly an excellent likeness of Queen Eleanor. It was done from the life at the time of her wedding in this cathedral, to Louis the King of France. She was only fifteen at the time...'

Jay was not listening. She could not understand what she was doing, sitting there, drinking stale water from a glass. Everything after the sight of Eleanor's head was a smudge in her memory. The blare of a car horn brought her to herself in the middle of the multi-lane traffic outside the cathedral. A taxi-driver was leaning out of his window and shouting at her something about committing suicide without his help.

Jay wondered how she had got there. She waited for a gap in the vehicles and hurried back to her own car, pulse racing. She sat shaking for several minutes, before turning her key in the ignition. Inside her head there was the sensation of something soft and heavy pressing down. Could one feel a tumour growing? she wondered. Would it press against the skull? How thorough had her father's examination been?

Chapter 11

The cottage was damp and chilly when Jay got back to St Denis. She had left two of the portable radiators burning but both were cold, the gas bottles empty. It was too late to change them at the local shop so she foraged in the barn for vine-prunings to use as kindling and lit a huge log fire in the open fireplace in the kitchen.

The farmhouse had been added to and rebuilt many times over the centuries. The kitchen wing was thought to be thirteenth-century or possibly even older. There were the remains of a roasting spit cemented into the smoke-blackened sides of the fireplace. A selection of heavy black wrought-iron fire tools hung from hand-forged hooks. A cauldron in which Jay's mother sometimes made soup for visitors, hung just out of the flames on its thick, ratcheted iron trammel.

Jay was not hungry after the heavy lunch she and Merlin had eaten at Châlus, but opened a bottle of local wine and a packet of biscuits from the pantry which the mice had missed.

The chill that had entered into her in the cathedral would not go; she wondered whether she had caught Leila's bug and pulled her chair closer to the fire, trying to get warm. Most of the heat went straight up the wide chimney. She moved a reading lamp closer and nudged the chair closer still towards the warmth until she was sitting almost within the huge fireplace, sipping the wine and nibbling biscuits. It was hard to concentrate on the books; the words kept floating on the page as she tried to remember what had happened in the cathedral.

She could remember standing in front of the pulpit, looking up at the carved head... and the pain in her brain from the noise of the organ. She recalled her eye following the sunbeam... but in her memory the carved features were unclear, as though there had been a veil in the way.

The phone rang, startling her. It was Merlin, calling from a phone box at Vienna's Schwechat airport. The line was not very good and he was having to shout: 'Glad I got through to you, Jay. I'm just ringing to apologise for what you walked into yesterday evening at Oradour.'

'That's okay.'

The line was silent except for the ghost of another conversation.

'I wanted you to know that doesn't often happen.' Merlin sounded awkward. 'And I wanted to say it was fun today at the castle.'

'I enjoyed it too,' she said, aware that she sounded still and formal.

'Did I wake you up?' he asked.

'No, I was reading.'

'You sound a long way away, Jay. And I'm running out of coins. The airport change office is closed – some kind of strike. I've just a few *schillings* they let me have at the Hertz desk. Oh, hell, I really rang to say this trip would have been a lot more fun if you'd come along.'

'I wish I was there,' she said.

'I'll ring again,' he shouted. 'G'night. The money's just...'

Jay replaced the receiver.

The thick biography of Eleanor had fallen to the floor when the phone rang. She picked it up, open at a random page, and found on it a detailed description of the siege of Châlus, including King Richard's death at the hands of a crossbowman by name of Pierre Basile.

The name nagged her. Then she shivered with fear as she deciphered another line of the *sirventès*. She wished Merlin had rung ten minutes later, so that she could have told him.

In Greek, she recalled, *basileos* meant king. Hence basilica, originally the king's house. Thus, the line 'Why King Peter did not grow old' must mean: why Pierre Basile, the slayer of King Richard, had to die.

A leaden heaviness fell on her. She sat, unable to move a finger, staring into the flickering fire in the large open fireplace with its heavy iron spit and blackened fire-irons.

* * *

The naked figure of a young man was hanging from an iron bar in front of the large open fireplace. His bloody trussed feet dangled clear of the ground. His hands and arms were lashed with brutal tightness to the bar by leather thongs. His bruised and bleeding head hung down, like Christ's upon the cross.

He groaned as consciousness returned. Lacking the strength to raise his head, his field of vision was the nightmare bloodscape of his own chest and belly, whose skin hung in agonizing strips and folds, peeled from his body inch by inch. Through swollen, bloody lips and toothless gums, he repeated, as he had in each interval of lucidity: 'I have the king's pardon. I have the king's pardon. I have...'

Two thickset, sweating men – Mercadier's specialists in the skills of the torture chamber – worked by the light of the fire and brace of thick tallow candles stolen from Châlus church. Their job was to prolong the youth's exquisite agony for as long as possible without actually killing him. A group of their comrades sat drinking looted wine and watching. One of the candles had been ringed at regular intervals, to serve as a rough time-keeper. The men were wagering with each other how many rings would have burnt away when the youth died.

Apart from pleading that the dying king had pardoned him of the crime of regicide, Pierre Basile had said nothing – or at any rate, nothing that Mercadier wanted to hear.

Outside, there was a tang of wood-smoke in the clean dry air as Eleanor left the hovel in which the king had just died and gathered her cloak around her against the frost. The *routiers* had set fire to everything combustible in the village of Châlus, preparatory to their withdrawal next morning. Several of the hovels in the village were still smouldering, an occasional shower of sparks erupting between roofless walls. There was a sound of drunken singing and a girl's scream.

Along the muddy track between the houses, Eleanor hurried, a cloaked and hooded figure. Ahead of her – for the moon was not yet up – a man dressed as a knight carried a sputtering pine-resin torch to light the way.

A group of drunken looters, carrying a heavy oak chest between them, staggered across their path. The queen's escort lowered the torch so that they could see the arms he bore on the linen surcoat worn over the hauberk of mail. William the Marshal's reputation as the greatest knight of his time cut a path through the drunken men more quickly than his sword would have done.

Outside Mercadier's headquarters, two of the *routiers* were taunting with a flaming torch a sullen, frightened peasant girl with dishevelled clothing and blood on her legs. Around her neck was a halter which one of the men was holding. William brushed them aside and stood back to let the queen enter first.

She confronted Mercadier like a whirlwind. 'This is the boy, Pierre Basile?'

'And if it is?' His brain was slow from the wine he had drunk.

'I command you to deliver him to me.'

'He's mine, so long as he lives,' Mercadier growled.

'And that won't be long,' laughed one of the drunken men. 'Look at the candle. It's nearly gone.'

'Leave us,' the queen ordered the men without looking at them.

'Stay,' said Mercadier.

Behind them, the tortured youth swayed back and forth on the iron bar. The queen's escort thrust his torch into a metal bracket on the wall in order to have both hands free. Manoeuvring to make sure that no-one stood behind him, William loosed his sword in its sheath.

'I command you, Mercadier.' The queen thrust in front of his eyes her right hand, to show him the signet ring she had taken from the dead king's finger. On it the three lions, which Richard had chosen as the arms of England, defied Mercadier to continue.

'By this ring I command you to leave our presence,' she repeated. 'And take your men with you.'

Mercadier hesitated. There was a hiss of steel on steel as William the Marshal half-drew his sword. With ill grace, Mercadier kissed the ring and ordered his men out of the room.

The boy was unconscious again. He recovered to find his entire body a network of pain on different wavelengths. First came the great slow waves that seemed to tear his chest and belly apart with each agonizing breath. Then the deeper stabs of pain from his twisted, broken arms and the sharp pulsation of damaged nerves in his skull from where the teeth had been torn out one by one. His swollen jaw was broken in two places.

He groaned and found his head lifted gently, a sponge soaked in water squeezed tenderly against his bruised and cut lips. Even that slight pressure hurt. A spasm of agony forced another groan from his lips. At a second touch of the sponge he opened his eyes to see a knight supporting his head and offering him the sponge again. Behind the knight a lady, dressed in such finery as the boy had never seen.

'Do you know who I am?' Queen Eleanor asked in a clear voice.

Pierre Basile's pain-filled eyes rested briefly on her and he shook his head imperceptibly.

She lifted her hand with the ring that had forced Mercadier's obedience. The boy recognised it as the one he had kissed on Richard's finger. 'The king,' he said pathetically, 'pardoned me.'

'I know that,' she said, speaking slowly and clearly. 'And I know also that you swore an oath of secrecy – that you would never divulge your secret knowledge. How I know such things is my affair. Now listen, boy. I am Queen Eleanor, mother of the king – and for the moment your lawful monarch. By this ring I do absolve you from your oath.'

Still he looked at her, wavering between consciousness and oblivion. The power of her eyes held him.

'Tell me. And then I bring you peace,' she promised.

He was aware only of her green eyes, holding him – and of a miracle. There was no pain. As long as he looked into her eyes, he knew she would hold the pain at bay by her will. As long as he clung to them, the pain would hover but not strike, like wolves keeping their distance at night from a fire.

'There will be no more pain,' she said, reading his mind. 'You have that on a queen's honour.'

Eleanor leaned forward to catch the words that could have saved the boy so much suffering, and listened intently.

'Do you swear to that?' she asked, raising to his cracked and swollen lips a crucifix worn on a cord around her neck. 'Do you swear it by Christ's passion on the Cross?'

'I do,' said Pierre Basile thickly, knowing they were his last words.

'Here, lad, your time is come.' William the Marshall spoke compassionately. With no more emotion that a butcher skinning a rabbit, he slipped the steel of his poignard between the exposed ribs and thrust straight and true to the heart. And Pierre Basile died, gazing into the eyes of a queen.

'The boy?' asked Mercadier anxiously as Eleanor left.

His bloodshot eyes took in the bright red stain on William's surcoat. The marshal's sword was in his right hand and a bloody poignard in the left, ready for combat. The knight who had served both Henry and Richard Plantagenet would not hesitate to take on a dozen of Mercadier's men.

'The boy's all yours, Mercadier,' the queen said unemotionally. 'Do with him what you will.'

* * *

Groggily Jay recognised Leila's face peering in through the small window above the sink. She shivered. The fire had gone out hours before, leaving her stiff and cold after spending the whole night in the uncomfortable chair. She was surprised, on opening the door, to find that it was already late-morning.

'Booze!' Leila accused her. 'I do that sometimes – fall asleep in a chair with a bottle of vino. You feel terrible the next day. Serves you right.'

Jay passed a hand over her eyes. 'The light's too bright.'

'Never,' Leila disagreed. 'Not for an artist. But since you're obviously not in the market for conversation, I'll deliver my message and be on my way.'

'Don't go.' Jay clutched her; she did not want to be left alone.

'You're lucky.'

'Why?'

'I sold a picture and paid the telephone bill yesterday.'

'That makes me lucky?'

'Merlin called me last night.'

'He did?' Jay groped for a switch and plugged in the coffee-maker.

Leila nibbled a biscuit and spat it out. 'Yugh! These are mouldy. He said he'd tried calling this number several times before giving up and trying me.'

She picked up the telephone on the kitchen table and listened to the dialling tone. 'Sounds okay now. Anyway, Merlin said he'd spoken to you earlier in the evening, but when he tried to ring you and say goodnight, he couldn't get through. He asked me to come round and make sure you were all right. Now why would he do that?'

'I don't know.'

Leila grinned. 'Sounds like love to me. Were you out, or just didn't want to answer the phone?'

Jay yawned. 'I was asleep.'

'Must have been the sleep of the dead,' said Leila.

'I feel like death.'

'Maybe you caught that 'flu bug I had.'

'Maybe.'

'Well, the conversation's great. I'll be off.' Leila waved a handful of bank-notes from her shoulder-bag. 'I have money. A rich man of impeccable taste has fallen in love with my paintings or my body – I don't know which as yet. I am going to share my good fortune by paying some of my creditors. It's a good day for the shopkeepers of St Denis.'

'Stay and have some coffee,' begged Jay.

'Lovely idea,' Leila laughed. 'But you forgot to put either water or coffee into the machine. Byeee.'

Jay went round the house throwing open the shutters to let daylight into every room. There was a faint glow of red in the embers of the fire, but when she knelt down to relight it, a wave of revulsion pushed her back from the open fire-place with the black fire-irons swinging from the bar of the spit and creaking slightly in the draught.

The coffee did not help. Jay sat on a chair in the sun-filled garden, nursing the cup but lacking the energy to do anything. This isn't like me, she thought. Twice in less than a week I've slept till nearly midday. And instead of feeling good afterwards, I feel a hundred and twenty years old...

There were large parts of the previous day for which she could not account: blank hours which she could not fill in. And in their place were flash-memories of scenes and events that belonged in someone else's mind: blood, pain and murder.

Am I going mad? Jay wondered. She thought of getting the car out of the barn and going after Leila – to have someone to talk to – but had not the energy. And even if she found Leila, what could she say to her?

93

Part 3

Chapter 1

Midday was chiming on an ornate Baroque clock in the main square of Dürnstein when Merlin drove into a parking lot outside the ancient ramparts of the little town. He chose a place between a Saab with an S plate and an English-registered Volvo, remembering from his in-flight reading that the town had been sacked in 1645 by the Swedes.

By the look of Dürnstein, he thought, the latter-day Vikings had not done a very thorough job on the town although little now remained of the massive fortress which had once dominated this stretch of the Danube valley. Above the car park, a ribbon of masonry straggled up the hill towards the remains of the castle where Richard the Lionheart had been held to ransom on his way home from the abortive Third Crusade in 1193.

Merlin locked the hire car and stretched. Why, he asked himself, had it seemed so imperative the previous day to say goodbye to Jay and rush off to the other end of Europe? For once there was no editor littering the world with cables, no deadline to set up the parabolic antenna for a transmission on the other side of the globe, no telephone messages waiting everywhere he arrived: 'Will Mr Freeman please call...'

So why the hustle for a story that was eight centuries old? There was no logical answer, just a gut feeling that could not be put into words.

And why hadn't he put more energy into persuading Jay to come along? It would have made the trip a whole lot more fun. The answer to that was easy: he'd been wary of appearing too pushy after the first evening when she had shown a hint of the toughness that had made her a top performer. But maybe he should have been more assertive, not less than usual? The problem was, he reflected, that he did not want to risk making a wrong move with Jay...

There was an hour to kill before the appointment with Baron Kempfer. To get some fresh air, Merlin decided to climb up to the castle ruins and take in what Baedecker recommended as a magnificent view worthy of one asterisk. At the top he sat on a section of wall reduced by the Swedes nearly to ground level and studied the town with the wide, slow-moving Danube River beyond. Swollen with winter rains, it was brownish-grey rather than blue. A burst of spring sunshine lit up a stream of barges ploughing their way upriver.

To the east the Danube wound down the valley towards Vienna which showed as a smudge of pollution on the horizon – and westwards to Linz, which would have been the capital of the world if everything had worked out according to Hitler's plans and those of the SS Division Das Reich. By habit, Merlin undid his camera case and took several shots on different lenses, despite the haze.

He strolled around what remained of the castle walls, wondering what Jay would make of them. Had these stones really echoed to Blondel's voice singing the two-part song of which only King Richard knew the descant? It was more likely, Merlin thought, that such a romantic story had been cooked up by the Lionheart's PR man, as a clever way of diverting attention from the fact that the king's release was going to be an expensive pleasure for his subjects on both sides of the Channel! The ransom of a million silver marks was worth in modern terms several billion dollars.

Ruins were not Merlin's scene; he knew almost nothing of medieval history and wished Jay were with him to make the place come alive, as she had for a moment at Châlus. He recalled her sitting on a pile of stones below the ruined keep and singing a song, which she said had been written by Richard during his captivity at Dürnstein.

> *'Ja nus hons pris ne dira sa raison*
> *adroitement, se dolantement non...'*

She had translated the words for Merlin: 'What prisoner can ever argue his own case? He can however write a poem to comfort himself.'

Strange words for a song, thought Merlin. Whoever wrote the song – whether Richard or the PR guy – certainly knew what it was like to be locked up in prison...

The gloomy train of thought led to memories of the months he had been locked in the dark cellar during the siege of Beirut. Some days he had not even been given food or water but cowered foetus-like round the clock on a filthy bug-ridden blanket, twitching and whimpering with each near impact as artillery pounded the buildings above. He had done everything the psychologists recommended a hostage should do, endeavouring to make contact with his hooded and masked captors by begging and arguing with them. He had told them about himself, his wife, his family... and ended up by talking to the walls and the rats and bugs, which were friendlier.

And since his escape he had thought a million times about it. The random shell breaching a prison and sparing the prisoner – that was permissible chance, okay. But there was no way of explaining away the veiled woman who had led him to safety.

He had seen her several times since that day. The first time had been a week or so after his release. It was at midnight, in the bar of the Intercontinental Hotel. Merlin had sat on one of the high stools, getting drunk, surrounded by the flushed faces of the press-gang, who were noisily trying to drown the war outside in alcohol. Absent friends, some of whom had vanished with a bang above ground and some with a whimper in rat-infested cellars, were traditionally remembered over drinks late at night when their favourite jokes were re-told as a requiem. Their memory was saluted by drunken, ribald laughs and hash-high giggles instead of a bugle playing the Last Post.

Merlin listened to the jokes but they didn't connect; no cathartic mirth came to release him. He had become an outsider, unable to drink and smoke his way into the old feeling of belonging to the noisy, boozy, risk-taking, live-for-the-moment fraternity in the bar. So he downed drink after useless drink and sat surrounded by an invisible curtain, cut off from the strangers with whom he had worked for years.

It did not surprise him to see the veiled woman standing at the end of the bar. That night she seemed more real than his flesh-and-blood companions.

A woman reporter from Italian television – universally loathed for stealing other people's stories – was congratulating Merlin on his escape. As she kissed him on the lips, Merlin saw the other woman watching. Next day the news came in that the Italian camera team had driven over a mine on the road to Tyre. All were dead. Two days later, despatching some film at the airport, he bumped into a French newspaper photographer he had known for years. Again the veiled woman was watching. Less than a month after the Frenchman had been buried, Merlin saw her again just after talking on the telephone to his mother on the day before she died in a car crash.

After the funeral, he resigned. The reaction from the New York office had been a raise in salary. After a three-month break, Merlin went back to work – not for the money but because it was the job he knew best. And as the months passed, he became used to grieving twice: once when he saw the veiled woman and again when Death rolled the dice. Merlin knew that his own number would not come up. On the contrary, he developed an uncanny ability to stay one step away from danger which, among the cynics of his profession, earned him the nickname of Merlin the Magician. In his own mind he thought of himself not as a magician, but rather as a modern counterpart of Coleridge's Ancient Mariner, condemned to sail the seas of life with a burden of unexpiable guilt.

He stood on the razed mound of Dürnstein castle overlooking the misty Danube valley, breathing in deep lungfuls of the cold spring air. Through a gap in the ruined walls he caught a glimpse of a woman with blonde hair. Her voice reminded him of Jay. He accelerated his pace and turned the corner fast, almost colliding with a couple of pale-skinned Swedish tourists. They were carrying folding chairs and a picnic box, looking for somewhere out of the wind to eat their lunch. Merlin nodded politely to them and sauntered on, killing time.

Chapter 2

Baron Kempfer's villa stood on a knoll overlooking the Danube. The driveway led through a well-kept garden of lawns and flower-beds just emerging from their winter wraps. There were two gardeners raking the grass and sprinkling moss-killer as Merlin drove in.

A maid kept him waiting in a room with picture windows on two walls which gave views both onto the river and the town. The furnishings were comfortable and tasteful, not ostentatious. It was the house of a successful provincial industrialist; in Krems, the nearest big town, the factory of Kempfer Chimie AG was a major employer.

To make the appointment Merlin had used an old journalist's trick: 'I have a lot more evidence but I don't want to talk on the telephone.' Since then the baron had had time to regain confidence. He limped into the room, an old and rather bent man, leaning heavily on a thick stick, who sat without shaking Merlin's hand.

'You're wasting your time, Freeman,' he said. He spoke English slowly but with an impeccable accent, gained during his years at a British public school before the war. 'You say you've discovered evidence that my company has been supplying ingredients for poison gas to Iraq? Whatever you have stumbled across, there is not one shred of evidence on paper. If you print a word, I shall sue your newspaper in every country in the world.'

Merlin sat down without being invited, then plunged straight in with: 'I don't care what you sold to Saddam Hussein, Baron. Plenty of bigger companies on both sides of the Atlantic went right on trading with Baghdad until August last year so why should I pick on you? What I really came to talk about is the same subject as last time: that sunny day in June 1944.'

The baron looked relieved. 'I can tell you nothing. I was not at Oradour. My *Kubelwagen* was machine-gunned on the eighth of June near Brive-la-Gaillarde by some terrorists – or Resistance heroes, as you would doubtless call them. My driver was killed and I...'

He tapped his right leg. 'I lay unconscious, wounded, and should have had my throat cut by those Communist swine, had not a Wehrmacht patrol come along in the nick of time. I spent the rest of June that year in a military hospital at Bad Flinsburg. It's all in the divisional medical records captured by the Americans. With your countrymen's passion for recording history, I imagine that my temperature chart may still be carefully preserved in the archives of some University campus in Minnesota or Iowa. At any rate, by the time I was fit to rejoin my unit...'

'It's a neat alibi,' Merlin interrupted.

Kempfer looked tired. 'It happens to be the truth. I conserve in a safe place my original paybook which shows the period of my sick leave. So I don't have to defend myself from the gutter press after all these years.'

Merlin noted that the baron was having difficulty with his breathing.

'What are you really after, Freeman? I'll give you five minutes of my time, no more.'

'The gold,' Merlin gambled. 'I know all about the gold of Oradour.'

The baron lifted his stiff leg on to a padded footstool. 'There was none. That was an excellent example of some journalist's febrile imagination running away with him.'

'At least it explains...'

'Oradour is very simple, Mr Freeman. Don't try and complicate the issue. It was an exemplary reprisal against the Resistance – nothing more nor less.'

'There was no Resistance in Oradour-sur-Glane.'

Kempfer patted his leg. 'You think I shot myself? I tell you, the terrorist swine were everywhere. They had to be taught a lesson.'

'This lesson cost seven hundred lives – mainly women and children.'

Kempfer took an aerosol from his pocket and squirted two bursts into his mouth. 'In war, these things happen – on both sides. You of all people should know that. I wonder whether – in the interest of journalistic balance – you would write the story of the hundreds of German soldiers who were taken prisoner-of-war and then shot by Eisenhower's nice, democratic, gum-chewing GIs?'

'SS men?'

'No, soldiers in uniform, Mr Freeman – protected by international law and the terms of the surrender. And would you write about the hundreds of thousands – maybe a million – of men who had simply fought for their country and were deliberately starved to death in Allied POW camps after the cessation of hostilities?'

Merlin tried another angle: 'Is it just a coincidence that you live here, Baron – under the very castle where Richard Coeur-de-Lion was held prisoner? I'm asking because it was Coeur-de-Lion's gold that was supposed to be buried at Oradour.'

The baron stroked his stiff leg, massaging the knee-cap. 'Go on,' he said quietly.

Merlin was floundering, like a wrestler who had pushed and found no resistance. 'How long have you lived here?'

Kempfer smiled. 'My family has lived in Dürnstein for eight hundred years. You know Kempfer means "fighter" or "warrior" in German?'

Merlin nodded.

'My first recorded ancestor, to whom a grant of land is still to be found in the town archives, was a man called Mercadier. He was a mercenary captain who served Richard the Lionheart. Sometime after the king's death, this Mercadier arrived in Dürnstein and married the widow of one of the French hostages who had died here. He took the name Kempfer when he settled among German-speaking people because it was more suitable than translating his real name which, I believe, means merchant.'

Merlin hovered. There were ten different ways to play it, but sometimes, to get the real story, it was necessary to stake everything on a hunch. 'And did this progenitor of yours perhaps bring with him from France an heirloom of some kind? Maybe a poem of a type known as *sirventès*?'

The baron's face was completely white. 'For a war correspondent,' he said slowly, 'you are unusually cultured.'

'May I see it?'

The baron was caught off-balance. 'Why not?' he muttered.

He limped, leaning on the cane, to a painting which slid sideways and revealed an ordinary domestic wall-safe from which he took a number of documents. He shuffled through them and held out to Merlin a piece of yellow-brown parchment with frayed edges, enclosed in a plastic envelope.

'I must ask you not to take it out of the envelope,' he said.

Merlin held the parchment to the light. The faded writing was in stylised Gothic script which he could not read. A bold signature sprawled across the bottom of the sheet.

The baron sat down, out of breath. 'The signature is genuine. I had it authenticated some years ago by an old comrade who is a scholar, highly respected in this area. He told me that the poem was written down by a clerk, but signed by the hand of Eleanor of Aquitaine, the mother of King Richard.'

Merlin moved to the window where the light was better. 'I can make out the last line: something about Chartres, Bordeaux and...'

'Fontevraud.'

'Never heard of it.'

It is an abbey where you will find the tombs of Eleanor and Richard the Lionheart.'

'Yeah?'

'And if you turn it over,' suggested the baron, 'you will find my friend's translation into German and also a translation into English which I myself did many years ago.'

Merlin read aloud the English text:

> 'The heathen maze is straight beside
> the trail that you must follow
> to the stone that is hollow
> and the church of the bride.
> Like a pilgrim onward go
> To Chartres, Bordeaux and Fontevraud.'

He checked the rhyming scheme. It was ABBACC but the words meant nothing to him.

'May I photograph this?' He expected the baron to refuse.

If you can work without flash,' Kempfer said tiredly. 'I am told that it damages old documents.'

Merlin laid the parchment on the carpet underneath the window where there was most light. It was difficult to avoid the reflections on the plastic so he took several shots and varied the exposure, bracketing the reading on the light meter. When he was satisfied, he packed the Pentax away in his camera case and handed the document back to its owner.

'A trade,' said the baron. 'I show you my heirloom. Now you tell me how you come to know about medieval poetry.'

Merlin shrugged. 'I'm working on this angle of the gold of Oradour and I happened to stumble over one of these rhymes, carved on Châlus castle.'

'And do you have the words of this other *sirventès* with you?'

'I'm sorry, I don't.'

The baron seemed unwell. 'Now I must ask you to leave. I am an old man and my health is not very good.'

Merlin picked up the camera case. He had got bewilderingly more than he had expected.

'Before you go...' The old man was wheezing so badly, he could only get out a few words at a time. 'Write down your address. This old comrade... whom I mentioned... has other material you may find interesting. I'll put him in touch with you.'

'Give me his address and I'll contact him.'

'That would not be a good idea. He is a very private person.'

Merlin took out a card with his office address in New York and wrote Leila's telephone number on the back: 'Your old comrade can reach me in France during the next few weeks.'

Driving out of the garden gates, Merlin saw three figures standing between the shrubs. Two were the gardeners who had been there when he arrived. The third was the veiled woman who had led him to safety ten years before in Beirut. He skidded on the gravel, narrowly missing the gate post and pulled up. By the time he had stepped out of the car there were only two figures to be seen in the garden.

Chapter 3

'I had a hell of a job prising your telephone number in France out of your mother.'

Jay had been sitting in the sun-warmed porch of the cottage at St Denis for two hours, her mind blank as a vegetable. The voice on the other end of the line said hallo several times before she recognised the Australian accent of Andy Burrows, a television producer who had been talking for months about making a series with her Early Music ensemble.

'I'm sorry, Andy,' she apologised. Her brain felt as though made of cotton wool. 'I'm taking a few days off, so I told Mummy not to pass on calls.'

'I really had to twist yer ma's arm.' He sounded a long way away. 'And I tried several times to call you last night.'

'I was working on some new repertoire and didn't want to be interrupted,' Jay excused herself. 'What can I do for you, Andy?'

'D'you want the good news or the bad news first?'

'Either way,' she said.

'The bad news,' he chuckled, 'is that I'm going to ask you to cut short your holiday, sweetheart.'

'Why's that, Andy?'

'Because of the good news. A programme's been cancelled and there's an Outside Broadcast unit going spare for two days. If I move smartish, I can use one day for travelling and the other to record you and your group as a pilot for a series. What do you say to that?'

Jay felt her brain slip into gear for the first time since she had woken that morning. To hell with her father's idea of a rest-cure... If she could just do this one programme and prove that her nerve had not gone, that would be the best cure of all for whatever had happened at Canterbury.

'Yes,' she said, mind made up.

He laughed. 'Good on yer. There's a catch. We have to get the programme into the can the day after tomorrow. Can you be there at such short notice?'

'What time's the call?'

'Ten am for a run-through without cameras. That okay? I hope to have pictures to look at about two-thirty. That gives me four hours' rehearsal-and-recording time excluding the tea-break. It's going to be a hell of a sweat, Jay. And what about your musicians? Can you be sure they're free at such short notice?'

'Don't worry, Andy,' she said. She felt calm and in control – her normal self again. 'If they have another job that conflicts, I'll see they'll put in deps. We'll all be there, ten am the day after tomorrow.'

'You're a beaut!'

Jay replaced the telephone and checked her wrist-watch. If she set out immediately and drove non-stop, she could catch a night sailing from Calais and be home by breakfast next day.

She grabbed some paper and started making lists.

Merlin drove into Vienna and checked the hire car into the Hertz downtown office. His overnight bag was in a locker at Schwechat airport. It was several years since he had been in the city, so he strolled through a light drizzle, past the Opera House and Sacher's. He wandered into a couple of bars used by pressmen but saw no familiar faces.

Since leaving Dürnstein he had had the feeling that the old baron had made everything too easy for him. Why had Kempfer been so co-operative?

Merlin went over everything he could remember about the first interview with him, years before. He had filed that story and flown off on another lead the next day. Yet he was certain he had made a note to follow up some anomaly in the baron's story, if he ever had the time. The gap in his memory would nag him until it was filled in by an alcoholic ex-pat in a smoke-filled Spanish bar…

He bought a martini in the cocktail bar of the Hilton, which entitled him to use a warm and comfortable telephone booth. There he sat down with his contact book and a pile of tokens to ring some Vienna-based colleagues, in the hope of getting more background on Kempfer. The first correspondent he called had been posted back to the States months before. Two others were out of town. And so it went on. After drawing blanks all round, Merlin called Jay's number in St Denis. No answer, so he re-dialled in case of faulty routing.

When she picked up the phone, Jay sounded breathless, as though she had been running. Merlin thought he detected disappointment in her voice. 'You were expecting someone else?' he guessed.

'I'd just locked up the house when the phone went,' Jay gasped. 'I had to unlock everything. That's why it took me so long to answer.'

'I'll be back in St Denis by midday tomorrow,' Merlin announced.

'And guess what? I've found another *sirventès*. Can I take you to lunch at Chez Dominique and talk about it?'

Jay explained that she was about to jump into her car and drive fast back to Britain. Merlin felt deflated; there was so much he wanted to tell her.

'I couldn't get through to you last night,' he apologised. 'I did try.'

'There was something wrong with the line,' said Jay.

'But you're okay?'

'Why shouldn't I be?'

Because I saw a veiled woman, thought Merlin. 'Listen,' he said, 'to what I found here in Dürnstein.'

He read her the words of the second *sirventès* over the phone.

'What does it mean?' Jay sounded more polite than interested.

'I don't know yet. The first poem at Châlus seemed to have a meaning in every line and this one seems to have none at all. But the important thing is that it was definitely written by Queen Eleanor. It even has her signature on it. Can you hear me?'

'Yes. You don't have to shout.'

'So you could be right about the one at Châlus. If we can find some way of matching them up, Jay...'

'Look.' She sounded impatient. 'This isn't the best time to talk, Merlin. I have to get back to England fast. The television recording is very important for me and I can't risk losing the boat.'

'Sure, I understand.' Merlin fed tokens into the telephone. 'When can we meet again? Are you coming back to St Denis after the recording?'

'I don't think so.'

'Can you give me your phone number and address in London, Jay?'

'I shan't be there.'

'Give me them anyway. Please.'

It was long after midnight when Frau Baronin Kempfer dialled the number of the telephone beside Hermann Kreuz's bed in the Valle de los Cantos.

He lifted the handset. 'Hallo.'

'Am I talking with Herr Doktor Hermann Kreuz?'

'What is it?' he asked.

'Do you recognise my voice?'

'Of course,' he said impatiently. 'Why are you ringing?'

'Rudi is dead.'

'That's no particular reason to call me at four am. When a man of his age and state of health dies, it is a perfectly natural event.'

'Yes,' faltered the widow, 'but I thought, in the circumstances...'

'There are no circumstances,' he said swiftly.

'No.' She pulled herself together. 'Except that Rudi asked me to call you just before he died.'

Kreuz sat up in bed, alert. 'Why should he do that?'

'The doctor had been in the afternoon and gave him an injection, some kind of sedative. He came again late in the evening.'

'You said Rudi asked you to call me. That wasn't about the doctor's visit.'

Kreuz heard the woman at the other end of the line swallowing a drink of water.

Her voice was stronger now: 'Just before the end, I was sitting beside Rudi's bed. I thought he was sleeping, but suddenly he sat upright and grasped my arm. He said: "You must call Hermann…" Rudi was always so disciplined, you know – even at the end.'

'Why were you to call me?' Kreuz prompted.

'He said I was to tell you about the American who came yesterday afternoon, just before Rudi was taken ill.'

'What did they talk about?'

'I don't know. But he wrote you a long letter after the reporter had gone. He insisted on finishing it before he let the doctor give him the injection, although he was in great pain.'

'Send it to me by express mail,' said Kreuz. 'No. Better would be by courier. So don't do a thing. There is a security company in Vienna owned by an old comrade who will look after it for me.'

'Am I as disappointing as all that?' Leila asked.

Merlin kissed both cheeks and lifted her clear of the ground. 'Never,' he whispered in her ear.

'Liar,' she accused him. 'I can see in your face that I am not the woman you'd like to be holding in your arms. And don't blow into my ears like that. You know what it does to me. Now put me down or I'll touch you.'

'Threat or promise?'

'I've a palette in one hand and a brush in the other.' Leila kissed him on the lips. 'You'll be marked and everyone will know.'

'The story of my life,' he said, releasing her.

'Jay's gone back to England.'

'I know.' Merlin busied himself pouring coffee from the pot on her stove. 'I caught her yesterday afternoon, just as she was leaving.'

Leila looked at the painting on the easel. It wasn't what she had set out to do. Something had gone wrong and she was making it worse by going on. She put down the palette and brushes, found a turps rag and cleaned the worst of the paint off her hands.

'Doesn't sound like you, actually bothering to call a girl when you're out of town. Oh, talking of telephone calls, guess who tried to talk with you on this number at five am this morning?'

'Jay?' Merlin sounded hopeful.

'Try again.'

'Surprise me.'

Leila turned on the hot tap at the sink. The water ran cold and there was no washing-up liquid. She rubbed her hands together vigorously, trying to get the turps off with cold water. 'I can't imitate the voice: it's about two octaves too low and even my quick-fire wit isn't fast enough for an impersonation of...'

'My favourite agent, Matty Perelmann. Go on.'

'It seems that his favourite client gave him my number to contact without telling him that France was six hours ahead of New York time, not the other way round.'

'Matty thinks Brooklyn is the centre of the universe.'

Leila grabbed the canvas off the easel and hurled it to the back of the room. 'He may be right, but here on the whirling periphery of the galaxy a call in the middle of the night destroys a masterpiece.'

'Come on, what did the old slave-driver want?'

'To tell you that your voice-overs have been rescheduled for the day after tomorrow. That you're to book your own ticket and the production company will reimburse you. I think that's all he said, but I was asleep. I often am at that time of night. Does it sound right?'

Merlin grunted. 'You wouldn't have an airline schedule?'

'You're right.' Leila laughed at the idea. Her arm described an arc of chaos. 'Does it look like I'm going to need one in the near future, Merl? A bus timetable maybe, if I raid the piggy bank.'

'Can I use your phone to call Bordeaux airport?'

Leila studied his face for a moment, close up. 'Oh dear, you look like a little boy whose playmate had to go home.'

'What's that supposed to mean?'

She poked him in the solar plexus. 'You're sulking because Jay isn't coming out to play and now Mommy Perelmann has said you've got to come in and do your homework.'

'I am not.'

'No?' There were more questions in Leila's smile than the Inquisition had come up with.

'Well,' she said, 'I am at least right about one thing, Merlin, old buddy. You've fallen in love. You really have.'

Her laugh was without malice. 'I hope it hurts, you bastard. It's about time you knew what it felt like.'

'Thanks for the sympathy.'

She released him and started hunting through a pile of books for the telephone directory. 'What's a voice-over? Matty made it sound exciting.'

'Matty was born and raised in Brooklyn. He can make paying him a ninety percent commission sound exciting.'

'No, seriously.'

'Voicing-over,' explained Merlin, 'is dubbing a commentary I wrote months ago to a film that should have died on the cutting-room floor. I sit in a viewing theatre with a film editor I've never seen before, watching a scratchy black-and-white print covered in chinagraph marks and trying not to miss the cues and to match my voice to what it sounded like half a year ago when I had sinusitis and spoke the in-vision bits against the background of revving tank engines and rather close mortar fire. That's what voicing-over is.'

'And what's the film about?'

He yawned. 'It's the story of my hundredth death-defying visit to the front line. I can't remember where.'

She threw the phone directory at him. 'Poor Merl! You are feeling sorry for yourself, aren't you? If you turn off the self-pity, I'll make you an omelette while you call the airport.'

'You're going to cook for me?' Merlin's amazement was genuine.

'The condemned man ate a hearty meal... If you stop crying, yes. Can you see a clean pan anywhere? I know there is one somewhere.'

Leila cleared the top of the stove with a sweep of her arm and a crash of crockery breaking. 'And pour me a dose of Cinzano. It's all I have alcoholic. At least breathing New York air will get Jay out of your system. Did you sleep together?'

He was thumbing through the pages. 'Not the way you mean.'

'Is there a new way?' Leila flashed her eyes at him. 'Something I've been missing, *noo*?'

Merlin held the glass of vermouth for her while she sipped it, an egg in each hand.

'If you have to know,' he said, 'we both slept in my camper – in separate bunks.'

'Merlin Freeman and a beautiful girl spending the night in separate beds,' Leila whistled. 'Now I've heard everything. This must be true love.'

Chapter 4

Beneath the smoking pine-resin torches in the heavy iron wall-brackets, all the colours of the Middle Ages were to be found in the costumes of silk, satin and velvet. The trestle tables of the banqueting hall sported plaster replicas of the delicacies of the period: roast sucking pig, venison and wild boar with a centre-piece of a silver-glazed swan with a gilded beak that floated on a lake of green pastry.

Only the dessert fruit was real: grapes, persimmons and pomegranates. The brightly dressed guests were all walk-ons. Carl Moritz helped himself to a handful of grapes off a properties trolley and earned a hard look from the girl SM.

One end of the medieval hall of Oakham Castle had been cleared of everything anachronistic. The other end, where Carl sat, was crammed with hi-tech television recording equipment. Between two cameras he could see Jay's group, dressed in medieval costume, in a pool of television lighting. They were accompanying her in a song of the Third Crusade.

Carl stood up and moved sideways to get a better view of Jay. Her powerful soprano voice rang out clearly above the sound of flute, lute, rebec and harp as she lamented her lover, far away on Crusade in the Holy Land:

> *'De ce sui molt deceüe*
> *Quant ne fui au convoier...'*

On the chorus, the other voices joined in:

> *'Dex, quant crieront Outree*
> *Sire, aidies au pelerin...'*

Carl could hear the director's voice coming from the nearest cameraman's headphones, directing the shot: 'Camera three, give me a big-close-up of Jay facing right. Hold it. On Two. Track and zoom in very slowly all the way to a BCU of Jay facing left. Now mix from Two to Three...'

Carl stood spell-bound by the music. He had never heard Jay sing so well. And her group was on top form, light years ahead of their standard the last time he had heard them perform.

A group of costume and make-up assistants clustered round the colour monitor where the SM was standing so that Carl was forced to watch the image in the camera viewfinder. It was small and black-and-white but Jay's high-boned face, framed by the severe lines of a wimple, was stunning, regal and powerful.

The song ended in total silence, to facilitate the editing. There was no applause; that would be dubbed on afterwards with the post-recorded links. After a short break and a consultation between the stage manager and Jay, the musicians changed instruments to play the final number in the programme, this time with Jay on the recorder. Carl shut his eyes and listened to every nuance of each note she played. From a banal little tune, Jay was making music. Her charisma suffused the other players, making the ensemble sound as one instrument.

Carl remembered the time when Jay and he had been music students. They had played duets together on summer evenings. It seemed a long time ago.

At the end of the recording he waited in the shadows until the crew had finished congratulating Jay and the others on their playing. Only then did he walk into the lit performance area. In his dark suit and camel-hair coat hung cloak-like over his shoulders, he made an incongruous figure among the jeans and shirt-sleeves of the television crew.

Jay turned to him, her eyes bright and cheeks full of colour. He took her hand and kissed it.

'You played superbly,' he said sincerely. 'I feel very humble.'

She laughed, high on the performance.

'I'm not joking.' He wanted her to understand. 'I've only heard playing like that a few times in my life. If I can give you one piece of advice...'

She was already turning away from him as the producer arrived with an entourage of assistance and a stills photographer in tow.

'...it's to throw away your real flute,' Carl held on to Jay's hand until he had finished. 'You were made for the music you played today. No one else ever played it like that.'

He was uncertain whether she had heard.

Anti-climax hung heavy in the air, as it always did for Jay after a performance. She sat in the dressing-room that had been set aside for the two women artistes.

She had changed into her street clothes and was packing away her instruments. The other musicians had gone. Outside only the riggers were left, rolling up cables and wheeling equipment away on trolleys.

The day had passed like lightning. It seemed only minutes since she had arrived and hung up her costume in the dressing room that morning. Then, her main worry had been the stiffness in her left hand where she had cut it at Châlus – and how much rather than whether it would harm her playing.

She had peeled Merlin's dressing off, to put on an ordinary sticking plaster which she had borrowed from Trish, the other girl in the ensemble – only to find no cut or even a scar. Her hand appeared to have healed without trace. In all the hustle of getting ready, there had been no time to wonder about it.

She opened the waste bin under the dressing-table and unfolded the pad of lint. There was dried blood in the centre of it, but no corresponding scar on her skin – and far from being stiff, her hands and fingers were more supple than she could ever remember.

Jay stroked the skin on the back of her hand. Merlin the Magician? He had said that was what other reporters called him. She was sorry he had not been there to see and hear her perform.

She recalled every note of the performance, as a musician can. Not only had she played as though possessed, she had also inspired the other musicians and pushed them far past their normal playing limits – as a single player can sometimes carry a whole team to victory on the sports field. Exactly how she had done it would have been impossible to describe to a non-musician. The praise from Andy Burrows and the crew meant little to her; of those who had been listening, only Carl had a musician's ear.

She gathered up the instrument cases and the holdall with her costume. Both hands full, she switched out the dressing room light with her elbow and backed into the corridor between the dressing rooms. The only light was coming from a green EXIT sign at the far end. From the corner of her eye Jay saw a woman waiting in the dim green light, dressed in some kind of veil. She thought Trish must have come back for something – a garment, an instrument rest, some music that had been left behind.

'Did you forget something?' she called.

There was no reply. Jay found the corridor light switch, put down her hold-all and pressed it. The corridor was empty. There was no one there.

114

Chapter 5

On the other side of the Atlantic, Merlin was trying to join in the group euphoria that comes when a programme is in the can.

'Great! Really great!' That's a fantastic job you've done on the commentary.' The producer pumped Merlin's hand and gripped his forearm to show extra sincerity. His smile showed an expensive amount of dentistry. 'I hope we get this thing together, Merl. I really do.'

To deflect the tide of bonhomie, Merlin indicated the editor standing beside them on the rain-slicked pavement. The taped-together cans under her arm contained the now commentated version of *Lebanon: The Forgotten War*.

'Thank Hannah,' he said. 'She did a really great job stitching all the bits together: film, tape, stock-shots... I couldn't even spot the joins myself.'

The producer's arm went around Hannah's shoulder in a brotherly hug. 'When this girl's edited a film, you can't tell the footage shot yesterday from a clip of an old D.W.Griffiths movie,' he enthused. 'The network has already seen a mute rough-cut. When they see a dubbed show print, they're gonna love it, I just know.'

'I hope so,' said Merlin.

He kept trying to press the auto-hype button; it seemed unfair to stay cool when all these nice things were being said. Over an expensive luncheon he had listened to the plans for a whole series entitled: *The Forgotten Wars of Merlin Freeman*. But all the while he had wanted to escape from his agent and the producer and the two grey-suited executives from the network with their Florida tans.

'It was great to work with you, Merl,' said Hannah. She dropped the cue sheets on to the wet pavement where they blew away into the gutter and disappeared into the neon-lit dusk of Manhattan. Merlin shut the door of the cab and watched them all drive away, leaving him outside the viewing theatre.

It was drizzling. He turned up his coat collar and started walking towards Times Square. He had tried ringing Jay's London number several times since arriving in New York. The first few times he had left messages but eventually had run out of things one could say to a machine.

He wandered through streets he had known – it seemed a lifetime ago – and past a block where he had lived briefly during his second marriage. For the first time ever, New York seemed a foreign city. It wasn't the place that had changed, but him. The idea of looking up old friends held no appeal but neither did an empty hotel room.

A Doubledays shop-sign drew Merlin across the road. He scanned the display of new war books in the window; several of the authors were friends. He went inside and browsed through the books, drifting slowly along the shelves to kill time and hoping that the rain would ease off.

In the History section there was a single copy of a thick biography of Eleanor of Aquitaine, which he bought without opening. He took it into the coffee shop next door and devoured the contents of page after page without skipping a word. Before falling asleep that night he finished reading all four hundred pages.

Next morning, Merlin rose early and took a cab north out of the city to Fort Tryon, overlooking the Hudson river. There he stood in the queue of tourists waiting for the Romanesque cloister to open. It was an annexe of the Metropolitan Museum of Art, built to house the medieval collections.

Inside the cloister, built from twelfth- and thirteenth-century stones brought over from Europe, he found what he was looking for. The book had described the carved capital sitting on its simple stone colour as being from a church near Langon in south-west France. It was said to be the finest likeness extant of Eleanor of Aquitaine, and had been carved to commemorate the visit to the town in 1153 of Duchess Eleanor and her new husband, Count Henry of Anjou, better known as Henry II of England.

Sheltered from erosion through eight centuries, the heads of the young duke and duchess were as cleanly chiselled as the day they had been carved. Merlin stared at the woman's face. There was no question it was Jay. The same high cheek bones and wide-open eyes, sensual lips and strong nose looked down at him with a half-smile as though savouring a joke that had lasted for the better part of a thousand years.

How long he stood there, Merlin had no idea. His mind was grappling with two sets of memories. There were his recent memories of Jay, but there were other, more troubling ones stirred up by the head on the column – memories that had pricked him in that first second when he met Jay on the tow-path with Leila. Jay and the veiled woman in Baron Kempfer's garden…

Aware of a museum attendant staring at him, Merlin wandered round

116

the other three sides of the cloister, looking idly around but seeing nothing as he racked his mind logically for clues. It was like opening drawers in a filing cabinet. If *Work/France* was empty, he tried *School/History Lessons* and so on. But every possible drawer was blank.

He waited until the attendant was answering a visitor's query and had his back turned before stepping up on to the stone bench beneath the column, to get as close as possible – and at the angle he wanted. The previous day's rain had cleared up. Sunlight poured through a small bull's eye window on the outside of the cloister.

Concealed beneath Merlin's lightweight raincoat was a camera with a 80–200 mm. zoom lens and a motor drive. Merlin adjusted exposure and focused on the head. Through the lens the likeness of Jay was uncanny.

'Hey! You can't do that, mister! It says Don't Climb On the Stones. Can't you read?'

Thanks to the speed of the motor-drive, Merlin had shot twelve close-ups of Eleanor's head before the attendant yanked him down from the bench. To convince the man that he had simply not understood the notice, Merlin spoke Arabic. He put the lens cap on the camera and through sign-language conveyed that he would not do it again. He left the attendant muttering rudenesses to a colleague and walked out of the cloister with a smile on his face and a story in his head.

'You don't have to sell it to me, Merlin. I'm your agent. I'm on your side, you know that.'

Matty Perelmann held up both hands in surrender and managed somehow to light another cigarette from the stub of the previous one, all in one gesture. The bags under his eyes looked like he was having a new face made and still had several fittings to go. He picked up a telephone that was ringing, growled into it a couple of times in his gravelly voice, picked up another one, finished both conversations and dropped the phones back onto their rests, pressed a button and growled into the intercom: 'No more calls.'

Then he sat back in his padded leather chair, stretched and yawned, 'Let me give you a one-word answer. How about: No?'

'Look at the pictures,' Merlin insisted.

'I got eyes.'

Merlin held up a close-up of Jay singing at Châlus. 'This is the girl.'

He held up a print of the head on the column at the Metropolitan Museum. 'And this is a likeness of Queen Eleanor of Aquitaine who is probably an ancestor of that same girl. She lived eight centuries ago, Matty. Eight hundred years. Right?'

'Thank you, Professor. Counting I know.'

'Now look at the black-and-white prints of those two shots I made last night.' Merlin held them up.

'So that's why I had to find you a darkroom to play around in at midnight? And me thinking you'd gone into hard porn...'

Merlin ignored that. 'This girl is the double of her ancestor, Matty. Without the colour and printed dark and grainy, you can hardly tell the statue from the girl, can you?'

'I agree, maestro. But what does that prove? Me, I go two months without shaving and I look like Moses, but even my own kids don't obey my commandments.'

Merlin pulled his chair round to Matty's side of the desk.

'You could sell this story to *National Geographic*,' he urged. 'Tell them it's a psychic treasure hunt. It's all there in front of you.'

He tapped the draft title: International Musician Hunts Treasure Hidden By Famous Ancestor. 'I borrowed the hotel porter's old typewriter and spent the whole of yesterday afternoon in my room, getting a treatment down on paper for you.'

'I think...' Matty pushed the pile of paper away. He spoke slowly, massaging the bridge of his nose and the tired eye muscles. 'I think that people should do what they're good at, Merlin. When it comes to war coverage, you're one of the best in the world.'

'So everyone keeps telling me.'

'Because it's true. And now, just when you could be getting your own network series and I want you accessible here in New York for meetings or whatever, what are you doing? You're going back to some god-forsaken part of Europe, messing around taking pictures on your own camera – that's what cameramen are for, by the way – and hammering out this spooky crap on a beat-up portable typewriter...'

'Listen...'

'No, you listen to me. What is this? Are you trying to put the clock back twenty-five years or something – Merlin Freeman the Boy Reporter?'

'I'll level with you.' Merlin tried another tack. 'The story's not the greatest, Matty. It's really just an excuse to spend some time with this girl.'

'Aah,' Matty beamed with satisfaction. He loved his clients' confessions. 'You're asking me to give you an alibi. Why didn't you say so?'

He picked up the colour photograph of Jay and nodded. 'I don't blame you. By the way, how's Carole?'

Merlin flinched at the name of his second wife. 'She's getting married again next month.'

'To a human being this time, I hope?'

Merlin sorted the prints and sheets of typescript into two piles. He picked one up and pushed the other back across the desk towards Matty. 'See what you can do. Sell the story to someone, promise?'

'How long have I got? It may take a decade or so. When do you go back to Europe?'

'Right now, if I can find a cab downstairs.'

'Oh great, I thought you were in a hurry! Now just supposing the network want to reach you and talk about this trivial million-dollar series they have on their mind – how do I reach you back in Europe, wise guy?'

'Same number I gave you before. You remember Leila Dor, the painter?'

'Do I?'

'You fixed an exhibition of her paintings once in Albany or Buffalo or someplace up-state as a favour to me.'

'Of course! Of course!' Matty clapped a hand to his forehead. 'I have total recall of all your old girlfriends. How could I ever forget one?'

Merlin stood grinning in the open doorway. 'Be a good guy, Matty. Help me set up this piece of harmless moonlighting. All I want out of you is an alibi.'

'Merlin, I'll do it. You know why?'

'I'm sure you'll tell me, Matty.'

'In the hope that it keeps you away from that goddam awful *Book of Blood*. Okay? Better you should spend some time making a play for – ,' Matty flicked Jay's photograph with a nicotine-stained thumbnail ' – this *schiksa*, this *goyische* Ice Princess here, then depress yourself again, working on all that massacre shit.'

'Thanks a lot.'

'And, Merlin!' Matty shouted through the closed door, 'For Christ's sake stay available near a telephone, will ya? If those guys at the network say they wanna talk to you, I want your little *tukhas* on the next plane back here. Right?'

Back against the door, Merlin placed his right hand across his chest, allegiance-to-the-flag style. 'I promise, Matty. I promise.'

The twice-weekly Olympic Airways flight from Athens touched down at Malaga International airport on the Costa del Sol with a mixed bag of passengers. Half were Greek and Spanish; the rest came from all over the Middle East and Asia, having come together in the transit lounge at Athens.

In the first-class compartment Salem Chakrouty undid his seat belt as the plane taxied towards the Arrivals building. In the next seat his brother Kassim awoke as the whine of the engines changed with reverse pitch. He had shaved off his luxurious black moustache before leaving Beirut. It made his face look younger, reminding Salem of boyhood holi-

119

days spent together – outings along the coast to Tyre and Sidon or expeditions into the mountains while their parents worked at the hotel. Then they had called each other Big Brother and Little Brother although the age difference between them was only four years. These were among Salem's happiest memories.

He looked up to find the hostess reminding him about his luggage in the overhead locker. He smiled thanks and started to follow the other passengers out of the plane when Kassim pulled him back into the seat. They were alone in the compartment.

'Just one thing, my brother,' he said quietly. 'As long as we are in the airport buildings, my name is Mohammed Ishaq and I am from Pakistan. We talked on the flight in English, if anyone should ask.'

He took from an inside pocket a worn blue British passport. 'So do not talk to me, in case you forget and call me Kassim. In fact, it would be better if you ignore me altogether. You are not used to these things. So I shall take a taxi from the airport and meet you tonight at our cousin's house.'

'Why should you need to use a different name?' Salem wondered.

'It is safer.'

'Have you enemies in Spain, my brother?'

The first-class passengers had all disembarked and a stream of tourist-class travellers were now slowly shuffling through the cabin.

Keeping his voice low, Kassim said, 'Don't forget: Mohammed Ishaq. But better you don't talk to me at all.'

By the door the hostess stood waiting. 'Thank you for flying with us today,' she said. 'Do fly Olympic again.'

'Oh, I shall,' smiled Kassim.

Behind her, the door to the flight deck was ajar. The co-pilot was still in his seat, going through a check-list. Kassim dropped his passport and airline ticket on the floor. As the hostess bent to pick them up for him, he pushed the door wider and took a good look at the instrument panel layout.

'It's called what?' Merlin clamped his free hand over his ear. The noise in the departure lounge at JFK made it hard to hear a word of Matty's gravel-voiced delivery.

'*The Other Side*,' Matty repeated.

'What the hell kind of magazine is that? I never heard of it.'

'It's printed in California – where else? – and sold to the recently bereaved who want to get in touch with the dear departed. You fill in a form at the mortician's agreeing to take out a year's subscription and Dr Death gets a kickback, so he's pleased, the publisher is pleased, and you get the magazine. That's how it works.'

'Are you putting me on?'

'I am not,' Matty shouted. 'You wanted a commission in a hurry, so I got you one. This is a magazine that'll buy any crap about the supernatural. But I warn you, Merlin, your text will be re-written in house style. You wouldn't wanna read it after those guys have finished working on it! Take my advice, let me strike out the by-line clause in the contract.'

'Whatever you say, Matty.'

'There's an advance of five hundred dollars, with five hundred on acceptance. Oh, and they want all rights in text and photographs.'

'I'll try not to spend it all at once.'

'You asked for it, Merl.'

'You're a wonder, Matty.'

'Have fun – and don't worry about those of us who sit in offices doing all the work for you.'

'I won't.' Merlin relinquished the phone to a polite Indian gentleman wearing polished black shoes and no socks. He squeezed on to a bench between two very fat African ladies in colourful dresses and sat smiling at the departure board, which winked conspiratorially at him. The London flight was delayed an hour, but that did not matter one bit.

Merlin closed his eyes and tried to remember when he had last felt euphoric at an airport. Angry, frustrated, worried, harried... yes, all those things. But happy? That had to be a long way back. It must have been on his embarkation leave before going to Vietnam - before everything changed at My Lai. The feeling he had inside him was called: Going Home.

Chapter 6

After the heady experience of being toasted in champagne by Andy Burrows at a sneak viewing of the unedited videotape, Jay's taxi deposited her back in the real world which had a pile of dirty laundry in the bathroom and unwashed dishes in the kitchen sink.

It was late but she was too psyched up to sleep. She switched on the television, flicked through the channels and switched it off again. There was a pile of letters behind the front door: bills and publicity circulars. There was nothing recent on the fax machine except Carl's list of the dates cancelled after the concert at Canterbury – which left the next two weeks blank in her diary.

Jay listened to the messages on her answering machine with a notepad beside her, her mind elsewhere. There were four calls from Merlin and Carl had sent a bouquet of roses by Interflora. They sat beside the telephone on the hall table with the hand-written card reading: I never heard playing like that in my life. Love, Carl.

Jay put into her video recorder the VHS copy of the tape that Andy Burrows had presented to her and sat down to watch it. There was no question that the performance of the group was almost perfect, but it was her own playing that astonished her: it was better than faultless. Whatever the cause of her trauma on stage in the Chapter House, it appeared to have lifted her musicianship on to a higher plane. The more she thought about it, the less it made sense.

She was still asleep five hours later when the door bell rang and she found Merlin standing on her doorstep in a creased denim suit and dark designer stubble, asking for change to pay the taxi: 'The cab-driver wants twenty-five pounds. Does that sound to you like the right amount?'

'Where have you come from?'

'Heathrow airport. I'll pay you back when the banks open.' He took her money and went back to pay the driver, dumped a pair of well-worn leather cases inside her hallway and asked, 'Am I welcome? You don't look too pleased to see me.'

Jay smoothed sleep-tousled hair back off her face. She was not certain what she did feel about Merlin's sudden reappearance.

'I'm pleased,' she said cautiously.

'I didn't plan to arrive like this. The intention was to knock on your door with a bouquet of roses but thanks to the jet-stream my flight got in before the shops were open.' He finished lamely, 'and I wanted to come straight here.'

'Someone else looked after the roses.'

'So I see.' Merlin picked up the card. 'Who's C?'

'A boyfriend,' she teased.

Merlin took a deep breath. He pointed to the bedroom door. 'Is he in there?'

Jay was looking at him, examining the curly hair, the brown eyes, the olive skin. He was somehow much cleaner-cut than she remembered, as though she had seen him before – in that Biblical expression – through a glass darkly and now saw him for the first time face-to-face. Out of nowhere came a physical desire to make love to him, so strong that it was a pain in her belly. She wanted to touch him, kiss him, get hold of his flesh and feel his hands on her face and neck and breasts.

Merlin was waiting for a reply.

Jay turned away to hide the flush of desire on her face. She could not recall ever wanting a man so strongly before.

'No,' she said. 'He's not.'

To cover her inner turmoil, she went into the kitchen and made coffee. They sat drinking it in her living room with its huge window overlooking Hampstead Heath and watched the sun come up.

'Must cost a fortune to have an apartment like this,' was Merlin's comment. Staring at her face framed by a halo of long blonde hair back-lit by the sun, he was inwardly just as disturbed as she was. Hard to see against the light, her face tugged at layers of memory.

Jay had pulled on a pair of jeans and a sweater. She sat, her feet curled under her on the window seat opposite Merlin. 'You look different,' she said, blaming him for her own feelings.

'It's the shiny nose,' he grinned. 'I'm a newshound that's picked up a scent.'

Merlin told her about the visit to Dürnstein and the second *sirventès* – and that he had sold the idea of a psychic treasure hunt to a magazine. To impress her, he lied and said it was *National Geographic*. He made no mention of finding the head of Eleanor in the museum.

'So the news-hound has set me up as his truffle pig,' Jay summed up. I snuffle around, leading you to medieval poems from which you deduce where the treasure is. You write the story and make a fortune.'

'Right!' he agreed. 'How do you feel about it?'

'What makes you think I have the time for all this in my busy schedule?'

Merlin's face fell. He had not even thought about that. 'Well,' he mumbled, feeling stupid, 'I guess we can do it in bits and pieces, a few days at a time, whenever you're free.'

Jay knew there were two whole weeks empty in her diary but there were things she wanted to sort out for herself. At Canterbury she had played worse than ever in her life; at Oakham she had played better than ever before. One day her brain wouldn't work at all, the next she could conquer the world...

And then there was the confusion of feelings about Merlin himself: that awful gut-wrench of desire fighting her brain that said, stay cool – this is a good-looking man who is far too used to having his own way with women.

'Do you always find a story to trap a girl with?' she asked. 'Or is this some special honour?'

Merlin stood up to stare out of the window at the view.

'Look, I won't fence around with you, Jay.' He turned to face her. 'I admit that the idea of making a story out of this treasure hunt began as a joke. But remember, at Châlus it was your joke, not mine. Then I wanted to use it as an excuse to get to know you, but it's more than that now. I think there really is a story here.'

'What made you change your mind?'

'A lot of things. One is: I bought a book about Queen Eleanor when I was in New York. She was one hell of a lady. I don't know quite where to begin.'

He left the room and Jay heard him unzipping his bags in the hallway. She cradled the coffee cup in her hands. On the window ledge sat the neighbours' cat. She could hear it purring through the glass as it watched three sparrows eating crumbs that someone had thrown onto the grass for them. I'm the cat, she thought. Merlin is what I want and this story of his is the crumbs that bring him within reach. So, if I pretend to go along with it...

The cat leaped. Two sparrows made it into the air. The other was a crumpled parcel of feathers in the cat's mouth.

Jay got up off the window seat, disgusted and thinking: This is not like me – it simply isn't the way my mind works. She decided to say no to his plan, whatever it was. First she had to sort out what was going on in her brain. Then, if Merlin was still around, she'd see...

He came back into the living room with a book that had several markers sticking from between the pages and a large brown envelope from which he took two black-and-white photographs.

'You told me you used to be a photographer.' Jay was unimpressed by the pictures. 'Why are they so fuzzy?'

'Grain,' he explained. 'It's deliberate. Now just answer one question. Who is the woman?'

'Me.' She picked up one of the photographs. 'This is the one you took at Châlus after we had climbed down from the arrow slit.'

'And the other? Where did I take that?'

She looked at the second photograph, trying to remember. 'I don't know where you took that one, Merlin. You've cropped it so tight on my face that I can't see the background.'

He tapped the photograph in her hand. 'This one is not you.'

She looked again and laughed uncertainly. 'Then it's my double.'

'It is the face of Queen Eleanor of Aquitaine.'

As Merlin told her about the carved column in the Metropolitan Museum, Jay's eyes went from the picture he was holding in front of her to his eyes and from there to the picture he had taken at Châlus.

'So,' he finished, 'if your family can trace itself back to the Plantagenet line, Queen Eleanor was almost certainly an ancestor of yours and – as you can see – you're her double.'

'That's creepy,' said Jay, meaning the picture.

'There's more.' Merlin opened the book on the table. 'Tell me where you made that television recording?'

Jay put down the two photographs. 'Oh, I never told you how it went.'

'Don't!' Merlin put a hand on her arm to stop her. 'Just answer my question. Where was it?'

'A place called Oakham Castle.'

'Oak-ham,' he murmured. 'In Rutlandshire, right?'

'Oakum,' she corrected his pronunciation. 'It's a twelfth-century castle near Leicester.'

'Whatever, I'm going to tell you how you played.' He looked very serious. 'You lost your nerve again completely. Am I right?'

Tight-lipped and angry at whatever game he was playing with her, Jay snapped, 'I told you, I didn't lose…'

'Okay,' he tried to calm her. 'Relax. Just tell me whether the same thing happened at Oak-ham as at Canterbury.'

'You couldn't be more wrong.' Despite herself, Jay had to laugh at Merlin's visible disappointment. 'I played like a bloody angel! I've got a video-tape you can watch, if you don't believe me.'

He looked puzzled. 'Well, that's another theory to chuck in the waste-bin. You're telling me that you played your flute perfectly, with no troubles at all?'

'It wasn't the flute,' she said. 'Flutes weren't invented in the Middle Ages. They're orchestral instruments that came in much later. In the

Chinon Ensemble, I play recorders – several different ones – some percussion and a bowed viol. And I sing, you know that. What are you getting at?'

'I made an inspired leap in the dark.' Merlin was mocking himself: 'Confucius say: Man who jump in dark land in wrong place.'

He hefted the book. 'According to this scholarly work, there are four known likenesses of Eleanor that have survived the centuries. One is from a church in Langon, France. That's the one I photographed in the cloister in New York.'

'And the others?'

'The second is in a place I never heard of, a little church at Chaniers, near Bordeaux.'

'I've never heard of it, either.'

'A third is in Bordeaux Cathedral where Eleanor was married to the French king, Louis.'

'I've seen it,' Jay interrupted. The image of the head lit by the shaft of sunlight in the cathedral was clear in her mind for a split second. It matched the face in the photograph perfectly, complete to the half-smile on the lips.

'When was this?'

She frowned. Why was it so hard to remember? She felt the panic come back and fought it, trying to remember. 'It was on the day... the day you went to Austria, I think.'

He put down the book and fixed her eyes. 'And what happened?'

'I don't know.' Jay shivered despite the central heating and the warm sunshine coming through the window. 'Oh God, Merlin, I don't remember! I felt so weird that day.'

Merlin's shoulders slumped; he had been hoping for a lead. 'Well, never mind. But guess where the fourth one is, Jay?'

'What are you trying to prove?'

'Just guess,' he shouted.

'Oh, don't play games!' She wanted to be alone to work out what was going on inside herself.

'I'll tell you. The only other likeness of Eleanor is right where you made your television programme, at Oak-ham Castle! It was carved to commemorate the queen's visit in twelve hundred and something. And I think it had something to do with your playing like an angel that day.'

'A carved head, eight hundred years old? You're saying it has some kind of magical properties?' Nothing would have surprised Jay; any kind of explanation would have been better than none.

Merlin was looking serious. 'Not the head itself. It's only important because it proves Queen Eleanor was there, as she had been at Canterbury.'

126

Jay wanted to tell him that he was wrong, that the success at Oakham had been all hers. But she knew that was not true. At Canterbury she had been playing within a few paces of where Becket had been murdered. Eleanor must have been there many times during Becket's friendship with King Henry and afterwards. Had she been there to watch Henry scourged by the monks on the cathedral steps in penance for the archbishop's death? Was that why she was so angry when she screamed, 'Damn Becket!'?

There was no question in Jay's mind that *something* had torn her fingers away from the flute, leaving her so shaken that she was physically unable to play a note. Whereas at Oakham, she remembered feeling taken over, as though...

She could not put it into words. There was a phenomenon that happened to musicians just a few times in their lives when the music they were playing entered into them and played itself effortlessly as though the spirit of the composer were breathing and fingering the notes for the player. But it wasn't that. This take-over at Oakham had been different, more intimate... almost like a physical embrace.

Canterbury, Oakham – and the memories of torture and violence – and the identical face of her ancestress – all seemed to add up to something she did not believe in: psychic possession.

Merlin repeated his question: 'This tape of the recording you made at Oakham Castle. I'd like to see it, if I may?'

Jay pulled the curtains to keep the light out. The cassette was still in the machine. Watching her performance, Merlin was looking for something. Halfway through the programme he leaped off the sofa to stop the video.

The shot that had attracted his attention was very brief. It began with a low-angle close-up of Trish's fingers playing her shawm, a medieval oboe. The cameraman panned right and pulled focus to a close-up of a woman's head. At first, it looked like Jay, then as the focus sharpened it became a carving on the pillar behind Trish. The picture mixed from that close-up facing right to a close-up of Jay's profile on another camera facing left. It was a television cliché.

Merlin back-tracked and pressed the Pause button. The stop-frame now held the two mirror-image profiles looking at each other. He knelt beside the video and turned to face Jay.

He was thinking aloud. 'Perhaps the fact that it went so well at Oakham is something to do with your playing a recorder, not a flute?'

'It's pronounced Oakum, not Oak-ham. I told you.' Jay spoke coldly. She was looking not at him but at the screen, thinking: One way or the other, I must lay this ghost. And one way of doing it is to say yes to Merlin's proposal and spend the next two weeks finding out everything I can about Eleanor of Aquitaine...

127

'What exactly do you get out of this story?' she asked.

'A chance to get to know you.' Merlin switched off the television and the video.

'No.' Jay turned to face him. She wanted to put the conversation onto a non-emotional, non-mystical level. 'I meant money-wise.'

He tried to make a joke of it. 'I never talk about the money side.'

'With me, you do. I put myself out for hire every day, Merlin. I'm quite used to haggling about my fees. Musicians have no false shame, talking about cash.'

Merlin had not expected his alibi to be tested. 'Well,' he swallowed. 'I get, er... I get an advance of five and another five when they accept my piece.'

'By "five" you mean five thousand dollars?'

'Er, yeah. That's right.'

'And it's for *National Geographic* magazine, you said?'

'Mm. Why?'

'I just wanted to make sure it was worth doing,' Jay said slowly. 'I've got two weeks free, so let's do it.'

'That's great...' he began.

She stopped him in his tracks. 'This is on a strictly business basis, Mr Freeman. We share expenses and we split the fee down the middle: five thousand to you and five thousand to me. How about that?'

Merlin laughed. 'Are you serious?'

'Always,' said Jay, 'when I'm talking about money.'

'Okay.' Merlin took a deep breath, thinking: You really talked yourself into this one, Freeman. The pleasure of getting to know the beautiful Miss Jay French is going to cost you four thousand dollars...

Chapter 7

To make a change from the all-too-familiar crossing from Dover, Jay had asked Merlin to ring the car ferry company at Southampton and check the sailing schedules for France while she was out doing some chores so that the flat would be tidy on her return.

Waiting for attention, with an electronic version of 'Jingle Bells' irritating his ear, he leafed absently through the pages of her telephone pad. Every sheet was covered in doodles. There was an entire garden of fantastic flowers and a zoo of weird animals decorating messages which Jay had crossed through. Merlin began deciphering her handwriting. The notes on the pad were all about dates, places and times. A musician's life, he thought, was not unlike his own.

The girl in the ferry office was halfway through reading out the list of sailing times when Merlin's eye was riveted by the repeated scrawl that covered the top half of the page on which he was writing. He rang off and sat studying it for several minutes. Before Jay returned, he sent two sheets from her fax machine to a number in Switzerland, together with a hand-written note.

At a nearby pub they ate a stodgy meal of heated-up pie and sausages, then strolled across the heath to Kenwood and back, to help the food go down. Back at Jay's flat, the fax machine had its tongue hanging out. She tore off the single sheet message.

'Dr Paul Glassner – Graphologie?' she queried. 'Never heard of him. It's from an address in Zurich. Must have come to the wrong number.'

'It's for me.' Merlin took the paper from her.

The message he read out was very simple:

Dear Mr Freeman,

So nice to hear from you again! This time you give me an easy job. There is no question. Both the signatures are from the same person – identical. Hundred percent so.

Regards to your beautiful wife,
Paul Glassner

'Are you married?' Jay asked. To her, Merlin did not look like a man who stayed still long enough to have a wife and home.

'Twice,' he admitted. 'I just got divorced.'

'And what does the rest of the message mean?'

Merlin's cases were still by the front door where he had dropped them on arrival. From the side pocket of the top one he took the page he had torn from Jay's telephone pad and pointed to her doodling. 'You wrote this?'

'Looks like it.'

'Did you or did you not, Jay?'

'It's my writing.'

'Where did you get this name from?'

Jay looked more closely. 'Ali Anor? I've no idea. Maybe it's a take-out kebab house?'

'You've written it a hundred times – up, down and sideways.'

'I always doodle when I'm on the phone.'

'But why write this name again and again?' he insisted. 'It was the top sheet, so I guess you did it last night.'

'It must have been while I was listening to the messages on the answering machine.'

Merlin looked from her face to the piece of paper in his hand. 'And you don't know what this means?'

'Oh come on, Merlin.' Jay felt impatient. 'What's all the mystery?'

'The mystery,' he said, 'is that Eleanor's real name was two words, spelled A - L - I - A and then A - N - O - R. Her mother's name was Anor, and because the daughter looked so like Mom, she was christened in Latin: Alia Anor. That means "the other Anor" or "the second Anor". I guess you'd know that much.'

'Go on.'

'Later the spelling changed to Ali Anor, then Alianor, Aliénor, Eliénor etc, but that…'

He waved the paper in front of Jay's eyes. 'That was how Queen Eleanor spelled her own name.'

Jay looked at the sheet covered with her writing. 'I don't think I knew that, Merlin. But then I have done lots of research from the period for songs and music, so maybe I read it somewhere.'

From his wallet Merlin took a colour print of the Dürnstein *sirventès* for which they had been trying to find meanings in the pub over lunch. 'Look at the signature,' he said.

Jay compared the two sheets of paper in his hands.

'When I saw your doodles,' Merlin continued, 'I sent them and the signed *sirventès* by fax to a man I know in Zurich. Doctor Glassner is a graphologist who works for the police there – mostly on forgery cases.'

She shrugged. 'I don't think people believe much in that sort of thing, here in Britain.'

'In Switzerland they do,' he argued. 'And in Germany it's used to analyse personality for every job application, accepted as proof of identity in court cases, and even for matching candidates in matrimonial agencies. I met this guy Glassner a year or two back while I was doing a piece on that Arab bank that went bust for a zillion dollars, all tied up with the Noriega drug money. It was a Zurich police inspector who told me just how good Glassner is. To him, handwriting is like finger-prints. He told me no two are ever the same, if you know what to look for.'

'So where does that get us?'

Merlin weighed the two pieces of paper in his hands. 'Glassner's reply means that the same person scribbled on your note-pad and signed this *sirventès* eight hundred years ago.'

'So I look like Eleanor.' Jay looked him straight in the eyes and, for a moment, the quizzical smile on her lips was exactly the smile on the column in the Metropolitan Museum. 'Then why shouldn't my handwriting resemble hers too?'

'Glassner is not talking about *resemblance*,' said Merlin. This is a man accustomed to giving evidence in court, so he doesn't use words lightly. These two samples of hand-writing are identical, Jay. That's like having the same finger-print as someone else.'

It was mid-afternoon when Jay's red sports car pulled into the traffic on the North Circular Road.

They had travelled two miles when Merlin hit the dashboard. 'Hell, I'm sorry. I'll have to ask you to go back.'

Jay swore. Once she had started on a journey, she hated turning back.

'The costumes,' he said. 'Forgive me, but it's important. I meant to tell you to bring along some of the dresses you wear when you play this Early Music.'

'What for?'

'It's part of the contract with *National Geographic* that I photograph you in costume at the sites we visit,' he lied.

'You could have said.'

'Blame the jet-lag,' he apologised. It was easier than trying to verbalise the plan that had just come into his mind.

Jay wheeled the Alpine round in an illicit U-turn to a chorus of protesting car horns from other drivers. Back at her flat she thrust several dresses and a couple of head-dresses – a wimple and a hennin – into a bag with a couple of recorders. When she returned to the car, Merlin was studying the maps in her AA book.

The car boot was already full of her luggage and Merlin's bags. Jay dumped the extra bag on the back seat and slammed the door.

'I don't need a navigator,' she announced. 'I could drive from here to St Denis without touching the wheel. The car knows the way.'

She screamed out of the cul-de-sac, burning rubber on the corners and cutting orange lights close. Despite a performance worthy of the circuit at Brands Hatch, by the time they were back on the North Circular, it was blocked with rush-hour traffic in both directions. It took an hour to reach the turn-off for Southampton, only to find that traffic was diverted from the motorway due to a multiple accident.

'I can't believe this,' Jay fumed, tapping the wheel in yet another jam. 'At this rate, we're going to miss the last sailing of the day.'

'There's no hurry,' said Merlin. 'Relax.'

'I thought newsmen were always in a hurry?'

'I'm on leave.'

Jay leap-frogged a couple of cars.

Buried in the map-book, he grunted. 'Sal-is-bury... You ever been there?'

'It's pronounced Saulsbry,' she corrected his pronunciation. 'And yes, I've played there. What about it?'

'It's where my family came from – oh, about four generations back. I always meant to visit the place one day, but somehow never got around to it.'

'I thought all you Americans rushed around tracing your roots, the first time you came to Europe?'

He grinned. 'That's like thinking that all you Britishers drive red buses, eat fish and chips and talk wiv a Cockney accent-like.'

'We're going to miss the boat anyway,' Jay decided. She was concentrating on her driving but the tension had gone from her voice, now that there was no question of catching the ferry.

'We could stay the night at Salisbury, if you like?' she suggested. 'It's not far out of the way, and you might meet a distant cousin or two...'

'Great,' said Merlin. 'I'd like that. According to your book, there's a wonderful little Tudor pub a few miles outside the town with exquisite French cuisine and a very good cellar. Let's spend the night there and catch the boat tomorrow morning.'

Jay accelerated savagely through a gap, throwing Merlin's head back against the rest. A lorry horn blared at them, very close.

'And by the way, dinner's on me,' he said.

'And by the way,' she reminded him, neatly manoeuvring the car onto the exit ramp between two lorries, 'you never paid me back the taxi fare this morning.'

They arrived at the pub after dark. It was called the Castle Mound and was miles outside Salisbury, near the small village of Old Sarum. Over dinner, Merlin persuaded Jay to talk about herself and her career, but this time she also made him tell some of the realities of his life in the media – not just the funny stories.

She listened, wondering how a man who had suffered twenty years of guilt for what he had done in Vietnam should choose a profession where he was constantly re-living his own trauma. It did not make sense, but then Merlin, she already knew, was far from being her idea of an unfeeling war correspondent. When they touched, it was pleasant. She liked his voice and his attentiveness, the way he dressed and moved. Watching him pay the bill, Jay thought: I can trust that man. If anyone can help me to unscramble what's happening to me, it'll be him.

She let Merlin hold her chair as she stood up.

'We have two bedrooms,' he murmured, inhaling her perfume.

'Yes.'

'And that's the way you want it?' he asked quietly.

'Yes.'

'Fine by me.'

They walked without talking up the dark oak staircase to the first floor, ancient boards creaking underfoot.

As Jay was putting the key in her door, she said, 'You know, I'd usually be really angry at missing the boat, but I'm not.'

'We're in no hurry.'

'Oh, it's not rational,' she said. 'I just have a musician's phobia of being late, that's all.'

'And tonight you're not angry?'

She kissed him on the cheek. 'It was a lovely dinner. Thank you.'

She closed the door before he could return the kiss, and left Merlin staring at the woodwork.

Inside the room, Jay leaned against the door. The desire for the man she had just touched hit her in the belly as it had that morning when he first arrived. It left her feeling weak. She moaned softly and grabbed the door-knob, hearing Merlin walk away along the corridor to his room. There was the same soft pressure inside her head that had made her think of tumours. Her body became too heavy to keep vertical. Clutching the furniture for support, she lay down on the bed fully clothed and was asleep in seconds.

Being a light sleeper had saved Merlin's life on more than one occasion.

The smallest alien sound – a metallic click in the jungle, a voice where there should be silence, or the faint whistle of the first incoming rocket – had him instantly awake and taking appropriate action.

It was the creak of floorboards in the corridor which woke him. His watch said two am. He lay still and listened. The noise came again, this time just outside his room, and the door handle turned. Briefly in the light from the end of the corridor he saw the gleam of Jay's blonde hair as she slipped inside the room. He heard the sound of her moving softly across the floor, then smelled her perfume as she knelt on the floor beside his bed.

Wide-awake, Merlin wondered what was going to be the result of his spur-of-the-moment decision to spend the night in a pub literally just across the road from the remains of the castle once known as Salisbury Tower, where Eleanor had been confined for fifteen years by Henry II. If Jay was affected by places where Eleanor had been, what effect would this place have on her?

An arm reached across him. He felt long soft hair brush his face and heard Jay's voice, low and husky: 'Kiss me.'

Merlin reached up and pulled her gently down. As they kissed a tremor ran right through her body and into his, like the subdued kick of a low-voltage electric shock. Her tongue and lips reached hungrily for him. A hand grabbed one of his and thrust it inside what felt like a dressing gown, to find that she was naked underneath.

He touched her breasts and Jay reacted with a moan of pleasure. 'Oh God,' she gasped. 'I've waited so long.'

The bedclothes thrust back, she scrambled into bed beside Merlin. Against his naked body, he felt the velvet of her garment and tried gently to undo the waist. It would not come undone, but the top was open and Jay's breasts were free and thrusting at him urgently. He caressed them, feeling their soft fullness and the swift hardening of her nipples that invited his lips. As he took them in his mouth, she moaned again with pleasure and crushed his face against her so hard that he could hardly breathe.

Merlin felt Jay's fingers explore the back of his neck, feeling for the scar behind the ear and slipping down his spine, kneading the flesh over his shoulder blades.

Slowly at first but with increasing urgency, they explored each other's bodies in the dark, Jay kissing his face and neck, running her fingers through the hairs on his chest and belly. And then her lips found his again and bore him back into the pillows. Her hair fell over his face, her perfume was in his nostrils. They rolled, first one on top and then the other.

Jay touched, explored and tantalised him with her lips and hands, surprising Merlin by her aggression. There was a kind of struggle until Jay straddled him and raised his hands to cup her breasts, then sank on to his belly, impaling herself, spreading the skirt and burying him in folds of velvet. Through it, her restless fingers explored his face, his neck, his chest, his arms – like a blind person trying to 'see' a statue.

He felt her lift herself, pulling the garment off, then her nakedness covered him. Jay's nails raked the skin of his ribs and found his nipples, to pluck them in time with the thrusting of her belly muscles, raising Merlin to a peak of sensation he had never known before.

Each time he approached climax, she stilled him artfully and then commenced again with kisses and caresses, thrusting her body against his fingers, his mouth, his chest, his belly. And when at last he groaned and called her name aloud, it was with pleasure spiced with pain from her nails raking his chest as she rode him to a small death in ecstasy.

Chapter 8

'You're winning,' said Queen Eleanor.

'I always win,' King Henry lifted her second bishop off the board.

They were alone in the sitting room of the queen's apartments. A huge fire of oak logs burned in the wide hearth but the high ceilinged room was cold. The king was drinking mulled wine which Eleanor had prepared the moment she heard the commotion late at night in the castle courtyard. During the long years of her confinement, that meant only one thing: the arrival of England's unpredictable king and his hard-riding court to pay respects to the queen who lived in prison.

The royal couple had exchanged greetings and fenced awhile as they always did – Henry wanting a favour in the lands that were hers across the Channel, Eleanor trading a privilege in return. Then they settled to a game of chess, which was one of the king's passions, as Eleanor knew well. Outside her windows, the hubbub of horses' hooves, shouts and the creak of waggons continued as the last stragglers from the king's baggage-train arrived and men fought with words and sometimes blows to find food and rest before the restless king's fancy should be to leave again – which might be in an hour or not for three days.

'I always let you win,' she smiled.

With an oath, he rose and leaned over the board to menace her. 'I win, Madam, because I'm the better player. I'm a king. If I can't play chess on a board who plays it daily across a kingdom with living bishops, knights and pawns, who can?'

Henry swept her ivory pieces from the board inlaid with aromatic woods and mother-of-pearl. They fell and scattered on the stone-flagged floor. He stomped heavily across the room to the fireplace, bandy-legged from spending more time in the saddle than on his own feet.

'It's an interesting philosophy,' Eleanor followed him and poured more wine into his cup. Baiting her husband's volatile Angevin temper was still her favourite sport. 'And who taught you the game, Henry?'

'You did.' He watched her suspiciously over the rim of his cup. 'But many a pupil comes to out-fight the man who taught him sword-play.'

'I'm sorry,' she said, looking meek for a moment as she put the jug down close to the fire. 'Of course you won. Or... you had my queen trapped, which comes to the same.'

'I'm good at trapping queens,' he laughed.

It was perhaps a cue. Eleanor never let one pass. 'You've had me locked up here for long enough, Henry,' she pleaded. 'Fifteen years is a lifetime for a woman past sixty. By now you've made your point, so let me go. I'll give you promises to cause no more trouble, in England or in France.'

'I'll keep you here until you die,' he growled.

'You're making yourself look ridiculous.' She laughed at him, the humble posture thrown away like a pawn that cost nothing. 'I'm an old woman, a grandmother, and you treat me as though...'

'Haven't you heard?' Henry came close to give himself the pleasure of his own reflection in Eleanor's wide, unblinking eyes. 'Those I hold dear are more precious than gold, so I lock them up securely. And since you are my queen, and thus the dearest of all my subjects, you must be guarded best of all.'

'Divorce me then and free yourself from this onerous chore.'

'Never!' he laughed. 'Even at your age, once free you'd roam Europe and set all the dogs in Christendom at my throat! No, by God, that was poor stupid Louis' greatest mistake. To be rid of a wife who was a pain in the arse, he let you go. But though I'd piles and ten of you to grieve my backside each time I climb into the saddle, I'll keep you wife until you die.'

'You'll die first, Henry.'

'I wouldn't give you the pleasure.'

'There won't be any,' said Eleanor. 'I'll mourn you with more tears than the little whore you keep at Woodstock. From what I hear, her bed will not long be cold after you're gone.'

Henry flinched as though she had hit him. 'You didn't know then – that she's dead, my Rosamund?'

'Poor Rosamund,' she mocked. 'Dead in that pretty bower you built her at Woodstock – your palace of love? And you couldn't bring yourself to tell me? Oh Henry, how cruel for you, to lose your one true love.'

'Aye,' he mocked her mockery. 'Poor Rosamund is dead. You knew, you bitch. You always know everything, no matter how I keep you close-confined. You have spies that work for you yet.'

'I have no spies. I'm an old woman, abandoned and forlorn.'

'You?' the king laughed at her denial. 'No spies, you say? Then, by God, you're a witch.'

He dragged her to the narrow, glazed window, thrusting Eleanor's face into the moonlight. 'Did you know that people say you fly on moonlit nights to rut with the devil at Stonehenge, you old hag?'

'Have they seen the horns?' Eleanor asked, ignoring the pain where he gripped her arm so viciously. 'And if they did, horns don't make a devil. You should know, Henry. I put horns on you times enough and still you came back for more, till you grew tired of me and took... Who was the first, Henry? Was it Alice, that poor child you bedded when she was but one week past her twelfth birthday? Say, where is the Princess Alice now? Do you still keep her locked up somewhere too, Henry?'

'I must,' the king growled. 'Who gets Alice, gets her dowry of the Vexin – and that's a piece of land I must have, to keep the French king uneasy in his bed.'

He drained his cup and pulled a fur mantle over his shoulders.

To detain him, Eleanor said, 'You're never sure about me, are you, Henry? Whenever your court is within a day's ride, you come to visit me – to make certain I'm still securely locked up here in Salisbury Tower.'

'I come to see you because I still care,' he said.

He reached for the queen's arm again, but this time in a half-caress. 'If you hadn't set my sons against me in rebellion, I'd not have locked you up, though you goaded me beyond endurance – which you always did.'

'Come now.' Eleanor touched his face. Her voice softened. 'I made you what you are, Henry. And you're not so ungrateful as to overlook that, whatever I've done since.'

'You witch! You bitch!' he laughed, letting go of her. 'God made me king, not you.'

'I made you king, not God,' she contradicted. 'The throne of England is not your Plantagenet birthright, Henry. If I had not chosen you – chosen you, I said – you'd still be the Count of Anjou, a mere vassal of my sometime husband Louis of France. It was my dowry of Aquitaine and Poitou, added to your own possessions, that tipped the balance and gave you the advantage over the other claimants to the English crown...'

'I've ridden far today,' he yawned. 'You take advantage of a man who's tired.'

'Eleanor stood looking down at the chessmen he had spilled in his tantrum. 'My dowry won you England,' she repeated. 'As it was your queen that won the game for you tonight.'

She stooped swiftly and picked the piece up off the floor, holding it in front of him. 'Do you remember, Henry, when first I taught you this game that I had learnt from the Saracen in the Holy Land? In those days, the pieces all had Oriental names.'

The king was wary of her now. 'So I recall,' he grunted.

'*Shakh-mat* we called the game then. It means – '

138

'I know what it means.'

' – in Persian: The king is dead. But this piece...'

She held the queen in front of his eyes and rolled it between thumb and fingers. The tired king watched through narrowed lids.

'This piece was then called *firz*, Henry,' she continued smoothly, lulling him with her voice that was still musical when she chose to make it so. 'The Arabs said it was the chess king's vizier or adviser, and so exempt from all the laws that bind the lesser pieces. Only thus can it outmanoeuvre all threats to the king and secure the final victory for him.'

'What's in your brain, woman?'

'*Firz*,' she said. 'Which in French became altered to *vierge*, the virgin. It sounds similar, but it was hardly a good name for the most dynamic piece on the board, was it, Henry? What blushing virgin could be allowed to unhorse a knight or deprive a bishop of his see as this piece does? On no, you men could not have that! So now, a scant three decades later, what's it called, Henry?'

'You're mad.'

The king pulled his cloak together across his chest and then heaved the oaken door open. A guard on the other side went to help and was pushed violently out of the way.

'Am I?' Eleanor called after Henry. 'I should be, after thirty years of marriage to you – and half of that in prison.'

Before the guard could close the door, she hurled the chess piece at the king. It struck him on the crown of the head where the grizzled hair was thin and fell to the floor.

Henry turned and gave the queen a look of such fury that Eleanor thought he was coming back into the room to strike her. The calloused hands that held the reins of state – and of the most spirited horses in the kingdom – clenched on empty air. His steel-shod heel slammed down on the stone floor, just missing the ivory chess piece which skidded sideways to safety between the feet of a second guard who had remained motionless throughout.

'Now it's called the queen, isn't it?' she shouted.

Through clenched teeth, Henry growled, 'You drive me to distraction, you old whore!'

'I haven't finished,' she shouted. 'That piece you cannot crush beneath your heel is now called "queen" after your Queen Eleanor, o husband mine! And why? Because I made the moves no one else in Europe could dream of, divorcing the King of France to marry Count Henry of Anjou and make him King of England and half of France.'

Eleanor's voice rose to a scream, pursuing the king's retreating back along the echoing corridors so that he clamped his hands over his ears to kill the sound: 'So I made you king, not God, Henry. Remember that until you die, you ungrateful bastard!'

* * *

Jay sat up in bed, her pulse racing. There was perspiration on her forehead and running down the cleft between her breasts – and more moistness between her legs.

But the dream from which she had just woken had been no erotic fantasy. The images growing fainter as she stared panicking into the darkness of Merlin's bedroom were of a chess board violently overturned and her own face bathed in moonlight, with a man hurting her. And in her ears was still the echo of a voice that Jay recognised now. It was the same voice that had shouted, just before the door slammed shut at Canterbury, 'Damn Becket!'

As the dream faded, Jay felt Merlin move in the bed beside her.

Drowsily he asked, 'You all right?'

She did not reply but sat still until his regular breathing told her he was asleep again. A thin strip of light from the corridor was coming under the door. Using it to orientate herself, Jay got quietly out of the bed and returned to her own room, where she was asleep again as soon as she lay down.

* * *

'It gives me no great pleasure to see you here, Marshal.'

Queen Eleanor spoke coldly. She pursed her lips and looked at the now battle-scarred face of William the Marshal. The man she had once thought more handsome than any troubadour now bore on his face and hands the marks of many combats. He held his left arm awkwardly from a wound of years before and walked with a slight limp. And yet he was still – in the words of a king not given easily to praise – 'the finest warrior in Christendom'. Henry also called him 'the only man I trust'.

William bowed his head and knelt on the cold flagstones before the queen.

'Rise,' she commanded. 'I hear that you're to be my new custodian, so why behave like a page-boy? Hypocrisy doesn't become you, of all people.'

She handed the royal warrant back to him. 'This makes you the new constable of Salisbury Tower, and thus my keeper.'

'It is an onerous but not an honourable task,' he said. 'I've little liking for it, Madam, as the king well knows.'

She sighed and then, unable to conceal her eagerness, asked, 'What news from Winchester? What are the new rules the king imposes?'

'You may go out riding each day.'

140

'Ah,' she breathed. 'So Henry's kept his word. It's years since I felt a horse beneath me or breathed air that didn't smell of damp stone.'

'And I'm to accompany you, whenever you set foot outside the castle walls.'

'...as my gallant squire, William?'

'As your keeper. Should you escape, my life is forfeit.'

'You'll live,' she said dryly, then caught at the chainmail sleeve of his hauberk. 'And may I have music? The king did promise that too.'

'You may,' said William, 'summon troubadours and musicians from France for your pleasure, Madam.'

Eleanor turned to her lady-in-waiting. Her face was transformed, radiant as that of a woman twenty years younger. 'Did you hear? We may have music and poetry again? We shall be alive, albeit living in a tomb.'

'One thing I tell you straight,' the marshal interrupted. 'I have strict orders from the king's own mouth. Should these musicians and poets be also spies from Prince Richard – should they be singing for your ears prettily couched messages disguised as songs, for example – they'll lose both their tuneful tongues and their amorous eyes before I let them quit these shores again.'

'There are no spies,' said the queen. 'Henry is obsessed...'

'The king says that there are.'

'He hopes there are.' Eleanor could not resist teasing bluff, honest William. 'It's less worrying than the other possibility.'

'That too.'

'And what do the people say, William?' She led him to the window, with the view over the rolling hills to the distant city. 'Do the loyal townsfolk of Salisbury believe I'm kept informed by spies – or that I can talk to the birds that fly so free?'

The old warrior met her eyes unflinching. 'They say you're a witch, my queen.'

Eleanor looked up into his eyes. She spoke softly: 'And what do you believe, old warrior? We've known each other three decades, nay more, so speak freely.'

'You've travelled to far countries,' the marshal said, confining himself as always to facts. 'That you have learnt much of the ancient arts from Saracen and Turk, I have no doubt.'

'And does that make me a witch?'

The scarred face relaxed into a smile. 'If you can escape from my custody,' he said, 'then I'll know you're a witch and no mistaking it.'

'*Touché*,' Eleanor smiled.

As he turned to leave her presence, she held him with: 'I greeted you uncivilly just now, William. Forgive me. It's not a fault that you are

Henry's loyal servant. If you were my man, you'd serve me just as well.'

'Aye.' The newly appointed constable of Salisbury Tower lifted his queen's hand to his lips. 'And with more joy in one day than in a year of my service to King Henry.'

Eleanor held him for a moment with her eyes, seeing again the handsome young squire that had been William on the day he won his spurs by saving her from an ambush by a greedy cousin, a minor noble with aspirations to rape. It had been shortly after the marriage with Henry, when she would have been a valuable prize indeed.

Heedless of personal danger, the unbelted squire had drawn his sword and ridden alone straight at the blocking party which included several knights and a small posse of men-at-arms. Secure in their numerical superiority, they had laughed at the untested youth and let him approach too near. While Eleanor watched, William had fought as though possessed, sparing no thought for his own safety as he hacked several men to death and putting the rest to flight single-handed. It had been a feat of arms for which even so jealous a husband as Henry could not refrain from awarding the knight's spurs.

But it was not the public accolade that Eleanor recalled now, rather the scene when they were alone after the ambush. Her small retinue of followers had fled the field, leaving her and William to confront the danger alone. She had drawn a dagger from her girdle, determined to draw blood before submitting to the inevitable, then quietened her nervous horse and watched the young hero risk his life in a dozen combats one after the other until her would-be ravishers were all put to flight.

Bleeding from several wounds, William had ridden back to her and wheeled his panting, sweating horse round inches from hers. Whatever words they had exchanged meant nothing by comparison with the burning passion in his eyes that said: *I would do all this again a thousand times if it would prove my love for you.*

His passion had been the more arousing for Eleanor because it was unspeakable. In her rich and varied life, many nobles, princes and troubadours had written poems and songs in honour of her beauty, protesting their affections for her, but the look in William's eye that day had been the yard-stick by which she measured all their protestations of love and found them wanting.

142

Chapter 9

Jay awoke to the sound of her wrist-watch bleeping on the bedside table.

Six am. She cancelled the alarm and closed her eyes again, feeling as though she had not slept all night. Half-asleep, half-awake, her mind was invaded by a confusion of memories: Merlin kissing her hand, a game of chess, the anger of a violent man. It was her erotic arousal by a scene of hand-to-hand combat and her urgent love-making with a man who had blood on his hands that told her these were not images from dreams but memories.

In the next room Merlin awoke as he always did, without an alarm. He switched on the light. The bed was in a mess, blankets and sheets tangled. He stepped out and felt velvet beneath his feet. What he had thought was a dressing gown turned out to be one of Jay's stage dresses.

Merlin pulled on a pair of trousers and padded along the corridor to her room. He tapped on the door. 'Jay!'

No reply. He tried the door. It was locked.

He rapped louder.

'I'm awake,' she called back.

'Five minutes,' he whispered.

They crept quietly downstairs into the grey light of dawn. As Merlin packed the bags inside the boot of Jay's car, she stretched both arms high and breathed a lungful of the clean cold air.

Merlin waited for her to make some reference by word or gesture to her midnight visit to his room. She had taken the crumpled velvet dress with a nod that meant nothing and stuffed it into one of her cases. Her eyes had not met his.

If anything, Jay seemed half-asleep as she scanned the open ground opposite the pub, where a series of grassy mounds poked their way through the clinging ground mist. Further away, remnants of walls loomed indistinctly, intermingled with some trees – all that remained of Salisbury Tower.

Memories flooded back into Jay's mind. She felt giddy and clutched the car roof. 'That wasn't me,' she said, suddenly recalling their love-making. It was not the pleasure that she remembered, but the feeling that someone else had been using her body.

'Are you okay?' Merlin hurried round to her side of the car.

As he came close, Jay clutched his shoulders. He saw an expression of anguish on her face.

'Oh, Merlin,' she shuddered. 'Please take me away from here!'

In a sparsely furnished room above an all-night kebab stall in Torremolinos, Kassim and Salem Chakrouty were arguing in low voices, trying not to wake up their cousin's wife and children on the other side of the flimsy partition wall. The cousin himself was still downstairs, clean-ing up at the end of a long night's work serving kebabs and *falafel* and *shwarma* to the hungry insomniacs of the Coast.

'Instead of helping me, you spend all your time hanging round the new mosque in Marbella and the coffee shops, my brother,' accused Salem. 'What is the point of spending all night drinking coffee and talking with Arabs? You could do that just as well in Lebanon.'

'Ever since I was a child,' replied Kassim levelly, 'you have criticised me for being an Arab. But an Arab is what I am, brother. What good did it ever do that our father tried to make us into Europeans? Tell me that.'

'Here in Europe it is a great advantage,' insisted Salem. 'Unlike most of your friends, we can pass as Europeans. We don't have to listen to bazaar rumour. We...'

'You do what you like,' Kassim cut him short. 'And I shall do things my way – the Arab way – by talking with friends, exchanging a thousand courtesies and gleaning a little here and a little there. Then we shall see who finds it first, this mysterious vale of muses, of which our ancestor wrote. Will it be clever, European Salem Chakrouty or his primitive little Arab brother Kassim, I wonder?'

On the ferry Merlin walked Jay around the deck of an hour, trying to keep her awake, before giving up and hiring a cabin where she could sleep for the rest of the long crossing. He sat in the bar, wondering what to make of his experiment in taking her to Old Sarum.

Once on French soil, he did all the driving while Jay slept in the passenger seat. They arrived in Chartres as dusk was falling. Driving into the first of the towns mentioned in the Dürnstein *sirventès*, Merlin wanted to stay in an old hotel near the cathedral but Jay refused quite adamantly. It was the first time she had spoken for hours.

'I hate old hotels,' she said vehemently. 'They're always draughty and cold and the beds are too soft.'

'What was wrong with the Castle Mound?' Merlin hinted. 'I like old-fashioned hotels. They have atmosphere.'

'Well, I need a good night's sleep.'

They booked into a new hotel on the ring road and strolled around the old quarter of the windy town, coming back to the hotel for an early dinner.

Over the meal, Merlin made most of the conversation. Jay seemed far away.

'You know the oddest thing about this second poem?' Merlin pulled out of an inside pocket the photograph of the yellowish parchment with the writing in faded ink. 'I was thinking about it as I drove along the autoroute this afternoon.'

Listening, Jay thought, I can't remember a thing about the journey. She rationalised her torpor as a reaction to the recording at Oakham: 'I'm always tired after a big show like the television recording. I get a big high and afterwards I sleep for days.'

'I understand.' Merlin touched her hand. She still had not made any reference to the night before. His chest and shoulders were sore from the scratches.

'I was trying to find some hidden meanings to fit Kempfer's poem,' he continued. 'On the face of it, this *sirventès* doesn't make much sense, but the uncanny thing is that it had to be the second or a subsequent one.'

'Why?'

'There's no mention of gold or treasure.' Merlin waved the photograph to make his point. 'This poem was never intended to set anyone off on a treasure hunt. It's useless as a first clue. If we hadn't fooled around that day at Châlus, deciphering the *sirventès* you found on the keep, Baron Kempfer's parchment wouldn't have meant a thing to me, or anyone else for that matter.'

'It meant something important to the Kempfer family, though,' Jay disagreed. 'Otherwise why did they preserve it so carefully through eight centuries?'

'A point,' he conceded. 'But, against that, why did he show it to me?'

'We're going round in circles.'

'I'm trying not to.' Merlin sounded frustrated. 'There seem to be so many things to think of at the same time.'

'Like what?'

'Well...' He let Jay take the photograph from him. 'Eleanor's your ancestor, right? But somehow all this tangle involves me too.'

'You mean the references in the first poem to the great seer of Arthur's court and the man from Atlantis or Atlanta?'

145

'Not just that.' Merlin shook his head. 'Think about it. How many other people could have been at Châlus that day and clicked on Dürnstein? The odds must be pretty long. And even if some medieval history buff was into Richard the Lionheart's story and bracketed the two places together – he wouldn't have known anything about Kempfer's SS connection with Oradour, would he? So he might have gone to Dürnstein and roamed around the ruins, but he'd never have found the baron's heirloom, and it would have been a dead end.'

Jay was trying to follow him but her brain kept slipping out of gear. She wanted to beg Merlin to leave Chartres right away but could not get the words out. Her grandfather had had a stroke; she wondered whether he had felt like this – urgently wanting to say something but unable to form the words.

'So what have we got here?' Merlin leaned over the photograph of Baron Kempfer's poem and read aloud:

> 'The heathen maze is straight beside
> the trail that you must follow
> to a stone that his hollow
> and the dome of the bride.
> Like a pilgrim onward go
> to Bordeaux, Chartres and Fontevraud.'

'The pilgrimage is the treasure hunt,' suggested Jay.

'I'll buy that.'

'And somehow we have to connect a maze, a dome and a stone with the names of three places that Eleanor knew well.'

'A maze, a dome and a stone that were there in her day, eight centuries ago,' he reminded her.

'Hang on.' Jay grabbed the *sirventès* from his hand. 'I know what the dome of the bride is.'

'You do?'

'It's Bordeaux cathedral.' She spoke excitedly, her mind clearing for the first time that day. 'Not now, but then.'

'Run that by me again!'

'Eleanor was married there to her first husband, King Louis. Since then the cathedral has been enlarged and the roof re-built, but then it was domed.'

'How do you know?' Merlin was curious.

'I bought some books in Bordeaux the day you disappeared off to Austria – and I paid a visit to the cathedral.'

'What did you see there?'

'I... don't know.'

Merlin was disappointed with her answer. The conversation rambled on getting nowhere until Jay picked up her room key and said: 'Bed.'

She was almost asleep when Merlin knocked on the door. 'What is it?' she called.

'May I come in for a moment?'

Jay opened the door to him, a house-coat thrown over her nightie. She slipped back between the sheets with no hint of invitation. Merlin sat in the chair farthest from the bed.

'I need some help,' he said, 'with translation. I was puzzling my way through a little pamphlet I bought in the bookshop by the cathedral. Would *labyrinthe* be the French word for maze?'

'*Dormir* is the French word for sleep,' she yawned. 'It goes: *Je dors, tu dors, il dort...*'

'I know, I know. *Tu dormiras très* soon. But am I right?'

'Yes.'

'Then it's two down and one to go,' said Merlin triumphantly. 'According to this weird little book – it's all about religious sites with magical properties – there's a pre-Christian maze picked out in mosaic on the floor of Chartres cathedral which apparently marks a powerful concentration of telluric energy.'

'What's that?' Jay asked, half-asleep.

'I hoped you wouldn't ask,' he laughed. 'I'm not entirely certain. It's something to do with ley lines – the lines of force that girdle the earth. People think that menhirs and dolmens were set up to mark where these lines intersect...'

'Sounds like a geometry lesson.'

Merlin was excited. '... which probably means that the stone that is hollow is a menhir with a hole in it.'

'A what?'

'A standing stone, pierced with a hole. They were used for healing magic before modern medicine. Country people used to pass sick children through the opening seven times by moonlight, to cure them of rickets – that sort of thing, you know.'

'I don't.'

'You got a better idea of what we should look for at Fontevraud?'

'Sleep,' she turned over and stretched one arm out of the bed to reach the light switch. 'Good night.'

Merlin stood up to leave. Jay's reaction to what had seemed a brilliant deduction in his own room, now made it seem tenuous and contrived.

He stopped at the door. Fontevraud... What had Kempfer said Fontevraud was? An abbey where both Eleanor and Richard were buried... No, he hadn't said that.

Merlin bent over Jay and shook her shoulder. 'Hey, I got it! The hollow stone is a sarcophagus.'

'Mm?' she opened one eye.

'I'll lay you a thousand to one that Eleanor was never buried,' he said excitedly. 'In those days the bodies of royalty were placed in tombs, not holes in the ground! So the hollow stone at Fontevraud abbey will be Eleanor's tomb. And now we've got all three clues worked out.'

Jay's regular breathing told him she was asleep. Merlin stood awhile looking at her. She looked so peaceful, lying there. Apart from a small love-bite just above the mole on her neck, there was no way he could have been sure this was the passionate woman with whom he had been making love only a few hours before in the sweating carnal frenzy they had shared in his room at the Castle Mound.

Chapter 10

Merlin rose early and paid his first visit to the cathedral while early Mass was being said in a side chapel.

He used the booklet he had bought the previous day to get his bearings. The maze was exactly where it was drawn on the ground plan; otherwise he would never have noticed it, covered by the rows of chairs. Inlaid in the stone floor, it was made up of concentric lines executed in grey and black marble with geometric precision. The chairs made the outline difficult to distinguish in the dim light filtering through the high stained-glass windows.

He picked his way along a row of seating and stood on the centre of the maze, looking carefully in all directions in case it was not the maze which was important, but what could be seen from there. Then he prowled through the whole building for another half-hour but found nothing of interest.

Back at the hotel, Jay's bags were beside his in the foyer, ready to leave. She was in the restaurant, enjoying a giant bowl of strong black coffee and croissants. When Merlin joined her, she showed him how to dunk his croissants like a real Frenchman. She was so full of sparkle and smiles that Merlin wondered whether she had been ill the previous day. Looking at her in the sunlit restaurant, he saw again the woman he had wanted that first day they met on the tow-path at St Denis.

He let the conversation lead banteringly here and there. It was a more normal way of getting to know a girl than the intense dialogues he had had with Jay since flying back from New York. For that, Merlin blamed himself. Once he started working on a story, he tended to get obsessed with it.

'I have to say it...' He stopped her getting up to leave the restaurant. 'And I know it sounds corny, but you're a very beautiful woman.'

Jay smiled. 'I have nothing against being told that.'

'Then may I tell you again?'

A small frown crossed her face. 'I feel good with you today.'

'And yesterday?'

She pushed her hair back from her forehead. 'I wasn't quite myself. It's amazing what a good sleep can do.'

'Perhaps you had a bug?'

She shrugged. 'Was I a bore? I can't remember a thing.'

He took her hand. 'I like today's girl a whole lot better.'

Jay felt his finger-tips glide over the back of her hand. The small touch left her almost breathless. She wanted to say: Do that again. And to say his name: Merlin. His touch was so arousing that she closed her eyes and murmured, 'You shouldn't do that to a girl in public.'

Merlin looked around the now-empty restaurant. 'There's no one watching.'

They kissed. Minutes later, Merlin whispered, 'It's a pity we've already checked out of the rooms. But we could check back in.'

'It's too obvious,' said Jay. 'I'd be embarrassed.'

Their faces were close, each searching the other's eyes. She eased herself away from his embrace and shook her head. 'No, Merlin. Let's not hurry things. I feel so... I don't know what I feel, but I want it to go on.'

Merlin felt desire surging. He wanted to make love to her then, not later. This was the way he had thought it would be with her: sunshine, smiles and getting to know each other in the best possible way...

'They change colour,' he said, meaning her eyes. 'Today they're so green, it's like looking down into a rock-pool at the sea-side.'

'And yours are so brown.' Jay traced the line of his eyebrows with one finger. 'Your irises are the colour of fresh-turned earth.'

'Earth and water,' he joked. 'Beware, the third element is fire when the first two come together.'

Touching Merlin and being touched made Jay want him physically, but not with the belly-wrenching ache she had felt when he walked into her flat or in the pub at Old Sarum. This was a gentler, floating sensation. She felt warm and caressed as they walked out of the restaurant holding hands.

Merlin paid the bill and carried the bags out to the car. They left it in the hotel car park and strolled in the sunshine along the river and uphill to the old quarter, dominated by the huge bulk of the twelfth-century cathedral.

Jay wanted to idle outside in the warm spring sunshine so Merlin, who was still irritated by his failure to find anything on his earlier visit, left her and went into the building alone. He picked his way along a row of empty chairs and stepped onto the centre point of the maze for another look round, to see whether the sunbeams pouring through the high stained-glass windows showed something that had been in shadow earlier that morning.

150

There was a flash of light as though a pure-white sunbeam had momentarily shone directly in his eyes. A shiver ran up the hairs on his legs and travelled up his body to leave his hair standing on end. At that second there was the loud bellow of a vehicle horn outside, a door crashed open and slammed shut again and a woman screamed something in Dutch.

With a reflex that had earned him awards for combat photography, Merlin leaped over the chairs and pushed past startled worshippers. Camera at the ready, he thrust his way through a group of tourists from the Netherlands standing in the doorway. He barged the baize-covered door open and ran outside to find Jay lying on the cobbles of the cathedral square, half of her body underneath the rear of a Dutch tourist coach.

The driver was apologising in fluent if eccentric English to anyone who would listen: 'Excuse, but I tell you the lady was not there. One second I am reversing the bus. In all three mirrors, nothing I see. Then, my God, from corner of eye I see lady running backwards. Truly so, backwards. My foot is so hard on the brake that cases are falling off the rack – you can see.'

'Okay. Okay.' Merlin halted the stream of words. He could see Jay's legs were not damaged. They lay a couple of inches clear of the huge double rear wheels of the coach that would have crushed them flat. Her face was white as chalk, the eyes open but unfocused.

'Help me get her up, will you?' Merlin ordered.

The driver helped him half-lift and half-pull Jay clear of the coach. They sat her on the boarding step of the open driver's door.

'Shut up,' Merlin snapped at the Dutchman who was still muttering his account of what had happened. 'Nobody's blaming you and she doesn't seem to be hurt, so just shut up.'

He took a handkerchief and wiped Jay's brow. What looked like a huge bruise came off, leaving a smudge of dirt right across her forehead. He felt her head through the hair but found no swellings or cuts. He moved her hands and arms, which seemed normal. Certainly no bones were broken. Throughout, Jay sat staring at the cathedral doorway through which Merlin had just run.

'You are this lady's husband, sir?' the driver asked anxiously.

'That's right.' And to Jay, Merlin said: 'Can you stand up?'

She stood up.

'No bones broken?' he asked.

Jay shook her head. 'I don't... think so.'

'Please be certain, lady,' said the driver. 'I have witnesses...'

A crowd had gathered. Merlin stood up and waved his arms to clear a passage. 'Okay, folks, the show's over. The lady had a fall but luckily the driver saw her in time. I don't think his vehicle even touched her.'

151

Merlin led Jay through the throng away from an approaching traffic policeman, and slipped inside a café where he ordered a large brandy for her. Jay swallowed the entire glass in one gulp as though it were water and choked. Some colour came back into her cheeks.

She turned to Merlin and searched his face.

'Oh, thank God it's you,' she said, clutching his hand with both of hers. They were icy cold.

'Who else would it be?' he asked.

She clung to him so tightly that he could feel her whole body wracked with sobs. 'Oh God, Merlin! Please take me away from this terrible, terrible place.'

Back at the hotel, Jay's room had not yet been made up. To calm Jay who insisted she wanted to get out of Chartres right away, he promised they would leave after she had had a rest.

He made her take a hot bath and drink a cup of sweet instant coffee which he prepared from the courtesy tray in the room. Then he insisted that she get under the bedclothes and keep warm while he sat on the edge of the bed, holding her hand until the shivering stopped. Only then did he ask what had happened.

'I was following you into the cathedral,' Jay closed her eyes. She did not want to talk about it.

'Take it slowly.' The pressure of his hand on hers said: It's okay. I'm here.

'You went on ahead.' She paused. 'I wanted to call after you, to wait for me. I didn't want you to leave me alone. But I couldn't talk, Merlin. I couldn't open my mouth. It was like at Canterbury when my fingers wouldn't play the flute.'

'And then?' he prompted.

'Then I was… pushed backwards.'

'Pushed? By whom?'

Jay shook her head. 'No one. There was nobody near enough. Not near me, but inside me… something sucked all the energy out of me and threw me away like an empty can.'

She searched his eyes. 'You think I'm mad?'

Merlin shook his head. He realised that Jay was talking about exactly the moment when he had felt that strange sensation in the maze but first he looked for a rational explanation: 'Perhaps you stumbled on the steps? Or caught your heel on an uneven stone?'

Jay shut her eyes to concentrate. There was something else too. Why was it so hard to remember and verbalise what had just happened?

'The same thing…' She ran out of words.

152

'The same thing what, honey?' Merlin was worried by the look of anguish on her face.

A shudder ran though Jay's whole body. 'I'm trying to remember.'

He waited until her eyes opened.

'I've got it!' she said. Please, her eyes begged him. Please don't say I'm going mad. 'The same thing happened at Bordeaux cathedral... I think.'

Merlin looked sharply at her. 'You didn't tell me.'

'I nearly walked under a taxi. It was... like my brain was switched off. One minute I was in the cathedral and the next thing I knew, I was standing in the middle of the road... I heard the brakes squeal and the driver shout at me but I didn't know how I'd got there. Oh God, what's happening to me?'

Jay was shivering uncontrollably. Merlin put another blanket on the bed and smoothed her hair. 'Right now I want you to have a sleep. Then we'll go back to the cathedral together and you can show me exactly where...'

'No!' Jay gripped his hand tight. 'I'm not going back there, Merlin. Ever.'

'Okay. Relax.' He spoke soothingly. 'You don't have to go back. But I do. There's something I have to check out. I shan't be long. Just give me an hour.'

Back at the cathedral, tourists filtered through the door past the spot where Jay had fallen. The Dutch coach had gone. Merlin walked into the ancient building and retraced his footsteps to the centre of the maze. He stepped on to and off the centre point several times. There was no effect, although, casting his mind back, he was certain that he had seen a flash of light and felt that strange sensation of goose pimples. No, he corrected himself. It had been more like the sensation when a comb is passed over the back of one's hand and the hairs all rise, attracted by the minute charge of static electricity – but a hundred times more powerful.

He sat in one of the chairs to reason out what might have occurred. From the little he had read about telluric energy, it functioned in some ways similarly to electricity. So... what if the centre point of the maze was like a terminal on a battery?

To complete a circuit, there had to be two terminals, a positive and a negative. Connect a bulb to one pole only and nothing happens - like when he stepped on to the centre of the maze and Jay was not near. But if she were somehow linked with him as far as the telluric forces were concerned, then she must have been in contact with the other terminal at the moment when...

He walked back to the door, opened it and found himself staring at Jay's face. It was, if anything, more of a likeness than the head on the

153

column in the Metropolitan Museum. The full-length carving was of a woman wearing a crown and with a prayer book in the right hand pressed piously against her breast. The drapery of the simple full-length dress was stylised but the face was startlingly natural. The sitter seemed to be repressing a smile at some inward knowledge. It was a portrait executed with loving attention to detail. Jay's broad brow, strong nose, full lips and her long hair, here coiled in tresses, were unmistakable.

The figure was one of a pair of carvings. The other was of a weak-faced, monk-like man who was looking disapprovingly at the woman beside him. There was nothing in the guide book to say who the two figures were, so Merlin asked one of the sacristans. The stream of information in rapid French was only comprehensible because he was already pretty certain what the man was saying.

The two carvings on the west portal were thought to be of King Louis and Queen Eleanor of France, placed there after a visit to Chartres by the royal couple to give thanks for their safe return from the Second Crusade in 1149.

Merlin walked back to the doorway to photograph the face of stone. In the view-finder, Jay seemed to be smiling at him. He zoomed in to check his focus. Through the telephoto lens he could clearly see a small bump in the stone, at the base of the neck on the left side. He had not seen it before because it was almost concealed by the low neck-line of the carved dress. A fault? A piece of bad carving? No, the workmanship was so precise and of such quality, it was no accident. The anonymous twelfth-century sculptor had intended the small bump to be there.

Merlin lowered the camera, walked back to the carving and put out a hand to touch the stone, running his fingers down the neck, across the bump and down to the collar bone. The small protrusion in the stone was exactly where the mole was on Jay's neck.

154

Chapter 11

'You're like two different women,' said Merlin.

He drove off the motorway and parked in a recreation area where they had walked hand in hand between the leafless trees. It was sunny but cold and both were wearing anoraks.

Merlin put an arm around Jay's shoulders, feeling protective. 'At one moment you're the beautiful woman I fell in love with on the tow-path, that day with Leila. And then some influence changes you completely – am I right?'

'It's more worrying than that,' said Jay. 'It's as if there are two people struggling for possession of my body and my brain. I think I'm going mad.'

'No.' Merlin tried to make himself sound certain.

'Then how do you account for what happens?'

He chose his words carefully. 'I think that you're a very sensitive person who should not be exposed to certain things or certain places that have a connection with this ancestress of yours.'

'Why?'

He grimaced, 'I don't know. But for Chrissakes – she was one hell of a powerful person, Jay! Think what it took in those days for a woman to get rid of the King of France for a husband and then marry the guy who becomes King of England, next day! And don't forget that Eleanor incited Henry's own sons to rebel against him, not once but several times. That's why he locked her up for fifteen years.

'Even after that, she grabbed the reins of power the day she was released and ruled England as regent until Richard could get there. After fifteen years in gaol and at the age of sixty-five, that took some doing! Before she died, her children or grandchildren were kings and queens of every country from Ireland to the Holy Land. The more I learn about her, the more I think she was the most powerful person in medieval Europe. If she'd been male and ruled in her own right, her name would be up there in lights alongside Alexander the Great and Julius Caesar.'

Jay leaned against Merlin's shoulder. She wanted him to go on talking. He was beginning to make sense of her own tortured wondering.

'So let's accept that you are – what's the word? – suggestible to her influence,' he continued. 'Instead of deliberately going to places with an Eleanor connection, we'll keep well away. And I'm betting all these... experiences will stop happening.'

Jay stopped and looked into his eyes. 'You really don't think I'm crazy, Merlin?'

For a second he was going to tell her about the veiled woman, but then decided it would not help her. Better she thinks I'm sane as a rock...

'Let's give it a try,' he said, hugging her. 'This damned ghost hunt, treasure hunt or whatever it was, is finished. We'll stop the night in St Denis and tomorrow we take off for somewhere warm, to lie on a beach and get to know each other like any normal couple.'

'Oh, Merlin!' Jay buried her face in his collar. He felt so strong, so dependable. She wanted him to hold her for a long time. There was none of the awful, gut-wrenching lust to use him for her pleasure, just a peaceful sensation of floating in his arms.

From across the river, St Denis was like an illustration to a book of fairy tales. The setting sun tinged the higgledy-piggledy buildings under their sheltering limestone cliff a delicate golden-pink colour.

Leila lifted her glass of wine. 'Cheers. Let's drink to my sense of balance.'

'Why?' asked Jay.

Leila lowered her voice mysteriously. 'Dom suspects I have a new lover. I have to walk a narrow line and not fall off either side.'

'Which means Dom's suspicions are well-founded?' Merlin guessed.

'Sort of,' Leila giggled. 'But the new guy is also jealous of Dom. So I've told him that's all over.'

'And it isn't?' Jay asked.

'No way!'

'How can you sort of have a new lover?' Merlin wondered.

'Sort of means it won't last,' Leila explained. 'But Mr Thisweek has bought three of my paintings, so I don't want it to end just yet.'

'What you're talking about,' he decided, 'is prostitution in kind.'

They were sitting on a makeshift verandah outside Leila's house watching the sun go down. At the end of the over-grown garden, the Dordogne flowed past in full flood.

For once the house was full of food which Leila had bought in a mad shopping spree. It had to be eaten because the fridge no longer worked, so Jay and Merlin were helping her to consume a bizarre mixture of oysters and *pâté de foie gras* and *terrine de rillettes* and smoked *magret de canard*, washed down with a local sparkling wine.

The food was marvellous but somehow the conversation only flowed in fits and starts, despite all Leila's efforts.

They were in the middle of a long silence when Leila said, 'Oh Christ, I quite forgot, Merlin. Your agent rang. He said to call him back.'

'Matty? He rang today?'

'No. Yesterday, or was it the day before?'

'Why didn't you tell me earlier?'

She smiled disarmingly. 'Too busy balancing. Didn't want to fall off the wire. Sorry.'

Merlin departed in the direction of the telephone.

When he had gone, Leila said, 'Jay, honey, it's none of my business, but I hope you guys know what you're doing. I mean, neither of you look like you're having fun, working on this crazy story of Merlin's. And frankly, you worry me. You look like you haven't slept for a week.'

Jay caught sight of her face distorted in her friend's enormous sunglasses.

'We're calling it a day, Leila,' she said. 'Tomorrow morning we drop everything and head for the Costa Brava – to lie on the beach and get to know each other.'

Leila crushed her cigarette in the ashtray and glanced at the door through which Merlin had disappeared. 'That sounds to me like a good idea.'

The door banged and Merlin returned, looking puzzled. 'Matty says he didn't call you.'

'Did I say Matty?' Leila looked surprised. 'No, it wasn't him that called. I'd have recognised the gravelly Satchmo voice and the rag-trade wit. So I wonder who it was?'

The conversation ground to a halt again. Suddenly Merlin turned to Leila and said: 'You've known Jay for years. How long?'

She started, her thoughts elsewhere. 'Oh, ten years, I guess. Let's see, I came here for the first time just to paint for a few weeks in the summer of 1981. So, ten years exactly.'

He placed the year in his own memory. 'I was in Lebanon that summer. And Jay, was she here? Did you meet her then?'

'Yeah. I remember it clearly.' Leila turned to Jay and put a hand on her arm. 'Don't take this wrong, honey, but your parents... At first they seemed such nice people, but they sure as hell were driving you pretty hard for a girl of nineteen.'

'In what way?' Merlin was chewing the food absently, tasting nothing.

'It's a long time ago, Merlin,' Leila pleaded.

'Well, try and remember.'

157

'I'm fed up with this whole thing,' Jay interrupted tensely. 'You promised…'

'Yeah, why in hell don't you leave the poor girl alone?' asked Leila. 'You're not on some fucking news story, Merlin, so leave it alone, huh?'

'I've got to know,' Merlin insisted.

His hand grasped Jay's firmly to stop her getting up. 'What did Leila mean, when she said your parents were driving you pretty hard?'

It was Leila who answered: 'You godammed journalists never give up, do you? So I'll tell you. Jay was a kid on holiday and they made her practise her flute six or eight hours a day.'

'Nobody made me,' Jay protested. 'Don't you understand? I wanted to become a professional musician more than anything in the world. I'd have practised twelve hours a day to make it.'

'What got me was their attitude to you.'

'Attitude?' from Merlin.

'They acted like they were Jay's keepers. She never went anywhere without one of them tagging along. I even had a struggle to get her mother to let her come swimming with me in the afternoons – as though she was six years old or something and couldn't go off with a friend for a dip in the river!'

She turned to Jay. 'Then there was that good-looking Swedish boy here who fancied you. Name like a burglar… Larsen, was it? The way your parents scared him off – wow!'

'They were possessive?' Merlin looked from Jay to Leila for confirmation.

'And how!' Leila laughed. Her earrings jingled. 'But the creepiest thing…' She grabbed Jay's arm. 'Do you know why I palled up with you, that summer?'

Jay shook her head. 'I didn't think about it.'

'Well, Christ, I was a divorcee of twenty-five,' Leila laughed. 'Worldly-wise and going through men like Mars bars! So why should I pal up with a sheltered virgin of nineteen?'

'Why did you?' asked Merlin.

'I felt sorry for Jay. She was a beautiful girl, being hidden away from the world. I thought she needed some fun. And as to those creepy hypnosis sessions every morning with her father… Yuck, I thought that was legalised incest!'

Merlin leaned forward and knocked the bottle over. He let it fall to the ground. Wine glug-glugged on to the grass.

'Why did you have hypnosis from your father?' he asked Jay.

'He's a doctor. He uses hypnosis for his patients.'

'But were you ill?'

Jay felt distressed. She looked from Leila to Merlin.

158

'If you weren't the two people I trust most in the whole world,' she said uncertainly, 'I'd just get up and walk away from this grilling.'

Merlin squeezed Jay's hand. Leila was still holding her other arm.

'Tell me about it,' he urged. 'If you had hypnosis regularly as a kid, that could explain why you're more than averagely suggestible. It's important.'

Jay licked her lips. They were dry. 'It started when I was fifteen,' she said.

'The hypnosis?' from Merlin.

A nod. 'At first Daddy said it was to help me relax. I used to get terrible pains in my neck muscles from playing too long. And then... It's so hard to remember, but... he said he could help me be a better player.'

'What did he do?'

'I had to count from five down to one backwards. Then I was like asleep and I suppose he talked to me.'

Leila lit a cigarette one-handed. 'It was worse than I knew, then. Your parents were trying to turn you into a musical zombie.'

Jay shook her head.'Sometimes it was a big help. There was a time I couldn't play at all. I lost my embouchure...'

'Explain,' ordered Merlin.

Jay pursed her lips and blew. He plainly didn't understand, so she explained: 'I couldn't get the proper sound when I blew into the flute, no matter how much I tried.'

'And why was that?' Leila asked.

'It happens to people. Some of them never play again.'

'And your father gave you a lot of hypnosis sessions to get you through this?'

'I suppose so.'

'But why did it happen to you in the first place?' Merlin asked.

Jay was silent.

'Something happened,' he suggested. 'Something triggered it off.'

Jay fought through the layers of suggestion that blocked her memories.

'I took... an overdose,' she stammered. 'That's what happened.'

'Let's get this straight.' Merlin was staring into her eyes, very close.

His voice was gentle. Jay knew this was not a reporter chasing a story, but a man who wanted to know these things because he cared.

'You took an overdose because you lost your embouchure?' he suggested.

'No...' Jay spoke slowly, groping for the details. 'I took some pills from Daddy's case – the one he carried when he did his house calls.'

'Why d'you do that?'

'I don't know.' Jay shook her head and tried to pull away from him.

'Tell me, Jay,' he insisted. 'You've got to tell me.'

159

She was choking on the words that would not come.

'It's simple,' said Leila calmly. 'Why does any girl of nineteen swallow a load of pills? You had boyfriend trouble, that's why.'

Merlin felt the tension drain out of the hand he was holding. Jay laughed and laughed until she felt too weak to continue and collapsed on Merlin's shoulder to get her breath back.

'I never had any boyfriends,' she gasped. 'I was too busy practising the flute for that. No boy was important enough to kill myself for.'

'So what was important?' Merlin asked quietly.

Jay felt her flesh crawl as the memory came back and then flitted away again. She licked her dry lips. Again she choked on the words, but this time they came out. 'We'd been to stay here in St Denis for the Easter holidays...'

They waited for her to go on. In the gathering dusk, there was a look of horror in Jay's eyes, as though she were witnessing events unfold on a screen in mid-air which the others could not see.

'On the way back to England...' She spoke very slowly. 'Daddy decided to make a diversion and visit Chinon Castle.'

'Chinon? Like the name of your ensemble?' Merlin's voice made Jay turn and search his face.

Uncertainly she returned his smile. 'It was there I saw... something terrible.'

'Like what?' Merlin's voice was a whisper.

'All I remember is that I fainted, right there in the castle courtyard. And the next day, when I picked up my flute to practise, I couldn't make a sound.'

'I feel so safe with you,' said Jay.

She lay with her head on Merlin's naked chest.

'You should.' His hand stroked her hair. 'I'm like St George. I stab the dragons of our time in the heart with a well-aimed paragraph. It's more effective than an oaken stake through a vampire's chest.'

'You're laughing at me now.'

'That...' Merlin raised himself on one elbow and looked down at her face framed by the blonde hair that spread over the pillow '... is one thing I'll never do, I promise.'

They were lying in her parents' large, old-fashioned double bed in the cottage.

Merlin traced Jay's profile with a finger. 'I told you my nickname when I put that dressing on your hand at Châlus. Did I magic the pain away this time?'

She shook her head playfully. 'I think you'll have to try again, doctor.'

'Where does it hurt?' His hand touched her breasts, and then her lips. 'Here? Or here?'

'Lower,' she breathed.

'I'll kiss you better.'

Jay closed her eyes and felt his fingers and lips and tongue loving her, lulling her with a gentle rhythm like a boat moving on a low swell. And then she was swimming in warm water, the colours changing as she blossomed like a flower, her body separating into petals as the climax welled up and up to finish in her brain.

She heard herself cry out his name and then Merlin was holding her to him and kissing her face and it all began again.

Much later he asked, 'Any pain now?'

'No,' she whispered. 'What are you thinking about, Merlin? You look so serious.'

He grinned. '*Post coitum omnia animalia tristia sunt.*'

'I didn't know you could speak Latin.'

'I can't. Just a few quotations, that's all.'

What was on Merlin's mind was the difference between Jay's responsive, tender, feminine love-making – and the almost masculine aggression of the way she had seduced him during the night at Old Sarum. The woman in his arms now was the one he had fallen in love with.

Looking at her head on the pillow beside him, he asked, 'Do you trust me?'

Jay's eyes searched his for a long time.

'Tell me,' he whispered. 'Tell me what you saw at Chinon.'

Immediately her body went rigid. 'No please,' she begged.

Merlin held her in his arms until she relaxed. 'It'll be okay,' he insisted.

'You promised, Merlin.'

'Just this once,' he urged. 'And then we'll never ever talk about it again. Tell me what you saw.'

Jay shivered in his arms but he held her tight.

'I almost can,' she said. 'It's as though I'm seeing someone I know at the end of a street and I run towards them but they get smaller and go round the corner. And when I get there, they're ever smaller and vanishing round the next corner. And the next. Like a diminuendo in vision instead of sound.'

'Let it go.' Merlin buried his head in her thick blonde hair. 'Let's try another angle. Tell me what happened after Chinon. When you got home to England, you swallowed the pills – to escape from whatever you saw?'

'I suppose so.'

'And you couldn't play a note?'

161

'The chronology's all mixed up,' she said. 'But it was something like that.'

'And you got your embouchure back through hypnotherapy?'

'No.' Jay lay still, remembering. In Merlin's arms, for the first time she wasn't frightened to grope through the mists.

'It was the strangest thing,' she said, wondering at it herself. 'After a couple of weeks I was really depressed. My mother went up to London one day to visit her sister. She bought me back a present, some music I'd never heard before. It was a set of cassettes by David Munrow.'

'I've heard the name.'

'That was the first medieval music I'd ever listened to. And something wonderful happened, Merlin.'

Jay swivelled her head to look into his face. In his eyes she saw only concern for her.

'When I heard Munrow's music, I knew that I could play again, but that I had to play Early Music, like he did. There was an old descant recorder in the house which I'd had at junior school. I picked it up and started playing medieval songs by ear from the cassettes. I remember the first one I learnt. I'll play it for you.'

She started getting out of bed.

'Where are you going?' from Merlin.

'To get one of my recorders.'

'Hold on.' He pulled her back in the bed. 'You're telling me that your block just disappeared the moment you began playing this medieval music?'

'That's right. I returned to music college the next day. From then on, I played recorders, shawms, pipes – all the medieval instruments. And overnight I became a far better musician than I had ever been before.'

'And you never had another problem until that evening, ten days ago, when whatever happened, happened in Canterbury cathedral?'

'That's right.'

Merlin watched Jay walk to the door. The sight of her nakedness aroused his lust. 'Don't be long,' he called after her.

Jay rummaged in her bags, dumped in the unheated small bedroom, and took out a simple descant recorder. She hurried shivering back to the warm bed where Merlin lay waiting.

'Later,' he said, trying to take the recorder from her.

'No,' she insisted. 'I want to play you the first song I taught myself.'

He lay on one elbow, watching. It was a strangely erotic experience: Jay's lips pursed on the mouthpiece, her long fingers caressing the instrument, her breasts resting on her arms, the nipples tantalisingly erect – and the strange, almost Oriental melody she was playing.

He lay spell-bound, unwilling to move in case he broke the magic of the moment.

Jay lowered the recorder to sing a verse of the song.

'What's it about?' he asked softly, kneeling over her.

'It's a strange song...' Jay watched Merlin's hands cup her breasts, gathering them like water into which he plunged his face.

'... not a love song, nor a lament. It was written by Bertrand de Born, a Crusader. He was a noble poet who was accused of being Eleanor of Aquitaine's lover.'

'And did he write songs in praise of her breasts or the little mole on her neck?' Merlin pulled her closer so that he could kiss it.

Jay rubbed her face in his curly hair, inhaling the smell of him.

'It's a warning,' she murmured, 'about false wearers of the Cross. Be on your guard against them, Bertrand says: *kar li sunt aussi felon que l' Sarazin* – for they are as treacherous as the Saracen.'

Part 4

Chapter 1

In the vineyards and the small ploughed fields of the narrow valleys that led down to the plain of the Dordogne, the heads of early-rising farm-workers turned to watch the unusual spectacle of an elderly man with crew-cut hair, clad in track suit and trainers, running hard through the clinging early-morning ground-mist. He was accompanied by an athletic-looking young man whose blond hair and blue eyes marked him as a for-eigner from the other side of the Rhine. As the runners passed, greetings were called in the patois: *Holá!* or *Adéou!*

Hermann Kreuz did not hear them; his entire attention was turned inward on the functioning of his body. With each step the iron-willed septuagenarian monitored his heart-beat, lung capacity and the perfor-mance of his muscles as he did each morning on the exercise track which followed the perimeter of the Valle de los Cantos. Alongside him, a blond bodyguard kept pace silently, running with the spring of youth in his step and a film of sweat on his naked chest.

Back at the hotel in St Denis, Kreuz handed his muddy outer clothes and shoes to the bodyguard. Naked except for a pair of brief shorts, he made himself comfortable among the puddles on the riverside terrace for the rest of his morning work-out – to the surprise of the other guests eat-ing their breakfast in the restaurant of Chez Dominique. Kreuz ignored their curious stares. One hundred press-ups were followed by a punishing schedule of pull-ups, knee-bends, then twisting and bending exercises on the wet tiles. He returned to his room where the bodyguard gave him a vigorous full-body massage followed by a cold shower, after which Kreuz ate his usual breakfast of dried fruit and nuts.

Merlin was waiting for the kettle to boil when he heard the peremptory knocking on the kitchen door.

'Who's there?' he called in English and repeated: *'Qu'y a-t-il?'*

He opened the door slightly and peered round the edge – to see, stand-

167

ing outside in the light drizzle, a visitor in a blue flannel blazer over a polo neck sweater and grey worsted trousers. With his air of well-groomed health and self-assurance, Hermann Kreuz would have looked more in place on the deck of a yacht in Cannes harbour than standing in the muddy driveway of a Dordogne cottage.

Taking him for one of Jay's neighbours, Merlin asked, '*Puis-je vous aider?*'

'You are Freeman?' The question was in English.

'That's right.' Merlin felt an instant dislike for the man on the doorstep.

'I may come in, out of the rain?' Taking the answer for granted, Kreuz stepped inside. He viewed the untidy kitchen with distaste and brought his gaze back approvingly to Merlin's well-muscled body, naked except for a pair of under-shorts.

'Kreuz!' He extended a hand which crushed Merlin's in a grip of steel.

'*Freut mich sehr*, Herr Kreuz.' Merlin winced at the unnecessary pressure.

The German smiled thinly. 'Herr Doktor Kreuz.'

'Doctor as in medicine?' Merlin poured hot water onto the coffee in the filter.

'I am an art historian, Mr Freeman.'

Merlin was searching in the wall-cupboards for sugar, opening one door after another. 'Are you a neighbour, Dr Kreuz?'

'I am here because I was given your name by an old comrade, Baron Rudolf Kempfer.'

'So, you're the friend Kempfer mentioned – the one who translated the Dürnstein *sirventès*.'

'That is correct.'

Merlin poured coffee into two cups for Jay and himself, and asked, 'Do you take coffee, Dr Kreuz?'

'Not since fifty years.'

'I beg pardon?'

'Caffeine,' Kreuz pronounced sternly, 'is like all drugs, very bad for the nervous system – therefore also for the brain. Take my advice and drink only pure spring water. A man with a good body like yours should take care of it.'

His back to the visitor, Merlin grinned to himself at Kreuz's little lecture. He picked up the two mugs. 'Well, thanks for the advice, doctor, but I'll risk the poisoned cup now and again.'

Kreuz nodded. He was aware that most people found his ideas cranky. 'I am here to discuss with you the matter of the *sirventès* at Châlus Castle.'

Merlin yawned, 'Well, I'm sorry about that, but the story's been dropped.'

'Why?'

'For personal reasons.'

Kreuz's alarm showed on his face. 'That is not possible. I have travelled a thousand kilometres to discuss with you...'

'Well, that's the way it is,' said Merlin. 'You could have checked before coming. I did give Kempfer a telephone number. And right now I'm getting cold and so's this poison I've been making...'

'Two cups?' queried Kreuz. 'You are staying here with a Miss French, according to my information.'

'It's her house.'

'Then kindly permit one more question. Would this lady be the person Kempfer referred to as your collaborator in the matter of the *sirventès*?'

'Yeah, but I told you. That's finished with. Sorry.'

Kreuz spoke as though he had not heard Merlin. 'I should like to invite both you and her to take lunch with me at the hotel where I am staying, Chez Dominique. There we may have a discussion.'

'Sorry, Doctor, but I already told you...'

'I have some information to which Miss French has a right, Mr Freeman,' said Kreuz smoothly. 'It is very important she should talk with me. Shall we say lunch at 12.30 hours?'

'I don't know if we'll be free.'

Merlin kicked the kitchen door closed, leaving Kreuz to let himself out. In the bedroom, his irritation with the visitor evaporated at the sight of Jay's head on the pillow.

'What kept you?' Jay asked.

Between laughs, Merlin impersonated for her the visitor's mannerisms, exaggerating Kreuz's German accent. 'You missed a great act, honey,' he finished out of breath.

'I heard the voices.' Jay sat up and sipped her coffee. 'So he invited us to lunch? It could be fun.'

Merlin disagreed. 'I have something in mind that will be a lot more fun than taking lunch with Herr Doktor Kreuz. Come here.'

Salem closed the door. They were in the small bedroom of his cousin's flat above the kebab stall in Torremolinos, where the children had been moved into their parents' room to make room for the brothers.

'Where have you been all night?' he asked Kassim who had just come in.

Kassim looked tired but had in his eye the glint of a hunter who knows that he is on the right trail. He threw himself on the bed fully clothed and shut his eyes.

'I looked for you at the mosque after evening prayers, but you were not there,' Salem complained. 'I looked all over Malaga and Torremolinos for you.'

Kassim sniggered at the idea of his brother trying to find him. He had spent the last thirty-six hours travelling to Munich and back, there to interview a lean blond man with needle-scarred arms who had recently been released from prison after serving seven years for drug offences that had got him thrown out of the German Olympic team at the 1984 Winter Olympics. The former athlete had talked freely to Kassim about the year he had spent as a bodyguard to Hermann Kreuz.

Salem looked at the children's drawings and paintings pinned to the wall above Kassim's head. 'I apologise,' he said. 'I did not mean to treat you like a child. I was worried, that is all.'

'About what?' There was a smugness in Kassim's voice.

'About these mysterious friends you spend all the time with, my brother. They sound like criminals to me, with their false names and papers, their expensive cars and fat wallets.'

'They are comrades in the struggle.'

'There's a war in Spain now?'

Salem's sarcasm fell flat.

'There is a war everywhere,' said Kassim. 'Those who pretend otherwise are conspiring with the enemy.'

Through the thin partition wall, Salem heard his cousin's wife reading a story in halting Spanish to her two children. The children were correcting her pronunciation. The small domestic scenes he witnessed daily in the flat were tugging at Salem's heart. It was a long time since he had thought so much about his dead wife and children.

'Then I am your enemy,' he muttered. 'I understand nothing of these things you say.'

'You understand nothing,' Kassim agreed. 'But you can be useful, all the same.'

He twisted in the bed and pulled a wad of bank notes from a hip pocket. He peeled off a handful and tossed them with a bunch of keys to Salem. 'There is a car outside, a Subaru pick-up with a covered back. Take it and buy the things on this list while I sleep. I shall need them tomorrow.'

Salem read the list. 'A rabbit?' he queried.

'It must be alive. Buy it in the market.'

'And a canister of CS gas? Where will I find that?'

'In a drugstore. Old ladies carry them in their handbags, so say it is for your widowed mother who is nervous of being mugged – if you are asked. You had better buy several cans but go to different shops and buy one in each.'

'Two used blankets, light brown or khaki…' Salem continued reading the shopping list.

170

'Buy them in a market, too.'

'One pair of Zeiss 7 x 42 B/GA binoculars...'

'If asked, say you want them for bird-watching.'

Salem threw the money and the list on to the bed beside his brother. 'What is all this?'

Kassim opened his eyes and rolled over on to one elbow. 'They are things we shall need.'

'For what?'

The scorn was evident in Kassim's voice. 'You, big brother, have been asking people since we arrived here for the whereabouts of the vale of muses. And you have been getting nowhere, while I now know where it is.'

Kassim smiled. 'With the help of my criminal friends, as you call them, I have obtained the map reference of a place called El Valle de los Cantos. It means the valley of songs – not muses – but the meaning is close. Maybe I mistranslated the word on the tile.'

'And is there a secret fortress there, built by the Crusaders?'

'No.' Kassim was enjoying his brother's mystification. 'The fortress in this hidden valley was built in 1950 with money from Swiss bank accounts belonging to the German SS.'

'Then it is not the place we seek. On the tile, our ancestor spoke of Crusaders – men of the Cross...'

'Not so, big brother.'

Looking smug, Kassim rolled over and took from his other hip pocket a much-folded piece of paper. It was a tracing he had made of the lettering on the tile with a rendering into modern Arabic below. He held it out for his brother to see.

Salem pointed: 'It says: "the secret fortress of the Cross".'

'Exactly!' Kassim rolled off the bed and sprang upright, grabbing both of Salem's shoulders. 'Exactly! The secret fortress of the Cross – which you with your clever European brain interpreted as a castle built by the Crusaders!'

'And what does it mean?'

Kassim laughed, his face close to Salem's. 'It means what it says, big brother. Nothing more and nothing less. The moral is that lesser men should believe what is written and not seek to interpret the writings of the wise.'

Kassim folded the paper carefully and returned it to his pocket.

'It is so simple when one believes.' He spoke softly, but his eyes burned with religious fervour. 'This secret fortress is owned by a man called Kreuz, which means Cross in German.'

On the other side of the wall, humdrum everyday life went on. One of the children was crying and the mother was shushing it before her husband was awoken. Salem sat on the bed, looking up at his brother. He

171

had not really believed his father's death-bed story of treasure and prophecy. To him the tile and its story had been primarily a lure which might entice his brother away from a way of life that must end in violent death sooner or later.

'How is it possible,' he asked slowly, 'that our ancestor eight hundred years ago could write of something which happened only in 1950?'

'Because all things are written,' sneered Kassim. 'Now – while I sleep – go and buy the articles on that list.'

Chapter 2

Jay stretched deliciously. Her skin still glowed from Merlin's caresses. Beside her, he breathed regularly, eyes closed.

On the dressing-table her flute-case reminded Jay that she had not touched the instrument for two days. She ought to get up now and practise for a couple of hours. That was the least work she had done on any normal day of her adult life.

'What are you thinking?' Merlin asked.

'So you are awake?'

'I was watching you through half-closed lids.'

'Sneaky.'

'So what were you thinking?'

'That it's nine o'clock. We're wasting the morning.'

He chuckled. 'What a funny thing to say.'

'I feel almost guilty, not to be up and working.'

'My, you do need a holiday.'

'We should be halfway to the Costa Brava by now. That was the plan, wasn't it, Merlin? We're way behind schedule.'

'Way behind geographically,' he admitted with a yawn. 'But emotionally we're ahead of schedule. Twice since dawn and...'

Merlin reached lazily for Jay, who dodged his embrace with a smile and: 'It's my turn to make the coffee.'

She scrambled out of the bed and wandered dreamily into the kitchen with Merlin's anorak tossed over her nightdress against the chill of the unheated room. There was an envelope pushed beneath the door, addressed to Miss J. French. Jay opened the door to see if there was anyone outside, and found a large bouquet of roses on the step. The handwritten card inside the envelope read: 'As a music-lover, I hope to have the pleasure of your company at luncheon. H.Kreuz.'

Above the signature there were two bars of music written in the same hand. Jay recognised them as the opening of Papageno's aria from The

Magic Flute. Obviously, she thought, the early-morning visitor who had so annoyed Merlin was more than just an ordinary music-lover.

Humming Mozart's catchy little tune while she made the coffee, Jay wished the flowers had come from Merlin.

'I,' he said on seeing the roses, 'have no intention of eating lunch with the guy, even if I hadn't taken an instinctive dislike to him. Apart from anything else, we agreed yesterday we'd drop all the Eleanor nonsense.'

'This mysterious Dr Kreuz is very persuasive.' Jay was arranging the roses in a vase. She felt secure after the night of making love during which she had brought out of the psychological closet so many old fears. One by one, in Merlin's arms, they had turned out to be no worse than bad dreams. Her anguish of the previous day at Chartres seemed now exaggerated. She wanted to show Merlin that she was not a hysterical schoolgirl.

'Flowers, an invitation and a polite note,' she said. 'And you say he came all the way from the south of Spain to talk to us? It's a bit rude just to push off and leave him in the lurch, isn't it?'

The rain had stopped. Jay threw open the window and took a deep breath. She could not remember feeling so carefree ever in her life. She heard Merlin roll off the bed and pad barefoot across the room. His hands slipped around her, gently cupping her breasts and pulling her back against him. She felt the touch of his lips on her neck and his hardness pressing against her buttocks.

Why had it never been like this with Carl and the others? she wondered. Everything felt so right with Merlin – like the old cliché: made for each other. With him, she did not have to close her eyes and concentrate. There was no hurry, no risk of all the delicious sensations slipping away at the last moment and leaving her empty and alone. When Merlin lifted her from one plateau of pleasure to the next, she abandoned herself to his caresses, knowing he would not let her fall. She felt as though they had a thousand peaceful years to get to know each other.

'Merlin…' she breathed the name and felt his fingers entering into her soul.

Merlin. It was the cry of a seagull, wheeling on the north-east gale. Merlin… was the lover who held her tightly when she called his name in the warm moist tumult of love. Merlin… was the ideal man she had dreamed of long ago, her knight on a white charger, the magician who magicked cuts away and healed the dark places in her soul, the man who would keep her safe from dragons…

But this Merlin holding her was no fantasy. He was flesh and blood and desire – the lover who gave her what she had always been seeking from a man. Jay let his hands travel up and down her body. She felt the strength of his desire and moaned with the soft pain of wanting him.

174

'Look!' he whispered.

She opened her eyes. In front of her was the familiar cottage garden with the rooftops of the nearby village showing through the leafless trees. Above them rose the whitish limestone escarpment with the ancient Templar tower on top. It was a scene she had known for most of her life and yet, that morning, it was different.

Or perhaps, she thought, I'm seeing it for the first time with Merlin's eyes.

All the muted hues of winter blended in the landscape. The lichen grey of the stone cottage outbuildings, the million shades of green and brown in trees and shrubs, the reddish tiles of the distant rooftops of the village, all melted together in a moment of perfection as the sun burned a hole through the overcast sky and made a million raindrops dance and sparkle on every branch.

For sheer perfection, it was like playing the second movement of a Mozart piano concerto.

'Why are you crying?' Merlin turned Jay to him and wiped the tears from her cheeks. His other hand pressed gently against the base of her spine, holding her belly against his.

Jay shook her head.

'Because you're happy? Or because you're sad?'

She looked deep into his brown eyes, searching, searching. 'It's not so simple as that.'

'Then what?' he urged her gently with the pressure of his arms.

Jay wanted him to understand. 'I feel as though all my life I've been running faster and faster, with never the time to stop and waste a morning like this.'

Merlin had his head on one side, puzzled.

'You don't understand, do you?' she asked.

'Not really.'

'Time,' said Jay softly, tracing his lips with her index finger, 'is the tyrant that rules musician's lives. And you, Merlin the magician, have made it stand still for me.'

The magic of that moment when rain-drops were transmuted by sunshine into jewels which only they could see, carried them further away from reality on a tide of warmth and loving. Their progress into this new dimension was as effortless as that of a straw in the vortex of a whirlpool or a feather in a gale. As pleasure grew into joy and joy turned into what they both perceived as the beginning of happiness, they made love again and again, exhausting their bodies and consciousness until it seemed that their very souls were entwined. And when at last they were cast ashore exhausted on the ebb-tide of passion, they lay love-wrecked on a foreign strand which neither of them had ever trodden before.

If Jay had decided at that moment to go to Peru or up into the Himalaya, Merlin would have said yes.

Instead she announced drowsily, 'It's too late to leave for Spain now, so we might as well accept the mad doctor's invitation and have lunch with him. And if conversation with Dr Kreuz is too boring, we can always make an excuse and leave early.'

Merlin did not argue. Although he would not have broken his promise of the night before to drop the whole idea, he had been intrigued at the speed with which Kreuz had followed up the visit to Dürnstein. Professional curiosity outweighed his dislike of the man.

Half an hour late, they wandered hand in hand into the restaurant. As Merlin afterwards realised, it was the point of no return.

Kreuz was munching a handful of dried banana when they arrived at the restaurant. He was standing by a reserved table with his back to them. As the waiter announced the arrival of his guests, Kreuz turned. His gaze brushed over Merlin without interest and settled on Jay. He stood stock-still, a sliver or whitish banana poised halfway to his mouth. Beneath the tan, his face paled and for a second a gleam of excitement shone in the cold blue eyes.

Kreuz swallowed the last piece of dried fruit and rubbed his hands together. 'So this is Miss French, who discovered the *sirventès*?'

Merlin performed the introductions: 'Jay French – Dr Kreuz.'

Jay flushed at Kreuz's intent examination. His eyes focused on the mole on her neck. Thinking that it was a love-bite which had attracted his attention, Jay pulled the collar of her sweater higher.

Kreuz took her hand and gave a half-bow, murmuring: '*Kuss die Hand.*'

He sat staring at Jay while she and Merlin ordered their meal, then engaged her in a conversation that excluded Merlin – all about music, musicians and conductors. Once or twice Jay tried to bring Merlin into the conversation, but there was nothing he could contribute.

By the time the main course arrived, Kreuz had charmed Jay completely. Cleverly he brought the conversation round to her interest in medieval music and from there to the subject of the two *sirventès*, which he agreed were almost certainly clues to the buried treasure of Châlus. He wanted to know what she and Merlin had been doing at Châlus Castle, why Jay had immediately recognised the poem for what it was, how Merlin had made the connection with Baron Kempfer and why they had now decided to abandon the trail after coming so far?

As a professional interviewer, Merlin had to admire Kreuz's manipulative skill; he was getting everything out of Jay and giving nothing back. To stop her answering yet another question, Merlin interrupted with:

'Unlike the steak, Dr Kreuz, we didn't come here to be grilled. You said you have some information which is important for Miss French.' He sounded so hostile that Jay gave him a nudge under the table.

Kreuz was oblivious. 'What kind of name is Freeman?' he asked.

'What kind of question is that?'

Kreuz pursed his lips. 'To my ears Freeman sounds Jewish. Would it be an anglicised form of Friedmann, perhaps?'

For a second Merlin contemplated getting up and walking away from the table. Only the weight of Jay's hand on his thigh restrained him.

'It happens,' he said in a very controlled voice, 'to be an old English name. My family were settled in Salisbury for centuries. Yeoman stock, I think they call it on Jay's side of the pond.'

'Excellent.' Kreuz nodded approvingly as though Merlin had passed a test. He popped another sliver of dried fruit into his mouth and washed it down with water.

'I'm a scholar, Mr Freeman. My passion is the art of the Middle Ages, especially poetry. When I heard from Kempfer that you had discovered a hitherto unknown *sirventès* written by Queen Eleanor, I could not wait to see it.'

'What do we get out of it?' asked Merlin.

'A great deal,' said Kreuz. 'I have the most extensive collection of medieval art and manuscripts in Europe. There is a great deal I can do to help you, but first I need to see this poem.'

'Not good enough,' said Merlin.

'Please,' said Jay. She smiled at him. 'Please show Dr Kreuz the poem we found at Châlus. It's only fair. Baron Kempfer showed you his.'

Merlin took out his pocket book and folded it at the page where he had copied both the *sirventès* and Jay's translation. Kreuz bent over it, absorbed.

'*Savies que la pucelle...*' He carried on reading and grunted with surprise at the translation. 'This is an excellent rendering, Miss French. I could not have done it better myself.'

'High praise,' muttered Merlin in Jay's ear.

And then the interrogation began again – to end abruptly when Jay mentioned being a descendent of Eleanor of Aquitaine. Kreuz made a clicking noise with his tongue and nodded to himself as though everything made sense. He left the table and walked outside on to the terrace where he stood looking out over the river, deep in thought.

'I told you the guy was weird,' commented Merlin.

'Why are you so rude to him?'

'I don't like being conned.'

'In what way?'

'Despite his promise to divulge information to which you have a right, you may not have noticed but so far the traffic's been one-way: from us to him.'

'Relax, Merlin.' Jay squeezed his hand. 'I'm so happy today. Please don't spoil things.'

She felt a growing fascination for Kreuz and could not see why Merlin disliked the man so strongly.

'Doctor Kreuz is a musician and a medieval scholar,' she said. 'We have a lot in common. I think you're jealous.'

'Of that guy?' Merlin laughed. 'You're kidding.'

They were sampling the cheese board when their host rejoined them.

'Sitting,' he announced, 'is very unnatural. For thinking, one should walk, or at least stand and breathe clean air.'

He caught the look that passed between Jay and Merlin. 'But I think you young people are not interested in my – what is that lovely English word like the German for sick? – my cranky ideas.'

'Oh no,' said Jay with a straight face. 'They're fascinating, Doctor.'

'I am an exceptional man,' said Kreuz straight-faced. He leaned across the table, admonishing Merlin with one finger. 'Those who listen, learn a great deal from me.'

To placate Merlin, Jay gave him a wink.

Kreuz took from a pocket the plastic-covered parchment that Merlin had last seen in Baron Kempfer's home. He placed it on the table beside Merlin's notebook and announced, 'Tantalising, aren't they? They seem to say so much yet really tell us little. We don't even know exactly what the treasure is.'

'It's a pile of gold,' said Merlin.

Kreuz laughed. The sound stopped in mid-breath as though he resented wasting the energy. 'Of course, the gold. Well, that must be worth between twenty and thirty million dollars in today's values. To find it, you will need my help.'

'And why would you help us, Doctor?' Merlin cut in.

'To please my vanity as a scholar,' Kreuz smiled. 'Many people have sought Queen Eleanor's gold and failed.'

'Like the SS Division Das Reich?' Merlin slipped the question in.

'I think so,' said Kreuz smoothly.

'Were you helping them too, Doctor?'

Kreuz shrugged. 'I am a scholar, not a soldier, Mr Freeman. And why do you try to irritate me when I am offering help?'

'Because I don't believe in Father Christmas. What exactly is in this for you?'

'Frankly, Mr Freeman, I disapprove of treasure-hunters like you, but Miss French who is a descendant of Queen Eleanor has a moral right to the gold hidden by her ancestor. That is different.'

'I repeat: what do you get out of it?'

'Something far more valuable than money – knowledge!'

Merlin laughed sourly. 'We're talking perpetual motion or the secret of eternal youth?' He stood up and threw his napkin on the table. 'I never heard such a load of shit in my life.'

Kreuz froze. For a moment, Jay thought he would strike Merlin.

Then he mastered his anger and turned to her. 'Miss French, I don't understand your friend's mentality.'

Jay looked after Merlin. His shoulders were hunched with anger as he left the restaurant. 'I'm sure he didn't mean to insult you.'

'On the contrary,' said Kreuz coldly. 'It's obvious that he did. But it is of no importance.'

He waited for Jay's eyes to leave Merlin and settle on his face again. 'My motive in assisting you to recover the lost hoard of Châlus is not material reward. On that you have my word. It is for me a privilege to place my humble talents at your disposal.'

Kreuz leaned forward and fixed his eyes on Jay. Wishing that Merlin had not gone, she tried without success to break the eye contact.

He was whispering so quietly that no one else in the restaurant could hear: 'You have a great destiny to fulfil. Am I not right?'

Chapter 3

Merlin did not trouble to keep his voice down: 'In the entire world only you could have made me apologise to that guy.' He could not remember ever meeting anyone who made him so unreasoningly angry as Hermann Kreuz.

'Sshh,' Jay squeezed Merlin's hand. After the excellent meal she would have liked to curl up in bed with him. Instead they were sitting in the rear seat of Kreuz's white BMW while he pored over a map spread out on the bonnet of the car and explained to the bodyguard in German the route to follow. The series of barked commands was too rapid for Merlin to understand.

'The last time I went for a ride with guys like these,' he grunted to Jay, 'it ended with a bag over my head and my wrists tied together with commo cable.'

'Commo cable?'

'Telephone wire to you.'

Jay took the remark as a joke. 'I don't know why you've taken such a dislike to Kreuz. I think he has a weird charisma. There's a sort of physical energy radiating from him that I find compelling. When he fixes those cold blue eyes on me, it sends shivers up my spine.'

'I saw.'

'Don't be so uptight, Merlin. I've known a couple of conductors like Kreuz. In any other job, you'd say they were megalomaniacs, but on the podium they're the ones that make an orchestra excel itself.'

Merlin snorted with derision.

She squeezed his hand. 'You're jealous, Merlin. I do believe you're jealous.'

He clammed up as Kreuz got into the car and sat in front beside the driver.

As they left the restaurant car park, he half-turned to look at Jay. 'You're wondering what is this post-prandial treat I have in store for you? It's a sample of what I can show you, a token of my good faith. So, be patient for fifteen minutes and you shall see something beautiful and unique. Now you must excuse me. At this time each day, I sleep.'

Kreuz pressed a button. His seat-back reclined, his eyelids closed like a garage door coming down. The cropped head lolled on the cushion of the head-rest.

In the mirror, Merlin was watching the driver's face, which had not changed expression since they had first seen him. 'Where exactly are we going?' he asked.

'*Versteh' nicht.*'

'*Wohin fahren wir?*' Merlin tried.

There was no reply. Merlin put his arm around Jay's shoulders and let her doze against him while he tried to follow the way. The driver used a hundred small and winding roads between vineyards, through woods and along marshy little valleys where there were no houses. Watching the compass mounted on the dashboard, Merlin could see that the route which Kreuz had told the driver to use was far from being the most direct way to wherever they were going.

Ten minutes later, Kreuz opened his eyes and announced, 'Two minutes and we are there.'

The car pulled up outside an ancient chapel hidden in the depths of a chestnut coppice. Through the trees was the outline of a larger building. There was none of the noise of the modern countryside: no tractors, no distant cars, no aeroplanes. Beside the chapel a spring gushed out of a low limestone cliff into a moss-lined pool. The only sounds were the ripple of water, the song of a few birds and the clicking of the car's cooling exhaust pipe.

'Where are we?' Merlin asked.

'The building,' replied Kreuz, 'is very old.'

He ran his long, sensitive fingers over the finely carved figures of knights and ladies that decorated the arch of the Merovingian doorway beneath the more simple Biblical scenes depicted higher up the façade.

'This stonework is ninth-century,' he explained to Jay. 'Parts of the building are older still, built on the ruins of a Romano-Gallic villa which was sacked and abandoned in the third century when the barbarian invasions put an end to what remained of the Pax Romana in Aquitaine. Later the ruins were occupied by hermits. When the first chapel was built and dedicated to St Florence, it became a place of pilgrimage because of the *source miraculeuse.*'

He pointed to the spring. 'The water is reputed to cure women's problems. I had it analysed. It is slightly radioactive. What they do with it, I don't know. Perhaps they drink it, perhaps they…'

He squatted to mime a woman douching herself. 'And the chapel we

181

now see was built by a rich woman in the twelfth century as a thanks offering for her cure.'

'…by Queen Eleanor?' asked Jay.

'Who knows?' Kreuz led the way into the chapel after opening the heavy, nail-studded door with a large iron key which he had taken from the glove pocket of the car.

Merlin ushered Jay ahead of him. As their eyes adjusted to the comparative darkness they saw that the building was not derelict nor even disused. There were fresh flowers and a clean cloth on the altar. The plastered walls had been recently lime-washed, the leaded lights had no holes and there was no dust on the terra cotta tiled floor.

'Local women,' explained Kreuz, 'still come here to perform their devotions and perhaps to ask for cures.

'Now…' He modulated his usually harsh voice, which took on an almost feminine quality, 'what I am about to show you has been seen by very few people. It is a great privilege.'

He strode to a purple velvet curtain which concealed the wall behind the altar, waited until Jay and Merlin were standing beside him, and then jerked the curtain along its rail to reveal a group of figures painted on the plastered wall.

Merlin was stunned. If the carved heads he had seen resembled Jay, the likeness of her in the woman's face painted on the wall in front of him was startling. The half-smile on the lips seemed to be mocking him, the green eyes gazing boldly at him, challenging…

'Eleanor of Aquitaine.' Kreuz looked from the fresco to Jay and back again several times.

'Is it not beautiful?' His voice caressed the silence. 'The colours are faded, but see the simplicity of the line, Miss French. The range of colours employed is small. In those days, the artist mixed his own pigments. And remember, to paint a fresco one must work fast in order to finish before the plaster dries. And yet, what a likeness! What art!'

The restored fresco showed Eleanor holding a *flûte à bec* or recorder. There was a second figure of a woman holding a lute. In the background stood two knights clad in chain mail, both holding swords. Their faces were part-hidden by the nose-pieces of the pointed Norman helmets which came down almost to the mouth. The unknown artist had painted one knight's eyes as brown as Merlin's. He was looking sideways towards Eleanor. The other knight had blue eyes and was watching the first one.

'I believe – ' Kreuz's voice held an almost sexual excitement – 'that this fresco was painted from the life when Eleanor came here for a cure. Just look at her face.'

They stared at it until Kreuz pulled the curtain back to conceal the fresco from view.

'Shit!' said Merlin. 'And me with no camera… '

'I could not allow photography.' Kreuz turned to Jay. 'This portrait is unknown to the world. When I discovered it, the chapel was derelict. I bought the place, had the structure restored and arranged for some local peasant women to look after it. They have no idea what they are guarding for me.'

'Why did you do all this?' asked Merlin.

Kreuz took his eyes off Jay's face and said, 'I am a rich man, Mr Freeman. I spend my wealth to conserve the beauty of past ages which this rotten modern world would otherwise allow to decay.'

He gestured at the roof and the walls. 'When I purchased this chapel, Mr Freeman, the roof was falling in and the walls crumbling under the onslaught of centuries. Nobody cared. Another few years and this thing of beauty would have vanished for ever.'

'How did you come to find this place?' Jay asked.

'Scholarship,' Kreuz smiled.

'Or maybe,' Merlin accused, 'you bought this place because you have a special interest in Eleanor of Aquitaine – and have had since you and your old comrades were hunting her treasure in June 1944!'

The accusation echoed off the stone walls and floor of the tiny chapel. Kreuz turned at the far end. The light from the small arched window behind lit his cropped grey hair but hid his face. 'I do not normally answer hostile questions, Mr Freeman. But in this case – for Miss French's sake – I will disabuse you. My interest in Queen Eleanor is not because of a buried treasure. It is because I respect above all other human qualities the power of the will.'

He raised both arms in unconscious imitation of a priest at the altar. His voice was harsh and strident again. '*Triunf des Willens*. The triumph of the will! The words mean nothing to you, I think.'

'Title of a pro-Hitler film by Leni Riefenstahl,' snapped Merlin.

Kreuz lowered his arms. 'Just so. Well, Eleanor of Aquitaine had a will, Mr Freeman. It was a will so…'

He groped with both hands in the air, seeking the right word. 'So colossal that we can still feel it today. She had a will that transcended her sex, the age she lived in, even her death!'

Kreuz shook his clenched hands as though he wished to shake compre- hension into his listeners. 'Eleanor's intellect was among the most superb Europe has ever known, but she lived in a time when power lay with men, so the history of her period is all of kings and battles. To the French she was an English queen; to the English merely a French duchess.

'Yet at fifteen, Mr Freeman, when she inherited the Duchy of Aquitaine, she was already statesman enough to sell herself in marriage to Louis the French king. It was the only way of keeping her inheritance intact. She defied the Pope to go on Crusade. She married two kings and begat two others – Richard and John.'

'We know all this,' interrupted Merlin.

'You may know, but you don't understand!' Kreuz shouted. 'It's not just a question of reading a few books! You must enter into the spirit of another age.'

He pushed past Jay and Merlin, and pulled back the curtain behind the altar, revealing the fresco again. 'This was a woman who, at the age of sixty-nine, dragged Berengaria to Cyprus for a forced wedding with Richard, so that he should have an heir – to prevent John becoming king which she rightly foresaw as a disaster. And she was seventy-seven when Richard was shot at Châlus. So what did she do, this incredible Eleanor of Aquitaine? Like a man in his twenties, she rode day and night to reach the stricken king before he died. And even later, she...'

Kreuz stopped and mopped his brow. His chest was heaving. Despite the chill in the chapel, he was sweating with excitement.

'I am getting carried away,' he gasped. 'Forgive me, Miss French. An old man's obsessions can be embarrassing.'

Chapter 4

'Sie dürfen weiterfahren!'

The blond guard in the black tee-shirt and slacks who had kept them waiting for five minutes, waved Jay past the barrier and dropped the boom inches behind the Alpine's rear bumper. Watching the car disappear along the dusty track, he spoke into his walkie-talkie.

Overhead, but inaudible to Jay and Merlin above the noise of the car's engine in low gear, a helicopter painted olive drab circled lazily like a vulture in a thermal, watching to make sure that the visitors did not stop to take any photographs on the way down the track.

'What a weird place!' Jay commented as they rounded the bend and saw down into the hidden valley. She twirled the power-assisted steering wheel, narrowly avoiding a large stone.

'Try slowing down,' Merlin suggested, 'if you don't want to lose the sump.'

Jay pressed the button to wind up her window and keep out the dust thrown up by their passage down the steep track. She put the blower full on and lifted her blouse with one hand to fan the sweat-moistened skin beneath.

'Those guards,' said Merlin, as the track began to level out and driving became easier, 'are not fooling. Did you see their weapons?'

'Some kind of rifles?'

He laughed at her description. 'Those, my love, are SA 80s. Beautiful assault rifles, but a helluva lot of firepower for the gate-house on someone's private estate.'

'It's like a location from a cowboy film.' Jay peered through the dust-covered windscreen. 'All these cactus plants. No shade anywhere.'

'There were some trees.' Merlin pointed to a stump they were passing. 'Looks like they were felled so as to leave no concealment near the houses. And, by the way, we're being followed.'

Jay squinted into the mirror on her door.

185

'Not behind,' he nudged her. 'See the shadow on the ground over to our right? That's a chopper flying quite low and more or less overhead, I'd say.'

As though on cue, the helicopter dipped just ahead of the windscreen as they reached the bottom of the escarpment. It skimmed along the now level track ahead, leading them to the largest of the guest houses in a storm of dust.

'Jesus!' exclaimed Merlin, recognising the 'copter. 'That's some toy for a non-military user to be playing with. It's a Messerschmidt-Bölkow-Blohm BO 105 – fast and very expensive.'

As Jay pulled up, he continued, 'My God! There's another blond clone coming out of the house. He matches the two on the gate. How many d'you think Kreuz has got?'

'Perhaps he breeds them in a secret laboratory down here?' Jay joked.

The helicopter peeled away, leaving Merlin and Jay stretching in the hot afternoon sun after the long journey south. The journey through the snow-capped Pyrenees and across the bleak, deserted plateau of León had begun in winter and taken them through spring into what felt now like full summer in the Valle de los Cantos, only twenty miles north of the Mediterranean coast.

'My name is Dieter.'

The soft voice belonged to a guard who was taking their bags out of the boot. He spoke in English with a slight lisp. 'Dr Kreuz presents his compliments, sir and madam. He invites you to make yourself at home and to join him for dinner in the main house at nineteen-thirty hours.'

'Fine,' said Merlin.

'If you need anything meantime, sir, just pick up the phone and I'll come right over.'

'Shouldn't we say hallo to Dr Kreuz when we've unpacked,' asked Jay, looking around at the semi-desert scenery.

Dieter smiled politely. 'I'm afraid that is not possible, Madame. The doctor works to a very strict timetable. He has an important meeting this afternoon. He asked me to give you his apologies. And by the way, you should not attempt to go outside after dark. Please wait in the house until I come to escort you to dinner.'

'Or what?' Jay was curious.

The guard pointed with one finger to a patch of shade where Jay saw two huge black Dobermanns sitting alert, their eyes watching her. 'At dusk,' he lisped, 'The dogs are loosed.'

'What is this place?' asked Merlin. 'You've got a snazzy little helicopter flying figures-of-eight overhead, the guards are armed and there are dogs running loose at night. Is this some kind of concentration camp you guys are running?'

186

Dieter walked ahead of them, two bags in each hand. Over his shoulder he said, 'Dr Kreuz has one of the greatest art collections in the world, sir. All the security measures are required by the insurance companies.'

They followed him inside the guest house, designed as a hollow square. On each side a row of rooms provided accommodation looking inward on to the startlingly blue pool which occupied the centre of the square. There were half a dozen sun loungers scattered on the pool surround and a huge air-bed of transparent plastic bobbing on the surface of the crystal clear water.

Dieter put their bags into two adjoining rooms and left.

Jay put her arms round Merlin's neck. 'Not sorry you came, now?'

'Let's say I've still got reservations about our generous host.'

'Well, relax.' She pulled his face down and kissed him on the lips. 'Don't be contrary. It was me who wanted to stop all the Eleanor nonsense. Then when I decided to come and see these mysterious relics that Kreuz offered to show us, you decided you didn't want to come.'

'I just don't like the guy.'

'All this...' Jay looked at the pool and the welcome bottle of champagne cooling in an ice bucket beside them. 'Kreuz must be a millionaire. D'you think the whole valley belongs to him?'

Merlin's eyes followed the flight of the BO 105 which dipped out of sight behind the roof ridge. It was making a series of low passes over the hills at the western end of the valley.

'I should think it probably does,' he grunted.

Jay slipped from his embrace, kicked off her shoes to sit on the top step of the pool ladder. She dipped a toe in the pool. 'The water's so cool and inviting. Let's swim.'

Merlin opened the champagne and poured two glasses. He knelt beside Jay on the edge of the pool, handed her a glass and stroked her hair. 'You look right, drinking champagne by your private pool.'

They chinked glasses. 'I suppose all you showbiz people live like this the whole time,' he teased.

'I'm a musician.' Jay sipped the cool champagne. 'I put on expensive dresses to perform. The rest of the time I wonder how I'm going to pay the rent, just like anyone else.'

'So what are you doing here, Miss French?'

'Since you came into my life, Mr Freeman, a lot of things have changed.'

'Put down that glass,' he said. 'I want you.'

'I'm all hot and sticky,' she warned.

'Then we'll make love in the pool.' Merlin slipped Jay's blouse free of the waistband of her skirt.

* * *

187

The helicopter pilot spoke into the microphone incorporated into his helmet: 'I've flown over this area a dozen times already. There's nobody here. And even if there is, the dogs will be loose in an hour. They'll take care of any poacher or snooper.'

The camouflaged BO 105 merged with the sun-baked landscape as he made one final sweep, skimming over the arid surface as low as safety permitted before heading for the landing pad in the valley, beside the main house.

Below, in the centre of the storm of dust and pebbles, Kassim Chakrouty held his breath and tried to block his ears against the *whup-whup-whup* of the rotors and the roar of the twin turbines. The old khaki blanket beneath which he lay was well weighted down with rocks. He had little fear of being discovered unless the helicopter should land and the guards come looking for him on foot.

Kassim gasped and sucked in clean air as the chopper tilted and dropped below the skyline. From his vantage point, now that he could risk lifting his head a few inches, he could see half the valley, from the main house to the single track that led into and out of the valley. Keeping the blanket over his head, he brought the powerful Zeiss binoculars to bear on the private courtyard of the main house, which he had been observing closely for over an hour.

Kreuz's important meeting which had prevented him welcoming his guests in person was with the two blonde masseuses. Describing his former employer's daily timetable, the athlete-turned-addict in Munich had described the specific activity which Kassim was now witnessing as: 'What Kreuz calls renewing himself from the fount of youth.'

Always conscientious in his research, Kassim had asked for all the details, 'You are telling me that this old man has sex each afternoon with both girls?'

A dirty nail scratched an infected needle-track. It was time for Kassim's informant to have a fix and he was finding it hard to concentrate. 'Not just sex. For Kreuz it's a process of rejuvenation, you know? He has all these crazy ideas.'

'Like what?' Kassim steered his informant back onto the subject by opening his wallet and starting to count out some notes.

'Like…' He read somewhere that ageing Roman men used to drink the milk of young mothers.'

'Kreuz does that?'

'Yeah. Believes he can absorb the essence of regeneration that way.'

It was obscene, Kassim thought. 'What else?' he asked.

A sniff. The dirty hand reached for Kassim's money. 'Kreuz thinks that daily consumption of the juices of young women has halted the ageing process in his cells. You know, sixty-nine, that sorta stuff…'

188

Kassim had been nauseated. His fear of women's bodies made the idea repulsive.

'I guess it works.' The man had started compulsively scratching himself; his skin was itching all over. 'It's ten years since I was down there working for Kreuz. He was over sixty then but the tough old bastard used to give me and the other guards a good hard run every morning. We were all Olympic or sub-Olympic standard, so what do you make of that?'

Kassim lay now watching in horrified fascination the athletic contortions of Kreuz's lean, tanned body, intermingled with the softer flesh of the two girls. He had heard that Westerners indulged in many perversions, but this was beyond his most erotic fantasy. Only when Kreuz discarded the girls and lay naked in the sun, did Kassim turn his binoculars to the guest house outside which the red sports car was parked.

He adjusted the focus. Two more naked, entwined bodies became sharp and clear, as though he could reach out a hand and touch them. Kassim hissed and licked dry lips. Truly the unbelievers would have much to atone for when called to their Maker...

Watching Jay and Merlin make love on the transparent air-bed floating on the square of blue water, Kassim's body went rigid with excitement. Through the lenses he watched Merlin kiss Jay's breasts, then stroke her belly and her thighs, parting the fair pubic hair and opening her lips to the sun and the eyes of the watcher on the hill.

Kassim was so engrossed in their love-making that he paid no heed to the increasingly lower angle of the sun which should have warned him that the time was approaching when the dogs would be loosed. Supine on the sharp stones, he kept his gaze fixed on the couple slowly and languorously making love, shifting his uncomfortable position in sympathy as the air-bed rocked to the gentle rhythm of the lovers' movements.

Throughout, Kassim concentrated on Jay's body. The man with her did not interest him, except as a remote agent who was manipulating the desirable parts of a woman's body. Only when Jay lay with her head in the crook of Merlin's arm trying to get back her breath, did Kassim look at Merlin's face for the first time. He dropped the binoculars, pushed back the edge of the blanket and raised his face for one incautious moment to the sky.

'Allah is merciful,' he said to the rocks around his hide. 'To the believer, He gives all things.'

He grabbed the glasses and looked again to make sure. There was no doubt: he was looking at the man who had been his prisoner during the siege of Beirut.

Aware suddenly that he lay in shadow – that it was late, with the sun not far to go before it vanished below the horizon – Kassim wriggled

189

back from the skyline and dismantled the hide, carefully concealing all traces of his day-long vigil in the broiling sun.

He ran crouching until it was safe to stand and then hurried across the broken ground, hoping the reach the dog-proof boundary fence in time.

Merlin stared up at the sky, his mind empty. The cloudless blue had turned mauve with dusk and was darkening rapidly.

Jay made a little noise in her sleep. Some water had slopped over the edge of the air-bed. It was cold and the air was chilling rapidly, now that the sun had gone.

Merlin liked the way Jay went to sleep on his shoulder after making love. He liked everything about her. He had never known with anyone else the heights of joy that he attained with her, the sweet, quiet calm they shared at moments together, nor the fiercely protective instinct she aroused in him.

On the negative side, on his brief trip to New York he had missed Jay more strongly than any other person in his life. He was not a hundred percent certain that he wanted to belong to anyone that much, but there didn't seem to be a choice...

Beside him, Jay dozed until he nudged her gently awake with: 'Time to get dressed for dinner with Count Dracula.'

Jay protested, 'Do I have to wear a wimple, Merlin? I'll be too hot. A velvet dress is bad enough.'

'Think of all the Arab women in the world, wearing veils all their lives.'

'They're welcome.'

Merlin unplugged the charging unit and inserted the battery into his flash-gun. 'Carry the wimple and put it on just for the pix, if you like. But this place is nearly a desert. You'll be surprised how swiftly it'll cool down, once the sun's gone. And I doubt if a fitness fanatic like Kreuz has central heating in his house.'

There were three of Jay's medieval dresses spread on the bed.

'The brown one,' Merlin decided. 'That'll look good in flash pictures. Nice and sombre as a background for whatever these relics are.'

'But we could photograph them tomorrow by daylight,' she objected. 'So why do it over dinner? Wearing one of these dresses is a real bore, Merlin. I can't even move around without holding the train up off the ground.'

Merlin was slipping on a crush-proof white tropical dinner jacket over a dress shirt and black trousers. He straightened his bow tie. 'With a guy like Kreuz, I do everything the first time. He may change his mind by tomorrow morning.'

Jay let him help her into the dress.

There was a light knock on the door of the guest house. The guard called Dieter entered and began discreetly tidying away the loungers around the pool.

When Merlin picked up his camera case, he asked quietly, 'Do you mind if I have a look inside, sir?'

'You're scared I'm packing a gun?'

Dieter smiled. 'I'm quite a keen photographer myself, sir. I'd love to see your cameras.'

Merlin opened the case. The manservant lifted the cameras and lenses out, examined them one by one and replaced them. 'Beautiful equipment,' he said softly.

They followed him outside. The clear sky was velvet black and full of stars. As Merlin had prophesied, the air was already cold. Halfway along the path to the main house, Jay sensed something in the darkness behind her. She turned and saw two of the Dobermanns following them, a couple of paces behind. In her shock, she nearly dropped the wimple. The two large black bodies were dimly outlined against the light pebbles. The dogs' eyes glowed in the starlight.

'You're quite safe,' said Dieter, sensing her unease. 'The dogs are a hundred percent obedient.'

'You could have tied them up,' she said. 'Just while we walked across.'

The guard sighed. 'I'm afraid Dr Kreuz is very strict about his rules – and one of them is that the dogs must be loose after nightfall.'

As they approached the main house, an infra-red beam was tripped and floodlights sprang on all around the building. As though this had been a signal, a distant but horrible noise broke out at the western end of the valley. It sounded like several of the dogs snarling and barking.

Dieter stopped with his head on one side, listening.

'The dogs are terrible killers.' He smiled, holding the main door open for them. 'I'm surprised there's any wildlife left on the estate, but occasionally a rabbit strays in from outside. The dogs tear it to pieces.'

Chapter 5

Kassim was within sight of the boundary fence when he heard the dogs. They were running silently on his scent, only the scuffle of stones giving them away.

It was dark in the valley below, but up on the hills the last faint glow of dusk revealed at first two, then three, and finally four dark shapes gaining on him fast. He was tempted to throw down the bundle wrapped in the old blanket in order to go faster, but to do that meant putting all his trust in speed.

His heart pounding with fear and exertion, he raced the last fifty metres to the boundary in the certain knowledge that he was not going to make it. He stopped just short of the fence and turned to face the dogs. They fanned out and kept coming. Only then did he open the bundle and throw the rabbit towards them; it was an old trick used a thousand times by *fellahin* slipping over the border between Lebanon and Israel. Whether or not it worked, depended on having the nerve to stand completely still, without moving so much as a hair whilst the dogs instinctively went for the decoy.

After a day spent in the dark, hot, airless sack, the rabbit moved in what seemed like slow motion to Kassim. Run, you little bastard! he prayed. He wanted to shoo it away or kick it from him, but he knew that a single movement could cost his life. Despite every muscle in his body screaming for oxygen, he held his breath and stayed motionless. Scenting the Dobermanns, the terrified rabbit shot sideways, hoping to escape between the man and the oncoming dogs. In panic, it scooted this way and that, seeking shelter in the unknown landscape. The dogs skidded round on a new course, following its desperate zigzags.

Kassim waited until he was sure their attention was locked on to the moving prey; he had at most twenty seconds. He threw the old blanket over the barbed wire strands that topped the fence. Behind him in the dusk, three of the dogs tore the rabbit literally limb from limb in a growling, snarling frenzy of blood lust. The high-pitched keening scream of the rabbit was clearly audible over the noise the dogs were making until it ceased abruptly.

The fourth Dobermann was too late to be able to grab a mouthful of fur and flesh before the game was over. Frustrated, it turned back to the larger prey just escaping over the fence, leaped ten feet into the air and clamped its teeth firmly into the calf muscle of Kassim's left leg.

He screamed with pain. Fuelled by terror, his muscles found the reserve of energy for one last desperate effort and heaved both his weight and the dog's upwards until most of Kassim's body was on the outside of the fence. Flesh tore and the dog fell. Released from its weight, Kassim overbalanced and fell. He would have dropped all the way to the ground and rolled clear of the fence, except that his clothing was tangled in the barbs, so that he ended upside-down on the far side of the fence, his head halfway to the ground and his injured leg trapped behind him, still on the inside.

With a furious snarl, the dog scrambled to its feet, scented the blood dripping from the torn leg and leaped to crunch bone and muscle between its powerful jaws. This time, the pain was almost paralysing. Desperately Kassim tried to twist his body round before the other dogs arrived at the fence and tore his face to pieces through the wide mesh. One hand scrabbled at his pockets for the canister of CS gas he carried. For one nightmare moment, he thought it had fallen out, then his fingers closed on the smooth metal and he wrenched it free, aiming for where he thought the dog's eyes must be.

There was no effect. The Dobermann was shaking his leg, the whole weight of its body swinging in the air as it tried to pull him back over the fence. Its violently scrabbling claws raked Kassim's skin through his clothing. The pendulum movement made it difficult to be sure where the canister was pointing.

Hearing the other Dobermann's coming, Kassim screamed from mingled pain and fear, nearly dropping the canister. His free hand felt through the wire and found the dog's neck, slippery with saliva dribbling down the narrow chin, mixed with Kassim's own blood. With a superhuman effort, he wrenched himself round and delivered a generous squirt of gas in the animal's eyes. The grip of the savage teeth loosened and the Dobermann fell to the stony ground with a thud, blinded and howling with pain.

The counter-balance gone, Kassim's body-weight tore flesh and clothing loose from the barbs. He fell to the ground clutching his injured leg and moaning with pain as the other three dogs hurled themselves in fury at the far side of the fence, their fangs only inches away from his flesh as they clamoured for his blood.

* * *

193

The heavy metal-lined door thudded shut behind Merlin as he followed Jay inside the main house. He noticed bolt sockets on both sides of the door-jamb as well as in the lintel and threshold; entering Kreuz's home was like walking into a bank vault.

The distant noise of the dogs was replaced by the muted strains of a Bach cello concerto that issued from small speakers discreetly hidden in the dark oak wall-panelling. At the top of a flight of wide stone stairs stood Hermann Kreuz, dressed in a black dinner jacket with a black shirt. One hand was fondling the head of another Dobermann sitting beside him. With a command for the dog to sit still, Kreuz bounded lithely down the stairs to greet his guests.

When Jay moved forward into the light, Kreuz smiled his appreciation of the brown velvet dress with the high bodice and the long train sweeping the floor.

'*Kuss die Hand*,' he murmured, his lips brushing the back of her hand.

He stood back, the better to appreciate her. 'If I may say so, that is a very beautiful dress. It's a style that suits you well.'

Jay turned completely round to show the dress off, one hand holding up the train, clear of the floor. 'I'm glad you like it. It's a stage costume I'm wearing at Merlin's request, so that he can take some pictures of me holding these relics of yours.'

The idea of photographs filled Kreuz with horror. 'It's out of the question,' he said. 'I am merely the custodian of all the precious things kept here. For any photography, I should have to obtain the owners' permission. They may have objections.'

Jay explained about the magazine article. Kreuz said nothing, but he kept his eyes on her even when Merlin was trying to reassure him: 'We won't say where we took the photographs, Dr Kreuz. "A private collection" is the usual euphemism.'

'And you expect me to rely on your discretion?' Kreuz queries.

'As a journalist, I'd be stupid to betray a confidence and risk losing a source.'

'Very well.'

The surrender came with surprising swiftness. After seeing Jay in her costume, Kreuz's mind was on something else. He excused himself with, 'I'll be with you in a moment.'

He left them in the hallway decorated with medieval Spanish armour and weapons. At the head of a broad flight of stairs leading up to the upper floor, the dog lay with its head on its paws, watching the visitors. A couple of minutes after Kreuz had gone, the lights went out.

'What's going on?' Jay asked.

'Power cut.' Merlin's voice came out of the darkness.

'If you weren't here,' she said, 'I'd be screaming.' She felt Merlin's arm go round her waist.

'Don't do that,' he said. 'Or you'll alarm our four-footed friend up there.'

'Can it see in the dark, d'you think?'

'No, but it's got a good sense of smell.'

She shuddered. 'I hate the way those animals sniff at me.'

They heard voices talking in German. A light appeared at the end of a long corridor.

It was Dieter holding a camping gas lamp. The valley was at the end of a power line, he explained, and cuts were frequent, but if they would like to follow him...

The house was bigger than it looked from outside. He led them down a long corridor. Jay was having trouble with the train of her dress, so Merlin helped her to free both hands by putting on the wimple by the light of Dieter's lamp. They continued along corridors, up steps and down and then across a courtyard garden, open to the sky.

Inside the chapel, another gas lamp showed Kreuz standing by a huge round table. On it were two objects covered by cloths like a conjuror's props on stage. He dismissed Dieter who withdrew, taking his lamp with him and leaving Merlin and Jay to pick their way through the semi-darkness of the chapel, aware of ancient, bulky furniture and statues all around.

The air they were breathing had that distinctive church-smell of old wood, almost like camphor. It was frustrating for them to see only what was on the table and the dim outlines of carved screens, a statue and some gleaming metal here and there in the darkness outside the pool of light. When Kreuz saw Jay's face framed in the severe lines of the wimple, his hand holding the lamp trembled with excitement so much that he had to put it down on the table. Merlin was surprised to see that he had changed out of the dinner jacket he had been wearing only a few minutes before; Kreuz now wore a dark hooded cape of some coarse fabric that came down to the ground. Only his tanned, wrinkle-free face caught the light against the shadowy background.

Kreuz licked his lips. His voice took on the same sibilant quality it had had in the little chapel near St Denis where he had showed them the fresco.

'I have two very precious objects for your delectation,' he said to Jay. 'The first is a mirror of polished bronze. Roman, second-century.'

He lifted the cloth off it and passed it to her.

'Roman?' Merlin queried.

Kreuz chuckled. 'Remember that in Eleanor's time, Mr Freeman, Europe was still waist-deep in the mud of the Dark Ages. What technology existed was very primitive. For that reason many Roman and Greek artifacts, although hundreds of years old, were still in use by those lucky enough and rich enough to possess them – as Queen Eleanor once possessed this mirror.'

Jay took it from him. The back was engraved with an intricate picture of satyrs and nymphs. The front had been re-polished and gave a soft and flattering reflection of her face, lit by the gas lamp.

Merlin was busy with his photographic equipment. 'Is this the best light we can have?' he asked.

'Can you manage?' asked Kreuz. 'The power might not come on again until the morning. We can leave the photography until tomorrow, if you like.'

In the mirror Jay saw Kreuz's pale blue eyes watching her intently. She swivelled the mirror away and pushed a stray hair back behind the veil of the wimple. The face framed by the wimple in the mirror mocked her. It was the face carved on the columns, the face painted on the wall of the mysterious chapel in the woods, but it was also her own face...

Merlin took several pictures, some by direct light and some using flash bounced off the white-washed walls while Kreuz kept well away from the lens. When Merlin had finished, he took the mirror back from Jay and wrapped it carefully in the cloth again.

'The other relic,' he said in his strange sibilant voice, 'I won't describe to you.'

Jay lifted the cover off. On the table was a pear-shaped vase, wider at the bottom than the top and made of crudely blown glass mounted in gold encrusted with large red gem-stones. The medieval style of crafts-manship was crude and lumpen beside the finesse of the Roman mirror.

'A wedding gift,' she said.

Her eyes met those of Kreuz. There was a silence. Merlin was busy loading the fresh film into his camera by the light of a gas lamp.

'But whose wedding?' teased Kreuz.

Jay ran her finger round the gold rim at the bottom of the vase. Without taking her eyes off Kreuz, she announced, 'It's inscribed: "*Hoc vas dedit rex Ludovicus sponsae suae Alianorae*". This vase was given by King Louis to his wife Eleanor.'

'You can read such a faint inscription in this poor light?' asked Kreuz.

'I made it up.' Jay felt pleased at the joke she had played on him. 'There's an identical vase mentioned in a book Merlin bought in New York. It was Eleanor's wedding gift to Louis. And that's inscribed : "*Hoc vas sponsa dedit Alianor rege Ludovico*".'

'Correct,' said Kreuz approvingly. 'This is the missing one of the pair.'

'How much would a thing like that be worth?' asked Merlin.

Kreuz took the vase from Jay and caressed it as a mother might a child. 'To a collector,' he smiled, 'this thing, as you call it, is priceless.'

Salem was growing nervous. He chain-smoked, throwing the cigarette ends out of the open window of the rusty and battered pick-up van.

By the dashboard clock he had been waiting at the rendezvous for half and hour when the dishevelled figure of his brother lurched out of the darkness and wrenched open the passenger door.

His hand about to turn the ignition key, Salem heard Kassim's ragged breathing. 'What is it, little brother?' he asked. 'What has happened to you?'

He switched on the courtesy light and saw Kassim's injured leg, bandaged by a strip from the torn trousers. Dark red blood was seeping through. Kassim's face was white from shock and contorted with pain.

'Turn off the light and drive to the coast,' he gasped. 'I need a doctor.'

'I'll take you to a hospital.'

'No!' Kassim grabbed the wheel. 'I'll give you directions. My friends will take care of me. Just get me to Malaga airport. I know the way from there.'

Salem drove carefully on the narrow, winding country road, heading north at first to pick up the main road to the town of Antequera, from where a dual carriageway lead south through the mountains to Malaga.

As Kassim explained briefly what had happened, the panic died out of his voice to be replaced by a note of triumph, 'God works in strange ways, my brother. But one thing is certain: the believer is always rewarded for his faith.'

Salem was coming to hate the pseudo-religious language his brother used; more than anything else it symbolised the gulf that had grown up between them during the years of war. 'Is this then your reward?' he scoffed. 'Where is it written that the believer shall be torn to pieces by dogs?'

'My injury is the result of my own carelessness.' Kassim clutched his injured leg. 'But my reward is that my enemy has been delivered into my hands, o brother.'

Salem took his eyes off the road for a moment and saw in the light of a passing car that his brother's eyes were bright with fanaticism – or delirium, he was not sure which. Was Kassim in shock? he wondered. If so, he should keep him talking…

'The enemy?' he asked cautiously.

Kassim laughed wildly. 'The fornicator! The American with his whore! He is the key to the whole thing. And to think: I had him in my power!'

There was an exaltation in the voice that sounded like madness to Salem.

'What American? What whore?' he asked in exasperation. 'We are here because of an ancestor who died three centuries before America was discovered. The tile contained no mention of Americans and whores.'

Kassim ignored the remark. 'His name is Freeman. I knew his face the second I saw it. He was my captive in Beirut until the Jews rescued him, on the day I received this.' He touched the shoulder still covered in scar tissue.

Salem concentrated on his driving. 'When was all this?'

'Nearly ten years ago,' said Kassim, 'during the siege of Beirut. Do you not see, my brother, how this is yet another proof that our ancestor foresaw everything. Absolutely everything!'

Chapter 6

They dined by candlelight. A dozen guttering tallow candles in a wrought iron candelabrum threw a warm amber glow over the oaken table and chairs, the white walls with their dark panelling and the arms and armour that decorated them.

The food was served by one of the blond guards. In the poor light it was impossible to distinguish which guard, or what exactly he was serving on to Jay's and Merlin's plates. Kreuz prowled about the room as he ate his usual diet of nuts and fruit, chewing each one separately and talking to himself as though in a reverie. With the cowl of his cape raised and half-covering his head, he looked like a mad monk.

'Fucking Rasputin himself,' Merlin whispered to Jay. He raised an eyebrow at his plate, on which a brown island of nut cutlet was being engulfed by a yellowish mud-slide of lentils – and made a grimace of revulsion.

Jay touched a finger to her lips. 'Don't think about it. Just eat,' she advised in a whisper.

The next time Kreuz's orbit brought him near to the table, he placed a hand on her shoulder. 'In addition to being a great queen, Miss French,' he murmured, 'your ancestor possessed a great intellect and reputedly also telepathic gifts. King Henry preferred to believe that she had a network of spies throughout the kingdom bringing her the latest news, but Henry was paranoid – which is why he survived so long. For myself, having examined all the evidence, I am inclined to believe that she did have supernatural powers.'

Merlin ate a pomegranate. That and the wine in the large carafe in front of his place were the only things on the table he could stomach. To his mind, Kreuz's monologue was getting weirder and weirder. He was resuming some abstruse scholastic disagreement he had had years before, ending: 'But in my humble opinion, Miss French, what the chroniclers say does not make sense.'

'What do they say, Dr Kreuz?' asked Merlin, unable to follow. 'I may have missed something.'

'That Eleanor retired to the abbey of Fontevraud after Richard's death and stayed there in pious retreat until she died.'

Merlin poked the food on his plate, unable to decide what it was. Some bits tasted brown and dry, the rest was yellow and wet. He tried another mouthful. So far as he was concerned, the evening had been a waste of time, apart from the photographs.

Kreuz was on his knees, looking more than ever monk-like as he pulled an ancient leather-bound tome from a low bookshelf. He lifted it on to a lectern lit by a pair of candles and leafed through the thick parchment pages, hunting for something.

'The fact is that during the last four years of her life Eleanor left the abbey of Fontevraud several times.' His voice was hardly audible as he leaned over the book. 'Indeed, within the year of Richard's death she was in Spain at the court of Castile where she arranged the marriage of one of her granddaughters to Philip of France, son of her ex-husband Louis. That much is a matter of record. I'm talking of Princess Blanca of Castile, better known as Queen Blanche, of course.'

'Oh, of course,' yawned Merlin.

Kreuz spun round, startling him. 'And why do I mention that, Mr Freeman?'

'I'm sure you'll tell us, Dr Kreuz.'

Jay shot him a look that said: Shut up, Merlin, you're behaving like an oaf.

Behind her, Kreuz raised a hand, like a priest sermonising. 'Because during her visit to Spain, Eleanor went missing for two months!'

He looked from one to the other of his guests, to see whether they had understood the importance of what he had just said. 'The chroniclers are vague on this, but I have proof that during this time she visited the Moorish court at Granada incognita! That was strange and dangerous business for a Christian woman of even half Eleanor's age, albeit in time of truce!'

His eyes stayed on Jay's face, seeking some reaction. 'Why should an old woman do that, do you think? Why should she travel all the way to the south of Spain on a journey that entailed going several hundred miles through Moorish territory? Can you imagine what that meant in those days, on horseback over appalling roads or none at all? The big question is: what was Eleanor seeking here in Andalucia? What did the Moors have that was so precious to her?'

Jay's mood had changed. The atmosphere in the candlelit room, the silence, the clothes that she and Kreuz were wearing, all seemed to exclude Merlin who belonged to another century. As the evening passed, she realised that Kreuz was talking to her alone.

'North of the Pyrenees, Miss French,' he intoned, 'twelfth century Europe lay in darkness and squalor. There ignorance was called God's holy work and learning was regarded as witchcraft. Yet here in Spain, nourished by the fertile soil of the Moorish kingdoms, flowered all the ancient arts and sciences of Egypt, Greece and Rome.'

Merlin watched the effect Kreuz's words were having on Jay. She followed the monk-like mumbling figure with her eyes and did not look at Merlin even when he nudged her gently under the table.

'What do you think?' Kreuz asked her. 'Did Eleanor come here for lessons in the new sciences of architecture, algebra and astronomy? Or perhaps to have her horoscope cast? We know from her own letters that she consulted astrologers before any important event.'

'What do you think, Doctor?' asked Merlin.

Kreuz turned to the last page of the book in front of him. His index finger traced the very last line. 'When Eleanor died, Miss French, the chroniclers recorded simply: *In hoc anno obiit Alianor.*'

Jay had said little all evening. She translated this line quietly: 'In this year, Eleanor died.'

Kreuz's eyes dwelled on her. 'Not much of an epitaph for the most influential single European of the whole Middle Ages. So what was she doing, those last five years of her life?'

Merlin stood up, irritated by Kreuz's scholarly mannerisms. 'If you can't tell us, who can? I think it's time for bed.'

He put out a hand for Jay. Kreuz moved swiftly and came between them with a slim carved wooden case which he laid on the table in front of Jay.

'A small gift for Miss French,' he said. 'Before you go, please accept this token of my gratitude for the pleasure your presence has given me tonight.'

Jay opened the case. Inside, lying on the green velvet lining, were a set of recorders, exquisitely hand-made in ebony and ivory.

'They're beautiful,' she said, lifting the descant recorder out and fitting the parts together.

'We could...' Kreuz hesitated. With his head on one side and his hands placed together, he looked like an obsequious monk craving a favour from some great lady. 'We could perhaps play a duet together before you retire for the night?'

He picked up another recorder. 'If it would not embarrass you to play with a mere amateur?'

Jay looked at Merlin, hand outstretched to her, waiting. 'I'd like that very much,' she said.

Merlin sank back on to his chair and poured another large glass of wine. The carafe, he saw, was nearly empty.

'Brandenburg Four?' suggested Kreuz. It was a piece of music he had practised for years, against just this moment.

He tuned his instrument to Jay's. He was, she thought, surprisingly good for an amateur. The musician in him, unlike the man, was attentive and responsive: he knew the music well enough to follow where she led.

Merlin up-ended the carafe over his glass. He had drunk too much that night. He felt angry at Jay and would have left, but there was no question of making his own way back to the guest house through the dark and past the Dobermanns.

When the music had ended, Jay's cheeks were flushed and her eyes bright. Kreuz's face too was bathed in pleasure. She put the recorder back into its case. Merlin drained the glass. His anger had faded with the music; he felt very drowsy and wanted to head for bed. He listened to Kreuz speaking to Jay in what sounded to him like Catalan Spanish.

'May we play one more before you leave?' Kreuz asked.

Why not? thought Jay. The recorder he had given her was a joy to play – and Kreuz was an excellent amateur musician.

'There's a song of the Third Crusade which I love,' he suggested. *'Chanterai por mon coratge*. You know it, I expect. It lies very well on two recorders.'

They played the duet and several other pieces of the same period. The room grew steadily darker. By this time Merlin was dozing in his chair at the table. He woke up to find Kreuz gone and Jay standing by Dieter with his lamp, waiting to walk back to the guest house.

Halfway there, the lights came back on. The cold air sobered Merlin fast. After Dieter had bidden them goodnight, Merlin yawned. 'I'm so glad you had a good time.'

Jay slipped the wimple off and shook out her hair. 'It was quite a rare experience, to play with an amateur and be able to make music together. You wouldn't understand.'

'No, I wouldn't. I also don't understand why I fell asleep like that.'

'As Leila would say: *troppo vino!*'

Merlin disagreed peevishly. 'I can hold my liquor. It wasn't that. Unless there was something in the wine…'

Jay laughed.

'There's one thing,' said Merlin. 'I also don't understand how you were suddenly able to completely exclude me from the conversation by talking Spanish with Kreuz. You said you couldn't speak it.'

'That wasn't Spanish.' Jay laughed at him again; she found his sulking amusing. 'We were talking medieval Langue d'Oc.'

'You were what?'

'The language of Eleanor's time.'

'Kreuz can speak that stuff?'

'Fluently,' she said. 'The more I learn of him, the more I realise that Kreuz is a most extraordinary man.'

Chapter 7

'I was right to shoot the pix last night.' Merlin threw the bags into the back of Jay's car angrily. 'And I sure as hell am not hanging around here all day, waiting for Kreuz to return from wherever he pissed off to in that fancy helicopter of his, just after day-break.'

'You were so rude to him last night at dinner, Merlin,' said Jay.

'Dinner?' he snorted at the memory of the meal. 'I'm supposed to say thank you for that crap?'

'Well, I thought Dr Kreuz was a very gracious host. I don't know why you're so hostile to him. This is his home and we're his guests. He doesn't have to be grilled by some aggressive reporter if he doesn't want to be.'

'Whose side are you on?' Merlin asked. 'Kreuz conned us into coming here to see a crappy mirror and a goblet...'

'It was a marriage vase.'

'...which, for all I know, were fakes.'

'What makes you think that?'

Merlin paused; he had no reason for his suspicions, except a gut reaction that told him Kreuz was a fraud of some description – a clever one, but a fraud all the same.

'Hang on,' he said, head cocked and listening. 'D'you hear that chugging noise? That's a diesel generator or I'm Jane Fonda. There was no power cut last night. I think that blackout spiel was just a typically Kreuzian way of not letting us see too much of what he's got stashed away here.'

Merlin slammed the boot lid shut.

'It's beautiful here.' Jay stretched, enjoying the sun on her bare arms. 'And Kreuz said we were welcome to stay on for a couple of days, if we wanted to. What's it matter if the food's a bit peculiar and our host has to go and do some work?'

She moved close to him invitingly. 'You weren't so angry yesterday afternoon. Why don't we just lock the door on the inside and...'

'Get in,' Merlin snapped. 'We're leaving.'

'Where are we going?'

'I'm going to do some checking up on our friendly host.'

'Where?' Jay was puzzled: how could the man who had spent hours making love to her yesterday, be so angry and so unloving today?

Merlin drove the Alpine so savagely over the bumps that she threatened to get out, halfway up the track: 'This is my car, Merlin. If you want to re-grade Dr Kreuz's roadway, go and get yourself a bull-dozer.'

'I'm sorry.' Merlin calmed down slightly and stopped the car. 'This place and guy who owns it are both bugging me pretty bad. Do you want to drive?'

'The way you're acting this morning, we'll be safer. What's got into you?' Jay manoeuvred her legs around the gear stick and moved into the driving seat.

Merlin had just closed the passenger door when one of the dogs was sniffing at the car window. He started with surprise. 'Where in hell did that beast spring from?'

Jay shuddered and let in the clutch. 'You're right, Merl. This place is creepy. Let's go.'

'I apologise.' Merlin placed a hand on her leg. 'That Kreuz just gets up my nose, I don't know why.'

'Well, for my sake, try and unwind,' she pleaded.

In the mirror Jay saw the dog loping along the track after them. With her hand on the horn, she kept going straight at the boom across the track by the gate-house. It swung up just ahead of the car's bumper and they drove past the two blond guards who watched them go with eyes as expressionless as the Dobermanns'.

The engine under the bonnet of the Subaru pick-up would have surprised the manufacturer. Kassim had no trouble keeping Jay's car in sight on the sparsely used local roads. With so few turn-offs, it was not even necessary to keep the target car in view all the time. He had insisted on driving, despite the pain in his injured leg.

They were entering Antequera, the first large town on the road to Granada, when Salem said. 'Look behind, my brother. We are being followed.'

Kassim swore.

'A black BMW, two hundred metres back,' Salem announced. Anyone who had lived through the civil war in Beirut checked the other vehicles on the road automatically.

'I see it.' Kassim looked in the door mirror. He was angry that the pain in his leg had stopped him seeing the other car first.

'Are these some more of your mysterious friends?' Salem asked.

Kassim wrenched the wheel over and bumped onto the forecourt of a service station where they waited in the shade on the far side of a pump island until the BMW had passed. Inside were two of the blond guards from Kreuz's estate.

'They are not following us,' said Kassim. 'They too are following the American.'

'So what do we do?'

Kassim gave his brother a wolfish grin. 'We follow them. They will make our job easier for us.'

After the lunar isolation of the Valle de los Cantos, Granada was back to modern life with a vengeance: traffic jams, pollution, noise and hustle.

To avoid the jams, Merlin map-read Jay through the narrow one-way streets of the old town. It was quicker than using the wider main thoroughfares of the city centre which were congested with traffic. They pulled up outside a *parador*, one of the government-owned luxury hotels dotted thinly over the map of Spain like a minor rash.

This one was a converted monastery, built around a Moorish courtyard garden where fountains played and two peacocks strutted along the gravel paths. Apart from electric light, there seemed to be no modern intrusions. A porter walked ahead of Jay and Merlin, wheeling their bags on a squeaking trolley. He bumped up the stairs to the gallery that ran round the courtyard and led them off it and down long, wide, empty corridors until he stopped and opened the door of a bedroom.

It was vast by modern hotel standards, with a polished terracotta-tiled floor and white walls against which the sombre black traditional furniture stood out like props on a stage set. The adjoining bathroom, with its enormous deep bath and Victorian plumbing, was almost as big.

The porter threw open a window and heaved at the heavy shutters. As they creaked open, Jay saw the Alhambra sitting on its hill above the town. In the hard sunlight the crenellated outline of the building was like a cardboard cut-out against the pure blue sky. On this side of the *parador*, the noise of the city's traffic was muted. The quiet timelessness of the scene made her wonder which was real: the modern hustle through which she had been driving or the fairy-tale landscape in front of her.

Merlin tipped the porter who closed the door and left them alone.

'Come and see this,' called Jay at the window.

'Later,' said Merlin. 'I've got some calls to make.'

He had been preoccupied on the journey.

'Please,' Jay insisted. 'This is beautiful, Merlin. Your phone calls can wait.'

He grunted something indistinct with his back to her and the view. Jay listened to him asking for old buddies whose numbers he carried every-where in his address book. Everyone he called seemed to be out of town.

At last Merlin slammed down the telephone in frustration. 'Well, that's just about the last guy in the world I'd ask for a favour.'

'Who is?'

'Bill Guzman.'

'American?'

'Mexican expat. He used to be a good newsman.'

'He's a reporter?'

'A stringer. A local guy who covers small stories or midwifes the big ones until the heavy brigade hits town.'

'And what's wrong with him?'

'He's a lush.'

'Where are you going, Merlin?'

'I'm meeting him in a bar.'

'And I'm not invited?'

Merlin shook his head. 'Wouldn't be a good idea. Bill's easily dis-tracted. If there's a bit of skirt around, he doesn't concentrate.'

'Hold on,' said Jay. She had put up with Merlin's moody silences on the journey, but this was too much. 'Is that all I am now, a bit of skirt?'

'That's not what I meant, honey.'

'I think it's exactly what you meant, Merlin.'

'Now look...'

'No, you look!' Jay placed herself between him and the door so that he could not avoid her eyes. 'I've stopped making excuses for you, Merlin. Last night, you did your best to ruin the conversation with Dr Kreuz, but I let it go. Now you're treating me like some tart you picked up in a bar. You go off to spend a boozy evening with some old pal and I'm supposed to wait patiently here until you return.'

'Have a look round the shops, or something,' Merlin suggested. 'I won't be more than an hour or two and then we'll go out and find some nice restaurant for dinner.'

Jay let her exasperation show. 'You are getting worse with every sen-tence. Who do you think you're talking to?'

Merlin caught in mid-air his jacket which Jay threw at him, then bent to pick up his contact book which had fallen onto the floor.

'Get out!' she shouted. 'I've had enough of you treating me like this.'

'I didn't mean to upset you,' he protested.

'You bring me to this beautiful city without a word of explanation what you're up to. You expect me to make love when you're in the mood and then just switch off and shut up when you want to play reporters. Well, I'm not that sort of girl, Merlin. I happen to have an identity of my own, d'you hear?'

Hands raised in surrender, he tried to placate her. 'Now look. I know I haven't explained anything.'

'No, you haven't.'

'Because I'm on to something, but I don't know what it is.'

Baffled, she made a peace offer: 'Then let's work on it together.'

He shook his head, wishing she could understand. 'I always work alone. That's the way it is, so you'll have to get used to it.'

'I don't have to get used to anything!' she snapped. 'Get that into your head, Merlin Freeman.'

He pulled a grimace and left the room without another word. Jay took off both her shoes and hurled them at the door after him. 'Well, fuck you!' she screamed.

When she was certain Merlin was not coming back, she threw herself on the enormous four-poster bed. What's wrong with him? she asked herself. Our last day in St Denis and the journey through Spain were an idyll of happiness in which we shared each second. I told him all my thoughts and plans and hopes. It felt as though we should never have a secret from one another...

She recalled lying on the air-bed with him twenty-four hours before, wrapped in tenderness and intimacy. She sat up on the bed and tried to work out exactly when Merlin had changed. The problem was that the whole of the previous evening which they had spent with Kreuz was a blur in her memory – a blur dominated by the hooded figure with his pale blue eyes fixed on hers. Somehow during those hours a psychic wedge had been driven between her and Merlin.

She thought of picking up her bags which were not yet unpacked and just walking out of the hotel. But that would be like a defeat. First, Merlin owed her an apology for his behaviour. Jay curled up and lay on top of the bed, staring out of the window at the Moorish fantasy on the hill above, turned blood-red by the setting sun. Somewhere nearby, a church bell started to chime the hour.

* * *

'Close the window,' commanded Eleanor. 'Since Richard's death, I've come to hate the sound of praying. Be it by monks or Moslems, the prating sound they make grates in my ears.'

'I'm no lady in waiting,' growled William the Marshal, getting up from his meal and closing the window. The voice of the *muezzin* calling the faithful to prayer from the minaret of Granada's mosque, was cut off in mid-wail.

They were staying in the house of a Jewish merchant who let rooms to Christians and pagans – non-Moslems who were in Granada on business or for pilgrimage and whom no devout believer wished to have under his

208

roof. Eleanor's room was large but sparsely furnished: a bed covered in furs, a trestle table and two chairs of wood and leather. Light came from candles on the table and a flaming torch in a wall-bracket. For sanitation, there was a crude earthenware chamber pot in one corner.

The only access was through another room where six other men from Eleanor's small retinue were lodged. Another two retainers slept with the horses in the stable beneath, their mounts saddled, ready to leave in a hurry.

'Here, Madam, you're supposed to be a knight.' William reminded the queen good-naturedly that she was wearing male clothing. 'When travelling without servants, men close the window for themselves.'

'I'm not supposed to be anything,' she corrected him. 'Clothes don't alter the fact that I'm still your queen and you are mine to command, Marshal. It just happens that I discovered in my youth the safest way for a woman of rank to travel is dressed as a knight, riding astride and with a small well-mounted escort. The risks are less than waiting for times of truce or begging letters of safe conduct, for truces can end swiftly and letters be revoked the day after they are granted.'

'Don't put too much faith in disguise,' William advised her. 'Remember the last time you were caught when thus attired.'

It was a reference to the fatal day when Henry's men had caught Eleanor fleeing across the scorched and wasted landscape north of Poitiers from the wreckage of her rebellion against him. She had been only a few hours' ride from the safety of the French court at Paris when trapped by the stroke of misfortune that had cost her fifteen years' imprisonment.

'I wasn't caught,' snapped Eleanor. 'I was betrayed to Henry by one of my own vassals.'

'The result was the same.'

'No,' she disagreed. 'The bitterness was twice as hard to bear.'

William listened to the ribaldry in the next room. 'I'll tell the Jew's steward to give the men no more wine. We'll need to be in the saddle tomorrow as soon as the Moors open the city gates at dawn – and we shall have to ride fast all day if we are to spirit away this witch the heathen devils value so highly.'

'The man's no witch, good William,' laughed Eleanor. 'He's a scholar, learned in strange matters – no more a witch than I.'

William moved to the window at the sound of the street gate being opened. He peered down into the courtyard and announced, 'It's the Jew returned with that rogue Mercadier.'

He made no secret of his dislike for Richard's old mercenary captain whom Eleanor had insisted on bringing to Granada. Half the men-at-arms carousing in the next room were Mercadier's men who owed no allegiance to the queen if Mercadier should change sides.

The marshal had begged Eleanor to bring anyone rather than Mercadier on this trip but she, reared in the quasi-Byzantine intrigues of the court of Aquitaine, preferred always to set one servant off against another. So Mercadier had been chosen expressly because of the hatred between him and William: Eleanor knew that, if it became necessary to fight their way back to the nearest Christian territory, each of these two redoubtable warriors would strive to excel the other in deeds of valour.

'I wish that I might escort you tonight,' said William. 'I mistrust the thought of you alone among these heathen with only that brute to guard you.'

The queen laughed at his concern. 'If I left Mercadier to guard my treasure chest, ere we returned it would be empty and he'd be far away.'

In Christian countries and on the recognised pilgrimage routes to and from the Holy Land, the Templars acted as bankers, honouring letters of credit. Because there was no Templar commandery in Granada the queen carried gold and jewels enough to pay for her needs, all locked securely in an iron-bound chest. Opening it now, she counted coins from a dozen countries into a small leather bag and pulled the draw-string tight. 'Give this to the Jew as we leave tomorrow morning, but not a moment before.'

'That means I'm last to go.'

'That's right,' Eleanor confirmed. 'But if I entrusted this small task to Mercadier, he'd stab the Jew and keep the gold – and we'd have half the emir's guard on our heels before we'd left the city gates.'

*   *   *

A second had passed, no more than the lapse between two chimes. Jay shook her head. Mingled with the last chimes of the church clock was the tinkle of coins in a leather bag. She wished that Merlin had not gone and left her alone.

Remembering that he had said he was going to see a man called Guzman, she reached for the telephone directory beside the bed but lacked the energy to open it. Then the telephone rang beside the bed. She picked it up and listened, half-asleep, to a voice she had not expected to hear again.

Chapter 8

Flabby, with the cough of a heavy smoker and the bloodshot eyes and blotchy face of a hard drinker, Bill Guzman balanced on the high bar stool like an overweight stork, one leg on the ground and the other wrapped around the leg of the stool to anchor him in position.

'I heard you are in town, Freeman,' he grinned. The Mexican accent and syntax were pure Hollywood, as was the Zapata moustache.

Merlin lifted his glass and swallowed. 'What is this fire-water you drink, Bill?'

'Spanish brandy. Is not-a cognac but is-a cheap.' The stringer lit another cigarette from the unfinished stub.

Merlin was angry with himself. I must be crazy, he thought, walking out on Jay to spend the evening with a slob like this. I could at least have explained to her that there's a loose end which has been nagging at me ever since I talked with Baron Kempfer...

He thought of picking up the phone behind the bar and calling Jay's room at the *parador* to apologise for shouting at her, but that wasn't his style. He preferred to sort things out face to face when he got back.

'You know anything about a Dr Kreuz, first name Hermann?' he asked.

A vague gesture of Guzman's hand was interpreted by the barman as a command for another generous measure of Centenario brandy splashed into the stringer's glass. 'Maybe,' he admitted. 'Whassa story?'

'Anything that would connect him with Oradour, June 1944?'

The stringer swallowed and pushed the glass forward with a nod to the barman. 'Sounds to me like Freeman is still a-writing that book of his.'

'Affirmative.'

Guzman laughed and ended up coughing. 'I tell ya, ya gotta be real smart to tie Kreuz in with that massacre. Sure, he is ex-SS and ex-Das Reich, but he don't a-talk to no journalist.'

'I had dinner last night at his ranch.'

211

Guzman's laugh ended in a coughing fit. 'How wassa steak?'

'It grew on a tree.'

Behind the boozy eyes, the stringer's brain was at work. 'What was in it for him, I wonder?'

'I don't know yet.' And that's the truth, thought Merlin.

'Well, don't push your luck,' was the advice. *'Der ehemalige Sturmbannfuhrer hat noch gute Kamaraden. Capito?'*

'You mean those blond bodyguards of his?'

An incredulous laugh. 'So you really have been out there, to that crazy hide-out in the Valley of Songs?'

'Are they what you meant by his friends?'

'No.' More brandy disappeared down Guzman's throat. 'Few months back, this-a poacher got beat up on Kreuz's spread. The guy is hurt bad, okay? So the police, they arrest two of those guards. Now what happen?'

'You tell me, Bill.'

'Do these guys spend a coupla months inside waiting for trial? No, sir! Kreuz, he make a coupla phone calls. Those two guys are on the afternoon flight back to der Vaterland. Nothing, *pero nada*, in the papers here. Me, I am writing a piece for the *Frankfurter Allgemeine*. They spike it. Kreuz, he has friends everywhere.'

'Where do all the blond clones come from?'

'The guards? Forget 'em, Freeman. They just come here for a one-year contract. They hand-picked by some old buddy of Kreuz – a guy who runs a security and courier service in Vienna.'

'Maybe I could find where they hang out off-duty and buy them a few drinks…'

'You wasting your time. They don't a-drink, those boys. They well-paid and well-trained. They don't a-talk – not to you, not to anyone.'

It was the knowing leer in Guzman's eye that prompted Merlin's next question: 'If they're here for a year, what do they do for women?'

Guzman laughed and choked on a mixture of brandy and cigarette smoke. 'Well, they sure don't get so much as a sniff of the pussy that Kreuz uses.'

Merlin recalled the blonde masseuse who had accompanied Kreuz to St Denis. 'What's the story there?' he asked.

'Those girls – they are supplied by the same outfit in Vienna. They come two at a time. I don't know whether Señor Kreuz gets fed up with them or they can't stand being locked up down in that valley, but they stay only six months. Then they go home.'

'Locked up, you said? They don't leave the place?'

'Nevair. Kreuz meet them at the airport when they arrive. He take them back there at the end of their stint. And Freeman…'

Guzman leaned perilously sideways to talk into Merlin's ear in a lowered voice. 'Once I hear this rumour – that several of these-a girls, they been pregnant when they get back to Austria.'

'That never made any scandal?' Merlin wondered aloud. 'The guy's over seventy by my reckoning.'

Guzman rocked the stool back on to an even keel. 'Seems like Kreuz adopt the kids and pays the mothers *mucho dinero*.'

'The randy old goat!' Merlin was remembering the way Kreuz had stared at Jay all evening. 'And what does our Señor Kreuz use for money?'

Another nod to the barman brought Guzman another drink. 'On his *carta de residencia* it say Kreuz, he is president of Santa Maria Hotels, SA.'

'And what's that?'

'Issa property company that own some hotels on the Costa del Sol. They got shares in marinas, that sort of thing. If you wanna know whose money, I save you research, Freeman. Santa Maria is wholly-owned subsidiary of Valhalla Investments in Zurich.'

At last something added up. Merlin remembered the name. 'So the Das Reich gold is now financing package holidays on the Costa del Sol?'

'My lips are seal.' Guzman made what he thought was a knowing gesture, tapping his nose. He missed and poked a finger into one eye, making it water.

Merlin tried another tack. 'Kreuz puts out that he's a scholar and an art historian. What's that all about?'

Guzman's hand was now clamped around the bottle. He was serving himself liberally. 'You try every angle, Freeman, I give you that. But you won't get nowhere with that story.'

'With what story, Bill?'

'The fake antique business.'

Merlin smiled. The fresco, the chalice, the mirror were probably all fakes, he thought. 'He sells them?'

'Nah. Kreuz too clever for that.'

'Then what?'

'For the right price, Dr Kreuz sell attributions, Freeman. Clever, huh? He cost a lot but some of these things go for millions in the saleroom – and I ain't talking pesetas.'

Merlin played with his empty glass and waved away the bottle when Guzman took it as a hint.

'Why, Bill?' he asked. 'If Kreuz has all the Das Reich money to play with from the Valhalla set-up in Zurich, why fart around with fake antiques?'

'Boredom.'

'What's that mean?'

'Kreuz, he is a very clever man,' said Guzman. 'The SS had some of the best brains in Europe, and don't you forget it.'

'So?'

'You wanna know what I think?'

'Tell me.'

'I think it amuse Kreuz to – what you say? – pit his wit against respected experts and prove them wrong when he knows all the time they are right.'

Merlin peeled two thousand-peseta notes from a roll and stood up to go.

The stringer picked the notes off the counter. 'Is this the going rate for all my help?'

'It's for the drinks,' said Merlin, 'but you can keep the change. I'll share the by-line with you, if you're a good boy.'

Bill Guzman lurched to his feet angrily. 'You a cheap bastard, Freeman, you know that?'

Merlin had not stopped to listen. He was in the street, hailing a taxi, with an uneasy premonition that he should not have left Jay alone so long. It would serve me right, he rationalised, if I got back to the hotel and found she'd walked out on me.

There were two dark-haired men signing the register as Merlin hurried up to the reception desk of the *parador*. Without paying them any special attention, he grabbed his key and hurried upstairs, two at a time, then ran along the corridor. The door was locked. He undid it and found the bedroom empty and Jay's bags gone.

Merlin leaned against the door jamb, cursing himself for being so stupid as to pick a fight with her. He ran back along the corridor towards the stairs, to see whether her car was still in the parking lot. Halfway to the stairs, he bumped into Jay coming out of another bedroom. She had changed into a dress he had not seen before.

'Where have you been?' he gasped, out of breath.

'None of your business,' she said curtly.

Merlin fell into step alongside her, eager to explain. 'I thought you'd checked out of the hotel.'

'I've moved to a room of my own.'

All he wanted was to smooth things over. 'Okay, whatever you like. But listen, Jay. About Kreuz. I've found out…'

'Leila was right.' Jay stopped. 'She said you journalists never give up. Haven't you understood yet, Merlin, I don't care what you've found out? I don't care where you go, who you talk to, what you do. You get right on with your life and I'll get on with mine.'

He spun round and stood in front of her. 'I don't believe this is happening!'

214

'If you'll get out of my way…'

'I'll do what?'

'You're blocking my way and holding my arm. Please let go.'

Merlin took a pace backwards. 'Jay, please! At least let me buy you dinner, to say I'm sorry.'

'The invitation is too late,' she said. 'I'm having dinner with someone else.'

'You don't know anyone else in Granada!'

'As it happens, I do. Now get out of my way!'

Merlin stood aside and watched her go. She swept past a cluster of people outside a bedroom near the stairs where the porter was opening the door for Salem and Kassim Chakrouty, the two men who had been checking in when Merlin was collecting his key.

Kassim did not expect the American to recognise him; he knew Merlin had never seen the face of any of his captors. All the same, he kept his back turned and pushed Salem ahead of him into the room. Once inside, he let his brother tip the porter and sat down at the dressing table, took out a sheet of headed notepaper and wrote on it Leila's address which Merlin had used for himself and Jay in the hotel register.

As the porter departed, Kassim was mentally thanking the French for making their addresses so simple to memorise: just a person's name, a village and a five-digit postcode.

Chapter 9

Jay was aware that the restaurant was full, but the other patrons were an out-of-focus blur behind the pale blue eyes fixed on hers. Kreuz rambled from one subject to another, mixing politics with history, genetic theories with musicology, religion with economics. The hard-to-follow monologue in his monotonous voice was like the hypnotherapy sessions Jay had had with her father.

She wondered at the start of the meal whether her host was trying to mesmerise her. Two hours later she could not remember anything about the meal: neither what she had eaten nor what Kreuz had been talking about. It was as though he had been talking at her but to another person. Her legs felt woolly as though she had taken alcohol, although in fact she had drunk only water at the meal. She found it difficult to unravel why she had agreed to go along with Kreuz's proposal – or even to be certain what it was that she had agreed to.

She walked with him out of the restaurant and back across the street to the *parador*. The fountains in the courtyard had been turned off and the peacocks were asleep in one corner like huge ungainly hens. There was some classical music being played as background music which Jay identified as Vivaldi's Winter from The Four Seasons.

Kreuz said goodnight at the bottom of the stairs that led to the bedrooms. When Jay turned at the top, he was still there, the pale blue eyes fixed on her. He bowed without speaking.

Her bedroom was stuffy. Jay threw the window open and gazed at the Alhambra, flood-lit on its hill. Below, in the shadows of an alleyway behind the hotel a veiled woman hurried out of sight round a corner, followed by the taller figure of a man.

*　*　*

The journey through the streets of the sleeping city led to a small gate in a blank wall, which opened at Mercadier's first knock. Inside the courtyard stood three huge black slaves clad in velvets and silk. Mutes, they communicated by a series of grunts. One of them closed and bolted the gate before showing Eleanor up a flight of stone steps leading to the first floor while the other two remained below on guard.

At the top of the steps, Mercadier went to open the door but was stopped by a thick and sinewy forearm. The mute signed for Eleanor to go in alone. He slipped the latch. Through the crack she saw only darkness.

'Where I go, he goes,' said the queen.

Her meaning was clear. The slave grunted several times, went inside and left them waiting. When he reappeared and motioned them both to go in, Eleanor and Mercadier heard the door close behind them. There was a loud *pop!* and a blinding burst of light which came from a pile of whitish powder atop a metal tripod, hissing and crackling as it burnt with a strong sulphurous smell, spitting sparks in all directions.

The intense light revealed a host of glass retorts, pottery bowls and metal devices covering several tables. Hanging from the ceiling were several alligators and a dried ostrich carcase. A cage held a pair of large rats, one green and one red. In another cage, a score of rainbow-hued mice scrambled over each other frenetically. In a third sat several huge green toads, their chests ballooning with each inhalation. A stuffed elephant's head watched them from the far wall. Beneath it, two lions stood on guard either side of the small figure in Arab robes that was chanting what sounded like a prayer in some strange tongue. The light fizzled and spat burning particles, casting a harsh white light that changed colour each time Yussef El-Kebir's hands passed above it.

'Sorcery!' hissed Mercadier.

'Be quiet,' ordered the queen. 'This is but trickery designed to impress the ignorant. The light is to blind us. Do not look at it!'

She ordered Mercadier to remain by the door and walked towards the crackling powder and the turbaned wizard beyond. He threw up a hand and called urgently in Latin. 'Stay, oh queen! Do not cross the mark or my magic is undone.'

There was a line chalked on the stone floor right in front of Eleanor. It was one side of a pentagram within which he stood, the powder hissed and coloured fluids coursed from one retort through tubes into the next. Eleanor stopped short – not because she was afraid of witchcraft but because one of the lions had just blinked and turned its head towards her.

She coughed as the sulphur fumes caught her throat. 'What magic?' she asked.

The light sputtered and went out. The shutter of a horn lantern was opened, lighting the wizard's face, thin and bearded with eyes that glittered as he reached with a pair of tongs into a small furnace. He took

217

something out of it and dropped it into a pot of water where it sizzled briefly. He removed the object from the water and placed it on a cushion, holding it in front of him as he approached Eleanor and bowed low.

'My gift,' he said, offering her a large ingot of gold.

Eleanor weighed it in her hand. 'All the pure gold in Granada belongs to the emir. That is the law here.'

'I can do with that what I will,' said the wizard, his glittering eyes fixed on here. 'Did you not see? I made it myself.'

Eleanor was amused by the little drama. 'You did this to impress me?' she asked.

Yussef el-Kebir's eyes flicked from her to Mercadier who was keeping well back in the shadows. 'I did it so you should know who I am, o Queen. In all the emirate of Granada there is only one man who makes gold for the emir!'

While most of the inhabitants of the walled city of Granada slept, Eleanor and Yussef el-Kebir talked through the night. They used Latin, their only common language, of which Mercadier had but little understanding.

It was a bizarre scene in the alchemist's den. The lions had been led away by two hunch-backed dwarfs; one of the giant slaves now crouched in a corner, his eyes never leaving Mercadier. Beneath the hanging crocodiles, surrounded by all the impedimenta of the alchemist's art, a scholar in silken turban and robes sat on a rich carpet, face to face with a woman dressed as a Christian knight.

Yussef el-Kebir began by treating Eleanor with condescending politeness: a queen she might be, but a queen was still a woman and therefore every man's inferior according to the law he served. Then, as Eleanor's extraordinary intellect and wide knowledge forced him to converse with her as with a man, came the delightful realisation that this woman who did not veil her face before him or flinch in argument was that rarity: another mind on the same plane as his own, a person whose sex and station in life were irrelevant.

The conversation was a fencing match between two scholars, embracing after the manner of the time when disciplines were yet undemarcated history and theology, politics and poetry, medicine and philosophy. Some time long after midnight, Eleanor abandoned the cut and thrust of disinterested and scholarly debate, to lead the conversation onto the subject of alchemy.

'Al-khimia,' she said. 'To us it's another science you Moslems have and which we lack, but the word is Greek – from khemeia meaning transmutation.

'A Greek name,' he agreed, 'for an Egyptian science.'

218

They thrust and parried, he citing Zosimus of Alexandria while she responded with relevant Socratic theory, he telling of his own long studies at the temple of Ptah in Memphis while she offered morsels of the teaching of Diodorus Siculus.

'You seem to know as much as I,' Yussef admitted at last. 'The truth is that we can make a small quantity of pure gold into more gold of a lesser quality. More than that no man has yet achieved.'

'...which is a truth revealed to anyone who brings a touch-stone to your den.'

Yussef toyed with the ingot she had handed back to him. He was puzzled. 'If you know so much, o queen from the north, then you could make gold yourself – or seem to do so as well as I or any other alchemist. You don't need me, so why do you come here at such risk to yourself?'

'Because,' said Eleanor, 'there are two strands of alchemy. The one concerns itself with the transmutation of metals, while the other, of which I know little...'

He interrupted her quickly: '...is a blasphemy in which no true believer could involve himself.'

Eleanor's green eyes challenged him. 'The other matter of alchemy concerns itself with the elixir of life and with reincarnation. Of this I know little and you know much.'

Yussef shifted uneasily; the slave was a mute whose tongue had been removed in infancy and Mercadier had given no sign of being able to follow the learned discourse in Latin, but even so. 'To admit such a thing would be to forfeit my life on the rack, my tongue and eyes torn out with red-hot pincers – as well you know.'

Eleanor was growing impatient. The dawn was not far off. As she led Yussef to an understanding of the reason for her visit to Granada, he sat still, fascinated.

'Now,' he breathed, 'I see why a Christian queen should take the risk of entering a Moslem citadel in disguise. If apprehended, the least you risk here is imprisonment and ransom.'

'At my age,' countered Eleanor, 'risking the remaining years of my life is a small price to pay for the pleasure of discourse with the greatest scholar of our age.'

'Flattery,' Yussef stroked his beard, 'is the braying of asses, as I think you know.'

'Tell me, Moor,' she said curtly, 'are you the man who can do this thing for me, or not?'

'It is impossible,' he said seriously. 'No man can raise the dead, Madam. And if I could, I'd not raise Melek Ric for you. Should I bring back your son, the monster who slaughtered thousands of Moslem

219

hostages? No, if you want to raise the dead, go to the priests of your own prophet. They say he worked such miracles in Galilee.'

'I was told,' tried Eleanor, 'that you have sought and acquired all the forbidden knowledge of Egypt.'

'I have learned much of the ancient wisdom. More than any man now alive, I'll grant you that.'

Eleanor tried to penetrate the Moor's integrity and find a chink where some vice showed through. 'If you will undertake this task for me, I'll reward you with gold and jewels - not false gold and valueless baubles, but the very treasure that caused Richard's death at Châlus. I hid it safe to bring him back. It is all yours, if you will do but this one thing.'

'You come too late,' he said.

'How so, too late?'

Yussef rose and stretched. Now he understood what had driven Eleanor to cross hundreds of miles of enemy territory to reach him. It was the strongest emotion known in Nature, the unreasoning love of a mother for her child.

'Do you think' he asked, 'that it's an easy thing, to prepare a soul to come back to this earth? Do you think I need but to mix a magic potion and wave my arms, muttering some incantation in a long-dead tongue? No, Madam. The science of the Egyptians demanded that the candidate for reincarnation spend the last years of his life preparing the inner self. It was a discipline that few accomplished in several thousand years. I doubt that Melek Ric would have been able to begin the course, let alone finish it.'

Eleanor was silent. The Moor had just dashed her last hopes. The pain of Richard's death still throbbed within her breast, but her mind was clear. 'Would I?' she asked sharply. 'Would I be able to prepare myself to live again?'

Yussef studied her a moment. Then he laughed, 'Of all the men and women I have met, I think perhaps you might, o Queen. But would you want to live again?'

'Wouldn't you?'

The Moor shook his head. 'I have sons. They and their sons and their sons' sons are my immortality. Why should I seek to live again? That sort of arrogance fits a Christian perhaps, not a Moslem. Your priests talk of everlasting life, I'm told.'

'They talk of sexless, disembodied angels singing praises till the Last Trumpet sounds,' Eleanor said scornfully. 'If that's what my first husband Louis Capet is doing right now, it's also how he spent his wedding night, as I recall. What a waste of my body! That is most certainly not what I want. This flesh which has served me well is dying and I don't want to be extinguished as a column of tallow is snuffed out at daybreak.

I want to walk the earth again, Moor. Can you magic that for me? Or is it just a dream?'

Yussef glanced at Mercadier. He moved closer to Eleanor on the carpet and lowered his voice. 'My researches in many lands have revealed that what you seek has been achieved – not often, but in exceptional cases.'

'And can be again?'

He stroked his long white beard. 'To make the journey from one body to another with the spirit intact takes not just preparation. It takes enormous strength of will, not to weaken on the way. The distance to be travelled and the time involved are vast, even though the Egyptians proved with their mathematics that time slows down in limbo so that what may be a century on earth passes as an hour or two in the realms of death. Whether they be right or wrong, I cannot say.'

'You talk of will? I have it.'

'Many have started but failed before their destination,' he cautioned her. 'They end like travellers who have strayed in the desert, driven mad by thirst and the sun. Neither dead nor alive, they find their way occasionally from limbo back to the scenes of their earthly life, there to trouble the living as ghosts, mere shades of their former selves.'

She cut him short; the first tinge of pink was in the eastern sky. 'How can such misadventure be avoided?'

Yussef stroked his beard. 'As on any uncharted journey, the prudent traveller hires a guide.'

'And where do I find such a guide, Moor?'

'The best – of that there is no doubt – were the priests of Egypt. They were the cartographers of this uncertain territory. None have excelled them since.'

'But you have studied their esoteric science...'

'...as few before me, and few after, I dare say.'

'And will you be my guide?'

'The journey which you contemplate is fraught with danger,' he warned. 'The will alone is not enough. And even when the weary traveller sets foot once more on earth, there remains the danger of madness. So many returned souls entered their second flesh to find themselves regarded as lunatics, gibbering tales of nonsense built around a grain of truth. "I was Caesar or Alexander or Socrates", they babble, and end confined in chains, insane.'

'Why so?'

'Perhaps from simple loneliness – the unutterable loneliness of being alive and friendless outside one's time. We Arabs have a curse. To an enemy we say: "May you outlive your friends!"'

'We Christians say the same.' Eleanor was one step ahead. 'But as to that, what do you think a queen is, if not alone? She has no friends. As soon as a princess can talk, she learns that her parents will one day sell her for an advantage or in endeavour to keep the realm intact, as was my lot. From womb to tomb, she is surrounded by servants who deceive, courtiers who lie and friends who betray her.'

She laughed, 'At fifteen when my father Duke William died and I became Duchess of Aquitaine, my tender young flesh was not mine to enjoy. It was the property of the duchy, to be used for the good of the duchy. And do you think I had friends at Louis' court when I was Queen of France? Not one! I was surrounded by spies and tricksters. Those whom I thought otherwise, turned out to be the most dangerous. And when in despair I took lovers openly, it was to outrage Louis' monkish morals and taunt him with his impotence, not because I felt for the men I bedded what lovers normally feel. So don't warn me about loneliness.'

'Yet Henry Plantagenet you loved?' Yussef whispered slyly.

He had caught her off her guard, this Moor who knew so much. Eleanor's face softened. 'Ah, yes. With Henry, for a while, I loved. We loved each other, Moor, with a passion and a violence that will echo down the centuries. For love of Henry, I threw away a throne. And Henry would have done no less for me. He would have thrown away the world for me. He would! He would!'

Her raised voice roused Mercadier who yawned, stretched and went to the window to check whether the sun was yet above the horizon.

Eleanor closed her eyes, the better to see Henry's bluff Plantagenet face as it had been when he first came, aged eighteen but already a belted knight, to Louis' mournful court. In memory she heard the sound of that voice which, rising from the courtyard as he dismounted, had been enough to make her moist with longing and sick with desire for a man, for the first time in her life. But Henry had also stolen fifteen years of her life, and now she had a chance to live those years again.

'I want to walk this earth once more,' she whispered. 'I want to thrill to a lover's caress, to hear poetry, to make music, to weep for happiness and grief. I want to feel!'

The Moor looked at Eleanor's wrinkled face, which she was trying to hide with her hands.

'There,' he cautioned her, 'lies the greatest obstacle. In the secret Books of the Dead at the temple of Ptah, so often I read the record of failure. After spending their entire lives awaiting the rebirth of a pharaoh or general or high priest, the temple servants could only watch helpless as the returned soul died a second time in torment.'

'Why?'

'From their descriptions, meticulous and detailed, it seems to be impossible for any mind, however great, to stay sane inside another body, whose intimate sensations every minute and second of the day are torture to the soul which does not belong there.'

Eleanor smiled. 'If that's God's last ambush, I know a detour.'

222

The Moor listened to her plan with growing admiration. The longer he talked with her, the more Eleanor's intelligence fascinated him.

Mercadier spoke from the window. On Eleanor's instructions he used English, a tongue which no one in Granada understood. 'It'll soon be dawn, my queen. Here they open the city gates at cock-crow. We must be gone within the hour.'

'Will you come with me, Moor?' asked Eleanor. 'Will you do this thing for me?'

Yussef raised a hand and indicated the sleeping town outside the window. 'Here I am rich and respected. Learned men from Syria and Greece and Egypt brave the danger of the long sea voyage to travel here and talk with me. The emir consults me daily and gives praise to Allah for sending him such a vizier as myself. I have but to ask for a thing and my ruler sends men running to satisfy my whim – be it ice from the mountains to cool my drink in summer or a manuscript from Alexandria or far Cathay to quench my thirst for knowledge.

'He has given me slaves and servants and a house where my library is replete with all the knowledge of past ages. I am known from Marrakesh to the Ganges as Yussef el-Kebir, Joseph the Great. Yet if I come with you, o Queen, I shall be at best a servant and at worst a mere prisoner in your power.'

'You are a prisoner here,' retorted Eleanor. 'The emir does not allow you to leave the city gates, for fear his enemies should snatch you away to make gold for them.'

'A prisoner with honour,' the Moor agreed.

'I offer you more than honour, Yussef,' she urged. 'I offer you the freedom to join me in the greatest adventure the human mind can encompass. And if wealth matters to you, the treasure of Châlus is yours for helping me on my way.'

'So you say.'

'You have my word on it!'

'Should I trust the word of a Christian and a woman at that?'

'I'll swear it on the Cross!'

Yussef snorted his derision. 'Melek Ric wore the Cross on both his chest and his back when he murdered the innocents at Acre.'

'Perhaps I misjudged you, Moor,' said Eleanor. 'Perhaps you're not the man to do what I ask. Perhaps indeed it can't be done by any mortal man.'

Yussef shook his head. 'You appeal to my vanity. In truth, fame means little to me now. You offer me gold and jewels; I need them not. Yet my cupidity for knowledge grows greater as my years advance. I'll come with you to your kingdom in the north. Together we shall find out there whether a spirit as strong as yours may survive the torment of limbo and return to walk this earth in a second flesh.'

223

Chapter 10

Merlin had not smoked for years. He lay on the bed, halfway through a packet of Spanish cigarettes and a bottle of cheap Spanish brandy.

The sight of Jay in the restaurant opposite the *parador* had triggered in him the most violent rage he had known for years. She had been sitting sideways to the window, gazing intently at Kreuz and obviously hanging on to every word he said. He had wanted to hurl the door open, grab Kreuz by the neck and strangle him. The urge had been so strong that Merlin had found himself standing outside in the street, literally quivering with anger and smashing his fist into the wall beneath a street-lamp again and again until the pain brought back his self-control.

The moment of pure blood-lust raked up from his memory banks all the incidents in his life that he most hated, when from some layer deep within his subconscious arose a spectre of violence that clouded all normal judgement and feeling, leaving him – only the Vikings had a word for it – berserk.

In the memory buried deepest of all – at My Lai, mowing down the screaming, weeping, pleading villagers crouched over their children in a hopeless attempt to block the bullets with their own bodies – everything had happened in a haze of dope and grief for buddies blown away or maimed for life by the same villagers. The whole mindless four-hour tragedy had been like a diabolical Sunday school outing when a group of over-stretched kids went on the rampage. There had been no hatred for their individual victims like the boiling fury that had made him want to kill Kreuz with his bare hands.

Now the fury had simmered down, Merlin rationalised his mood as partly anger at himself for spoiling the very special relationship with Jay in the same way that he had spoiled all the other relationships of his life – even to the point of using the same script. Each time, there had been a plane to catch or a rendezvous to keep in some sordid bar when he should have been taking the time to be what Matty Perelmann called a *mensch* – a human being instead of a news-gathering machine.

In the smoke-filled bedroom, Merlin's mind's eye kept flitting from Oradour to Châlus to Dürnstein to the Valle de los Cantos. And wherever his private video show took him, Kreuz's pale blue eyes were watching.

Another brandy was poured, another cigarette lit.

Kreuz and Kempfer, all the Ks... Mentally Merlin projected remembered faces and places on to the tobacco haze that wreathed above him. There was a connection somewhere, he was sure. And it wasn't just a couple of old comrades keeping in touch on the subject of medieval poetry, either.

Jealousy projected on to the smoke-screen the image of Jay talking to Kreuz in the restaurant. She had been leaning forward eagerly to hear what he was saying. What was Kreuz's fascination for her? Did he have some sexual power over women? Merlin wondered. Or was there some weird connection between him and Jay?

What else would explain why she had been so – enchanted, was the word – by Kreuz the previous evening at the Valle de los Cantos? Perhaps Jay had some kind of hang-up about older men – the result of being so close to her father during adolescence?

Images of her tormented Merlin: Jay on the air-bed in the swimming pool, Jay radiant in the breakfast room at Chartres, Jay sitting naked in bed at St Denis, playing the recorder for him.

That was it. He stubbed out the cigarette in the full ash-tray.

The song...

Merlin groped for the words of the song by Eleanor's lover which Jay had played and sung for him, the night before Kreuz walked into their lives.

The original words he could not remember. They had been in incomprehensible old Langue d'Oc. But Jay had translated them. The whole song had been a warning from this Bertrand de Whatsit who had been Queen Eleanor's lover. But a warning to whom? To Eleanor? It didn't matter. The message was in the warning itself. There had been something about the Cross. And Kreuz – meaning Cross – had arrived in St Denis the very next morning.

But it was more of a coincidence than that...

Jay had been singing about false wearers of the Cross being as dangerous as the Saracen!

Merlin swung his feet off the bed and reached for the telephone.

A woman's voice answered sleepily, *'No sé donde está.'*

'I left him in a bar a few hours back,' said Merlin.

'Sin duda,' she said. *'Se puede...* Maybe he still there, I don't know.'

The brandy did not help Merlin's sense of direction. He got lost several times before finding the bar, only to discover that Guzman had moved on. Merlin tracked his only contact in Granada from bar to bar and finally ran him to earth at two o'clock in the morning. The stringer looked no drunker than when Merlin had said goodbye, hours earlier. The same leg was locked round the leg of this bar stool, keeping him upright.

Guzman showed no surprise on seeing Merlin again. He called to the barman, '*Mi amigo quiere pagar la cuenta.*'

Merlin paid the drinks bill Guzman had run up and placed two hundred-dollar bills on the bar, with his hand firmly on top of the notes.

'Kreuz, Hermann. Real name?'

The stringer smiled a watery smile. 'You know, Freeman, for two hours I am wondering if you come back to ask me that question.'

'Did he keep the same initials?'

'Kinda funny how often these guys do.'

'Kempfer?'

'First name Heinz. His brother, he live in Austria… got a title of some kind. Dook, baron, I dunno what exactly.'

'I could kiss you.'

'Don't.' Guzman pushed Merlin away. 'In this-a town I am known as a harmless, drunken has-been. Nobody know what a mine of information is Bill Guzman. Ees to that I owe great peace of mind.'

'I'll not breathe a word.'

Guzman moved fast for a drunk. The money vanished into his breast pocket as he pulled Merlin back with the other hand. 'Freeman! On this story I do not, repeat not, want a by-line. My dreams of winning a Pulitzer prize are long behind me *amigo*. Now I dream only of the quiet life and just enough money to get drunk each day, okay?'

Merlin walked back to the *parador* a much relieved man, certain that when Jay heard what he had learned about Kreuz, she wouldn't want anything more to do with the man. He debated knocking on the door of her room as soon as he got back, to give her the news there and then, but decided that might lead to more misunderstandings.

Opening the window to let out the stale fug in his own room, he reasoned that it would be better to wait until the morning to give her the news. Then they would sort everything out together and life would be good again.

He booked a call for 8 am and fell instantly asleep. He was still fast asleep when Jay booked out of the hotel at 7.

Part 5

Chapter 1

The twelve-hour solo drive from Granada to St Denis passed in a blur. As Jay drove the red Alpine faster and faster over the bleak, depopulated plateau of León, among the bright, sharp-fingered Pyrenees and through the dark and mournful pine forests of Les Landes, more impressions flooded back into her memory with each mile past. Scene by scene and sequence by sequence they slipped into her mind, displacing the memories that made up the life of Jay French and gradually making up the violent sage of burning loves and passionate hatreds, imprisonment, adventure and murder that had been the life of Eleanor of Aquitaine.

There was nothing she could do about it. She had again that sensation of something soft but heavy pressing down inside her skull. It seemed almost laughable that she had been afraid of brain cancer or some other nameable disease when faced with the unspeakable truth of what was really happening to her.

Her style of driving changed; from being fast but skilful and cautious, she found herself taking bends much too fast and overtaking more and more recklessly. Twice she would have died in head-on collisions, had not Spanish truck drivers braked hard to let her get back on the right side of the white line in time. The second time, Jay found herself gripping the wheel and feeling sick while a part of her mind argued arrogantly that she had a greater right to be on the road than the truckers who had given way.

Just before the French-Spanish border Jay stopped briefly to fill up with petrol and drink enough coffee to keep her going for the rest of the journey. There was a line of drivers queuing to use the telephones. Who could she call for help? What could she say? Only Merlin might understand and he... Why had he changed from the tender and protective lover to a boorish, argumentative chauvinist pig?

Jay stood alone and frightened in the noisy truck-stop. She no longer had any illusion what would happen at the end of the journey. It was like...

229

She had been seduced by her flute teacher at the Academy halfway through the first term. Eighteen, overawed by his reputation, counting herself lucky to be taught by him, hanging on his every word and worshipping his superb instrumental technique, she had thought that her student infatuation was love and that he – a married man thirty years older than she – was in love too. Only a musical prodigy who had never had time for boyfriends could have been so innocent.

In the hours just before they first made love Jay had suddenly seen the situation clearly, known that it was all wrong, that he did not love her and was just using her. Yet she could not stop herself going to his apartment when his wife was out, knocking on the door in full knowledge of what was going to happen. She had shut her eyes as he pulled her inside the door.

'Look at me,' he had commanded after kissing her on the mouth and slipping off her coat.

She had opened her eyes and seen his confident, cocksure smile.

'You can still go,' he said. 'I haven't closed the door.'

But she couldn't. Compelled to go on and find out, she had closed the door and let it all happen.

It was the same now but a thousand times worse. After a short overnight stop in St Denis, she would head next day for the very place she should avoid like the plague – the place where Eleanor's spirit would be at its most powerful. At Fontevraud where she had spent the last years of her life mastering the esoteric arts with Yussef el-Kebir, something awful was going to happen, of that Jay had no doubt. She also knew that she could do nothing to stop it.

It was dusk when Kassim screwed up his courage to walk into the grimy back-street café in Pau. There was the sound of railway stock *clink-clink-clink* in the marshalling yard across the road. An articulated truck with a Spanish number-plate was being revved up on the waste ground outside while the driver and another man tinkered with the engine. From the exhaust a choking fog of diesel fumes oozed into the café through a broken window-pane.

Kassim's contact was a woman who used the masculine *nom de guerre* Ramón. She looked more like a harassed, hard-up housewife than a revolutionary, with her pinched, pale face, badly cut hair and cheap jumper and skirt. She wore no stockings and had on her feet a pair of old espadrilles, the backs trodden down flat. Three years in a Spanish prison had crushed whatever *joie de vivre* had once shown in her dark eyes.

Sweat was trickling down the small of Kassim's back. Inter-group contacts were among the most dangerous moments of a terrorist's life: it was all too easy to walk into a police trap or to be taken oneself for an *agent provacateur*, with equally fatal results. On both sides of the Pyrenees the Basque Liberation organisation ETA was riddled with informers who worked for the Spanish and French police. Two-thirds of the leaders were in gaol; others disappeared on lonely roads and were never heard of again – which made the rank and file jumpy.

The noise of the truck engine woke the baby, screaming. Ramón broke off the conversation with Kassim in order to jam a piece of cardboard into the broken window in the futile hope of keeping out the worst of the fumes. Then she picked the child out of the pram and comforted it while Kassim continued the cautious identification routine. There were no other customers; he had hung about outside for twenty minutes to be sure of that.

Ramón gave all the right answers in a surly voice and without a smile even for the child in her arms. A couple of Basque-speaking railwaymen came into the café for an *eau-de-vie de marc*. She chatted with them equally unsmilingly as she served them one-handed, the child balanced on her hip. The postman arrived with a thin bundle of mail and lingered for five minutes over a glass of Calvados. Not a smile passed between any of them, which worried Kassim who was accustomed to the frequent eye-contact between Arab men. The total incomprehensibility of their language unnerved him; they could have been discussing football scores, plotting the assassination of the Pope or arranging his own betrayal.

When the three customers had gone, Kassim moved back to the bar. To quieten the fretful baby, Ramón sat down at one of the tables and opened her dress for it to feed. If the conversation went on much longer, Kassim decided, he would walk out empty-handed and get away fast. His mistrust of women in general prompted him to believe that this one was an informer. For all he knew, the place was already surrounded.

After a few more questions and answers Ramón went to the door again, still holding the child to her breast. With her free hand she fiddled with the piece of cardboard as an excuse for checking the street. It was empty, the Spanish truck with the dirty exhaust disappearing round the corner.

'This is the sample.' She pulled back the baby's blankets and mattress to reveal a matt-black 9 mm. Uzi machine pistol with the collapsible stock that made it into a sub-machine gun.

Kassim's pulse quickened. There was no going back once he had picked up the weapon, no chance of talking his way out. He took a paper napkin from the dispenser beside a dish of congealed *tapas* on the counter and lifted the gun. It was brand-new and had never been fired. There were still traces of the manufacturer's packing grease clinging to the metal.

He weighed in his hand the legendary Israeli weapon that was probably the best compromise between size and fire-power in the world. 'It'll do,' he nodded approvingly. 'Ammunition?'

Ramón pulled the mattress further back to reveal a screw-on silencer and two full 32-round magazines. Kassim scooped them up and stuffed them with the gun into a cheap hold-all he had bought that morning on the way to the rendezvous.

'When shall I see you again, for the rest of the consignment?' she asked.

'I'll be in touch.'

'We need the money.' Ramón was thinking of the child's father, dying in a Spanish prison. 'With that much cash, we can spring a comrade from gaol.'

With a small gurgling sound the baby puked over her shoulder. Kassim left her burping it. He walked swiftly towards the city centre, checking regularly that he was not being followed. Once in the crowded city centre he breathed more easily and walked with a spring in his step, despite the injured leg. In a cluster of shoppers waiting to cross the road at some traffic lights, he felt agoraphobic, wanting to flee or at least push them all away from him. He imagined their faces if only he could sling the Uzi round his chest and swagger along the street as he had done for years in his own country. How they would respect him then! How eager they would be to get out of his way, fear showing in their eyes as he glared at them...

It took a conscious effort not to hurry, not to limp, and to avoid looking anyone in the face. Kassim stopped twice in different bars for cups of coffee which he was too tense to drink. Then he visited several clothing stores, buying one garment in each. In a public toilet he changed all his outer clothes, dumping the hold-all full of clothes and transferring the gun to a smart new brief-case that went with his expensive suit. Satisfied at last that he was not followed, he unlocked the boot of a Renault 25 he had hired earlier and slung the brief-case inside.

At the Campanile Motel outside town, Salem was hungry. Completely out of his depth when he saw Kassim return dressed as a businessman, driving an expensive new car, he started to ask questions. Where are your own clothes? What happened to the pick-up truck? Where did you get the money? His questions were brushed aside with a sneer by Kassim who replied with curt orders to get packed fast and check out of the motel right away.

Kassim insisted on driving the car despite the pain in his injured leg. They left Pau, heading north towards the address which Kassim had discovered so easily from the hotel register in Granada. As he drove, Kassim rehearsed Salem in their cover story. He kept it very simple, rightly mistrusting his brother's ability to lie.

The gun hidden in the brief-case on the back seat was almost as well travelled as Kassim himself. Made in the Uzi factory in Israel, it had been shipped to a bonded warehouse in Rotterdam, part of a small consignment of silenced weapons. From there, it had been sold by a Jewish arms dealer in New York to a ex-CIA man based in Tripoli who was making a perilous fortune as a front man for Colonel Ghaddafy. His brief was to obtain embargoed goods that could not be purchased openly by the Libyans; terrorist weapons like silenced Uzis fell clearly into that category.

The EUC or end-user certificate for the deal had specified that the weapons were for the Special Force of the Sultan of Oman. The crates had been shipped from Rotterdam on a Greek-owned vessel flying the Panamanian flag. At night off the Libyan coast a fast patrol boat had intercepted the ship for what the crew thought was a Customs check. Only the master with his altered ship's manifest and a bundle of dollars in his pocket knew what the Libyans had wanted. From Tripoli a dozen of the Uzis found their way to Ireland as a gesture of support for the Provisional IRA from Colonel Ghaddafy. From there, this particular weapon had travelled inside an HGV fuel tank to France as a fraternal present from the Provos to Basque liberationists.

The guns were now being sold by ETA – subject to acceptance of the sample and to due payment – to the Sons of the Islamic Jihad, as Kassim's comrades were known in revolutionary circles. They wanted the Uzis for a complicated scenario which would end in the assassination of a Hezbollah leader thought to be too accommodating to Tel Aviv. Both the man and his family were to be gunned down in front of witnesses by men wearing Israeli uniforms and armed with Israeli weapons that fired Israeli bullets. All of which explained why the money to pay for the Uzis had to be untraceable. Which in turn – had Salem but known – was the reason why Kassim had been sent by his revolutionary brothers to hunt for Queen Eleanor's gold.

Chapter 2

'Hi!' Merlin parted the bushes. 'Am I intruding?'

Leila was lying on a blanket in the late-morning sunshine, soaking up warmth like a cat. The unkempt shrubs in her wildly over-grown garden made a perfect wind-break.

'Not you,' she yawned, happy to see him. 'I was just bozing.'

'Another word for the dictionary?'

'I meant to say dozing and boozing but I've done too much of the second to pronounce the first – or whatever.' She pulled herself up on one elbow and took a good look at Merlin.

He had obviously not slept or shaved. There were smudges of tension around his eyes and his mouth was a tight, angry line. No trace of the famous Freeman smile today, she thought. 'There's some vino in the bottle, Merl. Help yourself. Looks like you could do with it.'

Merlin poured a glassful of the local red wine, took two cigarettes from her pack, lit them and passed one to Leila.

'You're smoking again?' she queried.

He raised the glass in a silent toast and noticed for the first time the bruise above her left eye.

'What happened?'

'Oh...' She touched the swelling and winced. 'A lover's tiff. Dom found out and got excited.'

'He hit you?'

'Let's say I walked into his fist. I think it was meant for the other guy but I'm not sure. Afterwards the two of them sat up all night drinking whisky together and telling each other what a two-timing whore I am. But you don't look very interested in my problems. I hear you and Jay split up too.'

The cigarette was the hundredth Merlin had smoked that morning, or tasted like it. After a couple of drags he flicked it away into the bushes and cleared some wet leaves from a plastic garden chair so that he could sit down.

'How did you know?' He avoided looking at Leila.

'She got back here late yesterday, driving that red machine of hers like a bat out of hell.'

'... while I was sitting in Madrid airport, waiting for a connecting flight that didn't happen. And did Jay talk to you?'

'A few terse sentences. Jay is not – surprise, surprise – one of the weepers of this world, Merlin, old boy.'

'What was the message of those terse sentences?'

Leila squinted at him through her smoke. 'It sounded like a repeat of one I've heard before.'

'All my fault, huh?'

'I didn't say that.'

'But you meant it. Feminine solidarity...'

'Oh, snap out of it, Merlin.' Leila was not in a mood to humour him; she had her own troubles. 'You always do the same goddam' thing. You make a girl think you're in love with her. Then you rush off on some damned news story and drop her flat. So what do you expect?'

'Is that what Jay said?'

Leila inhaled and blew the smoke at Venus which had just appeared in the sky. 'Not exactly. I'm making it up, extrapolating from my own great sorrow. To be honest, she said hardly a word.'

Merlin tried to interrupt but she continued talking: 'All she told me was that she had walked out on you in Granada – something about you leaving her to wait like Cinderella in a hotel room until midnight struck and you turned back into the green frog you really are.'

'She said that?'

'Did it sound like Jay? Come on, Merl, if the line drawing was hers, the full colour version is signed Leila Dor.'

Merlin was thinking. He had done little else since waking up in Granada the previous day and finding Jay gone. But he could not get anywhere on his own; he needed a patient pair of ears, preferably belonging to someone who knew both him and Jay very well.

He took the plunge: 'Leila, can I take up a couple of hours of your time?'

'... to talk about your tangled love life? Sure, why not?'

Merlin was sitting with head bowed, staring at the ground between his feet. 'I'm worried about Jay. How did she seem when you saw her yesterday?'

'You want me to say she was pining for you, you arrogant bastard?'

'Just tell me what she was like. Was she her normal self?

Leila thought about it. 'Impatient is the word that comes to mind.'

Merlin stood up and gazed up-river to where the chimney of Jay's farmhouse showed above the trees.

'She's not there,' said Leila. 'They left – as the military say – at first light.'

'They?'

'The German – Dr Whatsisname.'

Alarm showed in Merlin's voice. 'Kreuz came back here with Jay?'

'No…'

'Then what the hell d'you mean?' Merlin grabbed Leila's shoulder.

She broke his grip. 'Jesus! That hurt, Merlin. What is it about me that makes all you guys wanna play rough?'

He knelt on the blanket beside her. 'Just tell me what happened, Leila – for Chrissakes!'

She pushed him back from her. 'Okay. I will, but calm down. Jay came back first. When I heard she was alone – the neighbours see everything in a place like this – I thought she might need a shoulder to cry on, so I called round to have a cup of coffee with her.'

'And she was pleased to see you?'

Leila shook her head. 'More like she was trying to get rid of me. It was weird. I stuck it out for maybe an hour of one-way conversation – I guess I wanted to talk to someone about Dom and me splitting up. Then, peep-peep, up drove Dr Toad in his white BMW and I got a clear message to take my woes elsewhere.'

'How did Jay react when Kreuz arrived?'

'Is this some kind of jealous lover act?'

'I want to know how she reacted to him.'

'Thinking back, she didn't really react much to anything…'

'She was like a zombie?'

'I didn't say that. It was like… she had something important on her mind and no time to waste.'

'Kreuz stayed at Chez Dominique?'

'No. That was weird. He stayed the night at Jay's house. The driver had a blonde girl with him who only spoke German. They stayed at the hotel. In a place like this, the neighbours…'

'I know. You said. And they left at dawn: Jay, Kreuz, the driver and the girl?'

'That's right.'

'Where'd they go?'

'I did catch a name but it didn't mean a thing to me.'

'Was it Fontevraud?' Merlin guessed.

'Maybe.'

'It's an abbey where…'

'That's it,' Leila nodded. 'Jay said something to Dr Toad about: "… when we get to the abbey". I think Fontevraud was the name. I could be wrong.'

Merlin stood up again. He smashed his right fist into his left palm several times. The thought of Jay a hundred miles away with Kreuz – and at Fontevraud of all places – brought back all the violent physical anger he had felt at Granada.

'What's up?' Leila asked.

'How long have you known me?'

She smiled, 'I've used a lot of toothpaste since we used to sit talking all night in Greenwich Village, solving the world's problems.'

'And do you think I'm crazy?'

Leila looked up at him and took in the set of his face and the tightly closed fists. 'You asked for it. Yes, at times I do think you're crazy, Merlin.'

'Well, that's great.'

'What do you expect me to say? Frankly, how else can I account for a man who's been so nearly destroyed by war, choosing to earn his living as a war correspondent?'

Merlin took a deep breath and felt some of the tension drain away. 'Leila, I think you're just about the sanest person I know.'

'That doesn't say much for the others.'

'Seriously, I need to talk to you before I kill someone.'

Leila looked at Merlin's anguished, angry face for a long moment before she said, 'You're not kidding, are you?'

She pulled him down onto the blanket beside her and sat listening as the words poured out of him, telling her about his first instinctive reaction to Kreuz, how each time he saw the man he felt a surge of unreasoning anger so strong that it made him feel physically sick. He told her his fears that Kreuz seemed to have some hypnotic hold over Jay and ended: 'I don't even know the guy but whenever I'm near him, I can feel myself doing and saying everything wrong, acting like a real arse-hole and alienating Jay when I want to help her.'

'Give me some examples.'

'If Kreuz excludes me from the conversation, I sulk like a moron instead of pushing in and grabbing my share. If he gets between me and Jay, I get so angry that I drive her towards him. If he outwits me, instead of using my brain I want to smash his face in. I can't remember any person I've ever met who made me feel this way. I could kill that guy with my bare hands and feel good about it afterwards.'

'Wow!' Leila ran her hands through his hair. 'You do need to talk to someone, Merl. Well...'

She stood up and looked at the paint on her hands which had left a yellow smear in his hair. 'The world can do without another masterpiece. I'm all yours. Take as long as you want.'

'Where are you going?' he called after her.

237

'To get a couple more bottles. By the look of you, it's going to be a long talk, so we might as well get drunk.'

Some of the tension lines had gone from Merlin's face. He scrambled nimbly to his feet. 'No time for that,' he said. Things were beginning to come clearer in his own mind. 'I think we ought to get mobile.'

Chapter 3

In the first week of March the abbey of Fontevraud was devoid of tourists. The streets of sixteenth- and seventeenth-century buildings, which had replaced most of the original architecture, had the deserted, two-dimensional look of a film set.

In the square where they parked the cars, just in front of the abbey entrance, Kreuz met an archaeologist he knew, who was in charge of some excavations in the abbey church. Invited into the site-caravan, he discussed the finds: small bits of pottery and yellowed bones, pieces of carved stone re-used from former buildings, tiles and a coin or two. Jay stayed only a few minutes before excusing herself and heading for the abbey church where lay 'the stone that is hollow'.

Her feet seemed to know their way. They took her quickly through the later buildings to the oldest part of the abbey, the nuns' kitchen and the cloisters that led to the church itself – all of which had been built in Eleanor's day. Jay wanted to stop or even better to run away but with each step she had less control over her own movements. At the back of her mind she was wondering whether Leila had heard and remembered the slim clue she had left for Merlin. And would he get it before it was too late?

In the cloisters the cold, moist air transformed Jay's breath into puffs of steam. Distantly – as though the whole nightmarish reality was a plot in a novel she was reading – she wondered how many places had been alluded to in how many *sirventès*. Was Canterbury – where it had all begun – named in another poem which had not been found? And Oakham Castle too? Had Eleanor perhaps left hundreds of *sirventès*, or even thousands, scattered in old manuscripts, carved on church and castle walls, most of them now lost forever?

Jay had the image of a vast spider's web, each strand represented by a *sirventès*. The fly for whom it had been spun was herself, Jay French. No matter into which strand she had blundered, she would have been held fast while the vibrations of her entrapment travelled through the whole structure to alert the spider who had been waiting for so long.

She had expected the church to be as deserted as the rest of the abbey but as she turned the iron handle of the huge oaken door the midday siren sounded from the fire station in Fontevraud town and a dozen students and archaeologists downed their brushes and trowels in the trenches that dissected the floor of the church to depart noisily for lunch, leaving Jay alone.

At the far end, near the altar, lay the tombs of Eleanor, Henry Plantagenet and Richard Coeur-de-Lion. She followed the scaffolding-and-plank walkway that spanned the excavations and stood gazing down on Eleanor's effigy. It was a lifeless, stylised death mask. The aged queen's face was thin and reposeful, the gaze directed devoutly at an open prayer book held in her strong hands.

Jay heard Kreuz's voice in the cloister calling her name and moved swiftly behind a column to be out of sight. Two pairs of men's footsteps came through the doorway into the church, sounding hollowly on the planking. There was a murmur of voices, the archaeologist wanting to show his visitor something of interest which had been unearthed that morning. From snatches of the conversation that reached her, Jay understood that he and Kreuz were arguing about dating different medieval techniques of stone carving.

She sat on a stone bench that ran along the side wall and felt the cold of the unheated church enter into her. The two men climbed out of the trench, their voices growing fainter as they moved away and the heavy door at the end of the nave thudded shut, leaving Jay alone with her thoughts.

She knew now what had caused her to stop playing at Canterbury, to black out at Bordeaux – and why she had fallen near 'the heathen maze' at Chartres. The same thing was happening now. She tried to stand up in a last desperate panic to leave the church but her body weighed a hundred tons. She had a fear that she was going to wet herself. Her eyelids were growing heavier and heavier. There was a flash memory of her father saying years before: '... and when they close completely, you'll be asleep but you'll still be able to hear my voice.'

They set out in Leila's battered old *deux-chevaux* because Merlin had decided that his camping van was too slow and conspicuous. He stalled the engine three times before he had backed the car out of her garden on to the track that led to the main road.

'What is it,' he wondered, 'about you Europeans that makes a car with a manual gear box and a small engine so attractive?'

'If you're rude about her, she'll stop altogether,' Leila warned. 'Just be polite, if you want to get as far as Fontevraud.'

'I can't find top gear.'

'You're already in it.'

Merlin drove cautiously, getting the feel of the loose steering. To keep the car in a straight line it was necessary to keep his hands continually see-sawing the steering wheel. 'You should have something done about this,' he advised.

'Never mind about my car. Tell me what's on your mind.'

Merlin had forgotten what a good listener Leila could be. He went over all that had happened, trying to leave nothing out. At times Leila was so still that he thought she had fallen asleep. But then her heavy-lidded eyes turned on him and he saw that she was taking everything in – and treating it seriously.

'Did you ever hear a crazier story?' Merlin finished, expecting her to say he was mad. 'Or one with so many contradictions and coincidences, if that's what they are?' He fought the wheel around a bend and braked. At any speed above eighty kph the car became uncontrollable.

Leila thought about it. 'I never heard anything like this. But let's see what possible explanations there are.'

'Shoot.'

'Theory Number One is the obvious: Jay has some kind of crack-up.'

'That's what her father thought, the first time it happened,' said Merlin. 'But it does not explain...'

Leila patted his arm. 'Relax, it was only a theory. You're right, it doesn't explain what you call the coincidences – like you being there to put Oradour and Châlus together and make Dürnstein or you hustling all the way to Austria so you could get there a few hours before the baron died, after which that lead would have been dead. Nor does it explain why Jay's experiences have all occurred in places where Queen Eleanor is known to have been.'

'There isn't a rational explanation,' he said. 'God knows, I tried hard enough to find one.'

'You say Jay's never told you exactly what happens?' Leila asked.

Merlin shook his head. 'She's very vague. At Canterbury, she said it was like there were hands pulling her fingers away from the keys of the flute to stop her playing. The other recollections – at Chartres and Bordeaux – were even more nebulous, although she was obviously distressed.'

'Distressed!' Leila snorted. 'You're a wordsmith. Is that the only adjective you can come up with?'

Merlin drove for a while in silence, recalling Jay at Chartres lying pale and shivering in the hotel bed, drained of all energy and...

'Hang on!' He drove into the parking area of a wayside restaurant with a Routiers sign and stopped among all the heavy trucks.

241

'There was another incident…' he began.

It was odd to be sitting there telling Leila about the midnight visit to his room at Old Sarum, but he gave all the details and contrasted Jay's wild unloving passion on that night with their other tender and affectionate love-making.

'What are you telling me?' Leila asked. 'That Jay is schizophrenic, that she becomes another person from time to time? I guess that's Theory Number Two.'

Schizophrenia? No, it was the wrong label, Merlin knew. 'These experiences only happen to Jay when she's around one of these Eleanor sites. But that wasn't the point I was going to make.'

'For a normally lucid guy, Merlin, you're not being very clear.'

He ignored that. Fists clenched with the effort, he was trying to snatch something out of thin air. 'The point is that after each one of these events, Jay is completely drained of energy.'

'She's tired?'

'No!' Merlin knew he was on to something now. 'You have to use a stronger word than that. Look, normally Jay has more vitality than a team of athletes, you know that. She's a performer with the energy it takes to magnetise a couple of thousand people in a concert hall, but after…'

He ticked them off on his fingers, one by one. 'After that night at Old Sarum, she slept most of the next day while I drove her precious car. And after what happened at Chartres, she slept for hours and was still like a sleepwalker for the rest of the day until we got to your house. You saw what she was like then. Like she was ill or…' He stopped.

'Or what?' Leila prompted.

Merlin tried another tack: 'Something happened to Jay that night I tried to ring her from Vienna, you remember? She couldn't tell me exactly what. A dream of torture, she thought it was.'

'She had a nightmare?' Leila passed him a lit cigarette.

'Much worse than that. After it, Jay slept through about half a dozen of my calls. There was nothing wrong with the phone; I had the operator check out her line. Jay just slept through.'

'I saw her the next morning,' said Leila. 'She looked… drained.'

'Drained is the word,' he said. 'Drained of all energy – but how and by what?'

'That brings us to Theory Number Three.' Leila wanted to laugh at what she was about to say, except that she had an awful feeling that it was true. 'Perhaps there is some supernatural explanation for everything that has happened: the coincidences, the contradictions, Jay's experiences, your irrational acts – the lot.'

'A unified theory?' Merlin wanted her to finish. 'Come on, Miss Einstein, let's have it – this one explanation that covers everything.'

242

'If…' Leila took a deep breath. This was not really her scene at all. 'If this ancestor of Jay's really was such an extraordinary and powerful person, then perhaps her ghost – oh, I hate that word, let's say her spirit – is reaching out from the past to get her hands on Jay.'

'Why?' Merlin snapped.

Leila spoke hesitantly: 'If Jay's drained of energy after each happening, then perhaps this… spirit from the past takes her energy. Maybe that's what Eleanor wants, I don't know. Like the vampire legends, you know – sucking not blood but vitality from the victim and parasitizing her life-force.'

Merlin smoked in silence. Around them, cars and trucks were pulling up and others were driving away. It was a normal everyday scene of twentieth-century life.

'The only thing my theory doesn't cover,' said Leila 'is the good Dr Kreuz. Where does he come in? Or is he some fluke outsider just after the golden treasure of Châlus?'

Merlin wound down the window and breathed clean air. 'He's no fluke. Kreuz is descended from a crook called Mercadier who worked for Eleanor and King Richard. So he's a part of it all.'

'And what is the hold he has over Jay? When did it begin?'

Merlin thought back. He felt calmer now, talking to Leila. Everything was falling into place, although he still had no idea what to do when they arrived at Fontevraud. 'I'd say it began at their very first meeting.'

'That lunch the two of you ate with him at Dom's restaurant?'

'Right. There was a kind of conspiracy between him and Jay, right from the start.'

'Conspiracy's a big word,' said Leila.

'The whole thing between Kreuz and her is so diffuse…' Merlin's gesture conveyed the frustration he felt. 'All I know is, I felt excluded, as though the two of them had a secret I was not privy to. I can't put words to it better than that.'

'Okay, let it go. But if, as you say, you sensed what was going on, why didn't you warn Jay?'

'I tried to do that a hundred times but she made out I was exaggerating and said I was paranoid or jealous. And, as I told you, when Kreuz is around, I do everything wrong. I'm aware of it, but I can't help it.'

Leila was silent for a moment, then: 'I wonder if Kreuz's influence over Jay is anything to do with all that creepy hypnosis business with her father when she was a kid?'

'Someone as habituated to hypnosis as Jay was, must become very suggestible.'

'But I never met a stronger-willed person than her,' Leila objected.

243

'Have you any idea what guts and drive it took to fight her way up the showbiz ladder? So that's another contradiction.'

'The only thing I know about Kreuz,' Merlin burst out, 'is that I hate the guy!'

'That's pretty obvious, but why?'

'I'd like to tear him limb from limb.'

'Because of the hold he has on Jay?'

'Yeah, but also... It's more like, we have an old score to settle.'

Leila shivered. It was not just that the car's heating system did not work and they had left it too late to eat.

'The first day you met on the tow-path,' she said, 'Jay looked at you like she was seeing a ghost. You made a joke about people recognising you because they'd seen you on television, but you looked... I thought at the time you looked like it was just as much of a surprise for you to see her.'

'I thought for a moment we had met, like she said. But we couldn't have.'

'D'you ever have those things they call *déjà vu*?'

'Never. What are you getting at?'

'I don't know if this is helpful or not,' said Leila. 'But if, as you say, Kreuz is a descendant of this Mercadier who served Eleanor and King Richard... Okay, it's a big if. But if there is some kind of contact with the past going on, then...'

'Then, what?'

Leila laughed nervously. 'It's getting crazier and crazier, Merl, but maybe you and Jay and Kreuz all knew each other in some past life? Perhaps you and Dr Toad were once deadly enemies? That would explain what you feel for him.'

She broke the tension by bursting out laughing. 'Oh Jesus, Merl! I can't believe I'm sitting here with you, talking with a perfectly straight face about ghosts. I don't believe in them.'

Outside, the car park was nearly empty as the last lorries pulled out onto the highway.

'I have to tell you something.' Merlin's voice was hoarse. His hands were locked on the steering wheel and his eyes fixed on a distant horizon. 'I've just remembered where I saw Jay before that day she came running along the tow-path to meet us. Oh Christ!'

He saw again the veiled woman who had led him to safety, the day of his escape in Beirut. Against the sky her muffled face was indistinct but her eyes were Jay's; there was no doubt. And the voice was Jay's too.

Chapter 4

Jay's breathing was growing shallower; it was as though she had not enough energy to expand the chest cavity properly. A different kind of panic came now, on top of the other. She was frightened of suffocating to death as her brain cells clamoured for oxygen which the paralysed lungs could not supply.

There was too the sensation of being watched, as when she turned in a restaurant or on a street to find a man staring at her – but this had a thousand times more menace. Jay tried to move her head to find her observer, but could not. A smell of incense, very strong and pungent, assailed her nostrils. By looking out of the corner of her half-closed eyes, she could see only a narrow arc of the nave to one side of the column.

The floor was lower than it ought to have been – level with the bottom of the archaeologist's trench. And there were only two royal tombs, back in their original places in a side chapel. The light coming through the small high windows was obscured by a pall of incense as a long procession of monks walked past, swinging their censers and chanting the end of the burial service. In the middle of the procession was a coffin being carried by nuns. And on the far side of the aisle stood a woman, staring at her.

Jay's senses shut down and ceased feeding information to the brain as though a surgeon's scalpel were severing the nerves, one after another. Hearing ceased, then the sense of smell and lastly vision. As swiftly as if someone had turned off the light, her field of view narrowed to a piece of stonework and then nothing but empty blackness. Wherever she strained to look was black – not the blackness of velvet, soft and warm and cushioning, but a vast infinity of cold lightlessness, terrifying in its sheer inhuman emptiness.

It was like having vertigo in every direction, for every direction was down. Jay felt herself falling, accelerating faster and faster into a bottomless pit, an all-engulfing black hole where she – who a moment before had been a person of flesh and blood – shrank to nothing more than a lingering spark of consciousness, spinning in the abyss and waiting impotently for her final extinction.

I must cling on, she thought. I must fight back and not let go...

She had learned so many tricks to summon up will-power on stage and tried to use them now to regain her body, only to feel herself thrust aside by the psychic pressure wave of Eleanor's indomitable will. There was a flash image of herself as nothing more than a piece of paper blowing helplessly along a platform in the wake of a fast express train.

*   *   *

'Poor Princess Joanna. Poor sometime Queen of Sicily. Poor daughter mine, she's dead.' Eleanor stayed in her pew until the procession had left the church. Her voice was as matter-of-fact as if she had said: I'm hungry. Since Richard's death and the tears she had wept for her beloved son, nothing had touched her heart, and nothing would, ever again.

Yussef coughed, a racking spasm that had bothered him since he crossed the Pyrenees into the dampness of Aquitaine. He was dressed in the cowled robe of a monk, a costume in which he passed unnoticed among the fifteen thousand lay and religious brothers and sisters of the huge community after being introduced by the queen on her return from Spain as her new confessor. Brought up as a Moslem, he was fascinated by the behaviour of women in the Christian kingdoms north of the Pyrenees, especially in the community of Fontevraud where both monks and nuns were subject to the rule of the abbess – a thing unthinkable in a Muslim country. Eleanor herself conformed to no norms of her time, as he had learnt many times since leaving Granada with her three months before.

And as for the nun whose body was in the coffin... Some nun! he thought. Eleanor's daughter Joanna had been a very worldly princess – and a queen who had travelled to the Holy Land on Crusade. Hers had been no cloistered life of prayer! After being divorced by the King of Sicily, she had returned to her own country, only to be carried off and ravished by a robber baron. And it was less than three weeks since Yussef in his capacity as the queen's supposed confessor had attended a ceremony during which Princess Joanna had piously professed her vows as a virgin bride of Christ although visibly in the last weeks of pregnancy! Now at last, he thought, she had conformed to the lot of woman by dying in child-bed.

He coughed again and pulled his robe closer, more against the cold than as a disguise; the church was empty now, save for Eleanor and himself. He was careful not to speak when anyone was near; his Latin although fluent bore the accent of the Holy Land where he had been born and anyone who had been on Crusade would recognise the Arabic intonation. As he stood up to leave, Eleanor was still seated and intent with her head cocked on one side as though listening to the distant chanting.

'Stay!' she hissed, catching at Yussef's sleeve to pull him round and face the direction in which she was looking. 'Look there, Moor! What see you there?'

She rose and dragged him with her through the swirling incense smoke to the centre of the nave. There she stood behind Yussef and took his head in both her hands, turning it until he was looking at one of the columns behind which sat a shadowy form.

'*Veni!*' she ordered. 'Come forth and let this doubting pagan behold what I can see!'

On the queen's command, the faint pre-echo of Jay's body rose and glided forward through the smoke.

'Look!' Eleanor commanded.

'I see nothing,' Yussef protested. 'Only smoke and shadows.'

'Look harder!' The queen willed him to see what she was conjuring up by sheer will-power. 'Your mind is turned too much towards the past where you have searched for knowledge all your life. You see the present only darkly and the future hardly at all. So look hard – upward, where the future will be and see what I discern there. Look where the sunbeam cuts a path through the dust motes! There!'

I see only shadows,' said Yussef, 'and sunbeams playing on the smoke.'

From her reticule Eleanor took a small painting half the size of her hand. It was portrait that had been commissioned by Count Henry on their marriage in 1152 and showed her as a young woman aged twenty-nine.

'*Ecce!*' Eleanor thrust the portrait in front of Yussef's face: 'Look on this. Now tell me what you see!'

She jerked the portrait away and tilted his bearded chin, forcing him to look up until he found himself gazing at the shadowy outline of a long-haired boy, or so it seemed to the old man – a faint figure, half-hidden by the pillar and rendered insubstantial by the wreaths of smoke that hung unmoving in the damp and heavy air.

'Reveal your countenance!' cried Eleanor. 'Show yourself to us!'

Jay's wraith turned so that the sunlight fell full on her face. There was a tremor in Eleanor's voice which sank to a whisper. 'Now, Moor, tell me whose likeness you behold!'

'It is the face in the portrait.' Yussef strained his eyes, the better to see against the light. 'It is yourself when younger. Is this some shade you have conjured from the past, Madame?'

247

Eleanor laughed triumphantly. 'This is the shade I have magicked from the future, Moor. Look again! Was ever a Christian queen thus attired?'

A draught parted the clouds of incense smoke and for a second Yussef saw Jay dressed in jeans and anorak, her long blonde hair tumbling freely down over her shoulders, unconstrained by wimple, veil or braid. Then the smoke thinned in a draught and cleared completely. The image summoned by Eleanor's will quivered and vanished before his eyes.

Exhausted, the queen thrust the portrait into Yussef's hands. 'Take this,' she said. 'Gaze on it night and day in your cell. Thus, and in no other guise, I will return to life, surrounded – as the pharaohs planned it – by the faithful servants who have ministered to me in this earthly life.'

Yussef compared the painting with the ephemeral figure he had just seen. They were identical.

'Tell me one thing, o Queen,' he said. 'Why this insistence on physical resemblance? Surely to return in any human form would be enough?'

Eleanor snapped at him, angry that sometimes his brain was so much slower than hers. 'D'you think I want to return to earth a drivelling lunatic, my spirit confined in the wrong flesh? No, I'll return as me in the flesh of an identical descendant – or not at all. Once I was beautiful and will be so again. Look at me now, a bent and wrinkled old hag fit for charity! Would that my brain was enfeebled so I did not know how the living flesh decays.'

'It is the way of all creatures,' Yussef consoled her. 'I too was once young – and handsome, or so men said.'

'But no one stole the best years of your life,' said Eleanor bitterly.

'Stole? How so? Who can steal time?'

'My husband, for he was the king of thieves!' Eleanor's angry voice echoed off the bare stonework. Her outstretched arm pointed accusingly at Henry's tomb in the lady chapel.

'He stole fifteen years of my life, Moor! With the result that I who changed the face of Europe will go down in history merely as the wife of Henry Plantagenet and the mother of Richard and John – as though I were some cow-like creature of womb and tit who suffered coupling, bore his offspring and was fit for naught else.'

Eleanor's voice was quivering with rage. 'The years that Henry stole from me would have been my years of achievement! I was just past child-bearing and thus as free as any man to rule my domains and build an empire, when he locked me up in Salisbury Tower. I was still physically strong enough to ride all day and all night for a week without sleep. I was still beautiful, able to charm a poem or a song from handsome prince and troubadour alike.'

She fell silent as the anger passed and shrank into herself, recalling the scenes of which she spoke. Tears ran down her cheeks. Then her mouth tightened, the tears stopped and her green eyes flashed fire again. 'Henry no longer wanted me. I'd given him the sons he needed to ensure the succession of the monarchy and the daughters he could trade for an alliance here or a favour there. Yet he knew me too well to divorce me and leave me free to raise rebellion in the lands that owed allegiance to him only through my blood. So he locked me away from the world – away from life itself – for a decade and a half.'

Yussef watched her, fascinated by the swift changes of mood.

'For fifteen years I was dead,' Eleanor hissed, her long, thin arthritic fingers clenching the air as though she wished to claw back the time lost. 'I want those years back – with interest! I want to live again the years out of which Henry cheated me. I want to thrill once more to the sound of music, to dance and hear poetry by moonlight, to feel a lover's caress excite my skin.'

'I have told you many times,' Yussef protested, 'what you seek has never been accomplished. Not even the pharaohs were so arrogant as to hope for what you want!'

Eleanor grabbed the portrait from Yussef and held it in front of his eyes. Her voice was powerful for so old a woman. It rang through the empty church. 'That's how I'll walk the earth again, Moor. I don't care if it takes ten thousand years. I should rather wait in the anteroom of Hell throughout millennia in order to return as myself in the years of my prime than come back in five years' time as Cleopatra or the Queen of Sheba!'

Chapter 5

Eleanor wrote no letters, nor read any; she received no visitors and herself never left the abbey precincts. Between the death of Richard in 1199 and her own death four years later, the chroniclers recorded nothing in her name. In England her son King John showed genius only for alienating his allies and strengthening his enemies. In Aquitaine the duchy went to rack and ruin as each petty lordling vied with his neighbours in greed and violence and the country as a whole slipped back into another Dark Age. Eleanor did not intervene. Night and day – she needed little sleep at eighty-two years of age – the queen bent her still formidable energies to driving Yussef el-Kebir further and further along the mystic paths which led to her goal. Not that he needed persuasion to burn the midnight oil; with a pupil as apt and determined as Eleanor, any teacher would have excelled himself. Yussef laboured hard, slept little, grew leaner, ate less and coughed more.

At first Eleanor's forays into the limbo of eternity were brief, lasting seconds or minutes at most. There, as in dreams – and as the Egyptians had proved mathematically – she found that time was indeed elastic. Wherein lay a trap for the unwary: it would have been easy for a less strong will to stay overlong in these other realms and return to find the neglected physical body too soon dead. Only Yussef's training and Eleanor's strength of purpose averted this peril.

Stage by stage she mastered the arduous spiritual apprenticeship which Yussef had gleaned from the adepts of the mystic Books of the Dead in the temple of Ptah. Eleanor's absences from the body grew longer, her sojourns in the flesh of less and less interest to her. The breakthrough came after four years of rigid discipline and application when she acquired the ability to draw vital energy from the living, necessary to sustain her spirit throughout the long wait in darkness that lay ahead. From that moment on, she could choose when to die and when to live again. Impatiently she began the physical preparations for her return and sent Yussef with William the Marshal and a handful of men-at-arms to sow far and wide the cryptic *sirventès* which would one day draw together the far-flung strands of her cosmic net.

Hovering between this life and the next, she retreated even within the abbey, rarely emerging from her own quarters except for a daily walk in the cloister for an hour or so after Mass. There she could always find a shaded seat out of the sun or a warm dry corner on a day of cloud or rain. The herb garden that occupied the garth in the centre of the arcades filled the air with perfume. With the aid of a cane, the old queen walked the gravel paths between low rectilinear hedges of thyme and sage and rosemary while two ladies-in-waiting followed at a discreet distance. There was a nun guarding each entrance to the cloister to ensure privacy.

On some days the pain in Eleanor's joints would have kept in bed a less determined person but she insisted on rising in time for Mass and walking to the church. After the service she took exercise in the adjoining cloister. If movement was too painful, she would sit and rehearse long conversations she had had with kings and princes and popes now dead. There were whispers in the echoing corridors of the abbey that it was not just the queen's limbs that were nearing death but that her mind was also failing.

Only Yussef understood the reason for this so rapid decline. For days, then weeks and months during her spiritual re-training, Eleanor's body had been to all intents and purposes dead. Her teacher had barred even her own serving woman from the queen's apartments on the pretext that she was in retreat. To use the word thus amused him, for she was indeed in retreat from the flesh, but not praying. Her body lay unmoving in his care as her spirit roamed the first reaches of limbo to accustom itself by degrees to the greater immensity that lay beyond. It took all Yussef's medical skills to keep the queen's aged flesh alive as the spirit's absences grew longer.

Eleanor walked in silence, her thoughts far away. The only noise was the hum of insects and the crunch of her feet on the gravel. Occasionally a bell rang or the sound of chanting reached the cloisters. She was near the end of her self-imposed exercise period when the silence was shattered by the sound of a mailed fist hammering the door which opened to admit two men into the cloister. Eleanor's failing eyesight made out the figures of a monk and a knight.

Yussef greeted her in Langue d'Oc which he now spoke fluently. He slipped the cowl back from his head to reveal the balding dome, the long grey beard and the eyes that burned in his now cadaverously thin face. A respectful six paces from Eleanor, he touched his forehead in greeting, Arab-style while beside him William the Marshal stood bare-headed with his helmet under one arm.

Eleanor held out her hand. On it she still wore Richard's ring, which each man kissed in turn.

'How pleasant to have visitors who speak the language of my childhood,' she said vaguely, unable to put a name to either face. 'Come, sit beside me, both of you.'

She motioned to the ladies-in-waiting to place cushions on the sun-warmed stone.

'I'll stand,' said William bluffly. He felt it more fitting in the presence of his queen.

Yussef helped her to sit on the stone bench that ran around the cloister beside her. 'You've been remiss,' she said, still lacking a name for him. 'You should come and visit me more often.'

'I've been with William the Marshal,' Yussef spoke slowly, understanding her confusion. 'Since Easter we've ridden the length and breadth of your domains, my queen.'

'And are they at peace?' she asked vaguely. 'Is there peace in Aquitaine and Poitou?'

He muttered that there was peace. She nodded approvingly. 'Henry would have been pleased. He liked peace. The taxes come in more easily, he said.'

Yussef was racked by a fit of coughing and spat on the ground. Blood stained the gravel at the queen's feet.

'It is time I travelled south to breathe kinder air, Madam, after all these years you've kept me locked up in a nun's damp cell,' he gasped. 'My mission here is accomplished. The Marshal and I have ridden north and south and east and west throughout your domains. We have left carved on church and castle wall the *sirventès* which you and I wrote out together. We have secreted parchment copies in archives that will be handed safely down through the centuries. We have done all that can be done.'

He coughed again and spat. The behaviour was normal in a time that knew nothing of hygiene. Eleanor poked at the bloody sputum with her cane. She had no pity to spare for the man who had broken his health in her service.

'I thought...' The queen sounded petulant but her brain was alert enough to switch to Latin so that William could not follow. 'I thought you would be quicker, Moor. At times, your magic was so slow I feared that death would scythe down both you and me before our plan could reach fruition.'

'If I was slow, the fault is yours,' Yussef defended himself. 'By seeking to return in identical form, you trebled my work. You asked of me what no man has heretofore achieved. Not once in the three thousand years when the religion of the dead held sway in the land of the Nile is there mention of any physical resemblance with the past incarnation.'

There was nothing like argument to sharpen Eleanor's wits and bring a flush to her withered cheek. 'The pharaohs,' she countered, 'were a decadent and enfeebled species at the end of their line, while Henry and I founded a new and vigorous dynasty.'

She gestured at the nun standing by the doorway that led into the church. 'You've seen the effigy on his tomb, Moor. It doesn't do him justice.'

Eleanor smiled. Behind her rheumy eyes were images the Moor could not see. 'Now there was a man! Henry had a prick like a stallion. I bore him seven children.'

She cackled. 'If he hadn't been king, busy with the affairs of state from dawn to dusk each day, he'd have peopled half Europe with his bastards! Oh, yes, with that stallion's seed in my womb I know I have founded a dynasty so vital that one day the humours of my flesh will recur exactly in one of my descendants. In her body I shall live again.'

They sat in silence for several minutes before Eleanor roused herself. She looked at Yussef with piercing clear eyes. '*Vale, serve fidelis*,' she said softly. Farewell thou faithful servant!

'Stay!' Yussef half-rose. 'Before you quit this flesh, remember that you promised me reward.'

Eleanor looked at him with a hint of the smile that made Yussef wish he had known her younger. 'I promised you a bed of gold, so large that no part of you should touch the ground.'

'What would I do with gold?' Yussef studied the bright red blood on the gravel.

He was using a small nugget of yellow metal as a worry bead, rolling it between his fingers. 'From this small piece I can make all I need, Madam. In any case, like you I've little time to live. But I wish to die in a garden of orange and lemon trees, smelling the blossom and hearing the sound of my native tongue in my ears. The only reward I ask of you is safe conduct as far as the first Moslem kingdom across the Pyrenees. From there I'll make my own way south and ask for nothing more.'

'You may go,' said the queen. 'After I have left this flesh, I doubt a heathen wizard like you will find a patron in that half-witted son of mine who sits askew on England's throne with so grotesque a lack of the aplomb his father had.'

'I have one last favour to crave,' the Moor asked hurriedly. 'Give me William the Marshal as escort until I am safe in Moslem territory. He is an honourable man.'

Eleanor's mood changed again as abruptly as before. 'No, no,' she said irritably. 'I have decided to send Mercadier with you as escort. 'Tis all arranged.'

'I do not trust Mercadier,' said Yussef bluntly. 'He is an evil fellow, drunk or sober.'

'He carries out my orders,' said Eleanor. 'Have no fear.'

'Men fear the unknown,' Yussef corrected her. 'I did not say I fear him. But I'd be safer travelling alone than with such a brigand to keep me company.'

Eleanor's patience was gone. 'Choose. You can stay here coughing your lungs up for a few more months – or go with Mercadier. In either event, we shall not meet again.' To her there was no point in prolonging this life when the future lay so enticingly ahead of her.

Yussef kissed the huge ring on the queen's gloved hand. He knew that he would not die in a garden of lemons and oranges, yet he was a man at peace with himself, for he had solved the greatest problem a human brain had ever tackled. Eleanor's dispositions were complex. His own, more modest, hinged upon a single tile fired in the nun's cell which had served as his combined alchemist's den, scholar's library and workshop during the years he worked for her. That the tile had reached Granada safely, he knew from the Templar who had brought back his son's ring as a token for payment; Templars would do anything for a bag of alchemist's gold.

There was also the *sirventès* Yussef had given to Mercadier without Eleanor's knowledge, but he placed no great hope in the mercenary captain returning so nebulous a favour by letting him go free.

Without any false pride, Yussef knew that he had designed for Eleanor what would later have been called a programme of genius. If into it he had injected some viruses, he considered that his legitimate prerogative; he had long foreseen that the metal with which he was about to be paid was not the promised bed of warm yellow gold but a single piece of steel, both sharp and cold.

Chapter 6

Jay realised that she had achieved something by her resistance when momentary flashes of vision reached her from the eyes of the woman standing in the church. She saw first the stones of the column, then a sunlit window and the pious effigy on the tomb as Eleanor turned her head. She sensed the former queen's surprise at the alterations in the architecture since the twelfth century and the trenches dug by the archaeologists – a surprise swiftly overcome as Eleanor thought: Of course, there have been many changes...

There was an asthmatic wheeze and a groan as Eleanor heaved a deep draught of air into her lungs. Then came an orgasmic ripple of pleasure that spread through the whole body as she raised her face to the sunlight pouring in through a window and cried in Latin: '*Vivo atque senso!*' I live and feel again.

She raised her hands to explore her face, Jay's face: the lips, the nose, the eyes, the formation of the bones. Her fingers found no wrinkles. She lowered her hands to feel firm breasts and a flat belly. A once-familiar dull pain in the lower abdomen made her cry out with joy: 'I have the menses! I am young again!'

She felt Jay's will fighting for possession of her skin, her eyes, her hands. But Yussef's training had foreseen this. It was for this final confrontation that Jay had been progressively bled of her energy. With one last huge effort, Eleanor summoned all the vitality she had stolen from Jay and used it to shrug away into the void the mind which had inhabited the body that was to be hers.

Jay felt bruised and torn, as though the trillion synapses within the soft matter of her brain that made up her thoughts and feelings, her very identity and personality, had been squeezed between sharp claws, pried loose from her skull and thrust into the whirling, timeless limbo of space. It would have been so peaceful to let go and become nothing, but still she fought back.

As the form of the sunlit window receded to a dot of light in the blackness, she strained towards another pinpoint, which grew and resolved into a face. It was Merlin, sitting at the wheel of Leila's car, she laughing and saying: '...ghosts. I don't believe in them.' And Merlin, staring into the void so intensely that Jay was sure he could see her, saying: 'I've just remembered where I saw Jay before that day she came running along the tow-path...'

The anguish in his voice reached out to her.

'Merlin!' Jay cried as his face shrank to a dot and then disappeared completely. Despairingly she fought her way back to him. There was an untimeable moment when the combat with Eleanor's spirit was almost like an embrace, when Jay's mind picked up Eleanor's flash of pride that this descendant of hers was no spiritual weakling but a worthy opponent.

She understood in that second that Eleanor's thefts of energy were not a recent thing. They pre-dated Canterbury and even Chinon. They had been going on since the day Jay was born. As a child she had often awoken screaming in the night, to find her mother trying to calm her. It had always been the same nightmare, a creature immensely old and alien coming in the dark hours to crouch over the bed and suck something precious from her. But how could a terrified child put that into words when asked: 'What's wrong, darling?'

'You had another bad dream,' her mother would say. 'It's all right now, Jay. You can go back to sleep, I'm here. I'll leave the light on.'

The little girl had wanted to scream, 'It's not all right. It's all wrong!' But the anguished wisdom of the young told her that there was no way of explaining such things to a grown-up.

Now Jay knew how Eleanor had sustained herself throughout eight centuries. Like a spiritual vampire she had come in the night to suck not blood but their very life-force from her living victims, generation after generation.

The knowledge accounted for so many things. All her life, Jay had felt – she groped for images – not hollow exactly but... incomplete, that was the word! Except for once. Just once, she had been whole. When Merlin held her in his arms and together they wept at the beauty of rain-drops sparkling in the sunshine, she had been whole, made whole by him. Was that what true love was: the power to make someone whole, healed, healthy?

'Oh, Merlin!' she cried. 'Help me, Merlin.'

Eleanor took two experimental paces, one hand holding the column for support. The centuries she had spent in limbo were as seconds to her now. She wondered why was it so extraordinarily hard to co-ordinate the muscles of Jay's body. Of course, the answer was obvious! The body she remembered had been old and shrunken and bent, while Jay's was taller by several inches than Eleanor had been even in her prime. The difference in height made Eleanor feel as though she was toppling over. The soft-soled trainer shoes on her feet did not help; they seemed to give no purchase by which to steady herself. She thought of a stick to lean on and then forbade herself any such idea, forcing one foot and then the other to support her.

Patience, she cautioned herself. It was as the Moor had warned: there were the seeds of madness in this experience of feeling through another's skin, looking out through her eyes and hearing with her ears. Sensations once taken for granted were lacking; a million new ones kept hammering insistently at her consciousness, leading to nausea and dizziness.

Panic threatened as Eleanor felt Jay's chest muscles pumping air into her lungs. They were the expanded lungs of a flute-player, so filling them with oxygen made her more dizzy, not less. She forced herself to breathe shallowly until her vision cleared.

The body shivered. Why? I'm cold, she thought, that's all. She laughed. No need for fear – just take everything as it comes...

It took every ounce of Eleanor's will to fight the desire to relax control of a thousand rebellious muscles and simply collapse on the planking beneath her feet. Instead, clutching the hand-rail for support, she progressed several agonizing paces along the walkway into a patch of sunlight before stopping to work out what to do next. Here the sun was warm on her cheek.

What, she wondered, was the language people now spoke at Fontevraud? Was Latin still the international tongue among educated folk? But supposing she had come back to earth during another Dark Age, to find the world populated by brutish peasantry with no lingua franca, what then?

Beneath the walkway was her own effigy on the tomb, flanked by those of Richard and Henry. Ever vain, Eleanor was pleased that whoever made her death mask had been kind enough to smooth out the wrinkles in the face. She had been so proud of those long tapering fingers faithfully reproduced by the long-dead sculptor. She looked more closely at the hands of her new body. They were the same, but bare of rings.

She touched again her neck and hair. Nothing, not so much as an earring or a necklace. So, this unknown descendant of hers whose body she now inhabited had worn no jewellery with which to buy service in an emergency... That was a small problem she had not anticipated; in her other life she had never, from the cradle onwards, been without a bauble or two with which to bribe or buy service.

Eleanor felt in the pockets of the unfamiliar garments but found nothing of value as far as she could tell. So how, she wondered, would she find servants to look after her immediate needs? Suppose the Moor had not accomplished everything he promised?

In one pocket of the anorak Eleanor found a powder compact. She flicked the lid open to gaze at her reflection in the mirror for a long moment. The face in the glass was the exact match of the portrait Henry had commissioned on their wedding day. She smiled at herself, admiring the perfect teeth and the lips that the randy Count of Anjou had so lusted for. But Henry was long dead – an effigy in stone she could reach out and touch, if she chose – while she was alive. Nothing else mattered.

Another wave of nausea threatened to drag Eleanor down into the trench. She put away the compact, gripped the hand-rail more firmly and focused her eyes on one of the stained-glass windows above the altar. As her sense of balance returned, she smiled at the irony of falling off some scaffolding to injury or death in the very moment of re-birth.

'I have been looking everywhere for you.'

Eleanor turned at the sound of Kreuz's voice echoing along the nave. The language he spoke was unfamiliar, but the timbre of the voice was unmistakably Mercadier's. She stood in the pool of sunlight and sighed with relief at the sight of the man coming towards her.

I'll offer masses for your soul, Moor, she promised. You did your work well...

'Mercadier,' she said. '*Serve fidelis, adveni!*'

Kreuz halted in mid-stride at the sound of spoken Latin. It was not just the language but the tone in which Eleanor had spoken...

'Miss French?' he queried.

'*Adveni!*' Eleanor ordered again, holding out her right hand for him to kiss.

Kreuz walked slowly up to her. He ignored the outstretched hand, noting the way the woman in front of him held herself. There was something different about the eyes and the voice was more peremptory...

Eleanor recalled Yussef's words: '... an evil fellow, drunk or sober.' But this Mercadier walking into sunlight was thinner and had none of the low-browed cunning written so plainly on his ancestor's features. He looked an educated man to her, a priest perhaps? Suffice it that he resembled his ancestor enough for her to recognise him.

'*Alianor regina sum,*' she said slowly. Would he understand Latin, this descendant of Mercadier, or should she try Langue d'Oc? And what would she do, if he spoke neither tongue?

A huge excitement swelled in Kreuz's chest and a matching smile spread over his thin features. At the very moment for which he had planned so long, his Latin deserted him from sheer excitement. Then he flushed and stammered, '*Mater Ricardi regis atque sponsa Henrici es?*'

258

'*Et tu*,' Eleanor felt an immense relief, '*filius servi mei nomine Mercadier es.*'

Kreuz fell to his knees. The genuflexion was instinctive; it seemed natural to kneel in front of this woman and kiss the imperious hand. 'So, my queen,' he said in Latin. 'You have come back.'

The half-smile of satisfaction that had intrigued so many portraitists in paint and stone floated on Eleanor's face for an instant as she took stock of her situation. She was young and beautiful! She had a servant and a language in which to converse with him! Yussef could not have arranged a better beginning to her second span on earth...

'Are you to serve me in this life as your ancestor did before?' she asked.

A loud laugh escaped Kreuz's mouth, startling the queen. 'Where is your respect?' she chided him. 'I asked a question and you did not reply.'

Kreuz stood up and peals of laughter echoed round the church. He clutched the hand-rail for support and laughed until tears ran down his face. He was almost hysterical with a sense of his own power: all that he had planned over the years was going to be possible, once he had traded with Eleanor for the knowledge which she had.

He forced himself to calm down and wiped the tears from his eyes. 'We live in an age devoid of respect for greatness, Madam. You will see.'

'No respect for greatness?' Eleanor wondered. 'Then what do men worship now?'

'Possessions.'

'It was Eleanor's turn to be amused. 'Well, that was ever so, son-of-Mercadier – for thus I think of you: as fitz-Mercadier. In truth, man's nature does not change. The provisions I have made for my return depend on it. But what else is new?'

'Machines.'

'We had machines.'

'Outside,' he said, 'I have a machine that will transport you with the power of a hundred horses.'

Eleanor laughed at the idea of riding a hundred horses at one time. 'Surely one's enough? Even Henry Plantagenet never exhausted more than five or six mounts in a day and, God knows, he rode them hard. What are you, fitz-Mercadier? A soldier, like your forebear?'

'I am a scholar,' said Kreuz. 'And you must understand from the outset that I also have a great destiny to fulfil. We are equals, you and I. You need me as much as I need you.'

Some things will never change, thought Eleanor. Here I am, scarcely back from eternity, and already a servant is haggling with me over his reward...

'Speak on,' she ordered. 'Tell me, fitz-Mercadier, what's your price?'

Kreuz's hands were outstretched as though he would touch her but dared not. They hovered just short of her body. His cold blue eyes were wide and staring.

'The gold,' he stammered. 'I don't want any part of the treasure of Châlus.'

Eleanor laughed. 'From the mouth of a Mercadier, that surprises me.'

'Yet it's true.' He spoke eagerly. 'I'll help you recover the gold. All I want in return is knowledge.'

He told her where the treasure was hidden, which made Eleanor wary. Kreuz's hands were trembling. His lips were dry but spittle ran from one corner of his mouth down his chin. His usual coherence deserted him and made him stammer.

Dear God, Eleanor asked herself, have I survived death and re-birth, only to find myself at the mercy of a babbling madman? She turned at the sound of the party of diggers returning, talking loudly among themselves after a good lunch.

'Who are these people?' she asked haughtily. The effort of talking had tired her. 'And why are they digging up my church, fitz-Mercadier?'

'We must leave here,' said Kreuz, finding his voice at last.

'He took several deep breaths, forcing himself to calm down. 'Talk to no one,' he counselled her, 'and rely on me.'

He held out an arm, to lead her outside. Eleanor did not take it. The smile on her face was replaced by an expression of sheer terror. She stood unable to move, clutching the railing with a hand that trembled visibly. The muscles of the body that had given her such exquisite pleasure so shortly before now refused the brain's commands. She felt herself falling and could do nothing about it.

'Oh, fitz-Mercadier,' she said in a voice that betrayed her fear, 'I cannot move hand or foot!'

Chapter 7

No way, Merlin told himself. Except her instruments, that car is Jay's proudest possession. She'd never leave it unlocked in a strange town, with the keys in the ignition...

He sat brooding at a café table, his fingers toying with her bunch of keys as he watched the rain slant down on the cobbles of Fontevraud's market square in which the gleaming red Alpine looked forlornly out of place. A few yards away, Leila's ancient deux-chevaux crouched sheepishly at the next parking meter.

Her tour of the town's few hotels had been as fruitless as Merlin's search of the abbey, where the only suggestion that Jay had been there was a prickling of the hairs on the back of his neck when he stood by Eleanor's tomb, like an echo of what he had felt in Chartres cathedral. That something had happened to Jay right there, Merlin was certain.

A group of young people in anoraks were playing billiards and using the juke-box. Leila returned from the loo with one of them in tow: a plain-faced, bespectacled girl of about twenty.

'This is Elise,' she announced. 'She's an archaeology student, working on the dig in the abbey church.'

Merlin waited.

'Tell the man what you saw,' Leila prompted.

'En anglais ou en français?'

'In English, if you can. He doesn't speak much French.'

'Well...' Elise hesitated, then the words came out in a rush. 'It is just after the lunch-break – is that how you say?'

She got a nod from Leila and continued. 'There is this lady...'

She laughed. 'Not a lady. I mean she is a girl not so much older than I. She is in the church with a gentleman.'

'What colour was her hair?' Merlin glanced at his watch. Five hours had elapsed since the time the girl was talking about.

'Blonde,' said Elise. 'She is standing in a place of sunlight, yes? And she has long blond hair.'

'Dis à mon copain ce qui est arrivé,' prompted Leila.

'Eh bien...'

'In English,' said Merlin.

'So... well, the blonde lady, she falls.'

'Was she hurt?'

'No, the gentleman with her... he helps her to stand. He calls down to us in the trench that she er... *comment dit-on qu'elle s'évanouit?'*

'She's fainting,' translated Leila.

'Thank you. So I and another girl... we climb up to help her, while the gentleman goes to get some friends.'

'What kind of friends?' asked Merlin.

'Le monsieur est allemand... He is German and he comes back with two other German peoples – a man and a woman. They help the lady who is fainting. They have to carry her because she cannot walk.'

That explained the car being abandoned, thought Merlin. 'During the time you were alone with her, did she say anything, the blonde lady?'

'No.'

'You're sure of that?'

A shake of the head. 'She look very ill, I think. She don't talk to us but...'

The girl gave up and relapsed into a torrent of French.

'What was all that?' Merlin asked.

Leila looked from him to the girl and back. 'Well,' she hesitated, 'Elise says that she did hear Jay talking with the *monsieur allemand*, i.e. Kreuz.'

'What were they saying? Can she remember?'

Leila shook her head. 'Elise says they were talking... she's a bit confused about this...'

'About what?' Merlin's linguistic frustration caused him to raise his voice.

'Calm down,' Leila counselled. 'If you start shouting, you'll frighten the girl.'

And to Elise she said, 'Go on, tell my friend what you told me. Take your time.'

Elise played with her spectacles nervously. 'It sound so stupid, but you see, I am taking Classical studies for my *baccalauréat...*'

'And?' Merlin kept his voice calm.

'Well, this lady and gentleman... You know, I'm sure they are talking in Latin.' The girl looked from Leila to Merlin. She shrugged, 'I could be wrong. Maybe they are speaking Italian or Portuguese. Is possible...'

'Did you catch what they said?' Leila asked.

The girl shook her head. 'No. I was so surprised to hear Latin and they talk so fast, not like at school when we...'

'Okay,' Merlin cut in. 'You've been a great help.'

He took a hundred-franc note from his wallet and pressed it into the girl's hand.

'Are you a detective?' she asked.

'No.' Merlin had often been asked. 'The blonde lady is a friend, that's all.'

Elise looked excited. She handed the note back and turned to Leila, to ask her in French: 'He is her lover, is he not?'

'Yes.'

The plain round face behind the glasses lit up with a surprising, radiant beauty.

'How beautiful!' sighed the girl. 'He is pursuing his true love who has been stolen by the *monsieur allemand* – just like a knight of old would have done. It is so romantic!'

Eleanor lay face-down on a solid oak table. Cushioned by a layer of furs, it made a good massage bench.

There had been a moment when her spirit almost failed as Kreuz's bodyguard and his blonde companion carried her out of the church, unable to move a muscle to help herself. Fortunately Kreuz had foreseen the possibility and brought along his personal masseuse from the Valley of Songs. The girl knew her job; as her skilled fingers probed and dug and control of the paralysed muscles was restored, the fear which Eleanor had felt in the church began to ebb: the awful fear that for whatever reason this flesh would refuse the commands of her spirit.

As a queen, she had been used to female servants dressing and undressing her, but it was strange to have a man watching her naked. Twice she had told Kreuz to leave her presence but he had refused, saying that he had much to tell her which could not wait.

'After all, I am a doctor,' he had said.

The joke was lost on Eleanor; to her the word had only its Latin meaning: a learned person. Otherwise Kreuz's usage of the Roman tongue was stilted and mannered but they could understand each other well enough.

Eleanor flexed her fingers, enjoying the feel of suppleness in Jay's bones and joints. She listened to fitz-Mercadier's babbling. What was he saying now? Oh yes, this plan of his he wanted to tell her about...

'The age in which I live was not ripe for our magnificent dream. *Imperium mil annorum*, we called it: the Thousand-Year Reich! We wanted to build a society of excellence that should have lasted a millennium and changed the course of mankind's evolution.'

'So what went wrong?' she asked, to humour him.

'We lost a war…'

'And that's new?' Eleanor mocked him. 'It was ever thus with great designs, o fitz-Mercadier. You lose a war, you bide your time, you make new alliances, you start again.

'This was total war,' Kreuz argued. 'A hundred million died. We were defeated not by men of valour but by base people and their machines. It was the cult of the common man that foiled us.'

'And has the common man machines like the one in which you brought me here?' she wondered.

He laughed at her ignorance. 'Wars are now fought with engines that are many thousand times more powerful than my auto-mobile. We have flying-machines that drop fire-engines capable of destroying whole cities like that.' He snapped his fingers.

'Truly?' Eleanor toyed with the thought. Total war was an interesting concept. Richard would have liked to be alive in this new age, she thought. Given these wonderful engines of war, he would have conquered the world – or destroyed it in the process.

Oh, Richard! She closed her eyes and could picture him still with a pain that was a fresh as the day he died in the hovel below Châlus Castle.

Most beautiful of men! she said to his image. Would that I had sought out the Moor while you yet lived, to weave his spells and bend his wisdom in both our service so that we could have come back to life together…

They had shared so many wonderful times. She had taught her favourite son music and poetry and he had rewarded her adoration by excelling the troubadours at both arts. In return he had taught her the rudiments of manly skills, taking her hawking and teaching her to hold a sword and use a long-bow and shoot one of the new-fangled crossbows, like the one that had taken his life. He had once halted the fall of a besieged castle simply to bring Eleanor there so that she could share his boyish glee as Mercadier's siege-engine demolished the outer wall and brought a tower tumbling down in a confusion of stone and broken bodies.

Kreuz was striding around the chamber, gesticulating as he spoke. 'Now machines and baseness rule men's lives. All that is mean and ugly is lifted up. The lowest is exalted and all the excellence of mankind is devalued. Thus our great dream of a new society will not now be achieved even in my extended lifetime. It will be centuries before the time is ripe again. And when that time comes, we must not make the same errors. The knowledge I have accumulated from my study of Greece and Rome and Egypt must be available for the new Leader –' he used *dux imperatorque* to translate Führer ' – when our time comes again.'

264

Eleanor tried to follow his meaning. 'Who is this new leader?' she asked, flexing an arm. The blonde masseuse gave a professional smile and started working on her other side.

'He's not yet born,' said Kreuz, 'and may not be for centuries to come.' Even to Eleanor he was unwilling to reveal his ultimate ambition.

'You talk in mysteries, fitz-Mercadier,' yawned Eleanor. 'You say you're a scholar. If so, then write a book which this unborn Messiah can read. Isn't that what scholars do?'

'Books get lost,' said Kreuz, 'and messages fail to be understood. How many clues did you leave, o Queen? Of those only a handful survived the passage of eight centuries. No, no, no! I must return to earth in person – as you have done – in the body of a descendant. You were right; it is the only certain way.'

He waved an arm around the quarters he had prepared for her. 'So, this is the bargain I propose: everything you need, I have prepared for you. In return, you must tell me all that you learned from your servant Yussef the Moor, so that I can do as you have.'

He's clever or mad, thought Eleanor warily – perhaps both. To distract Kreuz, as the masseuse moved her onto her back, she parted her legs slightly.

'I had many children,' said the queen. She saw Kreuz's eyes fasten hungrily on her breasts and pubic hair. 'When I died, I knew that among the dynasties they founded I should find a suitable body in which to be re-born.'

Kreuz sniggered as the masseuse spread a towel over Eleanor's loins. 'For the last ten years,' he said slyly, 'ever since I was certain what you and the Moor had planned, I have begotten four children every twelve-month. They are raised in my homeland until the age of five and then adopted by rich and powerful families all over the world. Since I intend to live for at least another three decades and shall continue to procreate at the same rate, my available pool of descendants will be many times greater than yours.'

He came close to the table. 'Now, if one of them were to be your seed mingled with mine...'

Kreuz licked his lips and ran a trembling hand over Eleanor's firm breasts. 'If we were to beget a child, now that would be a union of genes to make the world tremble!'

The arrogance of the man! thought Eleanor. She would have slapped him if her muscles were under her control. Instead she closed her eyes, wishing he would leave her alone. When I take a lover, she promised her new body, he'll be of noble lineage, not some crazed descendant of a mercenary captain...

But for the moment she needed Kreuz. She had to admit that the provi-

265

sions he had made were excellent. Apart from the modern clothes which she had to get used to wearing, he had equipped this refuge to which she had been brought exclusively with replica furniture and artifacts of the twelfth century. It was a place where she could feel at ease and gather her strength, where none of the startling sights she had seen on the journey from Fontevraud could intrude and disturb until she was ready to handle them.

From the pine-resin torches on the stone walls that provided the only lighting, to the crude oaken furniture and the huge log fire in the open fireplace, everything was familiar to her. The dishes off which she had been fed could have come from her own apartments in the Boissy tower at Chinon. The food prepared by Kreuz himself had been exactly what she would have eaten eight hundred years before.

Yes, she had to humour him, but also to put him off his guard by pretending that the adjustment to her new body was more difficult than it really was, thus feeding his sense of power over her. Once she had complete control over Jay's reluctant nerves and muscles, she planned to act fast to recover the gold and then master whatever language was necessary. At that point her need of the man she called fitz-Mercadier would be over and she could get rid of him without a qualm. Eleanor had no intention of becoming Kreuz's prisoner as once she had been Henry's.

'You don't know what you're talking about,' she said coldly. 'You cannot understand the will-power it took for my determination not to weaken during the long wait in limbo. You, fitz-Mercadier, could never do what I have done. Perhaps no one else ever will.'

Kreuz disagreed. 'It is you who do not understand. There is so much to explain. Because history is written by the winners, this modern world misunderstands what my leaders sought to achieve. Today the SS is judged by a few isolated incidents – our excesses and our failures – but to give us the proper historical perspective, you must see our organisation very much as the medieval church.'

Eleanor yawned again.

'In 1930,' Kreuz continued, 'Germany was in as much chaos and flux as Europe in your day. I joined the SS in the same way as an ambitious and intelligent young man went into the church in, say, the fourteenth century. It was a ladder which I could climb to reach the top rung of society without any great initial advantage of birth or acquired wealth. To those like me, the wilder excesses of National Socialism were irrelevant. We never talked of Jews and Final Solutions, any more than Henry's Becket or King Louis' confessor Suger bothered their heads with the doctrine of the Immaculate Conception...'

With help, Eleanor sat upright. The masseuse slipped over her head a cotton nightdress from Jay's luggage, which they had removed from the Alpine before leaving Fontevraud.

A new feeling stole over Eleanor as the girl helped her to stand: there was a softening of the spasmed muscles. She yawned again and stopped listening to Kreuz, concentrating on identifying the sensation. It was drowsiness, pure and simple.

'I'm tired, fitz-Mercadier,' she closed her eyes.

'But I have so much to say…'

Eleanor stretched like a cat in the sunshine, revelling in the thousand sensations of the flesh.

'Then talk to yourself,' she said. 'For me, it's been a damned long day.'

Chapter 8

Merlin drove Jay's car to the local Renault garage where the owner agreed to store it until called for. There was no particular point in the exercise, but he felt better performing that small task than sitting, watching the rain.

On the way back to the café where Leila was waiting, he stopped to buy a large-scale map of the area. A few parking spaces away from her old *deux-chevaux* he noticed a new Renault 25 but paid it no particular attention. The two men sitting in it looked like a pair of sales reps waiting to make a call.

'It's one thing,' argued Salem, 'to come here and claim what is ours by right. But this shadowing of people, this changing of clothes and cars – it all smacks of dishonesty. Why is it necessary, my brother?'

'That girl we interviewed – the archaeology student,' said Kassim. 'She would have gone screaming to the police if I had not flashed my fake *Rensiegnements Généraux* card. You have to look the part. For that, the right car and clothes are vital. Now, thanks to her, we know as much as the American does. We know that the German from the Valley of Songs was here – and still is somewhere around, with the blonde woman. All we have to do is sit tight and follow the Yankee when he moves.'

Unhappily, Salem cleaned a hole in the condensation on the window and watched in the wing mirror as Merlin greeted Leila in the café. It was almost dusk. As the lights came on above the façade of the café, he gasped.

'What is it?' asked Kassim.

'The name of that café. Can you see, my brother? It is called Café Alianor. You remember what Yussef El-Kebir wrote on the tile? "Then shall arise my sons to wrest from the brood of Ali Anor what was my due"…?'

He was talking to an empty seat. Kassim was out of the car and walking across the square. He ordered a coffee at the bar, keeping his back to

Merlin and Leila but watching them in a Coco-Cola mirror by the cash register as he chatted to the North African boy serving behind the counter. Merlin was poring over the map which he had spread across the table.

Leila lit herself another cigarette and one for him. 'You know,' she said, 'we could just be like anyone else and go to the police. Or is that too obvious?'

Merlin took the cigarette and inhaled deeply. 'To tell them what exactly?'

'That Kreuz has kidnapped Jay.' Leila saw the anguish in his eyes.

'No proof,' he grunted sceptically. 'You know what happens if you report to the police that an adult has gone missing? One way or another, they tell you to mind your own business unless there's proof of foul play. On the face of it, Jay went with Kreuz of her own free will. We can't prove otherwise, so why should the police intervene – even if they knew where to look?'

'But she wasn't herself,' Leila tried. 'I saw her yesterday. She was under the influence...'

'... of a woman who died eight hundred years ago!' he finished. 'Great story, isn't it? Try telling that to the cops. Next thing you know, you'll be in an ambulance, with a nice guy in a white coat giving you an injection.'

'So what are you looking for on that map?'

'Inspiration, I suppose.'

'Can I help?'

'You could if I knew what I was looking for.'

Leila was baffled. 'If you don't know what you're looking for, what are you looking for?'

He stubbed out the half-smoked cigarette. 'Is that what they call feminine logic?'

'Perhaps.' Leila stood up. 'So's this. It's dinner time. We're both worried about Jay, but there's nothing we can do right now and I'm hungry. There's a hotel across the way. So let's check in for the night, eat and get some sleep.'

Merlin finished his meal and left Leila downstairs in the hotel bar in the company of the two polite businessmen who had been dining at the next table.

He wanted to be alone in order to think. It did cross his mind that the couple to whom Leila was happily chatting were undercover cops of some kind. They had a lot of questions and fitted exactly the universal two-man police team of Mr Nice and Mr Nasty: the older man with the sad eyes was softly spoken and friendly enough while the younger one was a mean little bastard, by the look of him.

269

It didn't matter what they were, Merlin decided, because neither he nor Leila had anything to hide from the authorities. Upstairs in his room, he dismissed them from his mind and took a piece of hotel stationery to start making notes, more as a way of ordering his thoughts than because they meant anything.

Jay, Jay, Jay, he wrote.

That magic morning in St Denis he had felt that their souls were one. But a couple of days later all the magic was gone. As soon as Kreuz fixed his crazy blue eyes on Jay, something had changed inside her. Did he have some hypnotic power over her?

Merlin had heard the rumours about the SS involvement in black magic, astrology, necromancy but never come across any hard evidence. So stick to the facts, he told himself.

He laughed ironically at the idea. Facts? There weren't any. Or were there? Write the headings down, Freeman, one by one – like you were trained. See where that gets you...

Chapel, he wrote. The visit to the chapel lost in the woods somewhere between St Denis and Fontevraud, irked Merlin still.

Why had Kreuz taken him and Jay there and shown them over the place so proudly? Correction, he hadn't shown them over all of it. The building was quite large and they had seen only a small part: the little chapel itself. What was the rest used for? Was it a...

Safe house? And if so, had Kreuz taken Jay there or...

Kidnapped her? Under normal circumstances, Jay would never have left her precious car unlocked in a strange town. Had she gone with Kreuz because she was ill or under duress?

Elise. She had said that the woman she had seen in the abbey church was ill. But against that Elise had also said that she had been talking with Kreuz in Latin. Why? For privacy Jay could have used English or old Langue d'Oc, so why choose Latin? As far as Merlin knew, it was Jay's least fluent language. A dead end, unless...

Is she mad? Was it possible that the whole tangle of events was due to some emotional disturbance in Jay, maybe connected with the childhood hypnosis sessions?

A mental breakdown? No, there were too many coincidences and certainly the *sirventès* were genuine. Jay could neither have written them nor known about them in advance. She could not have found her own way to Dürnstein and the second poem or met up with Kreuz without Merlin's help.

Experiences at: Chinon Castle, Canterbury Cathedral, Bordeaux Cathedral, Chartres Cathedral, Fontevraud Abbey, Old Sarum and Oakham Castle.

Every one of Jay's inexplicable experiences had happened at a place

270

with which Eleanor had had powerful connections. That could not be coincidence. It added up to...

Possession!

Leila had first voiced the possibility. However hard Merlin tried to find another explanation, it was the only one that accounted for everything that had happened so far, but why should it be happening to Jay?

Rejection.

Jay had rejected him in favour of Kreuz in Granada – but Merlin had to admit that he had set himself up for it.

Help me!

It was true that Jay had never once asked for Merlin's help in as many words, but sitting in the car outside the truck-stop restaurant with Leila, he could have sworn that Jay was in the car with them, whispering: *'Help me!'*

There was a scratching outside as though a bird had flown against the bedroom window, attracted by the light. Merlin opened it and let out some of the fug. Above the noise of the rain and the gurgling of gutters and down-pipes he thought he heard a seagull cry. How far was Fontevraud from the coast? He wondered. Perhaps the bird had been blown inland on the gale? He closed the window again and looked at the last heading he had scribbled.

Treasure. Why hidden and where?

Somehow this had to connect, Merlin thought.

'Oh my God!' he drew a double-ended arrow linking Possession! and Treasure.

Everything made sense: if Eleanor's spirit was possessing Jay, then... the treasure of Châlus was her bank account – the financial provision she had made for just this eventuality.

That explained the why. As to where... Wherever it was, might be the last place he had a chance of catching up with Jay.

Merlin lit a fresh cigarette. The likelihood was – from what he had learned of Eleanor – that she would have stashed away the treasure somewhere convenient to Fontevraud, somewhere she could swiftly get her hands on it after her return to earth...

He opened the map, smoothed it out on the bed and marked the position of the abbey with a felt pen. The treasure was last recorded at Châlus Castle, so he marked that with a second cross. Somewhere between the two marks lay a fortune in gold.

From Châlus, Merlin reasoned, Eleanor had departed on a route leading north-west to either Fontevraud or Chinon. He marked Chinon. Ah! It didn't much matter which had been Eleanor's destination, for they were only a few miles apart, so the route from Châlus was the same for a large part of the way.

271

With Mercadier and his greedy mercenaries tearing Châlus to pieces, it was unlikely that Eleanor would have left it in situ or reburied it there. So, she had taken it with her...

Merlin ignored the straighter new roads on the map and traced in red the queen's probable route along twisting old back-roads through villages with ancient names like Beaulieu and Champagnac. It was twelve kilometres or eight miles from Châlus to Oradour-sur-Vayre, where legend had it the treasure was buried. Merlin ringed the name. Had Oradour been the first night's stopping place? Not much distance to have covered in one day, he thought. Even on horseback, surely it should have been twice as far? But Eleanor's baggage-train had included a waggon of some kind carrying the king's coffin, which would have slowed the pace considerably.

Outside the bedroom window, the spring rains slanted down on the roofs of Fontevraud. Merlin guessed that it had probably been raining in March 1199 also. From his own experience in Vietnam, he knew what it was like manhandling primitive transport along unmetalled roads during heavy rain. That one heavy waggon would have cut down Queen Eleanor's speed to a few kilometres a day...

He turned back to the map. If Oradour-sur-Vayre had been the first night's stopping-place, Eleanor might have secreted the gold there, but it was simply too close to Châlus for someone as wily as the old queen. She had too much nerve to panic and dig a hole for the gold at the first possible place, with Mercadier doubtless riding close on her heels. More likely she had ridden on a short way ahead, leaving the coffin to follow in the care of a trusted servant while she prospected a better hiding place.

Merlin rifled through the pages of the much-thumbed book he had bought in New York. William the Marshal, that was the guy! He had served Henry and Richard and finally Eleanor as loyal retainer. The knight Henry had called 'the only honest man in France' had been with Eleanor at Châlus.

Merlin put down the book.

What had Leila said, to explain his instinctive apathy for Kreuz? 'Perhaps the three of you knew each other in another life?' If she was right... at Châlus, after Richard's death, the three principal actors had been Eleanor, Mercadier and William. So, if Kreuz was Mercadier's descendant and Jay descended from Eleanor, then Merlin Freeman was a son of a son of a son of William the Marshal!

He read again the chapter about Eleanor's incarceration in Salisbury Tower. William had been appointed constable of the tower for several years. A man in his prime years, it was likely he would have founded a family there, one of whom – a yeoman farmer perhaps – could later have become known as Freeman, the progenitor of a line that emigrated to America. So, like everything else, it was possible. The more Merlin thought about it, the harder it was to account for the part he had so far played in any other way.

On the map he drew in the probable line of the second day's travel for the coffin and marked the end with a question mark. There was no town or village where the royal party could have spent the night, but there was a place-name: Chassenon. Beside it were three dots.

He consulted the key to the symbols used on the map. Three dots signified a ruin. Merlin's pulse quickened. Was this a twelfth-century castle, another safe house where Kreuz had maybe taken Jay? No, slow down, Freeman. One step at a time.

Back to Michelin.

He found Chassenon in the index, to learn that the ruins were a Celtic temple complex and a Roman baths. The modern road running past was built over the east-west Roman highway known as the Via Agrippa that had led all the way from Lyons in the Rhône Valley to Saintes on the Atlantic coast. At Chassenon, he read, excavations had uncovered Roman baths and twenty or more underground chambers, cisterns and reservoirs.

Merlin closed the guide book. Everything fitted. A woman of Eleanor's intelligence would have chosen to hide the treasure near or in a landmark that would survive the centuries, to ensure she could locate it when she returned. But she would not have picked a castle, for she knew all too well that fortresses were built one year and mostly razed to the ground a decade or two later. Even Richard's supposedly impregnable castle at Château Gaillard had been totally destroyed by the French king a few years after the Lionheart's death. However, a deserted ruin in which nobody was interested in medieval times... that was something else! For someone as crafty as Eleanor, a Roman ruin made a much more likely hiding place.

Merlin lay back on the bed and lit his last cigarette.

If it was as easy as that, why had the SS Division Das Reich not found the treasure when they scoured the area in 1944?

Merlin went back to Michelin once again, to find that the excavations at Chassenon had only started in 1958. He let out a loud sigh as everything clicked into place: on 10 June 1944 when the Panzers of SS Das Reich had roared past Chassenon on the way to Oradour-sur-Glane, the ruins had been just a series of grass-covered mounds in a field.

Quod erat demonstrandum! he wrote.

He opened the window and stood for several minutes, his mind blank, breathing clean air. The rain had stopped and the night sky was washed clear of dust. The moon had set and the stars were bright, hard pinpoints of light in the pure black void. Again he thought he heard a seagull cry very faintly in the distance.

He closed the window and put out the light. His last thought before falling asleep was: *Help me, Jay! Help me to help you!*

Chapter 9

William the Marshal started awake as his mount whinnied, smelling other horses nearby. He had been dozing in the saddle for miles, letting the animal pick its own way between the potholes – of which there were many. The Via Agrippa had not been mended since the Romans left a thousand years before and the disrepair was made worse by the local peasants' custom of treating the ancient carriageway as a quarry for building material.

In the moonlight he saw, a stone's throw to the south, the ruins of the Roman baths, still rising five and six metres high in places. There were the best part of fifty men-at-arms camped there, clearly divided into two parties. Mercadier's men, lifelong campaigners, were sleeping in waggons and makeshift tents while those in the queen's retinue were huddled in ones and twos, wrapped in their damp and muddy travelling cloaks, wherever the ruins offered shelter from the weather. They lay beneath Roman arches and on stone benches below mouldering frescoes that told of a more gracious age.

William dismounted stiffly and handed the reins to a drowsy retainer. The queen, he learned, had made her quarters in the *caldarium* or hot room of the baths. It was the largest and most solid part of the complex still more or less intact. The gaping arch at one end had been closed with a sheet of coarse cloth that flapped and cracked in the wind, like the main-sail of a vessel in irons. The Marshal drew the cloth aside and walked in. Two torches jammed into cracks in the masonry cast an uneven, flickering light over frescoes of a hunting scene. Showing in places through the layers of cow dung on the floor, was a delicately inlaid mosaic of the four seasons. The current season, spring, was depicted as a cherub with pouting cheeks blowing puff-ball clouds across the sky obscured by the queen's cloak.

Eleanor was on her knees, praying beside the late king's chaplain at the foot of the waggon on which lay Richard's coffin. Her eyes took in

William's arrival without pausing in the litany. With a nod, she bid him refresh himself from the wine and meat laid out on a folding travelling table.

The sentry outside the queen's quarters edged closer to the billowing curtain, the better to listen to the murmur of praying within. His hopes of gleaning any news to sell to Mercadier were dashed by the noisy arrival of a hard-riding cavalcade. The outer sentries challenged the new arrivals and were brushed aside. As they rode into the small lit area in the centre of the encampment, the first rider dismounted revealed herself to be a woman – a woman in a temper.

Eleanor's sentry was prudent enough not to attempt to bar her way; the Princess Joanna was notorious for sharing her mother's temperament. She strode past him and confronted the kneeling queen inside. Their first words were lost to the sentry's ears as William the Marshal came out, a chicken carcase in his hand.

He adjusted the curtain and ordered the man curtly, 'Be off with you and get some sleep.'

'But I've another hour of duty.'

'You've been relieved,' said the knight.

William watched the man rejoin a group of his comrades trying to get comfortable in their sodden clothes around a smoky fire that refused to give much heat. The rain had eased off and clouds scudded through the night sky. Mercadier, who seemed never to sleep, appeared from nowhere and squatted beside the sentry who had been relieved, plying him with questions and keeping a wary eye on his rival, William.

Behind the canvas, both women's voices were raised in anger. William listened and thought: What passion! Passion was the first word that came to mind when thinking of Eleanor and her children. They were always either loving each other excessively or fighting each other – sometimes to the death.

He shifted his position. As an old campaigner, he knew better than to lie or even stand still while soaked to the skin. He stamped his feet and blew into his cupped hands, hoping for fine weather on the morrow; there were streams a-plenty to ford on the route to Fontevraud where Richard's funeral was to take place. The queen was insisting on travelling at the speed of the waggon which bore the king's coffin, despite William's argument in favour of speed. She knew as well as he that in the days after a king's death, any kingdom was at risk; the sooner they got Richard's testament back to Fontevraud, or better still, within the walls of Chinon Castle, the safer the realm would be. But would she listen? Not Eleanor. The most she had conceded was to send William ahead to summon reinforcements from Chinon which should arrive before day-break.

He sighed with fatigue. When this was all over and the king laid to rest at Fontevraud, he decided that he would ask Eleanor's permission to leave her service and return to his wife and family, still living on the other side of the Channel in Salisbury. There life was, if not safe, at least calm by comparison with the perpetual turmoil of the Plantagenet court.

Inside the *caldarium*, mother and daughter railed at each other like a pair of fish-wives. William shut his ears and stamped up and down to get warm. What was it about the Plantagenets, he wondered, that made them fight all the time and band together only when some outsider offered himself as prey to their violent natures? Henry II had been a grandson of William the Conqueror, with all the arrogant love of power that was the hall-mark of a true Norman, descended from the Vikings. But he had been a statesman and a lawgiver too, talents which Richard had not inherited.

In the coffin, thought William, lay a man ruined by his mother. Brave, skilled in all the arts of war, but greedy... oh, so insatiably greedy. As king, Richard had only ever visited his domains north of the Channel twice but yet had managed to bleed the once-rich realm of England almost dry of taxable wealth. And now his plunder was all gone, squandered on ill-advised campaigns, a failed Crusade, and lastly his inflated ransom, half of which was still unpaid. Hostages or their substitutes still languished in Austria and would forever, as far as William could see; there was no possibility of all the money being paid – which was their only hope of release. It was, he reflected, a tragedy for the realm that Richard had ever been ransomed.

But Eleanor...

Despite his weariness, the sound of her voice brought a smile to William's face. One minute she was cajoling and persuading Joanna, the next attacking her with a stream of accusations and abuse that would have crushed any other opponent flat.

Yes, Eleanor was of them all the greatest, the one who commanded by sheer stature the service which the others had to claim by virtue of their rank. This woman who had presided over the Courts of Love, where poetry and music held sway, had infatuated William with her beauty on the first day he set eyes on her. And he had been true to her, in the sense of courtly fidelity, even throughout the years when Henry's savage sense of irony had made him her captor. The feat of youthful valour which had won young William his spurs had been only the first offering on the altar of his love for Eleanor. He would have laid down his life on a command from the queen without a single regret. That she had tested his loyalty and tarnished his affection over the years he forgave her willingly, for what idol could be worshipped as close as he had been to her without the worshipper seeing from time to time the base metal that lay beneath the gilding?

277

There was a smile on William's face as he listened to the queen's voice now.

'We are in vigil, daughter mine. I remind you of that.'

'I need no reminding that Richard's dead.' Joanna, taller than her aging mother, glared across the crudely fashioned coffin in which lay the king's body.

In the faint, flickering light, the two women faced each other warily like a pair of gladiators each seeking an opening in the other's defences. Their bodies were hidden in voluminous mud-spattered travelling clothes of dull-coloured fustian which merged with the gloom and their faces were framed by wimples so that they appeared to float in mid-air. In the shadows the late king's chaplain, Milo, was praying at his improvised altar, doing his best to ignore the women. Two huge elk hounds stood guard at Eleanor's feet, snarling at Joanna when she raised her voice.

The first of Richard's siblings to reach Châlus, she had been furious to learn from Mercadier's rear-guard that Pierre Basile had been killed. Her own search of the castle and surrounding lands had confirmed what she was told: that, if treasure there had been, it was gone. Joanna had then departed in furious pursuit of Eleanor's retinue, reported to be heading northwards with a heavily laden waggon.

She accused the queen now of stealing and spiriting away the gold which should by rights be hers: 'For I'm the only woman that Richard ever loved,' she shouted.

The arrogant voice echoed off the ancient brickwork and peeling frescoes of the vault: loved, loved, loved...

'He never loved you,' she screamed at the queen. 'You nagged him and bribed him and manipulated him from the day he could talk, but Richard never loved you. He told me so.'

'You're an unnatural creature,' Eleanor hurled back at her daughter. 'What the two of you did, when you enticed him to your bed, is forbidden by the Church. D'you know the name for women who lie with their brothers?'

The priest crossed himself and kept his eyes closed. His lips moved in prayer. The two huge dogs slunk away into the shadows, whining.

'And what did he lie with after me?' sneered Princess Joanna.

'With pretty, red-lipped, rosy-cheeked boys, that's what!' She came close to the kneeling priest and thrust her belly at his startled face in a crude pantomime of fellatio.

'I recall that when you took Berengaria to Cyprus, your ship stopped in Sicily to re-provision and I met that poor bewildered princess you were dragging to my brother's bed. She was terrified – not for herself, but that he wouldn't be able to get it up! And he never could, could he,

278

poor Richard? It's thanks to you that I was the only female with whom he could be a man.'

'I beg you, Madam,' the priest remonstrated. 'This is the house of God. We are in presence of the Host...'

'Still your tongue, Chaplain!' snapped Joanna.

'No, you still your harlot's tongue!' Eleanor's eyes flashed in anger.

'Keep praying,' she ordered the priest. And to Joanna: 'I at least am in mourning. I was the late king's mother, after all.'

Joanna laughed scathingly. 'What kind of mother were you? As children we never saw you for years on end, until you wanted something – to marry me to an old man with the pox, to persuade Geoffrey and Richard to take arms against John and their father – or John and Richard to attack Geoffrey, whichever it was. Mother? You don't know what the word means.'

'Well, you soon will.' Eleanor lowered her voice. There was a sly smile on her face. 'Your belly's getting bigger by the day. And where will you find a father for this bastard, tell me that?'

'In there.' Joanna tapped the coffin between them.

Eleanor was warily silent as her daughter came round the ox-cart chassis on which the coffin lay. She knelt on the beast-fouled earth floor, her dress stained with the dung, to look into the queen's face close-up, clutching her hands in a mockery of supplication.

She's clever, thought the queen, this daughter of mine...

'And if I tell the world that it was Richard's seed,' Joanna hissed, 'what would you say to that, o mother mine? For there's enough that know it could be true. And he, poor sodomite, cannot deny it now. My brother, the king, is dead. Do you hear me, Mother? Your favourite's dead.'

She taunted the old woman again: 'Richard's dead and I'm alive. If John gets the throne, I want the gold. That's fair. One way or another, the gold I'll have.'

'You are an ingrate,' said Eleanor wearily. 'If it weren't for my diplomacy – my bullying the Pope himself on your behalf – you would at this moment be rotting in one of your ex-husband's dungeons on Sicily while he rutted with his new bride above your head. The least you can do is leave me in peace with my son's body.'

Joanna's gaze fell on the coffin.

'Is it the body you want to be close to?' she asked quietly. 'Or is it whatever else is in here?'

She pushed aside the kneeling priest who lost his balance and fell into the mire. He watched scandalised as Joanna grabbed the crucifix in front of which he had been praying. Using it as a lever, she defied his protests and forced the cover off the box – to find herself staring not at a pile of

279

gold but at Richard's bloated, stinking, discoloured corpse.

Eleanor said nothing. She put out an arm to hold back the priest. 'Leave the demented witch alone, Milo,' she said coldly. 'If she holds that cross long enough, it'll burn her sacrilegious hands off.'

Joanna prowled around the coffin, like a cat after a mouse. As a last gesture, watched by the priest and her silent mother, she lifted the dead king's arms and legs, one by one, to make sure Eleanor had not hidden anything among the wraps.

'If you must know,' said Eleanor dispiritedly, 'the boy Pierre Basile died before he spoke. You can thank Mercadier's brutes for that; they went too far. And even if the gold were here, it would legally be John's property now, since he has inherited the crown and all that goes with it.'

Her gaze went to the small iron-bound chest which Milo had been using as an altar. Inside it reposed Richard's testament – dictated by Eleanor, written by Milo and signed by the dying king – the testament that made John King of England.

'I want to see the will,' demanded Joanna.

'No doubt, but you won't.' Eleanor knew how to inject finality into the simplest phrase. 'You've insulted a queen and your mother, betrayed a king and a brother – oh, and blasphemed against God as well, I nearly forgot that small detail. It's enough for one night, even for a daughter of mine, I should have thought. So go now and find some rest. Someone has to pray for Richard's soul. Leave that to me, for I sleep but little at my age.'

With a typically Plantagenet about-face, Joanna thrust the crucifix into Milo's hands and ordered him to bless her.

He stammered and recoiled, muttering about Confession first.

'I'll bless you,' said Eleanor. 'Come to me.'

She embraced her daughter.

'Forgive me?' Joanna whispered.

'Of course,' said the queen. 'You're Henry's daughter. You have his temper, that's all. I understand.'

When the queen was sure Joanna had gone and would not return, she stopped praying and sighed.

'My sons, my daughters,' she complained to the priest beside her, 'have bickered and squabbled since they were weaned from the breast. Why did God curse me with such a troublesome brood?'

Milo was reluctant to leave her alone. He pointed to the Roman frescoes, repeating the current belief that the baths had been the work of giants and ghosts, in whose pagan company no Christian queen should be left alone.

Eleanor laughed at his pious entreaties. 'The fear of ghosts may be enough to keep the common people away from these ruins, Clerk Milo, but for me cross and candle are sufficient protection against any spirits. Now leave me, Chaplain. I would weep and pray alone.'

Alone, her tears were swiftly dried. After a few minutes she came to the curtain and pulled William inside.

'Help me,' she ordered him in a low voice, 'to lift the king's body. Now is the moment to lighten the coffin's load by half.'

William took a careful look around the sleeping encampment before slipping inside the drapes. He crossed himself and stooped to lift the dead weight of the king's body out of the coffin in one movement.

Renowned for her ability to cope with not two but several conflicting ideas at the same time, Eleanor ignored the bloated body that William was laying on the filthy floor.

'Come,' she said, pulling at the loose panel on which the corpse had been lying. 'We must hurry.'

Chapter 10

'Wake up!'

Merlin shook Leila's shoulder. She turned over in the bed and shielded her eyes from the light.

'I need a cigarette,' he said.

'What's the time?'

'Three o'clock or thereabouts.'

'And you wake me up for a smoke?'

'I had a prowl around downstairs to see if there was a cigarette machine, but there isn't.'

'Help yourself.' Leila pulled the sheet up, complaining, 'I only got to bed an hour ago.'

Merlin took a deep inhalation. 'You stayed up that late, talking with those two reps?'

Leila handed the cigarette back and shook her head.

'The rain's stopped,' he said.

'Good of you to wake me,' she yawned. 'I'd never have known otherwise.'

Merlin hesitated. Lying awake in the next room after the dream, everything had seemed clear, the choice of action simple. Now his head was full of a confusion of images: a furious princess, a dead king and the oh-so-clever queen. Eleanor... Jay... the veiled woman... and back to Eleanor. The images blurred and reformed.

Putting his thoughts into words for Leila was like trying to justify a midnight hunch to a sceptical news editor in the middle of a crowded news-room next day. Now, the strands of tangled coincidences seemed to be no more than a nebulous tissue of gossamer, woven together by the fragile stuff of dreams. He decided to say nothing to Leila about the dream.

'They're not reps,' said Leila.

'What? Who?'

282

'Those two guys downstairs. The older one I really fell for. His name's Salem. He couldn't take his eyes off me all night.'

'That's a good French name, Salem.'

'He's from Beirut. Something to do with the hotel business...'

Another coincidence? Merlin started. Of all the cities in the world, why should a man from Beirut show up now? 'What's his other name?'

'He did tell me. Hang on. It's something like thank you in Arabic, you know: *shoukran*.'

'Chakrouty?' Merlin guessed.

'That's it.'

It was more than a coincidence. 'I used to stay in their hotel years ago,' Merlin muttered.

She wanted to know where Salem had come from.

Merlin shrugged. 'What's Beirut like? It's a pile of rubble now. The old man – Yussef, that was his name – was a nice guy. He died a while back. I don't think I ever met the sons. So what's a Chakrouty doing in a one-horse town like this in the middle of France?'

'Some complicated deal – I couldn't work it out.'

'Has to be drugs or arms.'

'No way. Not Salem. Now Pierre, yes – I can believe that of him.'

'Pierre is the younger guy?'

'Yup. He says he's French, but I think he's Lebanese too.'

'Why d'you say that?'

'I heard them talking Arabic through the ventilation duct in the gents' loo.'

'I don't follow.'

'Well, I'm not at my most lucid when woken in the middle of the night, Merlin old boy, but I was going to tell you in the morning anyway.'

'Tell me what?'

'Pierre – the younger one – went off somewhere on his own quite early. He came back a couple of hours later and looked pretty angry to find that Salem and I were still talking. He grabbed Salem in mid-sentence and hustled him into the gents'. My Arabic's zilch but from what I could make out, Pierre was giving Salem orders to lay off me. From the tone of voice, he was pretty bossy about it.'

Despite everything on his mind, Merlin had to smile: Leila's tangled webs had no ghosts in them, just one lover crowding another. 'So maybe Pierre fancies you too?' he suggested.

Leila shuddered and pulled the sheet up. 'I'd run a mile. You've seen those eyes of his, Merl? That is a man who does not like women, period.'

'I don't go round gazing into men's eyes.'

'He's a killer,' she shuddered again. 'A hood, for sure.'

Merlin laughed outright. 'This is surreal.'

Leila shushed him. 'Keep your voice down. What is?'

'If Shakespeare's right and all the world's a stage, we have the *dramatis personae* of all time.'

He ticked them off on his fingers. 'A former war criminal has kidnapped a beautiful girl. Her friends can't go to the police because the real criminal has been dead for eight hundred years and they wouldn't believe us. I'm cast as Hercule Poirot and fluffing all my lines so far. You're the statutory beautiful nymphomaniac.'

'Oh, thanks.'

'Scene two opens. Enter a Lebanese who's mixed up with another Arab pretending to be a French gangster. They've got some kind of crooked deal going, but I don't see why they chose a place like this in which to consummate it.'

'Not Salem,' Leila smiled. 'He wouldn't be mixed up in anything dishonest.'

'Oh no!' Merlin stubbed out the cigarette in her ashtray. 'I know that throaty, purring voice… Leila, my dear, you are in love again.'

Leila stretched luxuriously on the pillows. 'I can't help it, Merl. It's the way I am.'

'In case you've forgotten, we're here trying to help Jay and…'

'Relax!' Leila's hand patted Merlin's knee. 'Salem is the most gorgeous man I've met in a long time but he's leaving in the morning, so it won't come to anything.'

'They all are the most gorgeous men, at the time.'

'Salem is different. I just know it here.' Leila placed her hand on the bed-clothes above her heart. 'And look, I'm as worried about Jay as you are, but what's that got to do with the way I feel about this man?'

'Nothing,' Merlin sighed. 'You're right.'

'What woke you up?' she asked. 'Or couldn't you sleep?'

'I had a dream.'

'What about?'

'I don't remember,' he lied.

But he did and, thanks to Jay, it was all so clear.

At Chassenon Merlin stopped Leila's car on the track leading to the ruins. Creaking on its rusty suspension, the *deux chevaux* rolled back on the slight incline. He ignored her instructions to wedge an old shoe beneath the hand-brake and left Leila to immobilise the vehicle after her own fashion while he walked towards what remained of the baths.

Halfway there, he stopped in his tracks.

This – it hit him now – was what people meant by having a *déjà vu*. He had been here before! In the dream the ground level had been lower and the ruined walls and arches much higher. Where the macadamed road ran, Roman flags lay concealed beneath the surface, he knew. In front of him stood the remains of the domed vault of the *caldarium* or hot bath, built of solid Roman concrete which defied the centuries.

A small notice by the gate advised that the site was closed until Easter. There was no sign of a guide or custodian, so Merlin crawled under the wire fence where some sheep had pushed through to get at the lush grass inside the enclosure. They scattered in front of him as he walked towards the archway where he had stood sentry while Joanna and Eleanor argued...

'No!' Merlin voiced a thought, stopping in mid-pace to light a cigarette.

Leila was sitting on the bonnet of the deux-chevaux with her arms crossed in front of her. 'What's up?' she called.

Merlin made a gesture: nothing.

He sat on the stump of a broken column with his back to her and thought: I refuse to get dragged into this spider's web. Wherever the memories in that dream came from, I'm still me. I am not, repeat not, the reincarnation of someone else...

And yet he knew where the gold was, as certainly as though he had put it there himself the previous night.

Merlin finished the cigarette and walked into the *caldarium*. The floor which, in the dream, had been deep in cow dung was now clean. A few vestiges of mosaic showed here and there, the rest filled in with cement on which lines had been scored to show where the design was missing.

On the exact spot where the coffin had stood, he looked around. On his right had been Milo's makeshift altar and there, behind a wall of tiles was the lead-lined cistern where Eleanor and he... Correction: where Eleanor and William had secreted the gold that had cost Richard's life. They had piled dirt from the floor over the hastily mortared tiles to conceal their work and left it to the centuries to do the rest of the work, so that now the false wall looked as solid as the rest of the building.

Merlin threw down his cigarette end and walked outside. There were some tools in a wheel-barrow beside the gate-house. He debated whether to break through the wall there and then, but decided against it. The treasure was the lure which would bring Eleanor sooner or later to this place. Or – Merlin kicked all the supernatural explanations metaphorically out of the window – put another way, it was the lure that would bring Kreuz here with Jay. At which point...

What the hell was he going to do then? Suppose he walked up to them and said, 'Jay, I've come to rescue you.' And what if she said, 'Go away.' What then? He couldn't compel her to leave Kreuz and come with him.

In the daylight the plan that had seemed so obvious after his dream was either preposterous or illegal.

And yet, standing alone among the ruins, watched by the chewing sheep and by Leila still sitting on the bonnet of the car, Merlin knew that Eleanor would be there soon. There was no point in trying to find where Kreuz had taken her. All he had to do was to wait at Chassenon and they would come to him.

But how long would he have to wait?

Not long, he decided. Eleanor was a woman who had never liked wasting time.

Kreuz was wearing his hooded cloak, in keeping with the medieval furnishings. The only incongruously modern note in the room was Eleanor herself. She had changed her clothes three times that morning, ignoring Kreuz's presence. Now she was studying herself in a polished bronze hand-mirror. From Jay's available wardrobe she liked best the effect of jeans, a man's shirt and a thin anorak, clothes which gave her a freedom she had never known before. Wearing her hair unbraided and unconfined by wimple or head-dress was another pleasure.

'Do you play chess?' she asked.

Kreuz looked at Eleanor as though she were mad.

'Well, do you?' she asked sharply.

'No, I don't play games. They are a waste of time.'

'A pity,' she said. 'It would pass the afternoon agreeably.'

After a good night's sleep, a hot bath and another massage, all traces of the hysterical paralysis had gone. She felt ready in body and mind to leave this sanctuary that Kreuz had prepared for her and begin her exploration of the new world outside. The problem of learning the right language did not bother her; she had spoken both Langue d'Oc and the northern French tongue fluently, as well as English, Latin and some Arabic, so she was confident of picking up any language swiftly. She had travelled many times to far countries with customs different from her own and enjoyed every experience of her life, except being locked up. She was now ready to tackle the exciting prospect of life in the twentieth century.

Twice Eleanor had proposed a visit to the nearest town and twice Kreuz had refused

It was time to show him who was mistress and who the servant. 'If you were a chess-player,' she added, 'you would understand what stalemate means.'

'I understand the term,' he said. 'It's a common enough metaphor.'

'Good.' Eleanor smiled and sat down beside him. 'In that case, my dear fitz-Mercadier, you will know that one of us must give way. I shall not tell you what you want to know before I have in my hands the treasure of Châlus. You say that you will not help me recover it before I have told you. That is a stalemate.'

'And how do we break it?'

She smiled, 'You give way.'

'I?' Kreuz raised an eyebrow. 'Why not you?'

Eleanor stroked her long fingers. She remembered them as old and knobbly with arthritis. Now they were smooth and beautiful. It was a pity that this descendant of Mercadier's was not someone younger and of noble blood with whom she could have passed the day in unemotional carnal pleasure. She put the thought away. Soon...

'I have already waited many generations for what I want,' she said, 'and I can wait more if necessary. Oh, I'd rather not, but I can. You, on the other hand, will be dead within a few years. And – as I found out with poor Richard – once you're dead, no one can bring you back. The work must begin before then. So you have no choice.'

Kreuz blinked. She was right.

Eleanor took a deep breath. This body – this young woman's body – would give her much pleasure, she was sure, but how wonderful that her mind was still her own. Henry himself, she thought, couldn't have played that stroke more neatly.

'You're right,' admitted Kreuz. There was no point in arguing.

'Of course I am,' said Eleanor. 'Tonight we shall recover the material provisions I have made for this new life. Perhaps we shall visit a town beforehand, I haven't decided yet. But first, let us pass an hour or so in music. Do you know a song that Richard wrote: *Ja nus hons Pris?* You take the tenor part and I'll play soprano.'

The Renault 25 was parked in a clump of trees, half a mile from the ruins.

Kassim shaded his eyes. There had been no time to replace the binoculars lost when he was attacked by the Dobermans, but he could see Merlin well enough at that distance and wished that he had a longer-range weapon than the Uzi. With a sniper rifle he could have killed the American with one shot at that range. He watched the man who had been his prisoner amble round the site, head down and deep in thought.

'What are they doing?' asked Salem from inside the car.

'Waiting,' said Kassim. 'It looks like a rendezvous of some sort.'

'So what do we do?'

'We wait too.'

After a while, Kassim added, 'In Fontevraud last night, while you were so obsessed with the Jew-woman, I was making enquiries. They told me in the town that this Queen Alianor lived eight hundred years ago. There is a legend that she buried a treasure somewhere in these parts.'

'So? There are legends like that, all over the world.'

'The tile of Yussef el-Kebir has been in our family's possession for forty generations, or so you told me. That matches: forty generations equal eight centuries, more or less. So this Queen Eleanor or Alianor was the person who cheated our ancestor, my brother! The treasure she buried must have been his due and is now ours.'

The tables have turned, thought Salem. To begin with it was me pretending to believe what was on the tile; now it is Kassim who does believe, with the same fanaticism as he holds all his other beliefs.

'How can she pay a debt,' he asked, 'if she's been dead so long?'

Kassim changed to English, quoting Tennyson: ' "Ours not to reason why".' And back to Arabic: 'Everything will come to pass as written, my brother. I think that whoever the American is meeting here is going to pay us this long overdue debt.'

Kassim stared at the two distant figures by the ruins. The Uzi was a close-quarters weapon. But if the treasure lay somewhere on the site, no one was going to risk digging it up in daylight. So he would keep his distance, wait if necessary all day and creep closer as soon as it grew dark. Then the Uzi would come into its own.

He opened the boot of the car, lifted out the brief-case containing the weapon and fitted it together. Even with the silencer screwed on to the muzzle, it was a weapon easily concealable beneath a loose coat or anorak.

On hearing the click of the magazine being rammed home, Salem got out of the car. He looked with horror at his brother holding the short, ugly metal weapon across his chest.

Unsmilingly Kassim said, 'I did not tell you about this, because you would not understand.'

Salem's face was pale. 'You are right that I would not understand,' he muttered. 'We are not in Lebanon now. The time of killing is past.'

He reached for the Uzi. 'Give that thing to me.'

Kassim clicked off the safety catch and stepped back to keep a constant distance between them.

'Keep away,' he ordered coldly. The Uzi was pointing at Salem's belly. 'This weapon is nothing to do with you.'

'Of course it is to do with me,' he said slowly. 'You are my brother, Kassim. If you kill someone in France, you will go to gaol. I cannot allow that.'

'They will never catch me,' Kassim sneered.

Salem took a step forward. His brother's face was now white with tension. His eyes glittered and his teeth were clenched. 'One more step and you die!' he promised.

288

Salem hesitated. Would Kassim pull the trigger? Reading the message in the fanatical staring eyes, he knew the answer was yes. He groaned inarticulately and turned away.

Kassim felt a thrill of power course through his veins. Since leaving the Beka'a Valley he had missed the stature conferred on him by a loaded weapon in his hands. The feel of the Uzi and the look of horror on Salem's face made him feel strong and authoritative once again.

'Your job,' he ordered his brother brusquely, 'is to drive the car. Nothing more. The rest you leave to me. Is that clear?'

Salem found his voice at last. 'And if I refuse?'

'Then I shall kill you.'

Kassim was looking right through Salem as he spoke.

'You will kill me?' he wondered aloud. 'Your own brother? Just to get your hands on some gold?'

'The gold is nothing,' Kassim sneered. 'It is a means to an end, no more.'

Salem subsided weakly back on to the passenger's seat, his feet still on the ground outside the car. He felt ill at what was happening. 'What kind of man have you become, my brother?' he asked rhetorically.

'I am not your brother,' said Kassim harshly. 'Your father is not mine, for my father is the Cause. I am a sworn son of the Jihad and know no other brothers except my comrades in the struggle. As it is written that a father must be obeyed, so I shall obey the orders of the Jihad. If it is necessary to kill you in order to safeguard my mission, I shall do so.'

Chapter 11

Kreuz's plan had assumed that Eleanor was bound to be disorientated for days or even weeks. During the time she was a helpless prisoner in his power, he had thought to plunder the esoteric knowledge she had acquired from Yussef El-Kebir.

It did not work like that. After waking from a good night's rest, she seemed in full possession of her faculties – and as capricious as any queen had ever been, changing her clothes and altering her make-up, ordering the driver and masseuse about despite an almost non-existent vocabulary, and throwing questions at Kreuz in Latin about every subject under the sun. He understood as he never had from all his research what hell had been the life of a medieval courtier, literally at beck and call both day and night. Halfway through the afternoon Eleanor ordered him to take her for a drive so that she could begin to familiarise herself with things modern. Only with great difficulty did he dissuade her from taking the wheel herself, so excited was she by what she called 'the new machines'.

Eleanor's confidence in herself grew by the minute, the fears of yesterday at Fontevraud forgotten the moment she discovered that by using rather than fighting Jay's neuro-muscular patterns she could operate zip fasteners, a slot machine, a radio, and even something as complex as a car.

At the railway station she made Kreuz explain to her how trains worked and television functioned, about the telephone system, the postal service, and all the medicines displayed in a pharmacy window. She bombarded him with a constant stream of questions that fed her insatiable curiosity.

At the same time, her gift for languages was allowing her to build up a reasonable working vocabulary of modern French. In a hardware shop she insisted on dealing with the salesman herself in pidgin-French, buying a hammer and chisel, a spade, sacks and torches. In a bar next to the store, some teenagers were dancing to a video clip. Eleanor was fascinated. She made Kreuz buy her a huge, succulent hamburger in a fast-food restaurant, mocking his vegetarianism which she called 'the diet of peasants.'

Then she had taken the wheel of his car and driven far too fast northwards to Chassenon. With difficulty Kreuz persuaded Eleanor to slow down through towns but her excitement as they came in sight of Chassenon and found the moonlit ruins still relatively intact, grew so much that she forgot to brake. She stopped Kreuz's car by crashing the bonnet through a hedge and stalling the engine. She strode ahead of him towards the ruins while he followed, burdened with the paraphernalia she had bought in the hardware shop.

In the *caldarium*, Kreuz set down the torch on a ledge in the masonry and selected a wide beam that lit the whole chamber dimly.

'There,' Eleanor showed him the place. 'Dig there, fitz-Mercadier. The wall is thin, you'll find.'

She left him tackling the masonry with hammer and chisel and walked outside into the crisp night air. There was time to be alone with her thoughts for a moment. The last time she had been at Chassenon, Richard had been dead but a few hours... his corpse had been dragged out of the coffin by William the Marshal... and there had been the confrontation with Joanna which Eleanor had won by sheerest bluff and the thickness of a single plank. Remembering her daughter's anger that night, Eleanor thought: God, how that woman loved screaming!

The only regret was that Richard was not there to share her new life. How he would have loved all the wonderful machines of which she was learning! Perhaps... She felt the firmness of her breasts and flat belly. Perhaps she would beget another Richard? No, that was not possible. To give Henry his due, the Plantagenet genes mingled with her own Aquitanian blood were what had made their third-born son so handsome, so fearless and so talented.

Eleanor sighed, picturing the Lionheart for a moment. It still hurt. Then the vision seemed to come to life! There he was, striding up the path past Kreuz's car, the same spring in his step. In her mind, Eleanor heard him cry out, 'Mother!'

She held her breath as the figure of a man came closer in the moonlight. Was it a man, or some wraith conjured up by her own associations with Chassenon, long said by peasants to be haunted by the earth-bound spirits of the giants who had built the baths?

Behind her the *chink-chink-chink* of hammer on chisel told her that Kreuz was labouring away. There was an echoing thud as a lump of masonry fell to the floor of the chamber.

But this was no apparition, Eleanor saw. This was a man of flesh and blood approaching her, holding some kind of weapon in his hand. For one wild moment she wondered whether the Moor had excelled his own expectations and magicked a descendant of her favourite son here to greet her. Had there been issue? Not from poor Berengaria's virgin womb, that was sure. But there had been rumour of one bastard by some serving wench.

The man came closer. Eleanor's spirits sank as the resemblance with Richard grew less at each step. Then disappointment changed to alarm: what could an intruder be doing at this isolated spot in the middle of the night? Until the gold had been recovered, they could not afford any interruption. Was this some peasant who lived nearby, awoken by the noise of them driving up in Kreuz's car? Was the resemblance to a beloved man just the figment of her over-stimulated imagination?

Alarm in turn changed to a gasp of astonishment as Eleanor recognised the man coming towards her. He was William the Marshal – not William battle-scarred and grizzled as he had been at the time of Richard's death but William in his prime, William with his sparkling eyes, William with his curly hair and the smile that warmed her heart.

With the realisation that there were no barriers to divide her as queen from him as commoner in this new life, that they were free to slake the passion they both had felt, a spasm of desire seized Eleanor.

'Nox mirabilis est!' She ran forward and reached out to him with both arms. *'Guilelmus, equitis optimus...'*

'Oh best of knights,' she sobbed, overcome with emotion surging within her breast and belly as love and lust intermingled in a great swirl of desire. 'Have you come to serve and love me once again with your unbounded devotion? Oh, William, truly this is a wondrous night!'

'Jay?' Merlin stopped two paces from her and repeated, 'Jay?'

The stream of Latin told him that although he was looking at Jay's body, it was inhabited by Eleanor's mind. He felt himself seized in an embrace. His arms went automatically around the body he knew. This woman smelt the same and felt the same and the voice was the voice he loved, breathing words he could not understand in his ear.

He felt Eleanor sobbing and quivering with desire, and found himself returning the fevered kisses of the woman in his arms as her hands clung to him. Behind her in the darkness came the *chink-chink-chink* of Kreuz's hammer and chisel.

Breathless, Eleanor pulled away to look upon Merlin's face and said in a clear voice, 'Beautiful!'

It was a word she had learned that afternoon from one of the dancers in the disco bar.

'Jay?' A smile of tremendous relief spread over Merlin's face. 'Oh my God, I love you. I thought...'

The heavy silencer of the Uzi caught him behind the left ear and he fell to the ground at Eleanor's feet, stunned. She saw standing where Merlin had been a small thin figure holding what was obviously some kind of weapon pointed straight at her. Beside him stood a much taller man. Their two faces together made that of Yussef el-Kebir.

The sweet blend of success and love curdled in her mouth. Of course, she thought, it stands to reason that Yussef would not have done everything for me and nothing for himself!

'Get inside, you whore!' snarled Kassim. If the words meant nothing to Eleanor, the gesture of the weapon was plain. She turned to walk into the *caldarium*, angry at herself of leaving Yussef's interest out of the equation. At the entrance she asked a question in Latin but received only an incomprehensible answer in English and a shove from the Uzi's silencer that sent her sprawling onto the mosaic floor.

Kreuz's body was half-in and half-out of the hole he had made in the false wall, a pile of golden objects beside him. On hearing the noise, he wriggled back into the main chamber and turned with a huge golden chalice gleaming in one hand and a solid gold statuette in the other. His eyes blinked, taking in the sight of Eleanor getting to her feet still threatened by Kassim's gun, while in the entrance to the *caldarium* Leila and Salem carried a groaning, semi-conscious Merlin between them.

'These men,' explained Eleanor in Latin, 'are the sons of Yussef el-Kebir.'

'Shut up!' snarled Kassim. 'Against the wall. Put your hands on your head!'

He menaced her with the gun. When she did not comply, his finger tightened on the trigger. He licked his lips. It was going to be a pleasure to execute this shameless whore whose dress revealed the swell of her breasts. In his nostrils, she stank of sex.

'No!' cried Kreuz. 'Don't shoot! She doesn't understand English.'

In his anguish at the thought that Eleanor might be killed before she had given him the information he needed for his own reincarnation, he rose and lurched off-balance towards Kassim, holding the golden objects before him.

The silencer swallowed most of the noise of the gun, turning it into the coughing of some subterranean beast. The impacting bullets lifted Kreuz bodily and hurled him back against the plastered wall above the hole through which gleamed the golden hoard of Châlus. Like Richard, struck by the crossbow-bolt eight hundred years before, his last thought was that it was all a mistake.

The body slumped to the ground on the heap of gold. In the eerie silence, the chalice and statuette fell from his lifeless hands and rolled heavily into a depression where the floor had subsided in the centre of the *caldarium*.

293

Merlin staggered to his feet as Kassim walked across the chamber and kicked Kreuz's body to make sure it was dead. Then he turned back to Eleanor. She had not seen exactly how the weapon in his hand worked but she had seen many other amazing machines that day and accepted that the man threatening her now intended to kill her too.

There was no language in which she could bargain with him or plead for her life so she slipped the dress off one shoulder, revealing her breasts in the hope of distracting him.

A wrong move, she thought, seeing his tongue lick dry lips. Kassim gripped the Uzi tighter to control the recoil and began slowly to squeeze the trigger. Eleanor's eyes watched the finger take up the first pressure.

Kassim felt a surge of sexual pleasure. He liked to see a victim watch the trigger-finger tighten, especially this bitch on heat...

'Yussef el-Kebir servus meus erat. Filii ejus estis.' The rapid Latin meant nothing to Kassim except for the name of his ancestor. His finger relaxed the pressure as he half-turned to Salem. Because his victim was only a woman he felt no need to be on his guard.

'What does the whore say about Yussef el-Kebir?' he asked. 'Do you understand?'

Leila had picked up Merlin's flash-gun when she helped Salem lift him off the ground. It was the only weapon they had thought to bring with them. She slipped it now into Merlin's hand. He hit the Test button as Kassim turned towards them. The flash blinded Kassim and everyone in the chamber except Eleanor who was sheltered from it by Kassim's body. In one swift movement she grabbed the heavy chalice at her feet and hit the armed man a vicious blow on the side of the head.

Kassim was sufficiently stunned to release his grip on the Uzi momentarily. Eleanor dropped the chalice, grabbed the weapon out of his hands and stepped back. In the first lesson in swordsmanship that Richard had ever given her, the golden rule had been: Always give yourself room to manoeuvre.

Because the unfamiliar weapon in her hands so resembled a lopsided crossbow, Eleanor placed the stock against her right shoulder and found the trigger – it was in the same place on a crossbow – with her right index finger. As Richard had showed her how to do, she sighted along the barrel and squeezed.

Kassim's head exploded in a spray of pink foam as the stream of 9 mm dum-dummed slugs atomised flesh and blood and bone and brain. If Eleanor's fingers had released the trigger after the first few rounds, she might have been safe. Instead, ignorant of the workings of the automatic firing mechanism which uses the hot gas from one charge to feed the next round into the chamber and fire it, she kept the trigger depressed.

The Uzi spat round after round into thin air where Kassim's face had been. It was the firing of the last bullet in the magazine which brought the temperature in the breech to the critical level at which this gun had been designed to explode.

Silenced Uzis were so obviously terrorist weapons that the whole consignment sold to Ghaddafy's front-man had been quietly replaced in the Rotterdam warehouse by a team of Mossad burglars. The substitute guns were identical except for a network of hair-line fractures that crisscrossed the roof of the breech. The deliberate defect was known in the arms trade as spiking.

If Eleanor had been holding the weapon in the conventional position at waist-level the small fire-ball of super-heated gas that emerged from the fractured breech would have blown her face away. As it was, most of the heat-energy blasted harmlessly at the roof of the chamber but enough had curled briefly around her face and hair to...

'I can't see!' she screamed and dropped the now useless gun.

Her ears, deafened by the blast, heard nothing. She raised her hands to her face and felt huge blisters growing on the scorched skin. The flesh of the long fingers, of which she had been so proud, had peeled off and was hanging in strips like the chest of Pierre Basile.

'No!' she cried in her sightless, soundless anguish. 'Oh no!'

She envisaged herself blind – and burnt hideous into the bargain. No man would ever look at her now, no lover desire this body she had acquired at such cost! Eleanor's plans crumbled around her and in a second that would last for all eternity she wished: O that I were dead again!

Chapter 12

'I love you, Jay!'

Somewhere in the darkness a bird cried. Jay struggled to put an image to the faintest of sounds. It was like fighting a general anaesthetic. She was tempted to stay a part of the cloying nothingness, an unthinking fragment of dust in interstellar space. But her mind, awoken by the faint echo of the bird's cry, refused to let go of the sound.

Not any bird this, but one she knew. The accelerando trill at the end of the Slow Movement of Beethoven's Pastoral Symphony was the call of the nightingale. But this was top F slurred to D, almost like a cat mewing... No, a seagull! And not just any gull: a seagull circling in the north-east gale.

Where? Jay forced herself to remember. It was above the storm-lashed promenade at Herne Bay after...

The gull cried again, louder this time.

She strained to hear it against the solar wind and fingered the notes in her mind: an F quaver slurring to a D minim. Mer-lin. Mer-lin. And again: Merlin.

Oh God, I love you, Merlin. Why did I never tell you? Why did I let Eleanor drive us apart? Why couldn't I see until it was too late what she was doing to us both?

There was a flash of light in the void as a supernova was born – a flash of light and then again the blackness of infinity and its twin, eternity. The rushing solar wind buffeted dust molecules and whole planets in its path.

Again the seagull cried, but this time much closer and a voice said urgently: 'Jay!'

It was Merlin's voice: 'Jay, can you hear me? Hang in there, will you? Don't give up.' And: 'I love you, Jay.'

A man's arm was around her shoulder. Jay knew it was his. She was lying on something soft but firm, being jerked from side to side. She

could hear small whimpering cries forced out of her body by each movement, through lips that would hardly open. Merlin, she sensed, was brac-
ing her and trying to spare her the worst of the jerking.

Her senses were coming back one by one. Hearing had been the first.

... because I'm a musician, she thought. In the background was the
low-frequency growl of a diesel engine in bottom gear. Behind that,
another voice was talking, distorted by the small speaker of a radio. A
man answering in French: something about the number of minutes before
they arrived at the hospital.

Sight? There was nothing but blackness still.

Smell? A strange mixture of odours in her nostrils: disinfectant, rubber
and burnt meat...

Touch? She could not move her hands. They hurt but she could not
feel anything with them. Yet there was some feeling... Her body was
being shaken, forcing more groans out of her. There were straps around
her legs and arms holding her on the firm narrow bed. Not a bed, a
stretcher. In an ambulance, of course. And... oh, such pain on the skin of
her face that she wanted to scream.

'Merlin?' Jay tried to lift a hand and touch him, to know that he was
near. But her hands were wrapped in masses of something soft and the
straps stopped any movement of her arms.

'Merlin?' She wanted to speak louder but the pain of opening her lips
wide was too much.

'It's okay. It's okay.' She felt the pressure of his arm around her. His
other hand squeezed her biceps.

'Just don't talk,' he said. 'You're gonna be okay.'

The rocking motion stopped as the ambulance turned onto the tarma-
cked road surface and picked up speed. A siren started wailing on the
roof and another on the police car ahead.

'I must know,' Jay whispered. 'What's happened to me? Why can't I
see anything or talk properly?'

'You've been burnt,' he said.

'My face?'

He hesitated. 'Yeah.'

'Is it bad?'

'Pretty bad.'

That means very bad, she thought. 'Am I going to die?'

He laughed a low throaty chuckle of relief: 'I can tell you, you are not
going to die.'

'I can't open my eyes. I can hardly open my mouth.'

'Don't try,' he advised. 'You're covered in gauze and some kind of
foam to stop fluid loss through the burnt tissue.'

Jay felt very calm. She was in an ambulance with Merlin looking after

297

her. Her face was burnt... but perhaps that wasn't the worst news. 'Merlin,' she panicked. 'My hands, are they burnt too?'

'Yes.'

'Oh God, will I ever be able to play again?'

'A gun blew up,' he explained.

'I was holding a gun?'

'Eleanor was. But that's all over.'

It was so tempting to drift into unconsciousness in order to escape the pain, but she refused to return to the comforting blackness.

'Talk to me, Merlin,' she whispered. 'Please. You've seen men injured like I am now. Haven't you?'

'Too many times.'

'And do they get better?'

'Of course they do.'

'I mean, are they scarred for life?'

'It depends... He cleared his throat. 'It depends how quickly they get to the right surgeon, honey. As soon as we arrive at the local hospital I'm gonna be on the telephone. I want you in the Val de Grace today.'

The valley of grace? she wondered. It sounded so medieval.

He answered the unspoken question. 'It's the biggest military hospital in France, where they looked after the French casualties in the Gulf War. And if they can't make you look beautiful again there, I'll have you on an Air Force plane to Walter Reed in Washington. They have the best plastic surgeons in the world in that place and I've got all the connections with the military to get you in there, you'll see.'

He carried on talking to give her something on which to focus as the pain ebbed and flowed – and to stop her sliding into shock.

Jay clung to Merlin's whispers. At the hospital she heard the ambulance doors being thrown open. Merlin's arm was pulled out from under her shoulders.

'Merlin!' Jay cried in the sightless blackness. 'Don't leave me!'

His voice was close to her ear as the stretcher was lifted. His hand squeezed her shoulder.

'I won't,' she heard him say. 'Never again, I promise.'

Part 6

Chapter 1

Leila watched Salem strike blow after blow with the jagged stone until the surface of the tile was pitted in so many places that the writing was now illegible. The staccato noises were almost drowned by the noise of a concrete mixer not far away where one of the other houses in Tel-el-Sultan was being rebuilt.

It had been an impulse, completely unthought out, that made her grab an armful of the golden artifacts and stuff them under the back seat of her beat-up little car before the police arrived. The rusty old *deux-chevaux* had actually been driven for her through the police cordon by one of the gendarmes.

When the questioning was over and Salem released for lack of any evidence to connect him with the faceless body with its false identification papers, Leila had accompanied him to the Swiss border. She had meant to hand him his share of the treasure of Châlus as a going-away present. But saying goodbye, he had looked so lost and helpless, she had thought: I have to look after you for a while.

So she had driven the gold into Switzerland among a pile of canvases in the back of her car and helped Salem find a bank in Basel where his treasure would be safe. And after that she had stayed on because Salem was too broken by Kassim's death to cope with even the simplest task like finding food or a hotel room for himself.

Her own patience had surprised Leila. She had never wanted to look after a man before, certainly not one as snarled up as Salem then was. During her marriage she had gone through the motions of what other wives did but without feeling any involvement. This was different...

When she had tried to draw Salem out about his plans, he had talked vaguely of settling in America or Argentina where he had cousins. The gold sitting in the safety deposit box would more than finance that. Leila had listened to his words and the spaces between the words, understanding that Salem did not really want to go anywhere new; it was just that he could not face up to the pain of going back to Beirut alone.

So she had ended up flying with him, to keep him company. 'For just a few days until you get settled.'

Two weeks later, she was still in Beirut, visiting the old house in Tel-el-Sultan for the first time.

'It's ended now.' Salem stood up and tossed the stone through the grilled opening in the wall. He scuffed the bits of broken tile with his foot.

A pile of old clothes caught his eye in the refuse behind the dried-up fountain. The parachutist's smock, shirt and pair of trousers were still lying where Kassim had thrown them, weeks before. Salem picked them up and lifted them to his face. They smelt of old leaves and dust, not a man. He bundled the clothes into a ball and threw it at the grille but it fell short.

'What a view!' said Leila, looking at the city and the blue Mediterranean beyond.

Salem was remembering the times when Kassim and he had looked through the telescope with their father to read the neon sign blinking on the seafront: Chakrouty – International – Hotel. But that was all in the past. Lebanon now belonged to the future.

He smiled at Leila's excitement in the colours, the smells, the view. In a sleeveless yellow cotton dress and with bare feet she walked about the courtyard, imagining the house as it must have been when it was a home and showering questions on Salem as he pointed out to her the landmarks of the city, or rather where they had been.

Her wide-eyed, bubbling enthusiasm up here made him see Leila as a different woman from the subdued tourist who had viewed with horror the devastation down in the city. At times, Beirut seemed to be peopled by black-clad widows and crippled children hobbling on crutches.

'Can we come up here again?' she asked.

'Of course. This is my house. It is my only house.'

'Next time, I'll bring my paints,' said Leila. She spoke to the view, aware that something important was happening in Salem's mind.

She stood on tiptoe and raised her arms as high as they would go, like an Indian saluting the sunrise. 'I think,' she said, 'that this must be the most beautiful place in the whole world.'

'If you like ruins,' he said, seeing only the desolation around them.

'I like this one.' Leila spun round and walked into the house. Salem followed her from one roofless room into another and another.

'It's a house that's crying out to be lived in,' Leila announced at the end of the brief tour.

She turned and took both his hands in hers, adding on an impulse, 'You asked me last night what you could do for me, in return for the help

I've given you these last few weeks. Well, there is something. Let me buy this place from you, Salem.'

'It's not worth anything.'

'Then give it to me. I'd like to do it up and live here.'

'You live in France.'

'I never belonged there.'

'And do you belong in Lebanon?' he asked.

'Who knows?' Leila shook her dark curly hair and sucked in a deep breath of the pine-scented air. 'My mother was Armenian, my father a Jew. My grandfather was a Turk. So what does that make me? Wherever they come from, it wasn't far from here, that's for sure.'

She led him outside and back onto the terrace with its view over the city now coming to life again.

'That,' said Leila, 'is the view I need to see when I wake up in the morning.'

'Salem took his eyes away from the city below with all its memories and looked at the woman beside him who was unlike any other he had ever known. He had thought that all desire was dead, crushed forever in the ruins with the crumpled bodies of his wife and children. Never again, he had vowed. Never again will I love, because of the pain it brings. Never will I feel desire, for the memories it calls back.

Yet Leila had somehow melted all those death-bound resolutions. Her smile, her heavy-lidded eyes, her soft olive-complexioned skin, her voice, the way she walked, her capacity to enjoy every second of the day for its own sake – all urged him to let the dead bury the dead.

'You could never live here,' he heard himself say. It was a voice from the past trying to convince her. 'A woman on her own…'

'I've managed pretty well, so far.'

'In Europe, maybe.'

'And in the States.'

'This is different.'

'You think I need a man to protect me?' Leila teased him.

Her nearness was disturbing him. 'In an Arab country, every woman needs a man…'

She stepped close, so that he smelt her perspiration on her neck and between her breasts. With a wrench in his bowels he thought, I want this woman.

Forgive me, he said to the ghosts, but I am a man of flesh – and flesh needs flesh to lust for. And I need her for a thousand other reasons too.

Leila parted her lips. She could feel what her closeness was doing to Salem. She wondered why he didn't touch her or kiss her like a European or American man would have done. To bridge the last narrow gap between them, she touched first one of his eyebrows and then the other.

She drew her finger down his nose and traced the outline of his lips. And still Salem kept the last few millimetres of distance from her.

'I'd like to paint you,' she said huskily. 'You're a beautiful man.'

Salem moistened his lips. 'Stay here,' he said.

'I wasn't going anywhere, right now.'

'I meant, stay in Lebanon with me.'

'Is that an offer?'

They stood looking into each other's eyes. The day was still, without a breeze. There was a rustle of leaves in the aged olive tree that shaded the bomb-blasted courtyard, as though the ghosts were whispering goodbye.

'I need you,' Salem said solemnly.

A spark kindled behind his eyes that Leila had not seen before. He was no longer the broken man who could not meet her gaze, but a strong man who had suffered much and was going to be strong again.

'You've come back to life,' she said wonderingly. A great ball of warmth grew within her belly at what she had done.

Salem took a deep breath. It felt good to be alive in his home and holding this beautiful creature in his arms.

'Make love to me,' she whispered.

He stepped backwards, shocked that a woman had voiced his own desire. 'Not before we are married.'

'Then kiss me!' Leila's eyes, her whole body invited him.

Salem took her hands in his and held them firmly to stop them touching him. 'With a woman like you, an embrace could never end in one kiss.'

'Oh God!' Leila closed her eyes and squeezed her thighs together. 'How can you do this to me?'

'Have you always satisfied your desires immediately?' he wondered.

'Since the day I started being me, I guess I have.'

'Then we will never make a good Arab woman out of you...' said Salem mock-seriously. The small joke was his first essay in humour for a long while.

He pulled her closer. 'There is obviously no point in trying to do the impossible.'

'Does that mean what I think it does?'

'Be quiet!' he ordered.

Leila let him close her lips with his. She felt his hands exploring her body through the thin fabric of the dress, tracing her vertebrae, the cleft between her buttocks, her rounded hips.

A sob – a final sob for all the memories – escaped him and he clung to her more tightly.

'Oh God!' Leila broke free to breathe. 'You're so damned strong.'

'What are you looking for?' he asked.

'A bed.'

'There is none here. We will have to wait.'

'No.' Leila pulled her arms free and took his head in her hands. 'This is too important to wait, Salem. Grab those old clothes you tried to throw away. Spread them out on the ground. They'll do.'

On my dead brother's clothes? thought Salem. What will the spirits make of that?

Reflected in Leila's dark eyes, he saw himself nod approval of her outlandish suggestion, then smile. He lifted his face to heaven and roared with laughter until he felt weak and subsided to his knees by the bundle of clothes.

'What did I say so funny?' she asked.

Salem was spreading the clothes on the tiles. He tore off his jacket and shirt, heedless of the buttons, to add them to the rough couch.

'Old ideas,' he said, 'are like old clothes. They should all be thrown away.'

He knelt up and held out a hand to her. Solemnly he said, 'My house is your house. Come, share my bed.'

Chapter 2

Five months later Merlin drove into the parking lot of the Massachusetts General Hospital in Boston. He took the lift to the top floor with a bunch of long-stemmed roses in one hand and a piece of paper in the other.

Jay had been practising the flute, eyes closed so that she could concentrate on the quality of sound to the exclusion of everything else. Merlin stood in the doorway of her room, watching. When she had finished playing there was a ripple of applause from the small crowd of nurses and patients who had been listening in the corridor.

Merlin closed the door behind him and asked quietly: 'What was that music?'

'Hi!' She was happy to see him.

Those green eyes, he thought. Will I ever forget them?

Jay felt good; the last operations were over, the grafts had all taken. She could begin life again. And the amazing truth was that her flute playing was better than it had ever been, with an indefinable quality and power that had not been there before when Eleanor was sucking her energy, drawing off each day a tithe of life-force and using it against her. At last, with Eleanor's spirit finally laid to rest, all Jay's health and vitality were her own.

'It's called Syrinx...' She put her arms around Merlin's neck and kissed him on the lips. '... by Debussy. Isn't it beautiful music?'

'And sad.' His embrace was perfunctory and passionless.

Jay put down her flute and took the flowers, inhaling the perfume. 'Thank you.'

His silence made her ask: 'What is it?'

'It's time for waving hankies on the platform. The schmaltzy shot from every showbiz film.'

Merlin felt stilted and awkward, handing her the fax message. 'I've been sitting on this for three days. It's your travel arrangements, with love from Sir Ewan himself. He's done a good job with the publicity angle – Star Fights Adversity. Should get you good audiences.'

Jay scanned the list of dates and venues. 'Is that sarcasm?' she asked.

'Professional admiration,' said Merlin. 'Sir Ewan is also giving you that nice guy Carl Moritz as tour manager. He'll look after you.'

Jay had done a lot of thinking about this moment, but it was one thing to work out what ought to be said and done – and quite another to say and do it. She turned away so that Merlin could not read her inner feelings.

In the window glass her face was almost back to normal; there was still a pink shiny area of skin near her right ear where the burns had been deepest, but it was hidden by her hair which had re-grown and was brushed further forward than before. By the unpredictable nature of explosions, the hottest gas from the ruptured breech had by-passed most of her face and the damage to her hands had been on the back, not the sensitive tips of her fingers.

'What's happened to your other instruments?' Merlin asked, to fill the silence. 'There was a whole pile of them here yesterday.'

'The recorders?' Jay kept her back to him. 'I've had enough of medieval music to last me several lifetimes so I gave them away to one of the nurses. She does music therapy with a group of handicapped kids.'

There was another awkward pause broken by Merlin.

'It's a helluva tour Sir Ewan has set up for you,' he said. 'He's got you into just about every major hall between the Atlantic and the Pacific.'

'I guess I'll need the money to pay back the medical loan.'

'Uh-huh.' Merlin took another piece of paper out of his pocket. 'Your bill's been settled. There's the receipt. I picked it up in the office down-stairs. And don't thank me – I wouldn't have that kind of cash. It's a wedding present from Leila and Salem. Apparently they got married last week.'

Jay took the receipted account from him. 'They can't do this!'

'They already did. I guess they can spare it.'

'Then it's really happening.' She turned away again, thinking of Leila.

Merlin thought she meant the tour. He came close and put his arms around Jay's waist. 'It's what you wanted, honey. You fought every inch of the way. That kind of courage deserves a great success.'

'It's what I want,' she agreed, 'but I'm going to miss you terribly. I've gotten used to seeing your face each morning. And I'm even learning your language – words like *gotten* and *in back of*.'

He buried his face in her hair. 'I'll miss you too. But it's time I got back to work as well. Matty's been hustling me for several weeks now to agree a date for the shooting of my network series and I can't put them off any longer.'

'You didn't tell me.'

307

'I figured my place was here until the day you walked out of that door without a date for a next visit.'

Jay twisted round to face him. 'That sounds kind of final, Merlin.'

'You've got your life and I've got mine.'

'And never the twain shall meet again? We've talked about this...'

He pulled away from her.

'No, we haven't,' he said harshly. 'We've lived a wonderful fantasy in between your stays in hospital. We've lain on the beaches of the Cape and made love all summer, pretending that a beautiful dream was real life. The chill reality of fall is that I'm not made to be a toyboy that hangs around a showbiz star.'

He put as much space between them as the room allowed. 'You, on the other hand, are hardly going to follow me round the world to – as Leila once put it so neatly – sit in rented apartments, waiting for the phone to ring and tell you I've got my arse blown away at last.'

Jay settled the flute in its case on the dressing table, beside the roses. In the mirror, she saw her face, her hands and the flute. She had everything back, despite Eleanor. But in the out-of-focus background behind her was Merlin and she wanted him too.

She felt a choking sensation in her throat. 'I love you,' she said. 'And I need you near me.'

She willed him to walk across the room and put his arms around her again.

'Ain't possible,' Merlin said with a twisted grin. His voice was strained. 'I'd like it too, but how could it ever work out?'

'We've talked about it. We planned...'

'Plans?' he snorted. 'You mean dreams. Which one of us would end up saying first: you're never there when I'm free? I don't want to wait for that scene.'

There was a pause until Jay could talk. 'When are you going?' she asked.

'I've got a flight out of Kennedy in a couple of hours.'

'Where to?'

'Lebanon. We start shooting the series in two days' time. I'll give your regards to Leila and Salem when I pass through Beirut.'

Jay watched the blurred image in the mirror as he blew a kiss and closed the door behind him.

The telephone rang. Merlin stood in the corridor with his back against the door, half-hoping that Jay would run after him, but knowing she wouldn't. On the other side of the door, the phone rang again and he heard her pick it up. The call was one he had booked to London for her. He listened for a moment to Jay talking with Sir Ewan about dates and halls and photo-calls, then pulled himself together and walked fast through the corridors and reception areas without meeting anyone's eyes.

Driving out of the parking lot, Merlin took a wrong turning and found himself passing the Boston Museum of Fine Arts. It hurt. He remembered taking Jay there – and how she had wept in front of Renoir's painting of the girl dancing in a white dress and red bonnet. Merlin had been wearing his blue denim suit that day and she had insisted on buying him a yellow hat, to match that of the man in the picture.

He turned the car around and headed for the expressway but missed another turn and found himself in Chinatown, driving past a restaurant where they had eaten *dim sum* together. Boston was full of memories of Jay.

He had shut up the rented house on Cape Cod that morning and handed back the key, driving into the city unable to rid his head of the words of the song: 'Why did summer go so quickly? Was it something that I said?'

To distract himself from the tune that still would not go away, Merlin tried to remember what Bret Harte said about Bostonians. Something about a stern-eyed Puritan being the perfect Boston man. And another quote – from where? – 'Boston has opened and kept open more turnpikes that lead straight to free speech and free deeds than any other city.'

Beside him on the passenger seat lay the thick shooting script for the first programme in the network series *The Forgotten Wars*, on which he had spent the summer working. And on the back seat lay two leather bags, covered in stickers, that contained all his clothes.

In the road-tunnel under the harbour, heading for Logan Airport, he could not see clearly. Each flashing brake-light triggered another image from the magical summer they had spent together. There was Jay tasting her first clam chowder in Provincetown. Jay running through the Atlantic surf with a mongrel dog that had adopted them on the beach several days running. Jay stepping off the ferry to Martha's Vineyard. Jay at Woods Hole. Jay at Hyannisport, by the Kennedy compound. Jay...

He drove out of the tunnel into daylight, checked the car into the Hertz lot and threw his bags into the courtesy bus. Dreams were dangerous, he thought. Reality was a pair of well-worn bags and a shooting script. He didn't need anything else. The connection with the flight to Beirut was tight, but he would make it. It seemed a long time since the day that spring when he had crossed the Atlantic feeling euphorically: *I'm coming home.*

Back in her room, Jay was trying to sound normal.

Sir Ewan was pleased with himself. 'Isn't life wonderful?' he said. 'Though I say it myself, that's a tour list to be proud of.'

'It is,' Jay swallowed the tears. 'I'm looking forward to playing again, Ewan. It's going to be wonderful. It's everything I could dream of.'

EPILOGUE: February 1992

'I think this is the most beautiful hotel I ever stayed in.' Jay raised her glass in a toast to Leila who was sitting on the low wall that surrounded the swimming pool of the Chakrouty el-Sultan hotel.

There was a new telescope for guests who wanted to enjoy the view of the city that was slowly re-building itself on the plain below. Swimming in the pool was a young couple, talking to each other in a language Jay could not identify.

'Greek honeymooners,' commented Leila *sotto voce*. 'He owns a hundred ships at anchor in the Bay of Piraeus and her father owns the rest, as far as I can make out.'

The hotel had been made by converting the old house and several other ruined dwellings of what had been Tel-el-Sultan. The result was a sprawling single-storey Arab-style hotel, with little white-washed bungalows for the guests instead of bedrooms, each set in its own garden.

Below the terrace the lights of Beirut were coming on. Beyond the city, the sea was as blind Homer had envisioned it - wine-dark against the sunset.

'Won't you have a drink?' Jay asked.

Leila made a grimace. 'Fizzy water for me,' she told the white-coated waiter.

They clinked glasses as the waiter left.

'You on the wagon?' Jay asked. 'Is that really necessary?'

Leila patted her swollen belly. 'No cigarettes either, would you believe?'

'Doctor's orders?'

'Salem's. He's far more strict than the doctor.'

'How long to go?'

'Three weeks or so.'

'Happy?'

'Like I was born here.' Leila took hold of Jay's hand and squeezed it. 'Can you understand that?'

311

,ot really. It's so… un-European.'

Leila laughed. 'And that should worry me, of all people? You're kidding.'

They talked with the same easy familiarity they had always shared – about Jay's life and travels, of St Denis and mutual acquaintances. Then they sat silently enjoying the sunset as the red orb changed shape to that of an hourglass, distorted by the atmosphere as it plunged beneath the sea with an almost audible sizzle.

Though she had seen it a hundred times, Leila gasped at the beauty of it all and, in a momentary osmosis, Jay understood something of why her friend had thrown away her previous life to live in that spot with Salem.

In the gardens of the hotel, hidden lights came on, illuminating the pathways between the trees. There was a discreet whisper of Arabic music from the small restaurant where the cook was preparing kebabs beside an open-air fireplace.

'You should have come to visit us earlier,' said Leila.

Jay shook her head. 'To tell the truth, this is the first real break I've had in a long while.'

'The tough schedule of success?'

'Something like that. In the last three months I spent fifteen nights in my own bed.'

'I know.' Leila sipped her glass of water. 'I talked to your damned answering machine every day for a month until you called me back and promised to come here.'

Jay smiled at the recollection of the increasingly abusive messages. 'And you didn't give up until I told you the flight number and date of my ticket.'

She leaned across to her friend's chair and planted a kiss on Leila's cheek. 'I'm glad you persisted.'

They watched the lights of a car on the road winding its way up the hill to Tel-el-Sultan.

'That'll be Salem,' Leila announced. 'I'm sorry he wasn't here to greet you. He had to go and pick up another guest.'

They heard the car doors slam and the sound of Salem's feet running along the tiled paths between the shrubs and trees. He greeted Jay with a kiss on both cheeks before standing, was obviously pleased to see her.

'I'm so glad you have come,' he grinned. 'Leila talks about you a lot.'

'She's looking wonderful, Salem, and I just love your hotel.'

He raised a glass of wine. '*L'chaim* as the Jews say. It's the best toast in the world. I drink to the life in Leila's belly – and to your return. I drink to make sure you come here again.'

'I certainly hope to, Salem.'

He put down the glass and looked stern. 'Hope to is not good enough.

312

Hope to is a European being polite. In Lebanon a promise must be ful-filled.'

'Then I promise as a Lebanese,' said Jay solemnly.

He relaxed. 'You know, when the child is born we are going to call her Jay and you will be her godmother, so you must come back often to watch her growing up.'

'It's going to be a girl?'

'Of course,' said Salem. 'I know these things.'

He sat down beside Leila, patted her belly and took her hand in his.

'He's just hoping,' she smiled at Jay. 'If it's a boy, we'll call him Merlin.'

Jay looked away. 'I suppose he's been here, to stay in your hotel?'

Salem laughed. 'Many times. Merlin also likes it here.'

He kissed Leila's hand. 'Shall we tell her our secret?'

Leila was watching Jay's face closely. 'Merlin is here right now. He was Salem's passenger in the car.'

There was a long pause before Jay asked: 'Does he know I'm here?'

'When I told him,' said Salem, 'he refused to come.'

'What!' exclaimed Leila.

'It's true,' said Salem. 'For you, my love, I have driven halfway to Jerusalem to find that man and his film crew in the middle of a desert. There I argued for two whole hours with the most stubborn person I know. And I had to drive him back here in my car to make sure he didn't change his mind on the way.'

He finished his drink.

'Come,' he said to Leila. 'It is time we dress for dinner. Tonight is a very special occasion.'

After they had gone, Jay sat in the darkness alone. She did not have long to wait. The familiar footsteps stopped short of her.

'This charade,' said Merlin's voice, 'wasn't my idea.'

He stood looking at the back of Jay's head, silhouetted against the sea of lights below.

Instead of turning round, she said, 'I know. Salem told me.'

'He and Leila set us up.'

'Yes.'

Jay heard Merlin take two paces closer but still she did not turn round.

'I followed your tour dates,' he said, 'and read all the notices.'

'You never answered my letters.'

'I had to be sure,' he said.

'Of what? What more could I have done or said or written, Merlin?'

She heard him sigh. 'Sure that I was me and not William. That I wasn't going to louse up this relationship like every other one I've had. That I loved you and not Eleanor. Oh, and a thousand other things. How could I put all that in letters?'

313

'And are you sure now?'

'Oh yes.'

'So why didn't you call me?' *If you knew the pain, Merlin...*

'I wanted to, but I was scared that this time you'd say no.'

At that moment the heavily overloaded electricity supply system gave up the unequal struggle and a power cut wiped out all the lights of the city. On the outskirts there were a few fires where nomads were encamped. In the city itself only the lights of cars pierced the gloom, while here and there on the sea acetylene flares showed where fishing boats were working.

The lights in the hotel garden went out too, leaving Jay and Merlin in darkness. The cook was cursing in Arabic and Leila was calling to Salem to bring candles. Jay felt Merlin's hands on her shoulders. A frisson of electricity ran through her and made her gasp as though he had touched every intimate part of her body.

She put her hands over his and squeezed.

Merlin gave a sharp intake of breath that told her that he was feeling the same. 'It's not going to be easy,' he said huskily.

'No.'

'And it's going to cost us fortune in air fares...'

'Yes.'

'... but we have to find a way of being together, don't we?'

Jay raised her face and saw the stars, partly blacked out by Merlin's head coming closer to kiss her. Between the whirling constellations was the void where her spirit had dwelt while Eleanor walked the earth in her flesh. If there was any music of the spheres, she had not found it. But there was no loneliness any longer, for she knew that she would always be able to hear the faint echo of a seagull's cry borne on the wind, whether the north-east gale or the solar wind of eternity.

'Merlin,' she said. Saying his name again after the months they had been apart was like a pain that cut her soul open. 'Oh, Merlin.'

And one by one the stars went out.